i

This book is dedicated to my father. Thank you for being my inspiration to be a writer and for always believing in me.

I Love you.

Acknowledgements

I would like to take this time to thank all of the people who have been part of this journey that I started nearly twelve years ago. First and foremost, I want to thank my wife Amanda. She's been right there day and night while I've worked so many hours, often times having to take time away from her and my children so I could finish it. She's been so supportive in helping me continue to accomplish this dream that I've had since I was a boy. Next, I need to thank my brother Cole. Without him joining me in this adventure, Black Winter wouldn't have turned into what it has become. Next, I think to thank our amazing cover designer Chelsea. I can still remember the terrible picture I drew and sent to her with the idea on how I wanted the cover to look. Cole and I couldn't have been happier with how it turned out and we look forward to you doing the rest of the series covers. Finally, I need to thank our amazing editor Sue. While working with you I was able to not only see the areas of my writing that needed work, it helped me to become a better writer during the process and want to continue working hard at improving my craft.

Again, thank you everyone for your part in making this book finally become a reality.

Updated cover design by Raphael Lucchini.

Just like Beau there are a few people I would like to thank for helping us make our dream become a reality. First, I would like to thank Beau for taking me on this amazing adventure with this series. I still remember being a 14-year-old kid when you first told me about this idea and too think that over the last 12 years, we have become partners is more than I could have ever dreamed of. Second, just like Beau I would like to thank Chelsea for the incredible cover you have given us and Sue for all the hard work and hours you put into editing this book for us. Finally, I would like to thank my wife Sarah. Since the day I told you about this series you have been nothing but supportive and your confidence in Beau and I gives me confidence to follow this dream.

Once again thank you to all of our family and friends who have been supportive and helped in so many different ways. This wouldn't be possible without you.

BLACK WINTER

Table of Contents

PROLOGUE

The last thing my dad said to me, just before he died was "You're a Captain. Be strong and lead them." He was gone only a moment later. Vanished in a burst of light, sacrificing himself to save us. I never got a chance to tell him sorry for being bitter towards him for all those years. I blamed him for everything, and all he was trying to do was protect me. He was trying to protect everyone. That was "his duty". He said it was my duty as well. If only he could see where his son is now, I doubt he would put such faith in me. Now I'm lying here on a table with no control over my body. Sometimes I wonder if I'm even in control of my mind. It feels like someone is reaching into my head with a hook and trying to pry information out. The blocks that my dad put in place seem to be keeping them out. For now. Sometimes it hurts, but so far I've been able to separate myself from the pain. I go to a place deep within my mind to find refuge. Something my dad taught me. He always said that if I ever found myself in so much pain and nowhere to go, to imagine a beautiful place where nothing can hurt me and to stay there. I can think of a place, but staying there is the hard part. The hook keeps pulling me out.

I don't know how long I've been here, wherever here is. Time seems to be lost. Or maybe time has simply forgotten me. I hear voices every so often in the background talking. They keep mentioning Captain Winter and that I have something they need. One of the voices is female. Her voice sounds scared. She sounds as if she doesn't want to be here doing whatever it is she's doing, as if she doesn't have a choice. Underneath the tremble in her voice I can sense a kind, softhearted person. I bet she's pretty. She sounds pretty. The other voice belongs to a man. I don't know what he looks like, but I don't like him. His voice is harsh every time he speaks. It's almost as if he hates me for something I've done to him. If only I knew what it was I did. All he ever talks about is getting the information he needs from me. He sure has an interesting way of interrogating someone. I can't even open my eyes, let alone speak. I know I'm conscious and that I'm not imagining the voices because I hear a fan from a computer to my left, spinning at a high rate to keep the computer cool. I hear fingers, gentle ones, pressing on a keyboard and clicking a mouse. They probably belong to the pretty lady. I can also feel an I.V. in my right arm, pumping something awful into my veins. My mind alerted me to the danger the moment the needle punctured my skin. Probably what they are using to keep me in this state where I can't control my own body. At least I hope that's all it's for.

"Are we ready to begin yet?" asks the harsh voice. "I'm getting impatient."

"I ju… just need to activate the machine."

"Then do it. I don't have all day."

I hear one last click on the machine and the sound of a mechanical arm lowering something above my head. Once the machine stops, I sense something on both sides of my head. Then, suddenly, a bright light turns on and a buzzing sound begins to pierce my ears. I try to block out the noise, but it seems as though it's traveling through my mind, trying to find a place to penetrate my defenses. Whatever it is, this must be what the man meant by "get his information." By breaking into my mind and stealing it. I can see images of my sister, my parents and everyone I ever cared for as they flash through my mind like a movie in rewind. Some of the images feel strange. They feel foreign. They don't feel like my memories, but they feel every bit as real as any memory that I know is mine. The bright light and buzzing sound disappear and a strange sensation washes over my body. I can't hear the computer anymore or the soft voice. I'm no longer in the room. I'm there, all those years ago, fighting to protect people. Struggling to keep them alive... and that familiar voice.

Black Winter

CHAPTER 1

I ce cold wind slams into my face as I sit against the mouth of the cave. The small traces of light that manage to sneak pass the thick storm clouds are fading quickly. Soon the small valley in front of me will be left in complete and utter darkness. Visibility is already low in these conditions, but at night, without the help from the stars or the moon, you can't see farther than ten feet. I struggle to keep my eyes open as the lack of sleep and food begins to take its toll. The ground where I sit, with my back against the jagged rock, is frozen and I find myself having to move constantly from discomfort. Finally, I find a patch of fresh snow to sit on and for the first time in hours, I'm comfortable and close my eyes. The wind continues to pound against my body as it whistles through the cave. Just inside the cave is a ten feet tall and five feet wide steel door. Next to the door, built into the rock, is a black box that conceals a keypad allowing access to those with authorization. The cave itself is large enough for about fifty people to fit inside, with the highest point about fifteen feet up. Other than the rough, jagged stone walls, nothing else is visible except for a thermometer hanging just inside the opening, only a few feet from where I sit, fading in and out of sleep.

"*Ashlee, stay where you are. It's too late for you to try and go anywhere now.*"

"*I don't know what to do, Al. Everyone here is panicking.*"

"*I'm on my way right now. I'll be there soon. Just stay inside the hospital until I get there. It's the safest place for you to be.*"

"*What about mom and dad?*"

"*They're on their way to the compound along with other people from Layton. They'll be fine.*"

"*Please hurry, Alec. I'm sca...*"

"*Ashlee? Ashlee!*"

I look at my phone and the signal is gone. I try calling her several more times, but can't get through. Eventually, I give up and decide to try and send her a text, telling her I'm coming for her. The text isn't going through either, so I set it to keep trying until it has a signal and I put the phone down. The snow is coming down hard. There are no longer any snow plows out on the roads and as a result, the snow is already getting really deep. Visibility is so bad that I have to turn off the headlights because they're reflecting off the falling snow, making it more difficult to see. I turn on the emergency flashers to provide a small flash of light, and it at least makes it possible to see about fifteen feet, even if it's momentarily.

"*Alec, I'm not sure we're gonna be able to make it there. We haven't even made it out of Layton yet and we've been driving for thirty minutes. How are we supposed to get to Salt Lake with the roads already this bad?*" asks Brian.

"*We'll make it,*" I respond. "*We'll make it.*"

"*Look man, I want to go get her just as bad as you, but the weather has gotten a lot worse than they said it would.*"

"*We'll make it!*" I look over at Brian. "*We have to,*" I say in a softer tone. I turn my eyes back to the road just in time to see the lights of another car shining into my eyes.

"Alec? Alec, wake up."

2

I open my eyes to see my friend, and adopted brother Brian Williams, looking at me, shaking his head.

"You're such a slacker," Brian says with humor in his voice. He's wearing a ski mask to shield himself from the wind. Only his brown eyes are visible through the small holes.

"Well, maybe you shouldn't take so damn long to come and relieve me. I'm turning into a snowman out here," I respond as I climb to my feet, shaking off a thin layer of snow that settled on me.

"Yeah, that's why I sit in the tunnel. It keeps you dry and warmish," Brian says as he points down towards the tunnel where trucks would come to deliver supplies before the storm.

"That's also why we only have two-hour shifts," I reply dryly.

"Yeah, sorry bro. Apparently there was some kind of a mix up on who's shift it was. I thought it was James' shift, while he thought it was mine." Brian scratches his head. "You know James and everyone else are all too afraid to come out here because they think there's "scary monster's lurking in the shadows". Plus, why didn't you just let yourself in?"

"Because. My access was revoked. And the only thing out there," I pause as I look into the black night, "is their own imaginations and a bunch of snow."

"I don't know Alec. I've heard strange noises out here lately that I've never heard before. It's actually kind of creepy."

"It's probably just some animal starving. A wolf eating a moose or maybe the moose is eating the wolf. You guys are seriously a bunch of little girls."

"Who you calling a little girl? You're the one who's too chicken to ask Emily out."

"I'm just taking my time."

"Oh please. What are you waiting for, an invitation?"

"I don't know," I throw my hands in the air as I make my way towards the door. "It's not like she's going anywhere."

"Good point, but if you wait too long, I'm gonna ask her out myself."

"I guess I better hurry then. She'll definitely not be interested in anyone after you get to her."

"Funny."

I envision a blank look of disappointment under the ski mask as he stands there motionless with his right hand up giving me the finger.

"There's really no point in you staying out here now. You pretty much let the whole day go by."

"I won't be out here for very long. As soon as those geriatrics who call themselves a council go to bed, I'm heading in."

"And I'm the slacker?" I say as I pull the large, heavy door open. "Watch out for the killer moose."

"I'll kick the killer moose's ass. Hey turn the light on for me, would ya?" Brian yells just as I close the door.

"You got it bro," I say softly knowing he can't hear.

I walk away from the door *without* turning on the light. Just inside the entrance to the compound is a large great room that everyone calls the main hall. The room is about a hundred feet wide and fifty feet deep. The outer walls are solid cement, painted white, and the inner walls are cinder block painted a dark grey to contrast. I'm not sure why the government cared so much about the color of walls in a military compound, but it does give the closed in environment some life. To my left is a long hallway that leads to all of the living quarters. The hallway goes a half mile into the mountain with two hundred apartments lining both sides of the hallway. Straight ahead is an elevator and a door that takes you to the stairwell down to the lower levels. To the right is a third hallway that also goes a half mile

4

deep, leading to the armory, storage, a gym, cafeteria, and a conference room and many others.

I pick the hallway on the right as I feel another rumble in my stomach. I walk down the long hall quickly, not stopping to talk with any of the people I see on the way. The cafeteria is at the end of the hall, so it takes a few minutes to get there. As I push my way through the double doors into the cafeteria, I see her instantly.

Emily Patterson.

She's bringing some food out of the kitchen on a tray to give to an older couple who are sitting at the corner table on the left side of the room. She's wearing a green t-shirt, a pair of dark blue jeans with holes in the thighs, a pair of black slip-on shoes and her black apron with the Army logo in the center. Emily and her mother, with the help of a few other people, work the kitchen, keeping everyone in the compound fed. My favorite part of the day is when I'm eating because I get to spend time with her. Emily and her parents arrived at the compound the same night we did. They had been trying to ride out the storm in their home when they decided that they should find somewhere better to go. Brian and I were on our way to Salt Lake on the night all the city services were stopped. That was when we found them. When we walked up on Emily's car, it was upside down and everyone in the car was unconscious. I can still remember the first time I saw her. Her green eyes glimmered when she smiled up at me with relief as I cradled her in my arms. I had to carry her while trekking through deep snow, six miles back to the compound.

"Hey Alec," she says with a big smile when she notices me.

"Hey Emily," I reply with a grin.

"Where've you been all day?"

"Oh—the other guys forgot who's shift it was and I sorta got left outside."

"I'm sorry. You've gotta be freezing."

"Yeah, I'm a little chilly, but I already feel a lot warmer now," I say this time with a smile.

"Why didn't you just let yourself in? I thought you had access."

I roll my eyes. "I thought I did too. I shouldn't be out there anyway," I say with a shake of my head. "I'm not gonna find anything."

"Well, just remember that's the only reason you found me and my parents."

"Actually, the only reason I found you is because we were in a car accident," I reply while taking a seat on a bar stool. "And that was a year ago."

"True, but you're the one who carried me back," she replies with another smile while raising an eyebrow. "Remember?" She disappears into the back before I can answer.

"I remember," I whisper. "How could I forget?"

"Will you be having the usual?" she calls to me.

"Sure am!"

I always order the exact same thing day and night. Chicken noodle soup. Due to our unfortunate circumstances, there aren't a lot of choices. I don't exactly enjoy the same thing every single meal, but it's the only thing that tastes good. Everything else is either too bland or just plain nasty. We ran out of the good food after only a month. The compound did have a large emergency supply of all kinds of different canned foods that would last this many people several years, but the good fresh food disappeared quickly, since we don't get regular deliveries.

"Hello, Alec."

I recognize the female voice behind me instantly. It belongs to someone I've known almost all my life. Someone that lived down the street from me and someone my parents tried over and over again to set me up with. She's also one of my least favorite people in the entire world.

6

"Hi Alisha," I say as politely as possible.

"Where've you been lately? I'm starting to wonder if you're avoiding me."

"Not avoiding anyone. I'm just always outside on watch lately." She takes the seat next to me.

Alisha is the type of girl that you would see going to clubs or always on those stupid reality shows. She wears expensive clothing and is always more concerned about her looks than anything else, including other people. Even inside the compound, when she can't go anywhere, she dresses up like she's preparing for something really important. Today she has on skin tight, black pants that make all her curves stand out. Her shirt is simple, with long sleeves, one of those loose hanging cotton shirts that droops off her left shoulder. The only good thing I ever could think about her is how attractive she really is. She has long blonde hair that never seems to be out of place, striking blue eyes and a stunning smile that could make anyone's heart miss a beat. Any guy would want to be seen with someone like her in public, but her arrogance and stupidity are too much for me. She cares about herself a little too much.

"It just seems like you don't ever have time to spend with me anymore."

"Well, your father and the rest of the council have me out on long shifts lately. All I want to do is sleep when I get done," I say as I spot Emily peeking through an opening above a counter that separates us from the back of the kitchen. She doesn't hide her annoyance as well as I am. "I don't really have time for anyone lately," I add.

Alisha spots me looking up at Emily as I finish my sentence and rolls her eyes. The two of them have never really gotten along very well. I assume it's because Alisha is jealous of Emily and Emily simply doesn't like her. Nobody does. Emily and I definitely have that in common.

"Well, I'll have to talk to my dad about keeping you out so much," she responds cheerfully.

"Yeah, that would be great," I say sarcastically, but Alisha doesn't notice.

That's one more thing I don't really like about her. She doesn't get my humor and can't even tell when she's being made fun of. She really is a dumb blonde. Just as I'm beginning to lose my mind, Emily walks out of the kitchen with my food.

"Here you go Alec. Chicken noodle soup. I also brought you a bowl of broccoli. You haven't been eating your vegetables. We need to keep your energy up if you're going to be out on watch as much as you have been lately."

"Hello, Emily," Alisha mutters in a condescending tone. "Having a good time in the kitchen?"

"Anything to keep me busy, I suppose. Are you having a good time with—well, what is it exactly that you do?"

"I sure don't cook food for anyone. Anything is better than that."

"That's because you don't do anything for anyone. All you do is play dress up all day. It must be nice having everyone waiting on you." Emily turns and walks back into the kitchen.

At this point I can tell that a serious argument is about to take place and I don't want to be in the middle of it, but I know it's too late for that now. I keep my eyes on my food as Alisha sits in her chair, turning red, ready to explode.

"Emily, this tastes delicious. Just the way I like it."

"Well, I'm glad you're enjoying it," Emily replies back just as she comes and stands next to the counter. "Can I get you anything el…"

Emily is suddenly splashed with water just before a glass shatters on the ground. Water is dripping down her face and she's drenched.

8

I instantly glare at Alisha as Emily stands there with the look of shock on her face, unable or unsure if she should move.

"What the hell was that?" I ask.

"She was being rude!"

"Only because you were."

"How can you take her side over mine, Alec?"

"Because I am. Now I think you better go," I continue while lowering my voice.

Alisha stomps out of the cafeteria without saying another word. Emily is still standing there frozen, refusing to make eye contact. Just as it looks as though she's about to cry, she turns quickly and walks back into the kitchen so I don't see. I instantly jump off my stool and follow. I find her standing next to the stove wiping away tears.

"Are you ok?"

"I'll be alright."

"Don't let her get to you like that, Emily."

"I know I shouldn't," she says as she glances up at me, trying to fight back more tears. "I just don't understand what I did to make her hate me so much."

"She doesn't' hate you. I think she's just jealous because she's no longer the prettiest girl around."

Emily smiles while wiping her eyes. "You know, her eyes never leave you when you're both in the same room."

"Too bad my eyes are never on her," I reply.

I want to wrap Emily in my arms and comfort her. I've been wanting to tell her how I feel and seeing her in this vulnerable position makes my feelings for her grow even more.

"How's Mya doing?" she asks, interrupting the awkward silence.

"She's good. I think she's pretty much back to full strength now. I'll bring her by to see you tomorrow."

"Good. I'd like that. I miss having her around."

"Yeah, me too and I think she misses you as well." I look at Emily, like a total fool, trying to think of something else to say, but decide just to walk over and grab the dustpan and broom that are sitting up against a tall metal cabinet.

"No Alec, let me get it," she says while taking a step towards me, reaching for the broom. I pull it away.

"You made me dinner. The least I can do is sweep up a small mess."

"Thank you."

"You're welcome. I could probably use a towel though," I reply as I begin sweeping the glass into the pan.

Once I've swept up all of the glass, I look up to see Emily standing there holding the towel. As she hands it to me, we lock eyes for a split second. While staring into her green eyes, I can't help but sense a feeling of longing from her. I'm certain she can sense it from me as well. Her eyes don't move like they're permanently fixed on me, as she bites her lower lip. Green has always been my favorite eye color on girls ever since I saw Emma Stone in a movie. Emily blushes when she realizes we're staring at each other and turns away. I grin and begin soaking up the water.

"Thank you," Emily says softly as she takes the wet towel and pan full of glass.

"You're welcome."

"You should finish your dinner," she mentions just before turning and walking back into the kitchen.

I take a seat back at the counter and quickly eat my food. I forgot how hungry I was with all the drama. After I finish, I pick up my tray and carry it back into the kitchen where Emily is standing at a sink washing some dishes.

"I'll take those," she says as I walk up to her.

"Would you like some help?"

"No, it's ok. I'm sure you're really tired anyway."

"Yeah, I am pretty exhausted."

"Alright, I'll see you tomorrow then?"

"Definitely. You working in the morning?"

"No-but I can be here."

"Great. I'll bring Mya with me in the morning then."

"Sounds good."

"Thanks again for dinner."

"Of course."

"Alright well-good night–Emily."

"Good night, Alec," she smiles back.

I turn and walk out of the cafeteria thinking I've been a complete idiot. I make my way down the long hallway thinking of Emily the entire way back into the main hall. When I enter the large space, the main hall is mostly empty except for a few teenagers who are still up, sitting on the couches in the middle of the room talking. I don't know any of them, but I see them every night. I assume this is their favorite place to hang out since they're always here. There really isn't anywhere else for them to go, so I can hardly blame them for spending their time here. I nod politely and continue walking along the right side of the room in the direction of the North wing where all of the apartments are. I nearly bump into a woman just as I round the corner.

"Hey Alec. Where've you been all day?"

"Hi mom. I've been out on watch for most of the day and I could really use some sleep."

My mom is 5'7" with short blond hair and blue eyes and still looks young for her age. She always dresses in nice business-like clothes and keeps herself very presentable. My father does the same. It doesn't matter if they are going out or staying in, they always look their best. They've both always said that getting yourself ready for the day makes you more likely to be productive.

Tonight, she's dressed in a nice pair of black slacks that show off her figure and a purple blouse.

"Yeah, you look pretty beat. I left some food out on the table if you want any."

"I'm good. I just ate in the cafeteria."

"Of course you did," she says with a smirk on her face.

My mom has known I liked Emily since the day I carried her through the front door of the facility. She always had a knack for knowing what I was thinking, even when I was younger. Plus, she can see the way I look at her. Everyone has to know by now. She knows me so well she could even tell I never cared for Alisha and finally stopped pressuring me years ago. It was mainly my father who continued to pressure me because of his friendship with Alisha's father, Michael.

"Emily was there, wasn't she?"

"Yeah, Emily was there. I wouldn't eat there if she wasn't. You know that. Where are *you* going by the way?"

"I was just running to tell your dad dinner is ready. He's in a council meeting trying to figure out what they are going to do about all the missing people. You know he's always trying to solve everything."

"Yeah—by risking the lives of his own children. Not to mention Mya falling down a hole and nearly dying. All those guys are full of great ideas."

"Oh, you know he's only doing what he thinks is right."

"Yeah, I know, but there's no way we are going to find anyone out there. There's no way to track them in the snow even if they are alive. They're sending us on searches that are only going to end up getting one of us killed." Brian and I both hate the missions with a passion. It's not that we don't care about the people who are missing. We both just know that under the current conditions,

12

nobody can survive without training and proper shelter. "The right thing to do would've been to never go outside in the first place."

"Well, maybe you need to say something in one of their meetings," she replies with a pat on my arm.

"I have. They don't listen to anything I say." Brian and I have been trying to talk sense into them for a while, but we've continuously failed to get through to them. We're only a couple of highly trained soldiers. What would we know? "Good night, mom."

"Good night, son."

I continue down the hallway until I reach my apartment. Number 142. I open the brown, wooden door and walk inside. I live in a small, two-bedroom apartment with my parents and Mya. Just inside the door is a living room area with a long, blue sectional couch and a chair. Fortunately, there's also a TV so that we can at least watch movies on long days. The kitchen and dining area are at the opposite side of the room. The dining area has a small square table that can seat four people with my parent's room on the left side and mine on the right. The entire apartment has plain, grey carpet throughout the living area and bedrooms along with a beige tile in the kitchen and bathrooms.

I walk over and open the door to my room and turn on the light. Mya looks up at me. She's curled up on the bed and quickly jumps onto the floor and begins to stretch by lowering the front of her body as if she's bowing, with her bum sticking straight up. She lets out a small, growl like groan as she always does when she sees me for the first time after a long day. The light reflects off of her bright blue eyes, making them sparkle.

"Hey girl. How's your leg doing?" I ask as I take a knee and put both of my hands on her front left leg, massaging it to check her reaction. She doesn't make any uncomfortable sounds and actually seems to enjoy it. This is good because only about a week ago she would still whimper whenever I touched it. The white fur on her leg had to be shaved in order to put the fifteen stitches to close up the wound.

We were out on one of the council's silly search missions when a sinkhole opened up underneath our feet. *A sinkhole!* Only one more bizarre thing to add to the already bizarre weather. She fell almost thirty feet, bouncing off jagged rocks all the way to the bottom. Her leg was sliced open on the way down. I watched in horror as my Siberian husky, my best friend, hit the bottom unconscious. The only reason I hadn't fallen down with her was because Brian barely grabbed on to my jacket. I thought she was dead as she laid there in the dark hole, motionless. Fortunately, she only suffered the cut and a lot of bruises.

"It's looking pretty good. Do you think you will be ready to come out with me tomorrow?"

She instantly starts barking and pacing back and forth with excitement.

"Ha, ha. In the morning big girl. Emily wants to see you too," I continue rubbing the soft fur around her ears and neck. "In the meantime, I need some sleep. And you could use some more rest too. But first, let's take you outside and then we both can sleep."

I take Mya outside to relieve herself quickly. Brian isn't there when we go out, meaning he didn't wait for the geriatrics to go to bed like he said he would. He's such a slacker. Rather than lingering outside for too long, I try to convince Mya to do her business quickly so we can come back inside. Fortunately, we're only out there for a few minutes and return to the apartment. I take a quick, hot shower and put on a pair of blue basketball shorts to sleep. Mya snuggles up against me on the bed and I start to drift off the moment the light is off. Clearly I was more tired than I thought.

NeVille

CHAPTER 2

I yank the wheel to the right, narrowly avoiding a head-on collision. I instantly lose control of the Hum-V and it slides off the road, down into a ditch so that the truck is almost perpendicular to the ground. We're stuck. I quickly look over to check Brian and he's looking back with the same look of relief on his face. I turn my attention around to find Mya smashed up against the back of Brian's seat, struggling to get on her feet. I unbuckle my belt and reach back to help Mya get her footing.

"Well—at least you didn't wrap us around a pole," mutters Brian.

"I might as well have. We're not going anywhere now." I feel a knot in my stomach begin to tighten. Now I have no way of getting to my sister. Realistically, I knew even before the accident, with the road conditions the way they are, that my chances were practically none. But now, without a vehicle, there is absolutely no chance. "Dammit!" I punch the dash several times.

"I'm sorry, Al," Brian says softly.

"It doesn't matter now. We need to check on the other car."

I open my door and instantly shiver from the chill of the storm. The wind is blowing hard and making it difficult to see. Since the truck is practically on its nose, I have to drop out of the car, landing in fresh, powdery snow up to my knees. Mya follows right behind me and is nearly consumed by the deep snow. I climb up the slope back to the road. At first, I don't see anything. I start walking in the direction the other car was headed as Brian catches up to me. After we walk about fifty feet, we see lights up ahead. My heart sinks when I

16

see the other vehicle upside down in the middle of the road. As we approach the SUV, it becomes clear that it rolled at least once. The windshield is smashed and all other windows are shattered. There are also dents over most of the vehicle. As I approach, I can see two people in the front seat and one in the back.

"Emily?" cries a female voice from inside the car. "Emily? Baby are you okay?"

"Mya, stay," I say to her. I step up to the vehicle and can see that there is a young female in the backseat, with her arms resting on the roof of the car. She isn't moving.

"Ma'am are you hurt?" I ask the woman in front.

"My daughter... is she okay?"

"I'm gonna check her right now. Are you hurt?"

"I... I don't think so."

"Okay, good. Brian here is gonna help get you out. I'll get your daughter."

I try opening the door from the outside, but it's jammed. I have to climb into the backseat by crawling in through the side window. The girl in the backseat is still unconscious and there is a mild laceration on the left side of her head. I position myself in the car so that I can wrap my left arm around her and release the belt with my right. Once I press the button, she instantly falls down, but I catch her with my right hand and lower her so that she is resting on my lap with her face up. I'm quickly taken aback. Even with her brown hair all matted up and blood on the side of her face, she's beautiful. I gently slide my hand across her forehead, moving hair out of her eyes. Brian's already removed the mother from the car and is now trying to get the father free. He's unconscious as well.

"Emily, baby? Wake up," her mother says as she climbs into the back.

It's evident that Emily got her looks from her mother. Her mom has the same long, wavy, brown hair and green eyes. I figure by the age of the girl in my arms, that the mother is probably in her forties.

"She must have hit her head on the window when your car rolled. I'm sure she'll be fine," I say to the nervous mother. "You should go check on your husband."

"I'm fine," replies a muffled voice from the front seat. "Stay with Emily."

17

I turn to see Brian helping the father down from his seat. I was paying so much attention to Emily and her mother that I didn't even notice what was going on up front. He looks like what you would expect your typical father to look like. He isn't out of shape but it does look like he has put on a few pounds naturally with age. He has a full head of dark brown hair and a little stubble on his face as if he hadn't shaved for a few days.

"I'm Alec, by the way," I say to the mom. "The ugly one is Brian."

"I heard that."

"I'm Emma. My husband is David, and this…"

"Is Emily," I finish.

I can tell Emma is extremely worried about her daughter. You didn't need to know her at all to see the worry in her eyes. I place my hand on her shoulder.

"She's going to be fine." Just as I finish my sentence, Mya comes into the car and immediately licks Emily's face and she stirs. "Mya, no," I say pushing her back. There isn't a lot of light, but when I look down, I see a set of tired, but beautiful green eyes looking up at me. I smile.

"Emily, are you okay?" Emma asks as she grabs her daughter's hand.

By this time David, Emily's father, has made his way into the backseat and kneels down beside his wife. He looks at me, giving me a nod of appreciation.

"My head hurts," responds Emily as she squints her eyes.

"You hit your head pretty good," I say, placing my hand gently near her cut. "I think you probably have a concussion as well."

"Alec, we need to get moving if we're gonna have any chance of making it back to the compound," says Brian as he pokes his head into the car.

"The compound?" asks David.

"It's a military facility, a few miles back up the road. That's where we were coming from," I reply.

"I didn't see anything like that on the map," David says confused.

"Because it isn't on a map," Brian says quickly.

"Do you guys have warmer clothes you can put on?" I ask as I motion towards their bodies.

None of them are dressed well enough to travel several miles in a blizzard. Emma is wearing a pair of black jeans, a thin grey sweater, and white tennis shoes. David also has on a pair of jeans, a red windbreaker jacket, but a heavy pair of leather work boots. Fortunately, even though the parents aren't dressed very well, Emily actually has on a pair of pink snowboard pants, and a long sleeve shirt with white and pink Nikes. She already seems like my kind of girl.

"We all have heavier jackets in the back with the rest of our stuff," responds David.

"Good, but what about better shoes for these two?" I look at women's shoes.

"Um, I don't have better shoes," replies Emma. "But her snowboard boots are back there with her jacket."

I turn and look at Brian. "Go see if we have anything in the truck that we can put over her feet to keep them dry." Brian gives me a nod and disappears without saying a word.

Emma and David go in the back of the car and start tearing through luggage. While they're busy looking for their jackets and boots, Mya crawls over and nudges Emily's hands up with her head. I go to push Mya away, but Emily catches me off guard.

"Hey sweetie," she says as she rubs Mya's head that is now resting on her chest. "What's your name?"

"This is Mya, and I think she likes you." I stare down at her, admiring the things I've already learned about her. The fact that she's beautiful, likes snowboarding and apparently dogs too, are just added bonuses. "I'm Alec, by the way," I say with a smile.

"Nice to meet you, Alec. I'm Em..."

"Here's your boots, sweetie," interrupts her mom as she returns to the backseat, now wearing a heavy blue winter coat. "And your jacket."

"I'm gonna sit you up so we can put your jacket on, okay?" I say.

Emily nods and I slowly lift her into a sitting position. She closes her eyes tightly and bites down on her lip as she lets out a groan.

"You're not hurt anywhere else, are you?" I ask.

"N-no. My head just really hurts." Emily leans her head against my chest, clearly already exhausted from the small amount of movement, and probably trying to relieve the pain.

"How's she supposed to walk several miles in a blizzard if she can barely even sit up?" Emma asks.

"I'll carry her."

I reach over and turn on the lamp next to my bed. Sitting on my nightstand is a picture of Brian, Ashlee and me. The photo was taken on the day Brian and I came home from a long tour about a year before the storm hit. Nearly two years ago today. I can't seem to get over that dreadful and wonderful night. Such conflicting emotions. Ashlee's blonde hair is falling over her face, making it so her blue eyes are barely visible. She has the biggest smile on her face as she wraps an arm around us both.

Mya hates being woken up early. She lifts up her head and shows me a look of irritation. She lays her head back down as a sign that she isn't getting out of bed. The bright red numbers on the clock show 6:05. It's early and I want to sleep more, but surprisingly I don't feel tired. I climb out of bed and walk into the bathroom to brush my teeth. The chill from the ice-cold floor sends a shiver up my spine. After my teeth are brushed, I wet my hair down and quickly put a comb through it. Once I'm finished in the bathroom, I quickly put my black cargo pants on, along with my boots. After I'm dressed, I look over at Mya, who's now watching me closely with a look of anticipation. Clearly, she isn't as tired as she led on. It looks like someone is more excited to get out of the house than sleep.

"Well—let's go big girl."

Mya wastes no time as she quickly jumps off the bed and stretches before following me out of the room. I grab my jacket that's hanging up on a coat rack by the door and we both leave the apartment. As we walk down the long, chilly hallway, I'm surprised to see that no one is up yet. The hallway is empty and none of the lights are on. I stop by one of the power boxes and open the plastic cover to turn them on. Each light makes a popping sound before lighting up the dark hallway. The lights let off only a slight glow at first as they warm up from being off all night. We continue our walk down to the main hall, not caring to wait for the lights to brighten the hallway completely. Just as we enter the main hall, I hear a commotion coming from one of the rooms down the north hall, towards the cafeteria.

"I'm not sending my son out on another suicide mission for people who are most likely dead," says my father in an unhappy tone. My father's reluctance to send me out comes as a surprise, since he was the biggest reason we went out the last time.

"Just because your son's stupid dog got hurt, doesn't mean we should leave people out there to die. Alec and Brian are the only ones with the training that are capable of going out there and making it back alive," replies a voice I don't recognize.

"That could have just as easily been one of my boys who fell down that hole. They could have been killed."

"Look Paul, we all know there are risks sending them out there. It's not like I'm not concerned for their safety too, it's just that the people who have lost loved ones deserve to know what happened to them."

The third voice I am familiar with, and one I don't care for any more than his daughter. Alisha's father, Michael Wilkinson. Mr. Wilkinson used to be the mayor of Layton City and always had a knack for throwing his authority around long before the storm came. Now, everyone inside the compound just stands idly by, letting him make the decisions.

"You're right Michael," responds my father softly. "They do deserve some closure, but I don't want them out there for more than a day."

"A day is all I'm asking for."

I quit listening after I hear the decision to send us outside and head for the front door so I can let Mya out to go to the bathroom. I truly feel bad for the people who lost someone, but I also know that going out to look for them won't do any good. With visibility almost zero most of the time and the snow up to your waist in most places, nobody could survive in this environment without the proper training and equipment. Even then it's risky. Besides, we've all lost people we care about. It's just part of this world we live in now.

"Alec? I haven't seen you in a couple days. How's my boy doing?" shouts my father just as I reach the door. Damn. I almost made it without being seen.

"I'm doing fine." I turn around slowly, trying to act nonchalant like I hadn't overheard their conversation.

My father's dark black hair, that had finally started to turn gray at fifty-two years of age, is neatly combed. He's wearing a pair of blue, faded jeans and a black button up dress shirt that make his dark eyes seem even darker. My father is a tall, strong, athletically built man like me. He's an inch shorter, standing at 6'3", but still in very good shape for his age. Before the storm, my father would run three and a half miles every morning before he left for work. Now, he gets his exercise in the compound's gym.

"Well, I hate to break it to you son, but…"

"Yeah, I overheard you and Mr. Wilkinson arguing back and forth. Dad, all we're going to find out there is some frozen bodies. And that's if they haven't been completely covered by the snow, which they most likely have anyway."

"I know son, but put yourself in their shoes. Wouldn't you want some closure as to what happened to them? I would if you went missing."

"Is Ashlee included in that?"

He starts to respond, but then chokes it back and lowers his head. After a moment of awkward silence, he looks back up at me with a painful look in his eyes.

"Son, I know you're mad at me for that, but I promise you I did everything I could to go and get her."

"Oh please. Your standing with the military, you could have easily sent a chopper to pick her up, or even sent a vehicle to get her. You were just more concerned about your job than your own daughter."

"That's not true," he says softly in a defeated voice.

I ignore him and turn to open the door. I pause, just before entering the code to open it. "When are we leaving?" I ask without turning to face him.

"First thing tomorrow morning. You and Brian aren't going to be doing any of your normal duties today so that you're both well rested for tomorrow."

"Well–I suppose we'll be ready to go." I enter the code and get a "NOT AUTHORIZED!" message. "Why has my access been changed for this door?" I ask trying to stay calm.

"I don't know," my father says as he steps up and enters in his own code. You can hear the locking mechanism release and the door slightly cracks open. Cold air quickly rushes through the small opening before the door is open a couple inches. "I'll make sure it gets restored though."

"See that you do. If I'm gonna be spending all my time outside, I need to be able to get in and out." Mya and I step outside and I close the door without looking back. Only I leave it slightly cracked so I can get back in.

I instantly feel the shock of the ice-cold air as it slams into my face. I check the temperature on the thermometer and it reads only five degrees. The wind howls as it passes through the valley and into the cave. I follow Mya out into the frozen wasteland, as she runs over the ledge into the clearing to pee. I wait patiently and gaze out towards the northwest in the direction of my home as I lean against the rock wall. I can only see to the edge of the snow bank, about twenty feet, because of the heavy snowfall and lack of light.

I imagine driving to my house and finding Ashlee sitting there on the couch watching a movie like we had done so many times. This had always been our thing to do together since we were kids. We were always the first ones in line to see the next big movie that was coming out. Now, I'm sure we'll never see another one together again. I've tried to deny it ever since that night, but the fear of the reality is too strong and that fear only grows stronger by the day.

The hair on the back of my neck suddenly stands up. I hear a faint, awkward noise in the wind come from the west, past where Mya went. I walk to the edge of the snowbank and peak over the ledge at Mya, to make sure she is close. She's only about fifteen feet away. I watch her as she paces back and forth, sniffing around as if she's trying to pick up the scent of something. I always wished I could smell, see or hear as well as she can. Having her senses would've made being a soldier easier. I could've smelled my enemies approaching. That kind of ability could've saved so many lives. Several moments pass as snow begins to build up on my shoulders and in my hair, when all of a sudden Mya's head jolts up and she freezes, looking in the direction from where the sound had come from. Whatever it is, she can either smell it, or see it. She stands motionless, like a statue, for about twenty seconds until I call to her.

"Let's go, Mya! Back inside now!" She turns her head, acknowledging she hears me, but continues standing there, returning her gaze to the shadows. "Mya!"

Just as I'm about to yell her name again, a loud shrieking noise, unlike anything I've ever heard before, echoes through the wind, sending more chills up my body. Mya quickly turns and runs up the ledge to stand next to me. I don't bother to wait and see what it is, since I'm not carrying a weapon and Mya, who usually shows no fear, clearly seems spooked. I grab her by the collar to make sure she follows, even though I doubt she wouldn't at this point. I quickly lead her back into the cave and over to the door. Just as I pull the door open, I hear the shrieking noise again and this time it sounds as if it's just outside the cave. Once we're both inside, I turn to pull the door closed, but not before seeing a shadowy figure near the entrance of the cave. I waste no more time to lock the door so that whatever is outside doesn't find its way in.

"Hey, there you are," says Brian and I nearly jump out of my shoes from the surprise. "Hi Mya." He kneels down and pulls her close, rubbing her sides. I stand there for a moment breathing deeply and Brian looks up at me and frowns.

"You okay?"

I take a deep breath and give a sheepish grin.

"Yeah. Thought I heard something."

Brian stands up and we consider it for a moment, looking at each other and we both grin.

"We've been cooped up too long, we're getting stir crazy man." I say, and we both laugh. Trying to ignore what just happened. "So, what's up, Brian?"

"You know yet?" Brian has that tone in his voice when he's unhappy with something. He knows about the mission. I knew he would be disappointed.

"Yeah, I know. I overheard my father fighting with the council about it. Those guys are a bunch of assholes."

"Well, we know from experience that the guys in charge usually are," he says with a grin and smacks me on the shoulder. "At least she'll be back out there with us," he adds, looking down at Mya.

"We shouldn't be out there at all. We're not gonna find anything."

"Yeah, I know. At least this will be the last time."

"We'll see," I reply as the three of us start towards the cafeteria.

"Tell her?"

"No. Not yet."

Emily's nowhere in sight when we walk through the double doors. There are only five people eating their breakfast for the day. I see Emily's mom sitting at the bar, so I decide to walk over and talk to her. I've grown fond of her in the last year. Always talking with her whenever I'm here eating. Mrs. Patterson is a really sweet person, just like her daughter and I enjoy our conversations. Whether she's telling stories about Emily or listening to mine, she's just a bright thing to look forward to after a long day in the gloomy outside. If only I could say the same about Mr. Patterson.

"Hello, Mrs. Patterson."

"Well, hello Alec. How are you?" She asks as she reaches over and gently squeezes my arm.

"I'm good. You?"

"Good. Emily will be back in a moment, by the way," she says with a smile as I take a seat next to her. Mrs. Patterson reaches down and rubs the fur on Mya's head. "How's *she* doing?"

"She's doing much better. After a couple weeks of rest, she healed really well. Today will be her first real day outside of the apartment for anything other than going to the bathroom."

"Yeah, she's looking pretty good. She sure is tough."

"Mya!"

26

Emily's voice echoes through the cafeteria and Mya runs over to her before I can turn around. She hasn't seen Emily in quite some time now, so I'm not surprised by her reaction. Hearing Emily's voice and seeing her in person still gives me butterflies. Today she's wearing blue faded capris with a red t-shirt–and her pink Nike's.

"Hi, Alec. Why are you here so early? I thought you'd sleep in longer."

"Mya couldn't wait to see you," I say with a smile.

"Well, lucky me. I wanted to see her too," she responds as she kneels down and wraps her arms tightly around Mya. "Her leg looks great."

"Yep. She's a quick healer, but she's also very lucky."

Emily continues to rub Mya's head for what seems like forever. She's enjoying this reunion with Mya so much that I begin to wonder how she'll handle letting her go back out. "I think she should just stay indoors permanently for now on. Both of you should."

Terrific.

"Yeah, about that…"

Emily's mood suddenly changes and her smile turns into a frown. "You're not really going back out there, are you?"

"The council wants us to look for the missing people one last time."

"Oh."

Emily is clearly upset now, but I wonder why. She's the one who felt like it was a good idea just last night.

"Oh, I do hope you find someone," says Mrs. Patterson.

"Mom, they probably aren't even alive. They've been out there way too long."

Emily feels the same way I do?

"Emily, honey, there is always a chance. I wouldn't just give up before trying at the very least."

27

"Yeah, I guess you're right. I'm just worried about Alec and Mya. They could really get hurt out there. Just look at what happened to Mya the last time they went out there, and they didn't even go very far. This time they could be out there for a week or more."

"Emily, Mya and I will be fine. Besides, it will actually only be a day. Plus, I've gone on dangerous missions where people are trying to kill me. It's my job. It's not like the snow is going to be shooting at us."

"I'll be fine too, by the way," interjects Brian.

Brian's comment makes Emily blush. Her mom and I both grin, but I might have turned a little red as well.

"*We'll* be fine, Emily," I reassure her.

"But what if Mya falls down another hole?" she asks as the color of her face fades back to normal. "She might not survive another fall like that."

"I've thought about that. She will be tied to Brian and me, so if either one of us falls, the other will be able to pull us up. We will be fine."

"It doesn't matter what you say to me. I'm still going to worry."

"I think somebody might have feelings for you, Alec," Mrs. Patterson mumbles under her breath.

Emily quickly shoots her mom a nasty look. I didn't even know she was capable of such a look, but she pulls it off nicely. The blush, however, she can't hide. Her cheeks are even redder.

"Alright, I'm going to leave you two kids alone to talk. It was nice seeing you, Alec. You too, Brian."

Emma pats Mya on the head before walking out of the cafeteria. The awkwardness in the room is almost overwhelming. I can sense that Emily is very embarrassed from what her mom said. She won't even look at me. She just keeps her eyes on Mya.

"So…" I say, scratching my head. "It was nice seeing your mom. I've always enjoyed talking to her."

"Yeah, she can be a bit obnoxious sometimes. Sorry about that."

"No really. I think your mom is great." Emily smiles at me and the awkwardness seems to fade, but then the smile quickly disappears as her mood appears to go sour again. She gets a sad look on her face as if someone has broken her heart.

"Do you really think you will be fine out there, or are you just saying that?"

I don't respond immediately. Instead, I just look into her eyes for a long moment, pondering what to say.

"Emily, I can't tell you that everything is going to go exactly as planned out there. But what I can tell you is that Brian and I have a lot of experience in things like this, so you have nothing to worry about. The thing that happened to Mya won't happen again." I pause and smile. "All three of us will come back, and if by some freak chance there are any survivors out there, we'll bring them back as well."

"I hope you're right." Emily looks down at Mya again. She's really having a hard time with this. I never imagined she would have such strong concern for Mya, let alone me. Her mom, my mom and Brian are all right. Now all I need to do is just tell her how I feel.

"Emily, I want to show you something. Will you come with me?"

"Now? What about the kitchen? Someone needs to be here if someone wants something to eat."

"I thought you were off?"

"I guess the other lady is sick, so I told my mom I would help today."

"Oh—well I guess it can wait," I say scratching my head.

"No," Emily shakes her head. "I mean—I'm sure everyone will get by without me for a little bit. But I should probably at least let my mom know."

"Perfect. While you're telling your mom, you can grab a jacket."

"You're taking me outside?" she asks with a look of excitement. "I haven't been out there since the day we arrived here." Emily says it as if she were someone remembering an old friend she hasn't seen in a long time. Although I hate going out in the snow, I also know that I am lucky to not be kept inside the compound all day, like someone in prison.

"Yeah, it hasn't changed too much. Just more snow."

Emily puts a "be back soon" sign on the counter and we start heading for her apartment. Emily and her parents' place is all the way in the back of the compound, so it's a good walk. Since her family was one of the last ones to arrive, they weren't left with much of a choice on where they could stay. So now they stay in the apartment that is farthest from the entrance.

"So why are you taking me outside?" she asks while twirling a finger in her hair.

"I thought it might be good for you to get some fresh air, that's all."

"It does get pretty boring being cooped up in this place all day, every day."

Mya is right beside Emily as we walk to her apartment. Sometimes, I wonder if Mya is my dog or hers. On the way, several people nod and wave to us. I don't recognize all of the people that we see because I'm always out on watch in the worst possible hours of the day and never have time to get to know anyone. We spend the majority of the walk talking about our days. Emily mentions a guy named Joe that is on the council and how he isn't very nice when he comes to eat in the cafeteria. She says he always orders her around as if she's the compound slave. I don't mention it to her, but I hope I get a chance to see this Joe character disrespecting her. I haven't punched anyone in a long time. Finally, after almost ten minutes of walking, we reach Emily's front door.

"Do you want to come in and say hi to my dad?"

30

"Um–sure."

Emily's dad doesn't really like me that much. We got into a bit of an argument not too long after they arrived here. The council, including her father, had wanted us to go out and find more people as usual. They expected us to find stragglers out in the snow and bring them here like it was a normal thing. After a long, not so friendly discussion, her dad said some pretty upsetting things to me about being "nothing but an ignorant soldier not caring about other people." I told him to go to hell and walked out. After that he's considered me to be a disrespectful punk. Or at least those are the words I remember him using. So I have the approval of the mom, but not the dad.

"Come on, Alec. He doesn't hate you. He just misunderstood you about the search thing. He really is great, once you get to know him. Plus, maybe since you're going out tomorrow, he might lighten up.

"I hope so," I smile.

Emily opens the door to her apartment and we walk in. Mya's right in step with us. This is the first time I've ever been in Emily's home. The apartment is identical to mine and every other apartment in the compound. Same sectional, only this one is grey instead of blue, and the same table and chairs next to the kitchen. I stop and look at the few pictures that the Patterson's were able to bring with them while Emily walks into her bedroom to grab her jacket. One of the pictures looks like a beach trip with about ten other people in the photo. Another is a family camping trip when Emily was a little girl. She couldn't have been more than seven or eight years old. She's super skinny with curly brown hair and freckles on her cheeks. I chuckle just as Emily comes out of her room and she gives me a stink eye when she sees what I'm looking at.

"Hey Ems," says David as Emily walks up to me, holding her jacket and wearing the pink snowboarding pants. I didn't notice him come out of his room.

"Hi, Dad."

"Alec." David gives me an irritated look to go along with his sorry version of hello. He even gives Mya a look of disapproval.

"Hello, Mr. Patterson."

"So what are you and–*Alec* up too?"

"Alec and I are going to hang out for a little while since he's leaving in the morning."

"Oh, right. The searches he thinks are a waste of time," he says as if I'm not in the room.

"Dad?" Emily says with a cautionary tone.

"I knew this was a bad idea. I'll be outside," I say and turn to walk to the door.

"Yeah and get your stupid dog out of my house too," he says with a hissing tone.

"On second thought," I turn back around and take a few steps towards him, completely unconcerned about what I'm about to say or who it might hurt. "You know something Mr. Patterson. You're a fool," I say with clenched teeth.

"How dare you?!" David unfolds his arms and narrows the gap between us.

"I'm only going out this one last time so that I can show how ignorant all of you old men are. If anyone without any kind of training tries to venture that storm, they will die. And the people that have been missing for months now are already dead."

I'm trying hard to suppress my anger. The last thing I want to do is give in, in front of Emily. Least of all to her father. I've never responded well to personal attacks on my integrity or my family, including Mya. Once, during my basic training, I knocked out my squad leader over a simple mama joke. Needless to say, my military career didn't start off on the best foot. Luckily, my martial arts training, schooling and leadership ability were too much for the Army to ignore.

"David, what's going on out here?" Mrs. Patterson asks as she walks into the room. I didn't know she was here.

"This punk here insulted me in my home!" he says while flailing his arms in my direction. His face has turned bright red.

"Only after you did first, dad. He was only defending himself." Mr. Patterson's angry expression instantly changes to one of surprise like a deer caught in the headlights. He didn't expect his daughter to take my side.

"Excuse me, Emily?" he says softer but still angry as he glares at her.

"You've been nothing but a jerk to him since we came here. You don't even care about his safety. He has more experience than any of you silly old men and yet you all still think you're right." Emily snaps at him. She then grabs me by the arm and leads me to the door and we walk out. Before closing the door, she turns and faces him. "And don't forget the one you call a punk and the dog you call stupid are the only reason we're alive," and she slams the door.

I'm stunned. Here I was worried about how I had just spoken to her father and how she might even react. She didn't hesitate to come to my defense. I still owe her an apology though. The three of us start walking down the hall when Mrs. Patterson opens the door.

"Emily?"

"What mom?" she replies, expecting a lecture.

"I know I asked you for your help today, but don't worry about that. You two go have fun," she smiles.

Emily lets out an exasperated breath.

"Thank you." She forces a smile in return and we start walking again.

We make it to the main hall without saying a word. The silence is extremely awkward and I don't know what to say. I feel kind of embarrassed for reacting the way I did.

"Well, don't let my father ruin our fun," she says, finally breaking the silence.

"Sorry. I shouldn't have reacted the way I did. I hope I didn't offend you."

"You didn't." she shakes her head. "My father was wrong to come at you like that. *I'm* sorry," she continues with a squeeze of my arm.

"If you say so," I reply as we stop at the main entrance to the compound. "Shall we?"

"Absolutely."

I enter the code with no idea if my father had managed to restore my access. I hope I don't look like an idiot. My stomach relaxes when I hear the door unlock. We listen to the sound of the door's internal heavy steel rods release as they slide back into the door so it can open. Mya's head tilts sideways as she listens to the strange sound. She does this every single time. Once the door is unlocked, it opens just a crack on its own, letting ice cold air rush into the compound. Emily steps back from the sudden shock of the freezing cold temperatures.

"Are you sure you're okay? We don't have to do this," I say softly as I reach into the chest pocket in my coat and pull out a black beanie.

"I'll be fine," she responds while trying not to shiver.

"Okay, but tell me if you get too cold. I don't need your dad to have another reason to hate me."

Emily smiles.

"You and Mya will keep me warm."

I return the smile and hand her the beanie. "Wear this." She takes it and places it on her head.

"How do I look?"

"You look good," I say with another smile.

To me she is the most beautiful woman in the world, with her thick wavy brown hair and eyes that are the glimmering color of emerald that I could get lost in all day. Everyone always seems to have an idea of what the perfect girl would look like and it's usually a mix of several popular actresses, but to me, Emily is that perfect girl.

I pull the door open just enough for us to fit through. Once Mya and Emily are clear of the door, I pull it shut without locking it. When I turn around, Emily is standing in the middle of the cave looking up, moving slowly in circles. Mya's nowhere in sight. I can't help but smile as I watch Emily take in the surroundings. After a moment of watching her enjoy the fresh air and the scenery, she looks over and sees me staring at her. A smirk spreads across her face.

"Never had the chance to look around that night you carried me here."

"Well, it's not much to look at. You didn't miss anything special."

"I kinda like it," she says, still smiling. "What's that?" She points at the wall to my left.

"Thermometer." I walk over and check the temperature. "Twelve degrees. That's the warmest I've seen in a while. Not to mention it was only five degrees less than an hour ago."

"What is the warmest that you've seen?"

"A few months ago it actually hit high twenties. It stayed there for nearly a week. I almost thought things might actually start to get better."

"Do you think it ever will?" Emily rubs her hand along the stone wall. I walk closely behind her.

I start to think about Ashlee and that night I met Emily for the first time. I remember that moment the truck slid off the road and realizing I wouldn't be going to get my sister like I promised her. I've never resented Emily or even her dad for what happened, but I still feel anger towards myself for failing Ashlee.

"I hope so."

Emily turns and reaches out her hand, taking hold of mine. We walk to the mouth of the cave. The wind is blowing lightly, at least in comparison with last night, but still enough that Emily covers her face from the icy chill. To our right is James Larson, sitting down looking the opposite direction, rubbing Mya's belly. James is a young kid, probably only eighteen to twenty years old. He's just under six feet tall and has long blonde hair that always covers his blue eyes. He volunteers to come out and stand watch from time to time.

"Hey James."

"What's up, Alec?" We walk up to him just as he stands to his feet. "My watch isn't over already, is it?"

"No. I just thought Emily might like to come outside for a change. It's been a long time since she's been out of the compound."

"Hi Emily," James says with a nod.

"Hi James. It's nice to see you."

"Nice to see you too. I don't know if I would want to be out here today though. I think a storm is coming."

"Oh, I don't mind. It isn't that bad," Emily responds with conviction.

James turns and looks out into the black clearing with an uneasy look in his eyes. He doesn't have the normal look of young arrogance on his face. He's usually calm and relaxed when he's out here as if he isn't afraid of anything. Now he's acting nervous and keeps looking out towards the valley.

"Is everything alright James? You seem a little spooked," I ask.

"Oh, I don't know. It's just been a little creepier out here than normal."

"What do you mean?" I keep my eyes on the young kid as he searches for a way to explain what's on his mind.

"I don't know. I heard some weird sounds earlier. Kind of like a howl mixed with a shrieking sound."

"It's probably just a wolf or something. The wind is just making it sound a little muffled," I reply, trying to boost James' confidence.

"Yeah, I thought that at first and then the noise was closer the second time I heard it. This time it was very distinct. I can tell the difference between Mya and a wolf and this was neither. I've never heard anything like it before."

"Maybe a deer or a moose then? They might sound like a howl out here too. Plus, whatever it is, it's probably starving and that would just make it sound more desperate," I add.

"Yeah, I guess so." James glances out into the dark clearing again.

I can tell that he's really freaked out. I can't help but wonder if it's the same sound I heard earlier. It has to be, and it certainly spooked me and Mya. I don't bother telling James or Emily that I heard similar noises. No need to frighten either of them any more than they already are. Causing a widespread panic over what is more than likely animals would be reckless. I consider offering to take James' watch, but then remember I have an early morning ahead of me.

"I'll give you two some space." James changes the topic. He walks over to the mouth of the cave and leans up against the rocky sides.

"Well Emily, how is it being outside?" I ask while trying to put everything James just told me and what happened earlier into the back of my mind.

"It's nice. I see what James means by "kinda creepy" though. I've only been outside for a few minutes and I'm already starting to get a little freaked out. I can't imagine being out here for hours not being able to see anything."

"Yeah, it can get a little spooky. That's why it's nice having Mya with me. Her senses are much better than ours, so she would let me know if something is out there." I point my hand towards the dark clearing. "It will be nice having her back."

"Alec, I've always wondered. How long can we stay here? At the compound, I mean." she asks, changing the subject.

"Well–that's a great question. Assuming we never run out of food, essentially we could stay here forever. This facility is powered by a nuclear reactor similar to one that powers a submarine. On top of that, there's giant water reserves buried deep in the mountain that could last fifty years or so. Hundreds of thousands of gallons. If we used that up, I'm sure we could figure out a way to use the snow for water."

"But we *are* running out of food," she says with concern in her voice as she kicks a clump of snow that has been shoveled to make a walkway.

"Yeah, we are. I could hunt and find enough food for maybe twenty people or so, but not for a hundred. That's just too many. With the storm never clearing up enough to see farther than twenty feet or so, it makes hunting extremely difficult."

"I see," she says while shuffling her feet.

I can tell she's cold, but she's trying her best to hide it and enjoy her time out here. I can't help but stand back and admire her as she starts to play with Mya. The two of them begin running back and forth, teasing one another. Emily occasionally reaches down and pokes her in the side as Mya nips up at Emily's clothes and hands. They do this for a couple minutes and I lose my train of thought as I stare out into the darkness. I'm looking into the shadows at

38

nothing for who knows how long when suddenly I'm struck in the side of the face by something cold.

Just as I recover from the instant freezing cold sensation in my face, another ice-cold ball of snow hits me in the chest. Emily has a grin on her face from ear to ear as she packs another one. I quickly kneel down and grab a handful of snow and start to pack one of my own as she releases the one she just made. The third throw narrowly misses me. I keep my eyes on her as I pack snow together in my hands. Snow is falling lightly onto Emily's head and she just has this wonderful glow about her. I smile as she realizes she's out of ammo and I'm only a second away from the perfect snowball. Just as she starts to pack another one, I release mine and it hits true, but Emily gets her arm up just in time to block it. We both start volleying snowballs at each other, going back and forth, both of us hitting each other over and over again. When I can see that she's getting tired, I run over and gently tackle her into the snow. We both start laughing as we roll over on each other. She gets the last laugh by smashing a handful of snow into my face. The shock from the cold nearly takes my breath away as I frantically wipe it clear. Emily notices my frantic attempt to clear off the snow and begins to wipe it away as well.

"That's what you get for tackling me," she laughs.

"Yeah, you definitely got me good." Mya starts licking the rest of the snow off my face and I have to push her away. "That's enough, Mya."

Emily grabs Mya and pulls her away from me, still laughing.

"He's just mad because he lost the fight," Emily says to her, just as Mya licks Emily's face.

"You laugh all you want. Next time I won't be so easy on you."

"Yeah you will," she grins.

I slide closer to Emily and Mya just sits down between us. James is still in the same place he's been since after we came out. I look back at Emily and she's staring at me. Her cheeks and her nose are red.

"What?"

Emily shakes her head and smiles.

"Nothing. I'm just glad you brought me out here."

I smile back.

"Me t..."

I'm interrupted by Mya jolting to a standing position with her hair standing straight up. She begins to growl softly, looking out in the same direction as James. I quickly climb to my feet and pull Emily to hers. I pull her back behind me instinctively.

"Emily, get back inside now," I say as calmly as possible. She doesn't say a word and quickly runs back into the cave.

"James, do you see anything?"

"No," he says shakily. I glance over at him and see his eyes are open as far as they will go and he's shaking.

Mya and I move over to James' side in order to try and make him more comfortable. Now I wish I had my thermal goggles and my rifle. All I have is my knife.

"Mya, what is it girl?"

She starts getting a little more worked up. Her growl is louder now and she starts barking. Whatever or whoever is out there, she doesn't like it. Suddenly, she leaps in the direction of our lurking visitor. I snatch her out of the air just as a large, shadowy creature crashes into us with a roar. I smack hard into the frozen ground on my back, and slowly roll to my feet to see a very large, angry grizzly bear. Mya is already on her feet jumping on the grizzly's back trying to defend me. I look for James and he's nowhere in sight. It's just me and Mya.

The grizzly snarls and whips around wildly trying to swipe Mya with its razor-sharp claws. It continues swinging its arms trying to defend against the small, but persistent pest. Multiple times, Mya

40

nips at the area near the grizzly's neck, but never causes any harm. Just making the dangerous predator even angrier. Multiple times, the grizzly swipes at Mya and each time she narrowly avoids getting hit. I watch as my fearless friend battles with such a large powerful animal. Finally, my gut twists as I see the grizzly get a hold of Mya and throw her to the ground. The grizzly quickly jumps towards Mya in an attempt to subdue her. I yell as loud as I can and pull out my ten-inch combat knife from its sheath. I charge the grizzly at full speed and jump onto its back. My fingers grip course, thick hair between them as I thrust my knife as hard as I can into the grizzly's flesh at the base of its head, over and over again. The grizzly lets out a roar and tries to shake me off. I hold on tightly as the angry beast swings me around violently. Then, like a flash of lighting, the grizzly grabs me with its powerful paws and throws me to the ground. I hit with more force than anything I've ever felt in my life and everything becomes a blur. I continue to hear Mya bark wildly until her bark becomes quieter and quieter and I no longer hear or see anything.

CHAPTER 3

My arms are beginning to burn from exhaustion as I march through the snow, cradling Emily. I've been carrying her for well over an hour and have to stop regularly to rest. Every time we do, Brian offers to carry her, but each time I decline. I refuse to let this beautiful girl see any sign of pain or frustration or weakness. She keeps her eyes on me the entire time. Hopefully, she can't see any signs on my face of how much I actually do hurt. While Emily isn't a heavy person, carrying her for such a long time through deep snow is causing my lower back to ache, and the muscles in my arms are burning from the constant strain.

Emma and David are both walking side by side just a few steps in front of me, with Mya and Brian in front of them leading the way. Emma has two heavy, nylon bags—the kind that the Army would hand out for recruiting, each wrapped around a foot to keep them both as dry as possible. I know that if we make it back to the compound without someone getting frostbite, it will be a miracle. Although David and Emma both have heavy jackets, gloves and something to cover their heads, David only has on a regular pair of work boots. They weren't meant for an extended trek like this in deep snow. We need to hurry for his sake. He could be in real danger of losing all his toes. Or maybe worse. Emily on the other hand, although she can't walk, is dressed warmer *than anybody in the group. She's wearing pink snowboard gear from head to toe. While she's the only one that was injured in the accident, she's also the warmest.*

After what seems like a lifetime of struggling through the snow, we finally arrive at the cave that conceals the door to the compound. It's taken us just over two hours to hike the three miles from where we crashed. Brian and Mya ran ahead of the group once we realized how close we were, so the door is open with a small group of people waiting as we walk into the cave. Both my parents and all the members of the council are present. Several people, including my father try and greet me as I walk into the cave, but I ignore them all and walk right past them into the compound. I feel instant relief as I gently set Emily down on a couch in the main hall. I look into her green eyes for the first time since I picked her up at the accident site.

"Are you alright?" I ask.

She nods her head.

"Are you alright? You look like you're in pain." Emily studies my face as she looks into my eyes, likely trying to read my expression.

"I'm fine. Just tired," I say breathing heavily. I gently brush the snow off her head and shoulders. "We need to have your head looked at."

I gently pull off her beanie. Emily bites down on her lip and winces from the pain. I notice her reaction and apologize.

"Thank you," she says while gently grabbing my hand.

"You're welcome."

I look over to our right, and Emily's parents are on the next couch and my father is attending to them. David's shoes and socks are off, showing his bare feet. I can see the discoloring in his toes and it's clear that the early stages of frostbite have started. I look over to Emma, who also has her bare feet showing, but hers appear fine. Just a little pink. The nylon bags worked after all.

"We need to get you over to the medical facility quickly," says my father. "Otherwise—you might lose your feet."

"Dad, as soon as you're finished helping them, I need you to look at her head. I think she has a concussion and probably needs a stitch or two."

"You'll have to bring her over to medical then. I can't do anything about it here."

It takes three members of the council to carry David down to the medical facility. I tell Emily that I'll carry her down there as well, but she refuses and insists on walking as long as she can lean on me for support. Once we're in medical, I find a bed for her to lie down on. The one thing that this building does not lack in, is medical equipment. The facilities in the compound are state of the art and better than most in the country. It takes my father only a few minutes to get a small pan of lukewarm water to have David place his feet in. Frostbite requires the area in question to be warmed up slowly until the skin appears red and warm. Once my father has made David as comfortable as possible, he comes and looks at Emily. He determines that she does in fact have a mild concussion and has to give her three stitches on the side of her head. He asks me if I can stay down here for a while to keep an eye on David. I quickly agree without giving my real reason for staying.

"Alec?" whispers a familiar voice. "Alec?"

I open my eyes to see Emily and quickly panic. Images of Mya getting thrown to the ground and the grizzly lashing out at her come rushing back to me, snapping me back to reality.

"Mya? Where's Mya?" I frantically look around the room several times trying to find her. Emily remains calm.

"Mya's fine," she says, placing her hand on mine. "She's with Brian. You've been out for most of the day. We had you carried to your room to rest and Mya's been pretty riled up since the attack, so Brian's keeping her occupied."

"What happened? I should be dead. The last thing I remember is being thrown to the ground and Mya barking."

Emily's calm, changes.

"We don't know."

"What do you mean?" I respond but quickly regret doing so. I have to squint from a sudden shot of pain in my head.

"Well–some people were looking for a place to camp and they saw our light–so they started heading towards it to find out what it was. When they heard the noise, they ran towards the compound to find you on the ground–and Mya standing next to the bear. Dead," she finishes while scratching her head, not believing her own words.

"Mya–my Siberian Husky–killed a grizzly bear?" Emily shrugs her shoulders, clearly unsure of what to say at this point. "That's impossible," I mutter as I try and sit up.

"But yeah, the other people," she continues.

"Oh right. How many are there?" I pull myself up and put my feet on the floor. The pain in my head isn't gone, but it's bearable.

"There's two of them. Both men, and they look like soldiers. Well, one is wearing a uniform. The other isn't."

"What else can you tell me about them?"

"Not much. Something about coming from the Layton Hills mall and other people are living there."

I nod my head, but look down, confused as I try and take everything in. First a grizzly attack then two random visitors. The thought of two people arriving at the same time as a grizzly bear attack seems odd. That can't be a coincidence.

"What's the matter?" Emily asks.

I don't finish the thought. I look up at Emily and smile.

"Nothing. My head just hurts a little, that's all."

I realize at this point that Emily is still holding my hand. Her hand feels smooth against my rough, dry skin. Her skin is soft and her touch gentle. Butterflies well up in my stomach from the intimate contact, even though it's just holding hands.

"Have you been with me the entire time?" I ask as I look into her eyes.

45

"You stayed with me all night when I was hurt. Besides, I wanted to."

Emily smiles, but this time I notice something different. It isn't the same smile she always has–the same one she gives to everyone. I don't know what it is, but now it seems like it's intended only for me. Ever since that night I carried her back to the compound and stayed up with her all night, even though I was tired and in pain, I've known I wanted to give my whole heart to her.

"I was just keeping an eye on your dad that night," I respond with a slight smirk. Emily tilts her head and raises her left eyebrow. "Well… I was, but he's not the reason I stayed."

I have a cheesy grin on my face, but I don't care. I just stare into Emily's eyes and she stares back. Slowly, I start to lean in. So close that I can smell her perfume. She mimics me. I don't know what the smell is, but it's a pleasant smell, like lavender. When our lips touch, I feel like a bolt of electricity rushes through me, warming my entire body and making me tingle all over. I quickly forget about the pain in my head. Just as I reach my hand up to her arm and pull her closer, I hear the front door close. She hears it as well and we both pull away from each other. She's grinning just as big as me.

"Hey Alec, good to see you're awake," Brian says as he walks into the room. "I was beginning to think I would be going on the search without you tomorrow."

Mya jumps up onto my lap, making me release my grip on Emily's hand.

"Hey girl. Nice to see you too. You're practically my little hero. I had no idea you could take on a grizzly."

She licks me in the face and then quickly changes course, making a beeline for Emily. She's too fast and licks Emily across the face as well. Emily just laughs and hugs her tightly.

"Thanks for keeping an eye on her," I say to Brian.

46

"Yeah, of course man. I'm just glad you're okay. When James came in with the look of panic in his eyes yelling "grizzly," I ran out there as fast as I could."

I try standing up and quickly feel a sharp pain in my back, making me let out a grumble.

"Man, I'm sore," I say, trying to stretch. "I feel like I got hit by a truck."

"I saw your knife sticking out of its neck, you crazy bastard. Too bad you didn't have a sword, you would've cut the damn thing's head off." Brian and I break out into a laugh.

"Oh, you boys are so immature. Of course you would find this funny."

Emily gives us both a nasty look and we just laugh more.

"Ow!" my back wrenches with more pain.

"Serves you right. Now maybe you will act a little more serious about this. You could have been killed tonight."

This time Emily's expression isn't angry, but concerned.

"Sorry Emily. You're right," I say calmly. "I'll be more serious," I continue with a grin. "So where are these two visitors?"

"They're in the cafeteria. They said they hadn't eaten a good meal in a couple days, so Emily's mom is making them some food," Brian replies.

"What about my parents? Where the hell are they?" I ask.

"They're in the cafeteria too," says Brian.

"Well, let's head down there then."

The three of us, with Mya in the lead as always, make our way to the cafeteria. Emily grabbed my hand as soon as we were out of the apartment. I think nothing of it other than giving it a gentle squeeze and we continue the rest of the way like that. As we approach the metal double swinging doors with CAFETERIA in big bold letters painted on them, I begin to think about everything that has taken place. Who am I about to meet? Where did they come from? Emily said one was military. Was the grizzly attack a random occurrence? And how was the grizzly killed? I know that Mya didn't do it. She couldn't kill a grizzly if her life depended on it. Could I have killed it with my knife and it just took the grizzly a few minutes to finally realize it was dead? Too many questions that need answers.

I spot the two strangers immediately. My parents, as well as Emily's and the majority of the council, are speaking with them. They look different than everyone else in the compound. One of them is wearing a camouflage military uniform. Air Force colors. I wonder if he's in the service or if he just purchased the gear in an Army surplus store. The other is dressed in hunting camo snow gear as if he was planning on going hunting. By the look of them, it's clear they've been outside for at least a day. Their cheeks and noses are rosy red as the warmth is starting to come back into them.

"Hey Alec," my mom says as we walk in. "How are you feeling, honey?"

"I'm fine. A little sore, but I'm fine," I reassure her.

"Alec…" my father motions towards them. "This is Jake Reed and Rider Nielson."

The one wearing the hunting gear my father says is Jake which would make the other one Rider. Jake reaches out his hand and Mya growls. He pulls his hand back quickly and shoots Mya a look of displeasure.

"Easy, Mya," I say and put my hand on her, but she doesn't listen and keeps growling. "Go over there," I command, pointing to the wall on the far side of the room. She reluctantly listens and walks over to the wall, but is still growling even as she sits down. "Sorry about that. She usually takes a minute to warm up to strangers," I lie as I extend my hand.

"It's no problem at all," says the one named Rider.

Jake hesitates before shaking my hand, still looking at Mya.

"Well, I guess I owe you both my thanks. I don't know how I could ever repay you guys for showing up when you did."

"Hey, don't thank us. The bear was already dead when we got there," replies Rider.

Rider has this surfer look to him. His hair is dirty blonde and long enough that it hangs down into his dark brown eyes. He's very tall. He stands a good six inches taller than Jake and probably two or three inches taller than me, which would make him close to 6'7".

"So wait, you're all telling me that you really do think Mya," I pause and look over at my two and a half foot tall dog, "killed a grizzly?"

"It must have been your knife that finally brought the bear down, son. You did stick him pretty good in the neck," replied my father.

"Yeah, that must have been it then," I say confidently, but still not convinced I'm the one who actually killed a grizzly. The grizzly still had way too much fight left in it when I was knocked out, so I know there has to be a better explanation. "Rider, were you in the service?"

"Yes. Air Force. I enlisted about three years before the storm."

"Good for you," I say with a nod of approval.

I look over at Jake to ask about him, but he has the same look of displeasure on his face. He has a dark complexion with long dark brown hair and a full beard. He's scanning the room and his eyes are focused, as if he's studying the place.

"So, where did you boys come from?"

"I was on a recon mission from Hill when my chopper went down a few days ago," responds Rider.

"Hill as in Hill Air Force Base?" interrupts Mr. Wilkinson. "Really?"

"Yeah, we're still fully operational."

"I knew it," Mr. Wilkinson says with excitement.

I think about the possibilities of Hill Air Force base being operational after so long with no contact with the compound. We'd been trying to reach someone on the radio for months after we first arrived here, but gave up when no response came after six months. Now, suddenly we learn they're fully operational. Where've they been all this time?

"So where are you from, Jake?" I ask.

"The Layton Hills Mall. There's a couple hundred people there, surviving just like you guys have here." Jake's voice is deep and commanding. Unlike his squirrely appearance.

"Wow. This is just getting better by the minute," says Mr. Wilkinson with more excitement.

"I think we have a few of your people there, actually. That's why we came here," adds Jake.

"Alec, did you hear that?" asks my mother. "Some of our people are alive after all. They must have been there all this time."

"Yeah, that's wonderful news," I reply without looking at her. "So how did you and Rider end up together?"

Brian and I give each other the same look. Everyone really seems to believe this nonsense. I watch Jake and Rider both closely to see if they give any signs of being untruthful. If one of them is lying, he won't be able to hide it completely. I get the feeling that Rider would have a great poker face. Not only is he military and trained not to give up information, but he has this aura about him. I can tell he's charismatic and most likely a good leader. He's probably good at charming the ladies as well. He keeps himself completely still, with his eyes steady on Jake to let him respond. Almost like someone waiting for their commanding officer to take the lead. Jake, on the other hand, isn't as smooth as Rider. There's no way Rider would take orders from this guy. I notice him shuffle his feet— a major sign of nervousness. His eyes, however, betray him completely. Jake's pupils dilate and move back and forth, looking

50

at everyone in the room, unable to focus on one thing at a time. He clearly feels uncomfortable with the question.

"I saw Rider's chopper go down about half way between here and the mall. I went to check it out and ended up pulling him out of the wreckage," Jake says with a shrug of his shoulders. "I was already on my way here, so Rider just came with me," he finishes with a hard swallow.

"So, you decided to go on a suicide mission by yourself just to tell us our people were alive?" Brian sneers.

"Brian..." My mom scolds him.

"It's alright, ma'am," Jake responds quickly. "The truth is, we would've wanted to know if our people were alive, so I volunteered to come and let you know, even with the risk." Jake gives Brian a smug look like he's trying to rub his reason in. "Plus, I've been hunting in pretty bad conditions for weeks at a time before all this. I knew I could make it here."

"Well, we're certainly glad you were willing to take the risk. Their families will be overjoyed to hear they are alive," continues my mom as she gives them both a pat on the shoulder before going to take a seat at the bar.

"Well boys, now you should just go to the mall," Mr. Wilkinson suggests as he looks at Brian and I.

"And what? Bring them back here?" I ask without hiding my contempt.

"Well, yeah. Why not?"

"Look, Mr. Wilkinson—I think it's great that some of our people are alive, but risking their lives in the storm for even a day is suicide."

"Alec, I think you're being unreasonable," my father says softly. I give him a wide-eyed look of concern. How can my father disregard my experience in these situations, the way he has been, as if my experience in these matters means nothing? "Wouldn't you want to see your family again too?"

I shake my head and glance over at Emily. She's looking at me.

"You have some nerve–father–to question whether or not I would want to see my family if I were in the same situation." My tone is cold and stern as I speak to him. "I've *been* in the same situation all along, since you seem to have forgotten," I say before returning my attention back to Jake and Rider. "Can you guys be ready to go in the morning?"

"What time would you like to leave?" asks Jake.

"0600. We'll meet you by the front door. If you're late, we'll leave without you," I respond with no emotion.

I'm done with this conversation and the entire search. They actually think we're just going to bring a group of people several miles across a frozen wasteland with no problem whatsoever. If what these two strangers are saying is even true.

"We'll be ready," Jake responds with a nod.

I motion for Mya to come and I turn and walk out of the cafeteria without saying another word or even looking at my father. Emily, Brian and Mya are right behind me. I wait until we are in the main hall before I say anything.

"Emily, wait here. I need to have a look at the grizzly."

"Why?" she responds confused.

"Because. I don't believe that I killed it with my knife."

"Okay," she nods. "I'll be waiting here in the main hall," she says and walks over and takes a seat on one of the chairs.

I unlock the door, pull it open and step out into the cold without a jacket, paying no mind to the fact that it is freezing and I have nothing but a shirt to shield me from the cold. Brian and Mya follow me and the three of us walk through the small cave and out onto the snowbank to find the grizzly still lying in the snow, undisturbed. The snow isn't falling and you can actually see a good fifty feet out into the clearing below the bank of snow, before the fog and lack of light prevent you from seeing any further.

The first thing I notice about the grizzly is my knife protruding from its back where I drove in the blade the final time before it threw me to the ground. As I get closer, I examine all of the different tracks in the snow to see if any of them are odd or out of place. Most of the tracks appear to be from a boot or shoe. I can tell from the different sizes that one set of prints is most likely Emily's. Another set, not much bigger than hers, probably belongs to James, and only one more set of human prints that I'm sure belong to me. The last two sets of prints belong to Mya and the grizzly. There aren't any more prints within ten feet of the body. Once I'm satisfied with my initial inspection, I step up to the large, furry creature and reach down and pull my knife out of its back. The blade is covered in hair, tissue and blood so I dig down into the snow to clean it off. I then kneel over the grizzly and examine the area where the knife had been. I can see around the grizzly's neck are other small incisions that were not caused by my knife and couldn't be from Mya. There's no way her bite would be strong enough to get through the grizzly's thick fur.

"That's strange," I mumble to myself.

"What is it?" asks Brian as he watches patiently.

"I'm not sure."

For no real reason other than curiosity, I pick up the grizzly's head and twist it back and forth. I'm more than surprised as the muscle and bone give no resistance from the twisting, making the hair on my neck stand up. I suddenly realize how cold I am. I look up at Brian with a blank expression, unsure of what to say.

"Alec, what is it?"

"There are deep cuts that weren't caused by my knife. And its neck is broken."

I stand up slowly while looking out into the dark terrain around me.

"Bullshit man. Don't mess with me."

I look straight into Brian's eyes long enough to say "I'm not" and look over to Mya. She's standing on the edge of the bank looking directly west, with her eyes focused on one spot. I walk over and kneel down beside her.

"What is it girl?"

She lets out a wine like she does when she wants something, while moving her two front paws back and forth, waiting for permission to run out into the shadows.

Brian ignores us and decides to examine the grizzly for himself. "What the hell. You weren't ki…"

He's interrupted by a loud shrieking noise, just like the one I heard earlier this morning. Brian slowly moves over to stand next to us and we stare out into the clearing trying to see what is making the noise. Mya continues to wine, but oddly the hair on her back never stands up showing signs of aggression.

"Whatever it is, I don't think it's dangerous," I say.

"And what makes you say that?"

"Because Mya doesn't seem to think so."

"Oh great. That makes me feel so much better after the day we've already had."

"You're such a baby. I'm the one that got attacked by the damn grizzly. Remember?"

"Yeah, you did and I'd like to keep it that way. I'm going inside."

"Seriously? We're in Utah. One grizzly is crazy enough. There's no way there is another."

"I'm still going in. There's no need for us to be out here anymore."

Brian turns and leaves without another word, walking quickly like a kid leaving a dark basement. I chuckle at the sight of my friend, a grown man who has served in the military and been shot at by trained maniacs trying to kill him, run like a girl from an unusual-sound. I continue to watch Mya as she stares out into the shadows, unafraid of whatever is out there. It's almost like she knows what it is.

"What is it girl?"

Mya doesn't break her concentration and continues to sit motionless. At this point, I can't help but again wish I had her senses. To be able to see, smell and hear as she does. I imagine what it would be like looking out into the clearing and being able to see a little farther in this weather. To hear the sound of an animal over the wind, trampling through the snow. To smell the scent of a deer that's several hundred yards away while I hunt. As I begin to get lost in my imagination, I'm suddenly interrupted by a whisper in the wind.

"*Alec.*"

I turn around to see if Brian is behind me trying to scare me. He isn't there.

"*Alec.*"

This time the voice is louder and clearly coming from out in the clearing. Or at least it seems to be. Chills creep up my spine and make me shiver again. I'm freezing. I've been so focused on what I was looking for, I completely forgot about not having a jacket on.

"Who's there?"

"*Alec, don't trust them.*"

"What the hell."

I become uneasy as I frantically scan my surroundings, squinting my eyes in hopes of seeing better, to find the source of the voice. I begin to wonder if I'm actually losing my mind. There's no way for a voice to travel, even in the wind like this at a whisper. The voice also sounds so familiar.

"*Don't trust them, Alec. They aren't who they say they are.*"

"Oh yeah? And why the hell should I trust you?"

"*Trust your heart, Alec. Trust your instincts.*"

"Who are you?"

"*Don't trust them.*"

I'm now standing. I stand motionless in the snow for several more minutes, waiting to hear the voice again. When I don't, I give up and decide it's time to go inside. This day has been so strange. Either I hit my head really hard and I'm imagining all of it, or something crazy is going on.

"Let's go, Mya," I say, trying to warm myself by folding my arms tightly.

Mya obeys the first time and follows me back into the compound. Brian and Emily, who's still sitting where I left her, are both waiting for me when I come through the door. I try to avoid eye contact with them as I lock the door behind me.

"Well, see anything?" asks Brian.

"No," I reply softly, still avoiding eye contact with him. Instead, I look over at Emily and she looks back at me with curious eyes.

"So, what's the verdict?"

"Brian didn't tell you?" I glance at Brian and back to Emily.

"No."

"Looks like it was my knife that killed it after all." I instantly feel sick to my stomach for lying to her, even though I know the truth will do nothing but harm. Probably even scare her.

"Well, I bet that makes you feel pretty good about yourself," she replies.

"Yeah–who knew I could kill a bear with a knife?" I say scratching my head.

Emily looks down with a look of disappointment and starts to fidget with her hands.

"So–I guess now you have to go pack, right?"

"Yeah I do, but I'd like you to come with me."

Her mood changes instantly.

"Okay," she smiles.

"Well, aren't you two adorable?" Brian says. Emily's face turns bright red and I glare at him. "I'm gonna go throw up and leave you two alone."

"Good night, Brian," Emily says with a chuckle.

"Night, Emily." Brian starts to head back towards the cafeteria.

"Hey Brian?" I call out to him.

"What?" he responds without looking.

"Pack heavy."

"I was already planning on it."

Pack heavy has a hidden meaning that we used within our military unit. It means to come prepared for anything. It also means to bring plenty of firepower. Brian disappears into the hallway and Emily and I start to walk back to my apartment with Mya by her side. I'll need some time to get used to that. Mya's only ever been this close with one other person. I take hold of Emily's left hand, interlocking my fingers with hers, without looking at her or saying anything. Emily shows her acceptance by gently squeezing her hand. I won't need time to get used to this at all.

"Alec, who's the girl in the picture with you by your bed?" she asks, breaking the silence. She must have seen it when she was in my room.

The image of Ashlee in the photograph, warm and safe between Brian and me at the airport pops in my head like I'm there that day, but the image instantly changes to one of her lifeless body, blue and frozen, huddled up against a wall. I quickly shake the image from my head.

"She's my sister."

"I thought so. You two look alike."

"Yeah, we're actually twins," I say, glancing over at her.

"Really? I never would have guessed that, with your black hair and hers being blonde."

"Yeah," I chuckle. "Most people say the same thing."

We're now at my door and we stop just outside.

"What's her name?"

"Ashlee. Her name is Ashlee."

I turn the handle and let Emily walk in first. Mya isn't as polite and forces her way past Emily, running through the front room and into the bedroom.

"How long were you in the military before the storm?"

"Ten years."

"Do you miss it?" she asks as she takes a seat on the couch.

I shake my head.

"No. Not at all, actually."

"How come?"

I hesitate to answer, unsure of how to explain it to her.

"Getting shot at and shooting at others isn't so much fun. I saw and did things that I wish I hadn't, I guess."

Emily looks down and nods her head. My response was pretty vague, so I decide to continue.

"When I first joined the Army, I was sent to Afghanistan—a place I've tried to forget. I hadn't been there for more than twenty-four hours when I had bullets shot at me for the first time in my life. The bullets weren't even half of it. Children—no more than twelve years old—had been taught since they were very young to hate Americans and were trained to kill us."

"So, what did you do when the kids were shooting at you?" she asks, even though I know she wouldn't want to hear the answer.

"We fired back at the enemy. It wasn't until after the shooting stopped that we knew we had killed children. My commanding officer acted as if he just killed regular soldiers and that it wasn't a big deal. I know he wasn't a ruthless killer, or even a bad person.

He just saw anyone shooting at him as the enemy, regardless of who they were. To him it was just war. I didn't feel quite the same way."

Emily is looking at me, thinking of what to say. I wouldn't know what to say in response to that. I shake my head in disgust of what I've told her and look away. I've tried so hard, for so long to bury these memories away as deep as I can. The one thing I'm ashamed of most of all and I've just told her all about it. Just when I think I'm about to have a panic attack from the images flashing through my head, Emily gently places her hand on mine, which had been on my lap and squeezes it gently and moves closer. The images fade away.

"Alec, there's no way you could have known, who or what you were shooting at. The only people to blame for the deaths of those children are the people who put them where they were," she replies in a calm, comforting voice.

I'm surprised by her reaction. I've never known someone with her ability to see no fault in what I've done. Everyone else, especially all the human rights activists that protested against us when we came home, treated us like monsters. Whether they were waiting for us at the airport when we returned home, or sending threats to our families in the mail, the hatred seemed like it would never end. Bunch of hypocrites they were. Protest the killing of others just to turn around and threaten harm on others. It didn't stop until we were shipped off for another war.

"I don't blame myself for shooting those children," I continue and look back up at her. "But seeing the bodies of lifeless children is not something I would wish on anybody. It's something I wish I had never been a part of."

Emily nods her head again. The light reflects off her eyes making them almost sparkle. I feel a knot forming in my stomach as I suddenly feel–nervous. Here I am with Emily, in my apartment, for the second time in less than an hour. I think back to the brief kiss we shared, just after I woke up to see her sitting next to me on my bed. I remember the tingling sensation and the butterflies after finally kissing the woman I've grown to love over the past year.

Now that I'm finally alone with her in an intimate situation, rather than a cafeteria with prying eyes and listening ears, being able to look at everything that she is, inside and out. I know I am in love with her. Love. That isn't an emotion I've really thought about until now. Not wanting my time with her tonight to come to an end, an idea pops in my head to keep her longer.

"So, do you wanna stay over for a while after I pack? We could watch a movie or something."

"Definitely," she smiles.

"Come on then." I climb to my feet and offer my hand to help her off the couch. "It will only take a few minutes to throw some things in a bag."

I lead Emily into my room by her hand. We find Mya passed out on the bed with her head resting on my pillow. I walk over to the bed and kneel down so I can pull my pack out from underneath. Emily takes a seat on the bed next to Mya, only to have her reposition herself so that her head is on Emily's lap. Emily welcomes Mya's affection by rubbing her head. I quickly start pulling clothes from my dresser and put them into the bottom of the pack. I grab six clean pairs of underwear and socks. I'm not really sure how long I'll be gone, but I don't want to be gone for more than five days at most. Especially now. Originally, we were only leaving for a day. A trip to the mall and back could take several days.

Emily sits on the bed quietly while continuing to massage Mya's head and rubbing her neck and belly. After a few minutes, I watch her grab the picture frame on the nightstand. She doesn't know I'm watching, but she smiles at the picture.

"When was this picture taken?"

"That was the day Brian and I came home after being gone for over a year."

I place my bag down against the door, satisfied I've packed enough extra clothes. All my other supplies that I'll need are in the weapons room, all except for my personal handgun that I don't want to get out in front of Emily. I don't want to give her any reason to worry. I take a seat next to her on the bed and reach for the photo. She hands it to me.

"It was about a year before the storm came. She saved up all her vacation time, so the three of us went on a road trip along the western coast for about two weeks, stopping anywhere that looked fun." I chuckle as I set the picture back on the nightstand. "I'd give almost anything to relive those weeks."

"What does she do for a living?"

"She's... she was a doctor," I look up at Emily and tuck a lock of her hair back behind her ear. "An Orthopedic specialist at Primary Children's in Salt Lake. The kids she worked with were her life. I told her she needed to get out of there, days in advance, but she refused to leave. She was always stubborn. We both are. I told her I would come and get her when I could."

I pause as I remember my last conversation with her and the panic in her voice, not knowing what to do. I can't help but imagine her huddled together with others in the hospital, either freezing to death or starving to death. Whichever came first. Both outcomes make my stomach hurt.

"How come you didn't go to her?"

"Once Brian and I helped our parents pack and got them on their way here, along with the majority of the people in here, we took a Hum-V out, knowing we probably wouldn't make it anyway. It was the same night that all government services stopped and the roads had gotten really bad."

"Wait," Emily says wrinkling her forehead. "That's where you and Brian were going that night?"

I regret answering her question immediately. The pain in Emily's eyes makes it clear that she thinks it is her family's fault I never made it to Ashlee.

"I'm so sorry, Alec." I start to shake my head, knowing what she's going to say. "If we hadn't been there that night, if we hadn't almost hit you…"

She climbs to her feet and starts to back away, with tears already streaming down her face. I hadn't meant to make her feel the blame for our crash. Even Brian was trying to tell me that we probably wouldn't make it. On one hand I'm angry with myself for not being able to get her and I will always carry that weight, but on the other hand I now have Emily. The fact that she is here now and alive is all that she needs to hear.

"Emily," I grab both of her hands and pull them away from her face, holding them gently. "Sit back down. If we hadn't been there that night, you, your mom, and your dad would be dead right now." I wipe a tear away from her cheek. "I'm glad I was dumb enough to think I could go get my sister. If I hadn't gone when I did, we never would have been in that accident with you. You and your parents wouldn't be here."

Emily pulls one of her hands free and wipes away more tears.

"But your sister," she continues.

"My sister made her choice. That's not your fault." It is someone's though. "I miss my sister and… I hope that by some chance she's still alive, but meeting you…" I cup her chin in my hand, "is the best thing that ever happened to me."

Emily's eyes are starting to look swollen from crying. I brush my thumb across her lips and pull my hand away. For a split second, I tense from surprise at her sudden kiss, but relax almost as if kissing her is normal. I simply close my eyes and enjoy the moment. The touch of her soft, smooth lips against mine makes me shiver as I place my left hand onto her side, just above her hip. Although I enjoyed our first kiss earlier, as brief as it was, this time I don't want it to end. I have no idea what tomorrow will bring and now leaving is the last thing I want to do. Things quickly heat up as we start to get carried away, when we are interrupted by Mya who decides to get in on the action. We both pull away the instant we feel Mya's fur and wet tongue and start laughing. I grab Mya in a bear hug and kiss her on the forehead. She lets out a howl of appreciation making Emily only laugh more.

"Looks like somebody's jealous of me," Emily chuckles just as the front door opens and closes.

"More likely that she's jealous of me," I wink at her. "I think my parents are back," I say slightly irritated.

Emily shrugs her shoulders and a second later my mom appears in the doorway. She looks surprised to see both of us, but it quickly changes to a pleased look.

"Hi mom."

"Hi," she replies, eyeing us with curiosity. "I was wondering when you two would finally get on with it," she smirks.

"Mom, really?"

"What? It's obvious that you two have liked each other for a long time. I think it's great."

I glance over at Emily and she has a grin on her face.

"Where's dad?"

"He's talking with Jake and Rider. I suspect he may be a while."

"Of course."

"You know your father. He's always involved with everything."

I don't say any more about the subject. Lately, I have nothing good to say about my father. I climb to my feet and walk over and give my mom a kiss on the cheek.

"Love you mom," I say, before grabbing my pack and walking out of the room.

"I love you too, son," she replies, before giving my arm a squeeze as I walk by. "Have either of you eaten anything?" she asks, returning her attention to Emily.

"Um—no we haven't. I was actually going to see if he wanted to go get something."

"Why don't the both of you eat here? I think we have some leftover deer meat from a week ago."

"That sounds good. Thank you, Mrs. Winter."

"You're welcome, but call me Susan," she says as she turns and walks into the kitchen. "No need to be formal."

I'm sifting through some movies that are inside a TV cabinet. Emily smiles at me when I look up and see her in the doorway. After watching me for only a moment, she walks over and takes a seat at the kitchen table. She seats herself against the back wall so that she can see into the kitchen as well as the living room. I can feel her eyes on me the entire time I'm looking through the movies. I finally find four for her to choose from. It's now time to indoctrinate her into my family tradition.

"Alright. I brought you a variety to choose from," I say as I set the movies on the table in front of her.

The four movies that I chose are: *The Man from Snowy River*, *Gladiator*, *Legends of the Fall* and *The Notebook*. Emily picks up *The Notebook* and gives me a puzzled look.

"Really?"

"I thought girls loved that movie," I reply, mimicking the look on her face.

"We do, but you strike me as more of the 'action' kind of guy."

"That's why I brought you *Gladiator*." I tap my finger on it. "And just so you know, I like pretty much all movies as long as they have a good story and good acting."

64

"Hmm…" she turns over each movie, with a blank face as if she's never seen any of them. "Well, I've seen these three, but I've never heard of this one."

"You've never heard of *Legends of the Fall?*"

She shakes her head no, curling her lip.

"What's it about?" She turns it over and reads the back of the case.

"Exactly what the back of the cover says. Forbidden love, betrayal and the bonds of blood."

Emily tilts her head to the side, unimpressed by my explanation. "You're gonna have to do a better job than that if you want me to be excited about watching it."

"It has Brad Pitt. What more do you need?"

"Do you have some sort of man crush on Brad Pitt?"

"The man is sexy, Emily and he's a good actor."

"So—you do have a man crush on him?"

"Okay, maybe a little," I smirk as I take a seat next to her. "Trust me. It's a good movie."

"Alright, I guess I'll trust you," she smiles.

We sit at the table talking for the next thirty minutes while my mom cooks dinner. Emily spends most of the time telling my mom and me about what she and her parents did for a living before the storm. Her father was a mechanic and her mom was a middle school teacher. Emily was attending Utah State in Logan, trying to get her teaching degree as well. She wanted to teach grade school. She had been home for the summer when the storm came. She told us they were out the night of the accident because her dad panicked about the storm and told them they had to leave. He had been watching the news and when the signal dropped, he decided it was time to go. He was trying to drive them south, hoping to outrun the storm.

"Dinner is ready," my mom interrupts as she brings over a plate of freshly cooked meat.

"Smells good, mom."

"Thank you for dinner, Susan," Emily says with a nod.

"You're welcome." She also places a bowl of corn on the table next to the meat and then sits opposite the table from me, next to Emily. "You're always cooking meals for us, so it's about time somebody cooked one for you for a change."

"I actually don't mind working in the kitchen. It keeps me occupied."

"Better than being out in the freezing cold all day that's for sure," I mutter as I place a steak about the size of my hand onto Emily's plate and then do the same for my mom.

"Yeah, it's freezing cold out there. I don't know how you do it Alec. Not to mention how creepy it is," Emily responds.

I cut into my steak and put a small piece into my mouth. The wild taste of the deer I killed only a couple weeks ago, ignites my taste buds. The combination of pepper, which my mom uses as a seasoning quite often, and the wild flavor of the deer meat is a drastic change from the same bland food I have on a daily basis. If I could hunt for food more often—or for everyone else in the compound, things would be much better. I glance over and see Emily digging into her steak with no hesitation like some girls tend to do when they eat their food. Emily certainly isn't making a mess of herself, but it's clear that she's enjoying the change of food as much as I am.

When I finish eating, I stay in my seat and listen to my mom tell stories about me when I was younger. Most of the stories she tells involve Ashlee, Brian and me, since we were always together growing up. This also meant that we always got into trouble together. My mom mentions one particular story about how the three of us made a slip and slide out of the hardwood floor in the house. It's amazing how well some liquid dish soap and a little bit of water can make a wooden floor as slick as an ice sheet. I can't help but grin at the memories of that day and the fun we had zipping down the hallway all the way through the kitchen and dining area. I chuckle as my mom recalls the horror she felt when she walked in and saw what we were doing to her precious floor.

While my mom continues to tell stories involving Ashlee, my thoughts are flooded with images of my sister sitting there in the hospital, frozen like before. Emily looks over and notices my sudden change of mood as I stare into the table with an empty gaze. She reaches her left hand and rests it on top of mine and gently squeezes. I return the gesture with a light squeeze of my own. I then give her a quick smile of appreciation before getting up from my seat to take my plate over to the sink. I still had a small piece of the meat left that I set aside to give to Mya. I wash my dirty dishes in silence, as I fight back the horrifying image of my sister sitting frozen, all huddled up trying to get warm.

"I'm gonna go take a shower, alright?" I say looking over at Emily when I finish, unable to shake the images.

"Okay. We still watching the movie?"

"Of course," I reply with a smile. "This way you two can have your little… girl chat."

Mya's still on the bed and looks up at me as I walk into my room. I toss the piece of meat at her and she catches it out of the air. She practically swallows it in one bite. I take off my shirt and toss it over at her. It lands directly on her head and she shakes it off with a groan of irritation. I close the bathroom door and turn on the shower. As soon as I'm out of the rest of my clothes, I climb into the already hot, steamy water. The feeling of hot water on my skin is soothing and helps me to relax my thoughts. I let the water run off of my head and down my neck and back. I stay with my hands pressed against the tile for several minutes until my mind is finally at ease and I'm no longer seeing awful images of my sister. I want to stay in the shower for a while, but I also don't want to keep Emily waiting for too long, so I decide to wash up quickly and get out.

As I'm drying off, I remember I haven't grabbed a change of clothes and I also didn't close my bedroom door. When I'm dry, I wrap my towel around my waist and quietly open the bathroom door so I can sneak to the bedroom door without Emily seeing me in a towel. I don't think it will be appropriate for her to see me this way yet. As soon as I open the door, I hear them talking about me.

"I've noticed that there's tension between Alec and his dad. Is that because of Ashlee?"

"It is," replies my mom. "He's mad at his dad because he thinks that Paul should have done more to bring Ashlee here."

There's a short break in the conversation as I move with my back against the wall. I'm barely blocked by the open door. Just as I place my hand on the door, my mom finishes what she has to say.

"Alec blames himself for Ashlee's… not being here. I think he's just taking his anger towards himself out on Paul. I… I don't know if she is alive, but I do know that Alec will never be the same, and he and his father will continue being bitter towards one another until he goes to Salt Lake. My biggest worry is that if Alec does go, and I know he will eventually, that I'll end up losing both my children. The bond between Alec and Ashlee is stronger than anything I've ever seen before. It could be the fact that they are twins maybe, but… a piece of my son will always be missing as long as they are apart."

I'm standing in my doorway, with my head down, and completely forget I'm trying not to be seen. I can hear soft sobs coming from my mom before she gets up from the table and walks to her room, closing the door behind her. I look over and see that Emily is also fighting back tears and has her hand on her chin, holding her head up. She looks over to see me standing in the doorway, but I have my eyes down at the floor, refusing to look at her and close my door.

After I finish getting dressed, I come out of my room to find Emily washing the dishes. Rather than trying to argue with her on the fact that she shouldn't be doing the dishes in my home, I simply go up beside her and take the one she just washed with soap and rinse it off, then set it on the dish rack to dry. The two of us stand there, side by side, in silence as we finish washing the dishes together. Even though we've only been transparent about our feelings towards each other for a couple hours, being here with her is something that just feels right. I could wash dishes with her every day and be perfectly happy. When Emily finishes the final plate, she hands it to me and takes a step back, leaning up against the counter to watch me. I don't notice her staring until after I set the plate on the rack and grab the towel to dry my hands. When I look up at her, she has a smile on her face and a glow in her eyes.

"What?" I ask as my face starts to feel warm.

"Nothing," she says, but continues looking at me.

I step towards her so that we are only inches apart, making it so she has to look up at me. I can smell her perfume. The sweet lavender smell. Emily places one hand around my waist and the other on my chest. My heart is pounding as I feel a sudden warmth rush through my entire body. I can't resist leaning down and kissing her gently on the lips. I make it a short one and pull away.

"Still wanna watch the movie?" I ask softly.

"As long as I get to stay with you—we can do anything."

"Good enough for me."

CHAPTER 4

F ive in the morning comes fast. I could have stayed in this position with Emily beside me on the couch forever. I fell asleep only half way through *Legends of the Fall*. Trystan had just returned home from his sorrowful adventures after leaving the war. I woke to find Emily snuggling up beside me. Mya must have climbed onto the couch sometime during the night, since she's down at the other end, on top of our legs, with her own legs sticking straight up in the air. I slowly slide Emily's arm off of my chest and quietly climb to my feet so I don't disturb her. The first thing I do when I walk into my room is shut off the alarm that had barely been audible in the living room. I'm lucky I didn't sleep in because Brian would've likely come pounding on the door at 6:00 AM wondering where I am. I quickly change into my black, heavy military issued cargo pants with thermals underneath to lock in the heat. I grab a thick pair of socks to wear underneath my boots. I put a simple, plain, grey t-shirt with a black, long sleeve Under Armor shirt underneath. When I'm fully dressed, I grab my pack with extra clothes and walk out of my room to wake up Mya and say goodbye to Emily, only to find her still sound asleep. I want to wake her but decide not to. She looks so peaceful and I don't have the heart to disturb her. Instead, I kiss her lightly on the forehead. I then whisper to Mya and give her a tap on the belly.

"Get up, Mya. It's time to go."

Mya rolls onto her side and gives me a disgusted look before slowly crawling off the couch. I walk over, with Mya sluggishly following and quietly open the door and then softly close it once Mya and I are both in the hall.

The main lights in the hallway are still off. There's only a faint glow from the nightlights in the floor illuminating the hallway just enough to see. We round the corner into the main hall only a few minutes later to find it also empty, but already well-lit. The lights in the main hall are activated by a motion sensor, so I figure Brian is already in the armory getting ready. Mya and I make our way down the south hall. As we near the door leading into the armory, I can hear arguing between Brian and a voice I recognize from yesterday.

"I'm not going to travel with a couple jarheads carrying assault weapons like they're going to war," Jake says with a snarky tone.

"Jarheads? Really?" responds Brian. "If you're too stupid to know the difference between Army and the Marines then I'm not sure I want you traveling with me. Your dumbass might drown in the snow."

"You know what..." Jake puffs up his chest and aggressively steps toward Brian. Brian doesn't move.

"Hey!" I yell as I walk into the room. "What the hell is going on in here?"

"Jacky over here doesn't want us bringing "assault weapons," Brian says back while simultaneously putting his fingers up in a quotation gesture. His mocking tone seems to anger Jake even more.

"Yeah, I heard that. What's that all about?" I ask Jake, who has an angry and shocked look on his face. He glances over at me, but returns his angered stare to Brian. "Don't look at him. I'm the one talking to you."

71

Jake reluctantly looks back with all the anger gone and just the confusion remains on his face. He's probably never had anyone speak to him the way Brian and I just did. I begin to think that Jake isn't all what he claims to be and doubt he runs the show where he comes from.

"I don't like the way I'm being talked to."

"That's understandable, but don't forget that you are in our home right now, so giving out orders isn't going to sit well with either of us," I respond in a commanding voice.

"I'm not comfortable with two people I don't know carrying those types of weapons." Jake is no longer making eye contact with us. He's just staring into the wall. He's not even looking at Rider, the man he came here with. I had barely noticed Rider was in the room myself. He appeared to be enjoying the commotion.

"I'm Captain Alec Winter of the United States Special Forces. If there are any two people in the world you should feel comfortable or safe with," I glance over at Brian, "it's with us. Besides, you have no say in the matter."

"Well, we are going to *my* home. You're not bringing those into my home."

"Look Jake—I don't know you or if anything you're claiming is true, but what I can tell you is that I'm being completely honest that the incident last night won't be the only one. Every living creature in this world is starving and after last night, I'm *never* going outside without protection again."

"I won't take you there if you refuse to leave the guns."

I step up real close to Jake and look him in the eyes. He tries to take a step back, but stops when he realizes he's up against a wall.

"We don't need you to take us there and we're taking whatever we feel is necessary. Do you understand?"

Jake's eyes dart back and forth at everyone in the room as he stands there in silence for several seconds with a defeated look on his face. For a moment, I actually feel bad for the guy. He does have two people joining forces against him while his companion stands in the corner with a smirk on his face the entire time he's being berated.

"I'll be waiting by the entrance," Jake finally says and walks out.

Jake doesn't make it more than a few steps out of the armory when Brian chuckles from amusement at Jake's childlike outburst. I can't help but grin as well, as I pull my M4 from a rack, along with a couple extra magazines of ammunition. As I put the strap over my head, so my rifle is resting on my back, I notice Rider eyeing the rifles on the wall. I don't trust him either. I especially don't trust him with a rifle, but I can't just tell him no. That would give away my suspicion.

"Help yourself, Rider," I say with a nod.

"Thank you," he responds as he steps closer to the rack without hesitation and pulls down an M-16.

As Rider is loading up on some ammunition, I walk over to the far wall and grab some rappelling rope to secure Mya to me. I also grab a pistol since I left mine under my bed. Once everyone has their supplies, I lock the door behind us, but not before calling Mya away from the water bowl in the corner. She had been there since we walked in and she sure was thirsty. While we're walking to the front door, Brian holds out a large, bulky, brown bag for me to grab. He had set it out in the hall and was waiting for this moment.

"No way, buddy. It's your turn to carry the tent."

"No. It's not," Brian challenges.

"Yes it is because I carried it last time. That makes it your turn."

Brian doesn't respond. Instead, he looks down at Mya and holds it out for her.

"Mya, you're a sled dog. You pull it."

She gives Brian a sound of disapproval and he pulls the bag back. He growls back and gives up, accepting that he's stuck carrying the tent.

When we walk into the main hall, I'm surprised to see multiple people waiting for us. Both my parents, Michael, Alisha, Emily's mom, and Emily are all there to see us off. I make a beeline for Emily the moment I see her, but my father stops me before I get to her.

"You guys all ready to go?"

"We're here, aren't we?" I respond without taking my eyes off Emily. Jake is talking to her and she looks uncomfortable. Her arms are folded and her stance is stiff. She looks over at me with pleading eyes to come and save her from Jake's stupidity.

"Alec, I know you don't want to make this trip, but everyone in the compound is grateful that you are going."

"Yeah, sure, dad. I just can't wait to get there and back," I reply, glancing at him quickly, but return my watchful gaze back to Emily.

"You boys just be careful out there. What's important is that you both come home," says my mom.

"We'll be fine, Susan," Brian responds with a smile. She gives Brian a hug and so does my father and then they give me one as well. The hug with my father is awkward. I sense he wants the hug to have more love or meaning, but I just resent him too much right now. I only gave the lousy hug I did because I felt like I had to.

"Love you mom," I say and give her a kiss on the cheek and then quickly walk over to Emily.

"...maybe one day, you'll come visit," I hear Jake say as I walk up to them.

Emily gives Jake a half smile. I waste no time and throw my arms around her tightly, pulling her close. Emily wraps her arms around me just as tightly and neither of us notice that over our shoulders is a very disappointed Alisha, with a crushed look on her face. I look over her at the last second before she turns around. I knew that it was only a matter of time before Alisha saw the two of us together this way and I'm glad she did. I've been trying for a very long time to get her to realize we would never work out. Hopefully my public embrace with Emily just made that possible. Although Alisha is clearly disappointed by her sudden realization that I'm no longer an option for her, she isn't the only one in the room who feels this way. Jake also has a very angry look on his face as if I just stole his big prize. His moment of unpleasantness lasts several seconds before he turns and walks over to the door next to Rider and waits to leave.

"For a moment there, I thought I was gonna be stuck talking to him forever," Emily whispers into my ear.

"What was he saying to you?"

"He was hitting on me and saying how pretty he thought I was."

"Well, the man made a good observation there," I smirk. Emily frowns.

"He also said that he would like to take me to the mall some time and a bunch of other stuff. I felt dirty talking to him."

"Well hopefully you won't see him again." I pull her close again and whisper into her ear that I won't let that happen and not to worry about it. Then I kiss her softly on the lips and then turn to face everyone. They're all staring at us.

"So—are you guys like a thing now? Because if you are, I should probably throw away the invite I made to the prom," jokes Brian.

"Dude, you were gonna ask me to the prom? I thought you never would," I say back.

Brian scowls as I walk up to him.

"I'll go to the prom with you, Brian. Alec can be our limo driver," Emily says with a squeeze of my arm.

"You guys can drive *me* around," I reply.

Everyone in the room looks at us like we're all crazy. The three of us just smile and ignore them. Emily reaches down and gives Mya a hug and kisses the top of her head. Mya licks her on the cheek and I kneel down so I can put her harness on and tie her to me. When I finish securing her, I stand up. "Okay, now we can go."

Everyone says goodbye and then Brian opens the door. Jake and Rider go out first, followed by Brian and then Mya and me. Just before I close the door, I turn and look back at Emily and say bye without any sound coming out. Emily does the same and I close the door, shutting Brian, Mya and me outside in the frozen wasteland with two strangers. Two people whom I don't trust and don't know what they might be planning, along with anything else that might be lurking in the darkness.

We've been trekking through deep snow for fifteen minutes and we haven't even made it through the large clearing in front of the compound. Jake is already moving at a really slow pace and I can't help but notice that it seems as though he isn't in any sort of hurry to get to the mall. Even though Brian and I both know the way there, we refrain from taking the lead to avoid another meltdown. I checked the temperature inside the cave before leaving and it was showing twenty-one degrees. One of the warmest days I've seen in quite some time. The weather is still every bit as crappy as usual, if not worse, to make up for the warmer temperature. The wind makes it feel colder than it actually is and makes it a little more difficult to walk.

As we continue marching through the frozen tundra, I notice we are coming up on the spot where Mya fell. I can still remember that day very clearly, like it happened yesterday.

76

Brian and I were out on a small search mission for food and the false hope the council had of finding survivors. We'd been out in the snow for almost half the day. We were trudging through the deep snow when the ground disappeared right below us. One second it was there and the next it was just... gone. Mya was standing right next to me when the hole opened up. It was like a dunk tank you see at the county fair, where someone is sitting on a platform above water and people are throwing a ball at a button trying to drop the person into the water. We didn't have water beneath us to soften our fall, but the drop was just as sudden and unexpected. As we began to fall, I desperately reached for Mya and the ledge at the same time. Mya slipped through my hand. Fear and panic overcame me like a rush as I saw her fall. Seeing her bounce off the side of a rocky wall like a rag doll as she fell into the darkness until she was no longer visible. I was lucky Brian had been close. He grabbed me when my grip began to slip.

I started climbing down to the bottom of the hole immediately, but Brian made me tie a rope to him to make sure I could get back up and that I didn't fall in. The climb down would've been nearly impossible without the rope since there wasn't much to grab onto near the top. Visibility was almost zero in all directions except for up. I had to shine a light down into the hole, but the darkness was too much and seemed to swallow the light. As I neared the bottom, the walls became easier to grab hold of with larger rocks sticking out far enough for support.

The moment I saw her, I thought she was dead. She was unconscious and bleeding from a large gash on her leg. Even when I saw her breathing, I felt sick to my stomach and unsure of her condition. She finally came to, as I was wrapping a bandage around her leg to stop the bleeding and my nervousness lessened a little. She woke in a panic not realizing where she was and I had to hold her down. She eventually calmed down when I placed my hand on her head and she heard my voice. Luckily, she recognized my voice before lashing out and biting me. Fortunately, I had thought to pack her harness. If only I had thought to put it on her sooner.

While I was putting it on her, I thought I heard something move in the shadows. I quickly raised my rifle and to my astonishment there was a large, dark tunnel leading somewhere. The tunnel appeared to have a smooth shiny side. I couldn't see how far it went. The darkness swallowed up the light too quickly. I figured it was just an animal I heard moving around, but the inability to see what kind of animal it was, made the hair on my neck stand up. I quickly tied the rope to Mya's harness, making it so that she dangled from my back and yelled for Brian to pull us up. Just before we cleared the top of the tunnel, I noticed two yellow eyes that appeared to glow, staring back at me. I don't know what kind of animal the eyes belonged to, but I still get chills thinking about it. I had never seen any eyes like them before in all my years hunting and camping.

"Alec, isn't this about where Mya fell?" asks Brian, pulling me back to reality.

"Yeah, it's just up ahead."

"Hey, I think I see it over there," Brian adds.

The five of us walk up to the hole. It looks exactly the way I remember it. Only now, the white snow is stained red from a trail of blood, along with a pattern of something being drug through the snow. Whatever tracks would have been visible were covered up. Almost as if whatever was dragging the dead animal, wanted to cover its tracks.

"Something was hungry," says Brian.

"Yeah, and I'd rather not wait around to see what it was," mutters Jake as he moves away from the hole.

I step up to the edge and slowly lean over to look inside. While peering over the side of the steep drop, into the black hole, I can hardly make out the jagged rock along the sides. I point my rifle down the hole and turn on the light. The light barely has an impact on all the darkness, but gives me enough light to see more blood until the trail disappears into the shadows. I move my light back and forth, over the entire area of the hole, in an attempt to see anything. Staring back into the hole sends chills down my spine as images of watching Mya fall and then looking down the dark tunnel as I knelt at the bottom, knowing something was staring back at me.

"Alec," says Rider, only I ignore him. "Alec?" he says again.

I turn and glance at him, but quickly look back down the hole. Mya steps closer to the hole so she can look down as well.

"Mya, no." I quickly grab her collar and pull her away.

"Alec?" Rider says again.

I look back at him, this time holding his gaze.

"What?"

Rider shakes his head and raises both his hands in a shrug. Snow has already begun to turn him white as it sticks to his clothes and his mask. "What are you doing?"

"Sorry," I say, pulling my eyes from him and looking back down into the hole. "Things didn't go so well the last time we were here."

"What do you think it was?" Rider steps up to the edge to look down into the dark hole.

"I don't know. The hole is too steep for a bear to climb up and down. Bobcat or cougar maybe."

"Well, we should probably get moving then, right?" Jake asks.

All of us look over at him. His mask is preventing us from seeing his face, but only a fool couldn't tell that he's scared. I suppress a smile as the others each let out a chuckle.

"You afraid of big kitties, Jake?" jokes Brian.

"Ah, you guys are really funny. Can we just get going?" he says nervously.

"Come on, man. They're more afraid of you than you are of them," Rider says to calm him down.

"I wouldn't put my money on that," Brian laughs as he starts walking again. He'll probably continue laughing at him for the rest of the day.

I can't help but smile underneath my own mask.

"This is why we brought our rifles," I say loud enough for Jake to hear. I take one last glance at the hole before Mya and I follow the rest of the group.

After a few, long, tiresome hours of hiking, I can tell the guys are running out of gas. Hiking through so much snow in the freezing cold is an exhausting ordeal, so I suggest we set up camp where we are. Nobody argues. The area we're in sits between a cluster of aspen and birch trees. With the low visibility, I can't tell if there are any buildings or homes. I figure we've made it only a few miles at most. Brian and I set our tent up between two pine trees. We are hoping the thickness of the trees will help to shield a little of the wind. Luckily, the snow hasn't built up quite as much in this spot, making it easier to lay our tent down on semi-level ground. Rider and Jake each have their own tents and set them fifteen feet away, under the same group of trees.

One major downside to all the snow is that building a fire is very difficult. Nearly impossible. Brian and I never really bothered because it's hard to find dry wood, and if you manage to, the wind almost always blows out the flames. The temperature must have dropped since we left because tonight is especially cold. The wind makes my face feel like it's turning into ice, even though it isn't blowing quite as hard. After maybe fifteen minutes of camp being set up, Jake starts to show his frustration.

"I can't take this anymore. I need a fire."

Brian and I exchange looks with each other. We know exactly how Jake is feeling, but also know that a fire is a lost cause. The three of us just sit and watch Jake frantically searching for dry wood. I figure I'll let him suffer for a little while because of his tantrum in the armory and for making Emily feel uncomfortable.

"Hey, how long do you think we should let him go at it by himself?" asks Rider.

"Who cares? If he wants a fire that badly he can start one himself," mutters Brian.

"You have to admit. A fire would be kinda nice," I say. "Besides, he looks pathetic."

"Well—you're not wrong there," Brian chuckles.

We all continue to watch him. He's about twenty-five to thirty feet away from camp, just walking in circles, looking up at the trees like he's lost. I wonder how he ever managed to make it from the mall alone.

"Alright guys, I'm gonna go help him," I say.

"I don't know why you'd bother. The guy's an asshole."

"Well—you're not wrong there either, Brian."

I hike through the snow towards Jake and leave Brian, Rider and Mya sitting by the tents. As I approach him, I notice something move in the trees, about fifty yards past where Jake is standing. My stomach tightens and I stop in my tracks instantly. I stare into the trees, waiting for more movement when Jake yells over to me.

"Alec? What are you staring at?"

"Nothing," I respond, keeping my eyes up in the trees. "Thought I saw something." My stomach loosens slightly and I walk over to him. "Thought I would come and give you a hand. Finding good burning wood in the snow can be difficult."

"Thanks, but I don't need any help," he replies without looking at me.

"Yeah, I noticed. You've been over here for what, twenty minutes and you haven't found any wood yet?"

Jake looks over at me. His forehead crinkles as he glares back.

"I'll find some eventually."

"At the rate you're going, the snow is likely to thaw first." Jake doesn't say anything. "Let me show you something." I pull out my knife and walk over to a tree and cut off the biggest piece of bark from the trunk as I can and hold it out for Jake to grab. "What does this feel like to you?" Jake reluctantly takes it and removes one of his gloves to feel it.

"It's dry," he responds sheepishly.

"Yeah, and it's probably the driest thing you will find out here. Get as much as you can. Hopefully it will burn long enough to dry out some branches."

Jake surprisingly nods his head in agreement and even a small hint of a smile. I know he isn't really happy to be getting help, but what guy would?

"I'll climb up this tree and break off some branches." I look up the tall pine.

"Sounds good to me."

I jump up and grab the lowest branch and then swing my legs up and hug the branch with them to help pull me up. Once I have my balance, I pull my knife back out and start hacking at some small branches that look like good wood to burn. My knife isn't capable of cutting through the wood quickly, so I also use my weight, by twisting and pulling to break most of them off. After I've broken off four large branches, I drop out of the tree. Jake has a large armful of bark.

"Do you think this is enough?"

"Yeah, if not we can cut some off the trees down there," I reply.

As we approach camp, Brian and Rider are both standing up, alert and looking into the trees opposite where we're coming from. Mya's nowhere in sight.

"What's going on you guys? Where's Mya?"

"We thought we saw something move up there in the trees. Mya's in the tent. I put her in there because I thought she might run off," says Brian without ever looking at me.

"Come on man. You know her better than that." I walk over to the tent to let her out.

"She went after a grizzly."

"Yeah, while trying to protect me. She won't leave your side unless she has to or you tell her to."

I unzip the tent and free Mya from her cage. She bolts past me and runs up to where Brian and Rider are standing.

"Mya leave it alone. Get back over here." She looks back at me, lets out a whining sound and then returns her gaze to the trees. "Get back over here, *now*!" She recognizes my tone and quickly turns around and walks back over to me with her head down. "Good girl," I say and pat her on the side.

"Do you think it was another grizzly?" Rider asks.

"In the tree?" responds Brian.

"Good point."

"Don't you think you give that dog a little too much credit?" asks Jake.

"Don't you think you're a bit of a pussy and a little stupid for a guy who used to go hunting all the time?" asks Brian.

Before Jake can go suicidal on Brian, I interject to distract him.

"I trust this dog more than I trust either of you," I say, pointing at Jake and Rider. "She'll never let me down."

"Whatever," Jake mumbles while giving Brian the look of someone with a sinister plan. Brian grins back.

"We need to get this fire started. It's gonna be dark soon," I say.

I begin cutting the top layer of skin off the branches since they're wet. Brian takes out his knife and does the same. After we have most of them done, I start setting the branches into a teepee. Once the branches are set, I grab the bark that Jake collected and cover the branches with it. When I feel like it's as ready as it will be, I pull out a lighter from my pack. The bark starts to smoke with the flame touching it, but it won't ignite.

"Let's hope this works," I mumble.

"Why don't we pour some lighter fluid on it to help get it started?" Jake suggests.

"Gee… I'll just head down to the local grocery store and get some," Brian replies snidely.

"This will work fine," I reply as I continue to hold the flame steady.

Finally, after holding the flame on the bark for at least a minute, a small flame begins to hold. I quickly move the lighter over to another part of the bark to get the other side started. Once I get another part burning, I repeat the process a couple more times until I have several, small, individual flames. Eventually, the flames start to burn the branches and it looks as though it might work.

"Wow," Brian says cheerfully.

"It's looking good," I reply.

We all sit in the snow patiently waiting for the flames to fully engulf all the wood. As I'm resting on the freezing snow, my stomach rumbles, so I get up and go over to grab my pack out of the tent. I'm not too excited about eating M.R.E.'s, but it is better than nothing. 'Meal, Ready to Eat'. That's what it stands for. They were adopted as the Department of Defense combat ration in 1975 and then mass distributed in 1978. They're perfect for use in the military because it's all the nutrition you need in a bag. The packaging can withstand rough conditions and exposure to the elements. I've never been a fan. What I wouldn't give to have a nice bowl of soup from Emily right now. It might be a while before I have another one of those. I grab a few M.R.E.'s and sit back down in the same spot, tossing a couple to Brian. If he's as dissatisfied about eating them as I am, he doesn't show it. He immediately opens one up and starts eating.

"Hungry girl?" I ask.

Mya starts licking her chops while I open one for her. The moment I have it completely out of the package, I drop it next to her to avoid getting my fingers chomped off. She's hungry after such a hard day. We all are. I start to open up the other one, when a loud shrieking sound echoes through the trees, making Jake and Rider jump to their feet.

"What the hell was that?" asks Rider.

"That's the same sound I heard last night, just before the grizzly attacked," I reply, still sitting down taking a bite out of my food. Mya's continuing to eat her food as well, not paying any attention to what is going on. I figure that if she isn't concerned about the noise, I won't be either. Whatever is making it, Mya clearly doesn't feel threatened.

"That was no grizzly man. That was something else. Something I've never heard before," Rider says nervously.

"I've heard that sound before too," Jake adds. "I've been hearing it around the mall."

They both stand there in the snow, listening like frightened children as they look into the trees, waiting for something to pounce on them from the shadows. Brian hasn't said a word. He's eating his food in silence.

"Well, whatever made that noise, I doubt it will come near our fire," I say.

All the individual flames I started had blended together and as a result, we had a small smoldering fire going. I can already feel the warmth on my face and it gives me a sense of relief.

After a few minutes of nervously looking around, Rider takes a seat and continues eating. Jake reluctantly follows, but continues looking around, clearly unsettled.

I stay where I am, in the snow, for almost an hour after finishing my food. Mya finished her food in only a few seconds so now she's just resting her head on my leg. As the last bit of light finally disappears, making it impossible to see more than a few feet without the fire, I decide it's time for some sleep.

"I'm headed to bed guys. Make sure you all get some rest too. We have another long day ahead of us tomorrow," I say and climb to my feet.

"I'll only be out here for a little while longer and then I'm headed to bed too," says Brian.

"I think I will head to bed now," Jake replies. "It's creepy out here."

"Let's go Mya," I say as I climb to my feet.

She walks right beside me over to the tent. Once there, I unzip the flap and let Mya in first. After she's in all the way, I step in and zip the flap back up. Outside of the compound, it's always too cold to take off any clothes at night, so I've already gotten used to sleeping with them on, including my shoes. I set my rifle down to the left of my sleeping bag and climb in. Mya usually sleeps at my feet or my head. Tonight, for whatever reason, she chooses my head and makes herself comfortable with her head up against mine. I'm only in the tent for about ten minutes, almost asleep, when Brian comes stumbling in like a drunk.

"Think you could be any louder, ya big ogre?" I ask.

"Quit your whining, princess. You weren't asleep anyway."

"Maybe I was. Did you ever think of that?"

"No—not really," he chuckles.

"Well, now I *am* going to sleep, so keep it down."

After I can tell Brian has finally gotten himself settled, sleep finally starts to come. The only thing I can hear is a light crackling sound from our sorry excuse for a fire, and soon I'm out.

CHAPTER 5

"Mya, knock it off," I mumble, half asleep. She nudges my head again. "Mya, what is your problem?"

"Alec?" Brian whispers. "Alec?" he says a little louder.

"What the hell is wrong with you two?" I say groggily, still half dozing out of consciousness.

"Shut up and listen man." Brian's tone changes. I sense urgency. I roll my eyes, knowing he won't be able to see, but listen anyway.

At first, I don't hear anything.

It's eerily quiet. The wind isn't even blowing.

I almost tell Brian it's nothing–then–as the anticipation starts to frustrate me, I hear the crunching sound of something walking in the snow. I quietly sit up and look in the direction of our fire. The fire was most likely out several hours ago so it isn't visible. It takes a few moments for my eyes to adjust to see Brian and Mya. Brian is also sitting up and Mya is on alert. Only she isn't growling and the fur on her back isn't standing up.

"What do you think it is?" asks Brian.

"I don't know. Let's go and find out," I say sarcastically.

"Okay."

"Dude, I'm kidding. Are you crazy?"

"Don't be such a pussy. We have *guns* this time. Remember?"

"Yeah, and we..."

A strange gurgling sound interrupts me. Almost like something breathing with a sort of muffled scratching sound, as if something is struggling for breath. Mya begins to whine.

"What the hell kind of animal sounds like that?" asks Brian.

"Nothing I've ever heard before."

We sit there quietly, cautiously waiting for something—anything—to happen. A chill rushes over my body as I realize that something has probably been tracking, or even hunting us all day. I slowly start reaching for my rifle, as quietly as possible. Mya continues to whine and starts pacing back and forth.

Suddenly, just as my hand makes contact with the M4, the same familiar shrieking sound echoes in my ears, piercing the silent night. I tighten my hand around the rifle and pull it towards me. And then something else happens. I hear nylon fabric ripping open.

"Hey, what the... Ahh!"

Brian and I scramble to our feet when we hear Rider scream. There are several loud pops, with flashes of light, before we have the tent open. Mya wastes no time and explodes out of the tent once there's an opening. We follow close behind her and run to Rider's aid as fast as we can. It's too dark to see anything, so I turn my light attachment on.

The side of Rider's tent is ripped open and he's inside groaning in agony. Rider's jacket is torn to shreds and he has large, open wounds in his chest. Suddenly, I feel as though I'm back in the middle of combat and one of my men was shot multiple times. Only the wounds in front of me weren't caused by gunfire. Some sort of animal came into Rider's tent trying to cause as much damage as possible. Almost as if the animal specifically targeted him. Blood is everywhere. It's on the sides of the tent, the ground, literally everything. Whatever attacked Rider—left its mark.

"What the hell did this Rider?" Brian yells. "Was it another grizzly?"

"N-no!" Rider groans. "Ugh… it w-was some… thing else," he replies shakily.

Rider appears to be convulsing from pain. He has the look of fear in his eyes. I can't be sure if he's more afraid of dying, or what he saw.

Mya barks in the distance.

"Ah shit! Mya!" I say, suddenly realizing I hadn't seen her since leaving our tent.

"Go," Brian says. "I got him."

"No, Alec," Rider says and reaches for me with a blood-stained hand.

I ignore Rider's plea and step out of the tent to listen for Mya. I don't hear anything and my heart begins to pound as I listen for any sign of her.

"Mya?!"

Nothing.

"Mya, where are you?"

My heart's racing and I'm already struggling for breath as I frantically shine my light on the ground looking for tracks. *Idiot*. I should have done that from the start. I spot some tracks leading past the fire, in the same direction I was gathering wood. I start running as fast as I can, my feet sinking into deep snow with each step, making my pursuit difficult. I have no idea what I'm running towards, or if I'm even running in the right direction. I gasp for air as I trudge uphill through the snow. The instant I stop to take a quick breath, I hear Mya bark not too far ahead.

"Mya! I'm coming!"

I continue running in the direction of where her bark is coming from. I have to ignore the burning in my legs as I charge forward.

My throat's drying out and each breath starts to sound almost the same as the scratchy throat sound the animal made outside the tent.

Mya's bark is getting louder and louder.

Finally, after what seems like miles of running, I shine the light towards the sound of her barking and the light reflects off her white fur. The knot in my stomach loosens. She's standing below a large cluster of trees, with her front paws on the trunk of one, barking up at the sky.

"What is it Mya? What's up there?"

I approach her and look up into the black pine trees. I point my rifle into them, with hopes of seeing what it is. The trees are extremely tall and very thick from the base all the way to the top, making it difficult to see anything. The cloud cover is too thick to allow very much light through. If not for my light, I likely wouldn't be able to see more than ten feet or so.

"Mya, stop," I say and place my hand on her head.

She stops instantly at my command and we both stand there quietly listening. Not a sound. I contemplate firing a few rounds into the darkness to see if I can scare the animal, but decide it will most likely worry Brian. Instead, I move my light slowly, back and forth, scanning the area. I do this for a few seconds when the light passes by something that catches my attention.

I move the light back and stop on something black. Black like the sky, but there clearly aren't any stars. Whatever it is, looks like polished leather. I move the light up a couple inches to see more of it. I freeze and the hair on my neck stands up. Looking down at me are the same yellow eyes that I saw in the sink hole—down the dark tunnel. I can't make out what it is. It's too dark for me to see its face clearly, but the skin appears to be the same as the rest of the body. And the eyes. Bright–yellow–menacing eyes looking down on me.

"Alec," the creature says in a whispering voice.

I'm surprised to hear a low, scratchy, male voice talking to me, but oddly relieved it isn't an animal. Or at least I don't think it is. If it can talk, it can be reasoned with.

"Who are you?"

Suddenly, a feeling of dread comes over me. This entire time I thought I had been losing my mind. Is this the voice that was talking to me outside the compound? My gut feeling tells me it's not. The voice outside the compound sounded female and I felt as though I'd known that voice for a long time.

"You're in danger, Alec."

"Who are you?" I reply, keeping my rifle pointed directly at it. I know my heart is racing and all I can do to try and remain calm is focus on my breathing. Deep, slow breaths.

"You know exactly who we are, Captain Winter," the creature says with a bitterness to its voice.

All of a sudden, several of the trees begin to shake as a hissing sound echoes in every direction. I grab Mya by the collar and slowly start backing away from the tree, towards camp.

"You can't trust them, Alec."

The hissing continues getting increasingly louder, almost as if the creatures are getting impatient. I'm surrounded and I don't know how many there are.

"Hsss…"

The hissing sound becomes so loud that I can barely hear my own footsteps in the snow, as I stumble my way towards camp, still holding on to Mya's collar. Periodically, I flash my light back up into the trees. At first, I don't see anything, but then I spot one. The light reflects off of more pitched black, leathery skin. Whatever it is, it looks reptilian with a defined, zigzag pattern, like the shape of diamonds all over. The overall structure of the body is human like. It has two legs, two arms. The creature has claws that are several inches long and just as black as the rest of its body. The face

91

is the most eerie part. Looking down at me is a black face, covered in the same black, reptilian skin, with razor sharp teeth smiling down at me. Oddly, it looks like it has a grin on its face, as if it wants to laugh at me. I let the light lower a bit and I discover that the creature is wearing a pair of cargo pants and boots, similar to my own. It's sitting in a slight crouched position like a predator.

"WHO ARE YOU?"

"You know who we are, Winter." The creature says my name with a bitter tone as its smile is replaced by a snarl.

"Answer me!" I step forward with my finger on the trigger. The creature lets out a loud shrieking sound in disagreement with my action.

"Alec?" shouts Jake from somewhere behind me, but at a distance.

I keep my light on the creature, ignoring Jake.

"Alec?"

A light reflects off the snow next to me, and I take my eyes off the creature for only a split second. The creature is gone when I look back.

"Damn."

I lower my gun and look over at Jake. He's now standing next to me, shining his light towards the tree the creature was in.

"What—was it?" he asks, panting like he's been running.

"I don't know. Let's get back to camp before they come back," I say as I step past him.

"They?" Jake replies in surprise. "How many of them are there?"

"I don't know. And unless you want to be here alone, I suggest you follow me back to camp."

When we're back at camp, Brian is inside Rider's tent pressing a lot of bandages onto Rider's chest to slow the bleeding. Seeing Brian working on Rider reminds me of a trauma tent during the war. Bandages and pieces of clothing, mixed with blood are scattered about the tent. Brian looks up at me when I walk into the tent with a *look* I'm all too familiar with. It's a look that my men and I had come to know.

Rider is dying.

"Did you see what it was?" Brian asks.

"We can talk about that later. Let's just focus on getting him back to the compound," I reply.

Brian nods and starts to help Rider to his feet, but Rider quickly waives him off and tells him that he wants to do it on his own. He starts to sit up and quickly groans from the pain, falling back down. After a brief moment, he tries a different approach and rolls over so that he's on his hands and knees. Once he feels comfortable, he pushes himself up with his hands. I watch as Rider uses all the leg strength he has to get himself all the way up.

"There we go. Now let's–get this show on the road," he groans with a slight hunch in his stance.

I nod to Rider in approval of his strength. The guy had several large cuts carved into him by some unknown creature and he isn't going to let that stop him. I still don't trust him, but I can't ignore the man's courage and strength. Rider would've made a great addition to our team, so long as he was honorable. It's rare to see a guy who can fight through this kind of pain the way he is. The kind I only allowed in my unit. It's what set us apart from others.

His bandages are already soaked through. We need to get him some proper medical attention soon. I step out of the tent and realize that Jake is nowhere to be seen. I look around for him and spot him standing behind a heavy cluster of trees. Curious that Jake isn't with the group in this type of moment, I decide to sneak over and see what he's doing. As I get closer, I hear the very distinct sound of a radio. I try to make out what Jake and the voice on the radio are saying, but the radio is down to low and Jake is whispering quietly. Disappointed I can't hear, I decide to surprise him and see how he'll react.

"Hey Jake, what are you doing?"

"Oh, hey, I-I was just radioing my people to let them know that we were having to turn around," he says nervously.

"You have a radio?"

"Yeah, that way I can keep in contact with them if anything happens."

I glare at him without saying a word. If I ever had an issue with trusting Jake before, I definitely do now. I want to question him more about the radio, but given the circumstances, I don't have the time.

"We need to get Rider back to the compound quickly," I say without taking my eyes off him. "We won't be packing up the tents, so if there is anything important you need, I suggest you grab it."

I turn and walk back to the tent to see if I can help Brian or Rider with anything. We're on our way back to the compound only five minutes later and I keep Jake in my sight the entire time. The hike back is even worse than it had been the day before. The wind picked up and is blowing hard again and it feels colder. I figure the temperature has to be closer to zero. Even though the hike is harder, we are moving at a much faster pace than the day before. We're moving with a sense of urgency, knowing Rider needs medical attention fast. He's already struggling to walk on his own and we still have a distance to go.

Along the way, Rider says he needs to rest for a few minutes, so I take the time to tell Brian about the radio. I almost have to restrain him from walking over and pounding the truth out of Jake right there. The last thing we need is another injured traveler. Fortunately, I'm able to convince him that we have more important things to worry about. Rider is our priority and we can deal with Jake when we're back at the compound. We let Rider rest for about ten minutes and then we pick him up and practically carry him the rest of the way. Brian and I are each under one of Rider's arms, and maintain that position for nearly two miles. Carrying him brings back memories of carrying Emily through the snow that day we met each other. A day I have mixed emotions about. I abandoned my sister and met a woman I would eventually fall in love with.

"Hey Alec, I think we are coming up on your sinkhole again. I say we stay wide," says Brian.

"I'm with Brian on this one," mumbles Rider as he coughs up blood. I don't argue.

Finally, after about a third of the time as our trip took us yesterday, I see the light from the compound and feel a bit of relief. I'm extremely tired from lack of sleep and the near nonstop hike for miles, through several feet of snow, while carrying a grown man. My legs are burning and feel like they might give out on me at any moment. As soon as I can get Rider to my father and make sure he's going to live, I plan on sleeping for as long as possible. Just as we come up over the edge of the snow bank, James is sitting near the entrance to the cave.

"Alec? What are you guys doing back?" he says as he jumps to his feet.

James's look of surprise quickly changes to horror when he gets a glimpse of Rider.

"Go get my father. Tell him to meet us down in Medical and that Rider is in critical condition."

"Got it," he responds and turns and runs back into the compound.

"Let's get him inside quickly," I say to Brian.

Brian and I lift Rider off the ground and create a stretcher for him with our arms crisscrossed over each other. Once inside the door, I order Jake to close it behind him without checking to ensure that he does. We quickly start towards the medical facility that's located next to the armory. Just as we start down the long hallway, my father shouts from behind us.

"Boys, we need to move him to the facility downstairs," he says sharply.

"Downstairs? You said downstairs was nothing but a bunch of storage," I say confused.

"Son, we don't have time for that right now," he says with a nervous voice. "Help me get him over to the elevator."

For the moment, I ignore the sudden news that we have a medical facility on the lower level. Not to mention the fact that I can tell he's hiding something. Why would he be nervous? He knows something. The doors to the elevator open instantly and we move inside, pressing the button for level two. Just before the doors close, I notice Jake standing in the center of the main hall, with the look of someone who's planning something and it makes me uncomfortable. What is he up to?

Once on the lower level, we carry Rider into the hall. The main hall on the second level is much smaller than the one on the main level. This one is in the shape of a pentagon and doesn't have any hallways leading anywhere. Instead, there are five doors—the elevator we exited from—the stairwell to the left and four others ahead that are evenly spread out throughout the room. I never had any reason to come down to this level before, since my father always told me it was for storage. One of the three doors has the words: Prototype Weapons scribed above it and looks like a vault. The second has swinging, double glass doors with two windows and Nano-Gen-Research above it. The final door says Receiving and I assume would lead you to the tunnel.

"Mya, stay here," I say to her but don't look to see if she actually does.

When we enter the room with the double glass doors, we come into a room that has several operating tables lined in a row, with heavy duty restraints attached to them. My father has us put Rider on the one closest to the door. The room appears to be larger than the cafeteria and has all kinds of medical instruments, electronic equipment and other things I've never seen before in my life. In one corner there is a table with several strange looking canisters that are so black they appear to absorb the light. In another corner there is a cabinet with glass doors. All the shelves are empty except for a small vial containing a blue liquid.

"Alec, pay attention. I need you to remove his bandages and then you and Brian need to hold him down while I clean the wound," my father says in a direct, but calm manner.

I gently pull the crimson-soaked bandages off and set them down on the table next to the bed. Rider is groaning from the pain, but his eyes are now closed. As my father sterilizes the deep cuts in Rider's chest, I can see Rider clenching his teeth as the muscles in his cheeks tighten. His breathing is light and slow and I know that he probably has a minimal chance at best. My father is an amazing surgeon, but I've seen plenty of men die before with wounds not as serious as these. It doesn't take long for my father to stitch up the wounds and for Rider to lose consciousness. The only indication any of us have that Rider is still alive is the faint movement of his chest. My father sets up an I.V. and starts a blood transfusion to supplement all the lost blood. When my father feels like he's done everything he can for Rider, he tells me and Brian to go clean up at the sink.

"Alec, was this another bear?" he asks as I wash my hands. I look over my shoulder and make eye contact for just a second and then turn and look back down into the sink.

"No."

"Did you see what it was?"

"Yes." I dry my hands off with some paper towels and toss them into the trash next to the sink. "Yeah, I saw *them*. I don't know what

97

they are and I don't think now is the time to talk about it." I start to walk out, without saying another word to him.

"Alec, I have good reason for keeping all of this down here a secret from you," he says as I push through the door. "Alec?"

I keep walking and ignore him. I find Mya laying down right where I told her to stay. She sits up with anticipation as I walk up and pat her on the head. We walk towards the elevator doors and I press the button to bring it down. While we wait for the elevator, I turn and look at the names of the rooms above the doors. I shake my head, disappointed that my father kept all this from me. I begin to wonder who my father actually is and if I really know him. When the door finally opens, I go to step inside, but Michael Wilkinson comes out, nearly running into me.

"Alec," he says without apologizing.

I don't say anything and walk into the elevator and press the number 1 to go to the first floor. As soon as the doors open, I start heading towards the cafeteria to find Emily, with Mya at my side. I see her the moment I walk through the doors. She's standing next to a far table to the left of the room taking an order for Jake, who has his back to the doors.

Some guy. He doesn't even care if Rider's going to live.

I walk over and take a seat at the bar, where I always do, occasionally glancing over at Emily to see what is taking her so long. The cafeteria is full tonight, so it's loud with chatter, making it difficult for me to hear her conversation. She looks over at me with pleading eyes. Everything seems normal at first, with Emily smiling as she writes down Jake's order, when suddenly her face turns beat red and she shakes her head no. When she starts to walk away, Jake reaches up and grabs onto her wrist.

I jump from the bar stool so fast that it falls down. Mya was also watching her and she lets out a loud growl as she springs to her feet and runs straight at them. Jake releases Emily's wrist just as he hears the sound of Mya's growl. Mya bites down on his arm hard and Jake cries out in pain. She releases after only one bite, taking a step back, getting between him and Emily and continues growling at him. I give her a command to stay when it looks like she might strike again.

Emily is shaking when I put my arm around her. The room is silent as the dozen or so people inside the cafeteria are watching.

"I think it's time you left, Jake," I say with a sharp voice.

"Why, because she can't control herself?" he replies through clenched teeth as he grips his wrist tightly. There's a small amount of blood visible through the fingers of his good hand.

"Please!" Emily counters. "You're disgusting!"

"Jake, I'll give you an hour. If you're not gone by then, I'll throw you out."

Jake grabs a small hand towel and wraps it around the wound. He stares back at Emily with dark, hungry eyes, holds his gaze for only a second and then makes eye contact with me. Jake did a good job of hiding it before, but now he has a bloodlust look in his eyes. He's killed men before. He then turns his eyes on Mya and lets out a low growl before returning his gaze back to Emily one last time. The room is still silent as everyone waits to see what will happen next.

Jakes glare suddenly changes to a grin.

"I'll see you again soon."

He turns and walks out of the cafeteria without another word.

Once he is gone, Emily finally relaxes and releases the tight grip she had on my arm. She gently starts massaging the wrist Jake grabbed and turns and walks into the back of the kitchen. I follow her. When we're alone in the back, Emily throws her arms around me and starts trembling all over.

"Are you alright?"

"He just scared me is all. I've never had anyone grab me like that before," she says with a shaky voice.

"What did he say right before he grabbed you? I saw the look on your face." She lets go of me and looks into my eyes, but quickly looks down.

"Just something really dirty. I'd rather not repeat it."

"At least he'll be gone and we won't have to see him again."

"Yeah. Are you hungry?" She tries to force a smile and I ignore the fact that she's changing the subject.

"No, I'm just tired. Brian and I practically carried Rider back here and it took a lot out of me."

"Is he gonna make it?"

I shrug my shoulders.

"We don't know. All we can do now is hope he recovers."

"What was it that attacked him?"

I'm not sure of how to answer her. I don't want to lie to her, but I also don't want to frighten her. How exactly am I supposed to tell someone that what I saw appeared to be human, but also appeared not to be? Also, that it had been talking to me for several days without me knowing about it. It would all sound crazy.

"We don't know," I reply, shaking my head.

"What did you see, Alec? You can tell me."

I look into Emily's eyes. She's watching me like someone trying to comfort somebody when they're frightened. I don't think I'm frightened, but can I be? I haven't really taken the time to think about it. Everything happened so fast, I just acted as if I was in battle again. No. I'm not frightened at all. I just don't like the unknown.

"Alec, what did you see?"

"I don't know," I reply while biting down on my tongue. "I've never seen anything like them."

"Them?"

"Yeah. There were several of them," I continue as the night plays back in my head and I break eye contact. "Mya ran after the one that attacked Rider. I found her barking up at a tree, so I shined my light up into it, hoping that I might see what it was. At first, I couldn't see anything. Then…"

"Then what, Alec?" She places her hand on my cheek and I focus on her eyes again.

I open my mouth to tell her the rest, but before I have the chance, I'm interrupted by my father storming into the kitchen with a shocked look on his face.

"Alec, I need you to come downstairs right away," he says, breathing heavily.

"Is something wrong with Rider?"

"Well… you really should just come downstairs. It's better if I show you."

I look back at Emily and she smiles.

"Go. I need to get back to work anyway."

"I'll come back up to see you after," I say and give her a quick kiss.

"I'll be here waiting."

Mya and I follow my father out of the cafeteria. We've barely made it to the main hall, when I stop.

"Dad, hold up."

"Hold up? I said we need to go downstairs."

"I know what you said. I'm not going."

"Son, this is important. You need to s…"

"No, it's not!"

"What's this about?"

"How did you know about this facility?" He starts to speak, but I cut him off. "And don't you dare lie to me."

He stands there–looking at me– studying me– as he considers how to respond. I've had suspicions about him for days now. Ever

101

since the grizzly attack, he's been acting differently. Not necessarily mad, or even scared like others, but alarmed. As if he's waiting for the worst possible thing to happen. His lack of surprise to Rider coming back as he did and also what I had told him made it clearer to me. Now that I have him alone, I want answers.

"I've been working on a Top Secret project for the government for many years. That Top Secret project is what you and Rider had the misfortune of meeting. This facility is where it all began." He just blurted it out.

The idea that he'd known about this facility and that he'd been working for the government made me wonder. Is it possible that he could've done something? Or that he knew more before the rest of us? I always thought it was strange that he knew where to go so quickly when the storm hit.

"If you knew about this facility, did you have pull with the military?"

"I don't know what you mea…"

"Stop playing games with me! I want the truth! Did you—or did you not—have the power to send help to Ashlee when she needed it? Did you know the storm was going to get worse? Or better yet. Did you know it was coming and not tell us?"

"I did everything I could for Ash…"

"ANSWER ME!"

Several people are present in the main hall. The group of kids I always see hanging out on the sofas and chairs are wide eyed as they witness a son berate his father. Others were simply passing through, but now are stopped, probably afraid that if they cross my path, they might become victim to my wrath as well.

"Alright! I knew about the storm, and I could've sent a chopper. Are you happy?"

"Happy? HAPPY! My sister... your *daughter* is *dead*, because you were more concerned about a stupid project that could have killed us, rather than taking care of your family."

"I'm sorry son," he says, with a defeated look on his face.

"I don't believe you," I say, choking back tears. "You did nothing."

"Son," he calls to me as I start walking away.

"No!" I quickly spin around and get up in his face. "Don't ever speak to me again. As far as I'm concerned, you're dead to me too."

Mya senses something is wrong and she starts nuzzling my hand. I gently squeeze behind her ear and start walking to my apartment. I held so much respect for him my entire life, and now all I want to do is strangle the life out of him. My sister is gone because he cared more about his work than his family. I feel like I'm going to be sick and can't wait to get back to my room. I make it a few steps around the corner when I feel a cold breeze blowing past me. I think nothing of it, since James was out on his watch. He's probably just switching out with someone, or done for the day all together. I just keep walking to my apartment and don't look back.

Once back in my apartment, I go into my room and close the door. I lay down on my bed, and Mya climbs on as well, resting her head down on my chest as she snuggles up against me. How could my father abandon my sister that way? How could he abandon my family? I reach over and grab the picture of Ashlee. I miss her more than words can express. My mom was right the other night when she said I might not ever be the same. How can any of us be the same after losing her? Ashlee and I were inseparable our entire lives. We did everything together. It was always her, Brian and me. I start to rub Mya's ears and close my eyes and try to relax. I'm still angry from yelling at my father so I try to focus on taking calm, deep breaths in order to relax. After a few minutes, I start to fall asleep with the picture still in my hand. I'm so exhausted—enough to sleep the day away.

CHAPTER 6

J ust before I drift into a dream, Mya shoots up to a sitting position and looks at the door. She begins tilting her head back and forth, trying to listen for something.

"What is it, girl?"

She glances at me before jumping off the bed. She runs over to the door and begins clawing at it.

"What's the matter?"

I must have fallen asleep with it in my hand, so I set the picture down before getting up and walking over to the door.

She runs out of the room as soon as I open it, and goes straight to the front door and starts doing the same thing. I hear the gunshots just as my hand touches the handle. Fear for my family quickly washes over me as I open the door and sprint down the hall. Mya runs ahead of me.

More gunshots, along with yelling voices, echo through the hallway as I run towards the main hall. The voices become clearer as I come closer to the corner. Mya is already out of sight by the time I approach the corner, but then she growls and a man screams out in pain.

I round the corner to find her wrestling with a man in a soldier's uniform and a ski mask. She has a mouth full of his right arm and there's a rifle on the ground. I quickly run over to help her just as the man tries to pull out a knife with his other hand. The blade is still partially in its sheath when I strike him across the face as hard as I can with my forearm. I instantly feel the orbital bone in his right eye break. He falls to the ground with Mya still latched onto his arm. The man begins to scream, but quickly stops as I pull out my own knife and thrust it into his chest, causing blood to spill out onto his jacket and my hand.

Suddenly, I hear more shots coming from the cafeteria, so I leave the man's lifeless body on the floor and cautiously start that way, but first I pick up the dead man's rifle. I hear screaming, a female voice, as I make my way down the south hallway. Several armed men, dressed the same as the one I killed, are walking towards me. Jake is with them, and he has Emily.

"Alec!" she screams when she sees me. "Alec, help me!"

"Kill him!" Jake orders the men.

I quickly reach down and wrap my arm around Mya and dive through the door to the lower level. Rounds hit the door behind me and shatter the window. We take cover behind the thick concrete wall as rounds continue to fly into the stairwell. In the process of grabbing Mya, I dropped the rifle, so now I'm defenseless against their guns. Finally, the gunfire stops.

"I'll take care of him," I hear one of them shout near the door.

Mya and I are hiding, just inside the door to the right, when he comes in. The soldier spots us as he steps into the stairwell and manages to get off a few rounds, but I'm too quick. The bullets hit the ground, narrowly missing Mya, as I push his gun downward and away from him, and then stick my knife into his throat. He lets out a gurgling sound before I pull the blade free and let him fall to the ground.

"Hey, do you guys have some bandages?" I shout out the door. "This guy's hurt pretty bad."

"No, you idiot," Jake snaps at one of his men. "We have the girl. Let's go."

"No!" Emily screams. "Alec! Alec!"

I slowly peak my head out of the stairwell to see them moving towards the door. One of the men sees me and fires off a few rounds, making me take cover again. I want to fire back, but there's too good a chance I might hit Emily. I wait until they are out the front door and out of sight before exiting the stairwell and breaking my cover.

"Alec?" says Brian as he comes from the hall leading to the cafeteria. "Jake and some men…"

"I know," I say through clenched teeth.

"Go get some weapons. I'm going after them." Mya and I walk towards the front door.

"Right behind you," Brian yells as he turns and runs towards the armory.

I turn off the exterior lights before I step outside so that if anyone is still waiting for me to come out, I won't be an easy target. That's when I hear the sound of engines starting. Things went from bad to worse. If they have snowmobiles to travel on the snow, I'll never catch them. I realize I have no choice but to step outside to try and prevent them from escaping. The wind is blowing extremely hard and pounding into my face before I'm even out of the cave. It's ice cold and I wish I had my mask, but I don't have time to worry about my body temperature. Emily's life is in danger and they already have a head start. I step up to the entrance of the cave and peak out into the clearing. Nothing is there except for the snow and darkness. I don't see anything. I wait for a few seconds to make sure there isn't someone waiting to ambush me, then I step out into the open and look down at the ground to find some snowmobile tracks.

"Dammit!"

I look back into the cave and try to decide if I should wait for Brian. I make my decision only a second later.

"Let's go Mya," I say and start off into the dark, cold snow.

I push myself as fast and as hard as I can. My legs are already tired and extremely sore from having to haul Rider back several miles. All I can do is clench my teeth as I fight back the pain and continue to push, no matter how bad it hurts. My face is starting to go numb and my legs begin to burn as I slow down against my will. I'm simply too tired and no matter how hard I push, I'm never going to catch them. I'm moving hardly at all and about to collapse from exhaustion, when I hear an engine.

"Mya, stop," I command her as I raise my rifle and scan the area. The sound is directly in front of me and getting closer. "Alright Mya, get ready."

Suddenly, as I'm waiting for the approaching enemy, the ground starts shaking below me. I instantly know what's happening and panic takes over me. My heart stops in the split second that I realize Mya isn't tied to me. The ground below us starts to sink and I dive to the side. I have no time to decide if I should grab onto the edge and continue after Emily, or if I will follow Mya down the hole. I just react. I hear a yelp towards the bottom as I pull myself up and turn to look down into the hole. I shine my light down, hoping I can see her and feel instant relief. She's standing there looking back up at me and appears to be fine.

"Sorry girl, I need to leave you here," I say with a knot twisting in my stomach. "I'm sorry."

I turn to walk away, leaving a part of me down in the hole, but don't see the soldier in front me before he strikes me in the head. The last two thoughts I have are of Mya in need, and Emily in danger.

A bright light shines into my eyes, blinding me as I struggle to see where I am. I have a splitting headache. I can feel dried blood on the side of my face. As my eyes struggle to adjust, I see that I'm in a room with no windows, just white walls and a dark gray, tile floor. The door appears to be a commercial office door. Stainless steel handle, all black, including the frame and a window. There's also a desk pushed into the corner. I'm sitting in a chair and my hands are restrained behind my back with handcuffs. The metal feels cold against my bare skin and gives me chills. I can hear voices coming from outside the door, but they're too muffled for me to make out what they're saying. The voices carry on their conversation for several minutes, until they stop and a few seconds later the door opens and Jake walks in, accompanied by a very big, muscular guy.

"What have you done with Emily?" I shout as I wince from a sharp pain in my head.

"Nothing yet," Jake smiles. "But I'll have my way with her soon."

I give Jake a cold stare before replying. "I'm gonna enjoy stabbing you in the throat," I say in a calm voice.

Jake smirks in response and gives the other guy a nod. The big, muscular guy strikes me across the face, splitting my lip in one blow. I smile and spit some blood at Jake's feet and stare back at him with no expression. I'm hit in the face again and stars quickly fill my vision. I would welcome the pain I felt only a moment ago, but I can't let Jake think he won.

"Seth can keep this up for days if you'd like, Alec."

"Seth? Really, that's your name? Does Sef have a wisp?" I laugh just before Seth hits me with his elbow, this time knocking me over. With my hands cuffed behind me, I hit the ground hard. I spit some more blood onto the floor.

"Pick him up," Jake orders. Seth pulls me back up so that I'm sitting upright. "Alec, look at me."

I can hear Jake speaking to me, but his voice is a muffled echo and my vision is still blurry.

"Alec, look at me," he says calmly while snapping his fingers in my face.

I lift my head and strain to look at him. Everything is white and my vision slowly starts to come back. I get dizzy again and start to fall back over. Jake quickly steadies me with his right arm until I can hold myself up.

"Alec, I want you to know what I'm gonna do to Emily. First... hey look at me," he says while grabbing a fist full of my hair to stabilize my head. "First, I'm going to beat her like Seth is beating you. Then, after she's been taught a lesson and can't fight back... Well–I think you can imagine what I'll do next." Jake chuckles and takes a step back from me. "I can't wait to taste her soft lips and enjoy that lovely aroma she gives off. You know what I'm talking about, don't you?" he grins.

My vision clears up enough for me to see and I look Jake straight in the eyes.

"Jake, I killed a lot of people while serving my country, but you'll be the first one that I'll enjoy."

Seth raises his hand to strike me again, but Jake puts up a hand to stop him. I'm looking down at the ground now and Jake kneels down so that we're eye to eye.

"The world is a different place now, Alec. There are those like me who take what they want and those who get in my way. There aren't any heroes in this story." He stands up and walks over to the door. "When you're finished having fun, take him outside and kill him," Jake says to Seth.

"My pleasure," Seth says, just as Jake walks out of the room, closing the door behind him.

NeVille

Seth takes off his orange-colored hunting jacket and sets it on the table. Underneath, he's wearing a green shirt that looks too small for him, making his muscles stand out. He then pulls out a knife that I recognize. My knife.

"Seth?" I say, trying to look up at him with my vision still a little blurry.

"What?" Seth has an indifferent look on his face. Almost as if he doesn't care either way if I live or die. Most likely he's a paid mercenary.

"What do you think of my knife? It's pretty sweet, huh?"

Seth turns the ten-inch blade over a couple times examining its beauty. I've owned the knife for nearly ten years. I bought it one summer when my family took a trip to Yellowstone. It was a custom knife, with a curved, brown handle. I found it in a small shop, just outside the main entrance to the park, near the grizzly and wolf exhibits. I carried it with me on every single mission during my time in the military. It was the perfect tool for cutting things. Or killing. I never imagined someone might use it on me.

"Yeah, it's a good knife. Too bad I have to kill you with it now."

"You're telling me."

"I thought some in the Special Forces were supposed to be hard to kill," he says with a smirk.

"I'm cuffed to a chair, Seth. Not exactly an honest kill. Plus, I thought Jake said to do that outside."

Seth shrugs his shoulders.

"Jake isn't here."

"Good point. You better get on with it then."

"Sorry, buddy."

Seth tosses the knife up into the air like he's some sort of badass, showing off before executing me. I grin from his arrogance, and see this as my chance to escape. While Seth is watching the knife spin through the air, I kick my unrestrained legs straight into his

111

kneecaps. I feel his knees give easily under the weight of my feet
and he drops to the ground at the same moment the knife lands
next to him, with the sound of metal clanking on tile. I then push
my feet hard off the ground, making me lift into the air, and I pull
my head down towards my chest to swing the chair in a flipping
motion. I manage to do a full front flip before bringing the chair
down onto Seth's back. He was already screaming out in pain from
the blow he took to his knees, but stops the moment the metal chair
lands on him. I half expect someone to come running in from
Seth's screams, but nobody does, probably because they figure it's
me doing the screaming.

I begin searching through Seth's pant pockets for a key to get my
cuffs off. I have to do it blind, since my hands are behind me and
with them cuffed together, it makes it even more difficult. In order
to get my hands into his pocket I have to contort my body and then
force my hands in the direction of a pocket, causing the cuffs to
put an uncomfortable amount of pressure on my wrists. The first
pocket is empty, but I get lucky on the second one. It takes me a
minute of trying to grip the key in my fingertips. Doing it blind is
something I've had practice with, but not after being punched in
the head several times.

Finally, I get a firm grip on the key and I'm able to slide the key
into the hole and turn it, making the cuff on my left hand release.
Once my second hand is free, I pick up my knife and slide it into
the sheath in my jacket. Seth isn't moving, but he's still breathing.
I'm not sure of what to do with him, so I leave him for a moment
while I open the door to peek outside. The hallway is clear. I start
to exit the room, but as I take a step out, Seth groans loudly. I step
back into the room and quietly close the door and kneel down
beside him.

"Sorry, buddy. Can't have you sounding the alarm."

I take hold of Seth's head and twist it violently until I feel his spine snap. It's been a while since I took someone's life and I've already killed three men today. I'm not sure how long it will be before someone comes to check on Seth, so I press in the lock on the door before stepping into the hall and my cell becomes someone else's tomb.

The hallway is narrow and not very long. It has the same simple light gray tile floor and white walls as the office. There are a couple more open doors that lead into rooms just like the one I was in. They're all empty except for a desk and chair in each one. Once I get to the end of the hall, I stop and peek around the corner. It's another hallway with one room at the end on the right and also a door leading out into what looks like a large open room. I creep along the right wall, until I reach the room at the end. Once there, I slowly open the door and look in.

Inside the room is a set of surveillance screens and another guy, sitting in a chair, not paying attention to any of the cameras. He's reading a book. On one of the screens, I can see myself standing in the doorway. I turn and look up and there's a camera placed in the ceiling, just to the left of the door that leads out of the hallway. Fortunately, this guy isn't paying attention to his duties, but I still can't have him sounding the alarm later on. The last thing I want is to take another life, especially one that isn't directly causing me harm, but he should've thought of that before he enlisted to work with someone like Jake. Emily is the most important thing to me right now, so I can't let my moral compass get in the way. I slowly move in behind him and grab him in a chokehold. The man quickly starts to struggle as he tries to fight free, but it's no use. I snap his neck and then drag him back into a small closet to the right of the surveillance screens.

"Alright Jake, let's see where you went off to." I begin looking at the screens, hoping that I might find him.

While looking at the screens, I quickly realize where I am. I'm at the Layton Hills mall. This is a place I've been to hundreds of times in my life, so it isn't difficult to figure out, once I see all the stores on camera. Plus, it makes sense since Jake did say this is where he was living. On the screens, I notice there are several men walking around with rifles in their hands. Probably more of Jake's goons. I don't see Jake or Emily on any of them. Frustration starts to sink in. One thing that does strike me as odd is there are four cameras on the bottom that don't show anything. I continue staring at the screens for several more minutes, trying to see anything that might give me a clue and to watch for patterns in the other men's movements. Once I'm satisfied, I decide it's time to go look for her and hope for the best. I turn to move to the door, but someone starts coming through on the other side, so I quickly step back into the small closet to hide with the dead body.

The person who comes through the door isn't who I would expect. It's a woman, and she's carrying a tray of food. I quietly wait for her to set the food down and as soon as it's on the desk and her back is to me, I step out of the closet and grab her from behind and cover her mouth. She freezes instantly and doesn't make a sound, but then quickly starts to tremble.

"I'm not going to hurt you," I whisper in her ear. "A woman was brought here recently. Do you know where she was taken?"

The woman nods her head. She's still trembling and breathing heavily.

"Alright. I'm going to let you go. You're not going to scream, are you?"

She shakes her head and I release my grip. I step around her so that I can look her in the eyes. She has a striking resemblance to my mom. Similar long, blonde, curly hair and blue eyes. My mom's hair is straight, but otherwise she looks almost identical. Instead of a more pointed nose like my moms, this woman's nose is round.

She's about 5'7" and in her mid-thirties. There's also a bruise on her left cheek to go along with a black eye that's maybe a couple days old.

"What's your name?"

"Su-Susan," she says, wide eyed and flushed. Even has the same name as my mom.

"Susan, I'm Alec. The woman?"

"I'm not a hundred percent sure," she responds sheepishly.

"Then why did you tell me you did?"

"I thought you might kill me if I said no."

I tilt my head to the side.

"Understandable. Well, I'm not going to hurt you even if you don't know." Susan glances down at what I'm holding in my hand and I realize that I'm still holding my knife, so I slide it back into its sheath. "Susan, I need to find her fast before Jake does something to her. If you have any idea where she might be, tell me."

Susan looks over and sees the lifeless body stuffed in the closet and exhales.

"Are you going to kill Jake if you find him?" she asks with no emotion.

"Yeah."

"He probably has her inside Macy's. That's where he always takes the girls he's interested in."

"Is that something he does there?" I motion towards the bruise on her face.

Susan looks down as if she's ashamed of something. I instantly feel pity for this woman and the pain Jake most likely caused her. She's just another one of his victims.

"Among *other* things, yes," she replies, just barely loud enough for me to hear.

"How did you end up here? I ask.

"I came with my brother. He said this would be a good place to wait for the storm to clear."

Susan stops talking for a brief moment. I can see that she's suffered a lot. I know there's more to the story, including her brother, but I don't have the heart to ask her.

"We better hurry though," she finally says. "I passed Jake on my way here and I'm pretty sure he's heading to where he has her."

"I should go alone. If they catch you helping me, they might kill you."

"Do you know your way around?"

"This is the Layton Hills mall, right?"

"Yes."

"Then I do."

"But there's something else you should know." She grabs my arm when I start to walk by.

"What?"

"All the men here are soldiers–and they aren't very friendly."

"Neither am I."

"I can see that," she replies while glancing over at the body again, "but there's one more thing you should know. Jake isn't the person you really need to worry about. There's another one. He's worse than Jake and also the one who's in charge."

"Jake isn't their leader?"

"No. Jake is just second in command. The guy who leads all of them goes by the General. Only I didn't see him come back with them, so I don't think he's here."

Could it be?

"This… General you speak of. Do you know his name?"

"We're not allowed to call him anything other than General, but I've overheard a couple of the soldiers call him Rider."

The sound of Rider's name makes my stomach churn. A man that came into my home and dazzled everyone into believing his story is the mastermind behind everything. These so-called people of ours that are here in the mall were never found. They were either killed, or taken if they are still alive. Now, Rider's back at the compound dying.

"I don't think you need to worry about him anymore."

"Oh–you've met him."

"Yeah." A look of confusion comes across Susan's face. "It's a long story."

"Maybe you can tell me about it some time."

"Maybe. Thank you, Susan. I won't forget your kindness," I say with a smile. "If I can come back for you, I will."

"Don't worry about me. I'll be fine. Just get this girl of yours out of here. She doesn't deserve what Jake has planned. Nobody does."

I nod my head one last time and leave the room. I step up to the double doors in the hallway and peek out so I can see what's on the other side. I notice that I'm on the bottom level and underneath the North wing where the food court is, in the center of the mall. In front of me is a play area for kids that I assume is now being used as a place for people to sleep since there are blankets and pillows on the benches that line the barrier on the inside. To the right of the play area is a store that changes every few months. Or at least it did back before the storm. A Halloween banner is hanging above the store now. They were always selling Halloween stuff months before. I can't see what it's being used for at the moment. There are tons of metal shelves blocking the entryway with sheets hanging on them.

I step out of the hallway and into the open area of the mall, closing the door behind me. This door, the one blocking the hallway, is a new addition. I can remember this hallway being open so anyone could access the public restrooms across from the surveillance room. I start walking slowly along the wall, away from the Halloween store, towards the circular center of the mall that has two escalators, one leading up to the top floor and the food court. In between the escalators is an elevator that I doubt they used in order to conserve power—power I'm shocked they have to begin with. There's not a single person in sight, but trash and all kinds of debris is scattered across the floor. The halls look as though people ransacked the mall in the wake of society shutting down.

I cautiously walk up to the corner of the North wing, staying close to the wall to avoid being seen from the upper level, and peer down both the East and West wings. Both wings appear to be clear of people, but I can hear two men on the upper level directly above me talking. Avoiding them will be easy, since I can stay on the lower level until I reach Macy's, but I still have no idea where any others might be. I only saw the two men on camera, but there could be more inside one of the stores that I need to walk by and I wouldn't know until it was too late. I decide the best option is to simply walk through the mall and act like I belong, but stay close to the wall to be safe. If I'm stopped by someone, I'll just have to hope they don't suspect anything. Or worse… already know who I am.

The Layton Hills mall is what I consider to be a standard looking mall. It has two levels. From the bottom level where I am, you can see up to the upper levels from the middle of the lower corridor. The end of the mall where I need to go has a stairway.

I begin walking casually along the tile floor, down the east wing. I step over scattered trash, keeping my guard up, occasionally looking through the opening to the top floor to make sure nobody spots me from above. As I make my way down the hall, I begin to wonder why the halls are so empty. Where are all the people? Each store I pass is barricaded, or at least concealed from seeing inside, just as the Halloween store had been. It's strange.

"Hey you!" shouts a voice from above. I look up to see a soldier in uniform. "What are 'you doing walking around? Curfew is in effect."

That kind of answers my question.

"I was told Jake needed to see me."

"Jake doesn't see anybody this late. Go back to your quarters before I have you beaten and locked up."

"Do you wanna tell Jake I'm not coming then?" I ask as he turns to walk away.

"Ahhh… hold on. Meet me at the top of the stairs," he says while pointing to the stairs at the end of the wing.

As I walk towards Macy's, I'm unsure of what to do when I face the soldier. As I near the stairway, I notice that the gate is pulled down so I won't be able to get in from this level. Before I reach the top of the stairs, I pull out my knife and slide it under the sleeve of my jacket with the blade down. Once I reach the top, the soldier is standing there waiting for me, with his rifle slung around his back. He's wearing the same uniform Rider had been.

"What is it he wanted you for?" asks the dark haired, bearded soldier.

"How should I know?" I shrug my shoulders. "I just do what I'm told."

"What were you doing on the lower level?"

I really don't have a response to the question, and since I really don't understand whatever system they have in place, I could say anything and it would be the wrong response. I look around to see if there are any other soldiers, and when I see there aren't any, I decide to act.

"Sorry," I say casually.

"You will be," he says as he reaches out and grabs my left arm. "A night in lockup will certainly make you."

I let the knife slide down into my hand and just as the soldier goes to say something or even scream—I stab him in the chest while placing my other hand over his mouth. The soldier struggles for a few seconds before going limp. I step behind him to prevent him

119

from falling and drag him into Macy's and around the right corner in the men's section, where I know the dressing rooms are. Once I'm in the dressing room, I put the soldier down and grab his rifle and pistol. Knowing I won't need to be as cautious, since I'll be able to defend myself better, I grab all his ammo as well.

I step out of the dressing room and begin making my way through the clothes for cover, with my rifle in the ready position. Macy's looks as though it hasn't really been touched. All the clothing racks are still in their normal positions and appear to have most of the clothes. As I cautiously continue making my way through them, I start to hear screaming in the back end of the store, where all the home goods are.

"No!" screams a female voice with fear.

I quicken my pace, but quietly move towards the screaming. The woman yells again. "Please don't!" she says.

I recognize Emily's voice. There's a crash a moment later as she's thrown into some shelves.

"Shut up, bitch!" says Jake.

My heart starts pounding as I realize I'm only steps away from Emily. My heart has never pounded this fast in my entire life, but I also never had to rescue someone I loved from a psychopath.

"You know, I just came from seeing your stupid boyfriend," Jake says as I step up to a shelf of comforters, with them just on the other side.

"Alec? He's here?" Emily sobs.

"He is," he says with pleasure in his voice, "but not for much longer."

"No!"

Emily screams again as Jake jumps on top of her and tries to force her onto her stomach. I step out from behind the shelf at the same time, not waiting another second.

"Hey, asshole," I say through clenched teeth.

"Huh? What?" Jake gasps as he turns to see me standing over him. "No. Impossible!"

I grab Jake by the back of his shirt and throw him into the wall. He staggers to his feet as I approach him.

"You'll never get out of here alive," he says as he spits into my face.

I wipe the saliva away with a sleeve. I pull out my knife and move towards him. Jake takes a halfhearted swing towards me, trying to avoid the knife. I lunge forward and give several quick, deliberate thrusts into his gut and chest. Jake quickly begins gasping for air and he reaches up and clenches his chest with his left hand. I reach up and grab a fist full of his hair like he had done to me. He tries to knock my hand free, but he's too weak. I shake my head and thrust the knife up into Jakes throat. His arms start flailing back and forth, hitting me a few times as he struggles with terror in his eyes. Blood spurts onto my arm and down Jake's chest. "I told you I'd stab you in the throat." I release my grip on Jake and let him fall to the ground and turn to face Emily.

"Ale…" she chokes unable to finish. I drop the knife and quickly move to her side and throw my arms around her tightly. "I thought you were dead," she manages to say as she begins to cry.

"Shhh," I try to sooth her. "I'm fine. We're fine."

She has light bruising on her face from where Jake or someone struck her. I hold her in my arms for what seems like an eternity and I want it to last longer. The tightness in my chest and stomach is gone for the first time since she was taken and I feel like I can breathe again. Holding her in my arms brings me instant comfort.

"How did you escape?" she asks as she pulls away from me.

"Idiots didn't restrain my feet. I saw my chance to break free and I took it."

"Your face looks like it hurts," she says as she lifts her hand to touch it, but instead rests it on my chest. I smile and hold back a laugh. "What?"

"Here you are worrying about me and you're the one that needed to be rescued."

"Even the hero needs someone to take care of him, Alec."

"I guess."

"Just make sure you don't forget that," she grins and hugs me tightly.

I want to hold on to her forever, but we're still very much in danger. Other men could come check on Jake at any time, and I still have no idea as to how many men there are. I force myself to pull away from her.

"We need to get out of here."

Emily nods. I stop and pick my knife up and wipe the blood on Jake's lifeless body. I then grab her by the hand and begin leading her out, when all of a sudden, she starts kicking Jake's corpse. She kicks him hard several times before letting up, and then we both walk back to the exit without talking about it. She had every right to do that, and I don't need an explanation.

"Do you know where they brought you in from?" I ask her softly.

"They brought me in where there were a bunch of offices downstairs."

"That's what I was afraid of." I look at Emily seriously for the first time since finding her. "Are you ready?"

"Yes."

"This is what we're gonna do. Hold my hand and act as natural as you can while we walk through the mall. As long as we avoid Rider's men, we should be ok."

She nods and we walk out of Macy's, heading straight for the stairs. Once at the bottom, I lead her up against the wall as closely as possible, to avoid being seen from the soldiers up top. We move quickly as we pass store after store until we reach the center. We're walking towards Dick's Sporting Goods when Emily stops me.

"Alec, it's this way," she mutters quietly as she points the opposite direction.

"We need to get you some warmer clothes," I counter while pointing at what she is wearing. She has on a pair of jeans and white t-shirt.

"Good idea," she replies as she looks at herself.

We hurry into Dick's Sporting Goods and go to where the skiing equipment would be. As we walk through the store, I'm surprised to see how most of the store's merchandise hasn't been touched. Everyone should have ransacked the place by now, but that clearly isn't the case. Once we're in the women's section of the ski equipment, I tell Emily to grab what she can and quickly. She frantically begins sifting through the rack of ski pants until she finds a pair of black ones that she thinks might fit. She quickly pulls them on over her jeans and they're a little loose.

"They might fall off," she mutters.

"Try pulling the straps tighter," I reply as I point towards the straps that work like a drawstring. She pulls them tighter until she seems satisfied they will work. "Go find a pair of boots," I say pointing to the shelf behind her. "I'll get everything else."

"Okay."

I'm amazed at how much Emily is keeping her composure. With everything that she's been through in the past few hours, most people would be useless, and dangerous. Emily, however, is the exact opposite. While standing next to a coat rack, I observe the way she moves. Quickly and yet gracefully through the different types of shoes. Her wavy, long, brown hair falls into her face as she tries on a pair of boots, concealing a view of her face. She looks up at me suddenly, sensing I'm watching her and catches me staring.

She cracks a smile as she looks at me with gleaming eyes. I continue staring at her long enough to smile back, but then return my attention to the task at hand.

I pull a teal and silver colored jacket from the rack that looks big enough to fit. I then move to the shelves where the gloves and beanies are. I grab a pair of simple black gloves and a black beanie for Emily and a beanie for myself.

"Found some boots," she says as she walks up to me wearing a pair of white ones.

"Perfect. Put these on and let's get out of here."

"You don't need to tell me twice," she replies as she puts her gloves and beanie on. "Let's go."

I give her a nod and we start making our way back to the mall entrance. Once we're at the door, I step up to the far-left wall and slowly make my way with her right beside me. We continue to stay close to the wall to avoid being caught in the open. When we reach the end of the hallway, I stop at the corner and look both ways, searching for any soldiers on either level. I step out into the open to cross over to the other side of the main hallway, trying to act as natural as possible. When I look up I almost gasp.

In the ceiling—in the central part of the mall—is a strange circular machine that I've never seen in all the years I've come here. The machine looks like one of those toys you would spin on a point and watch it move around. A top. Only the point of this machine is above ground spinning silently and fast. It's also giving off a red glow.

"What is that?" Emily asks with the same curious look on her face.

"I don't know, but whatever it is, I bet it's what is powering the mall."

I look at it for a few more seconds, studying it as if that will accomplish something. Before I realize I'm distracted, I pull my eyes away from the strange machine and grab Emily by her hand. Just when I think we'll make it into the hallway leading back to the area I was being held, a soldier starts coming down the escalator to our right and spots us.

"Hey, where are you going with that woman?" he yells.

I motion for Emily to stay where she is and start walking towards him. This soldier has a heavy red beard and a bald head. He's a good inch taller than I and probably outweighs me by thirty pounds. "I asked you a question!"

"Sorry, Jake told me I could bring her down and have some fun with her, if you know what I mean?" I say as I turn to look back at Emily, concealing the right side of my body. I slide my knife back out as the soldier steps up to me. "I thought you knew…"

Blood quickly sprays out onto the soldier's chest, staining his clothes and turning his already red beard, crimson. I had stuck my knife into his throat in the same manner I had done to Jake. He makes an uncomfortable gurgling sound and then falls to the floor in a pool of blood. I wipe the knife on my pants to clean the blood and I turn to see Emily staring down at the soldier with a sick look in her eyes.

"Hey," I say as I walk over and place my arm onto her shoulder. She doesn't respond and keeps staring at the lifeless body. The reality of the situation is now clearly having its toll on her. The adrenaline that's been keeping her going is fading.

"Emily?" I say softly as I step in front of her, blocking her view of the bloody scene. She blinks and looks up at me with a pale face. It pains me to see her like this and to also see me kill someone the way I did, but I have no choice.

"Are you with me?" She nods her head, but her expression doesn't change. "We have to move Emily. More soldiers are eventually going to come this way, and we don't want to be here when they do." Her wide eyes narrow as color starts to come back into her face and she begins to breathe for the first time in nearly a minute. "Let's go," I say as I hold out my left hand for her and she takes it.

I quickly lead Emily out of the central hall of the mall and we make our way past the kiddy play area and into the hallway where I was held captive. As we enter the hallway and are almost to the surveillance room, Susan steps out of the room in front of us.

"Alec, you need to hurry. The exit is this way," she says, leading us down the hall. "I was watching everything on the cameras. They just found Jake's body and there will be at least a dozen soldiers here any second now," she continues as she stops at what appears to be a service door.

"You need to get moving Susan. If they catch you helping us, they'll kill you." She doesn't respond to my warning but instead looks over at Emily.

"I can see why you're willing to risk your life for her," she says with sadness in her eyes. "Take good care of him."

"I will," replies Emily as she grabs my arm and smiles up at me.

"Susan, come with us," I reply.

"No, I think I'll stay," she says. "My brother died trying to defend me when these soldiers showed up." Susan's eyes begin to swell. "He was all I had left. Now I'd like to get back at them if I can."

I shake my head and look down at the ground, trying to think of a way to convince her to stay.

"Give me a gun," she says as she reaches out her hand. "I can buy you a little more time. There's a snowmobile on the other side of the door."

I pull out one of the pistols I took from the soldiers and hand it to her. I've known this woman for only a few short moments, but I find myself having to fight back tears of my own as I look her in the eyes one last time. All she does is smile before turning and

126

walking back towards the surveillance room. We hear the gunfire and her screaming as the metal door closes behind us. We're in a loading dock area and there are multiple snowmobiles lining the room with a large garage door.

"Get on this one," I say as I walk by the first sled towards the door, trying to shake what just took place.

I pull on the chain that's dangling to the left of the door and it lifts open. A bitter cold air rushes into the room. When I turn around to get on the sled, I spot an M4 on the back wall, along with other supplies like more guns and ammo. I discard the rifle I had for the M4 and a couple more magazines of ammo. I leave everything else behind. Just before I start up the engine, the gunfire in the hallway stops, meaning only one thing. Susan is dead, and they will be on us any moment now. I hop on the sled, in front of where Emily is already sitting, and I turn the key and fire up the sled without waiting another second and drive out into the freezing cold darkness—without looking to see what's behind us.

CHAPTER 7

The storm is especially brutal tonight, unlike any other in the past few weeks. Just a raging tempest of wind and snow. Visibility is worse than I've ever seen it before. It's as if some unseen force knew we were trying to escape and is doing everything it can to stop us from getting away. I try turning on the headlights, hoping for a little help, but the bright lights only reflect off the snow making it more difficult. I turn the lights off and pray that my internal compass has me heading in the right direction. I drive up a road that I think is 1000 N. in Layton, heading east towards the mountain and the compound. Our shelter and safety. I know that 1000 N. will eventually turn into Rainbow Drive and lead us straight onto the Valley View golf course. I also know there won't be much cover on the golf course, but since it will be the fastest and easiest route, the risk will need to be taken. After only about fifteen minutes of riding in the bitter cold darkness, my worst fear happens. The snowmobile jerks a couple times as it loses power, letting me know we're out of gas. The sled holds on to the last ounce of power it has for about another hundred yards and then the motor sputters and gives one last flutter before finally dying.

"Why are we stopping?" Emily yells over the wind.

"Uh, we ran out of gas!"

"Oh."

"Sorry. We'll have to continue on foot from here."

I can tell Emily isn't thrilled about a long trek in the snow, but neither am I.

"Where are we, Alec?"

"I'm not sure," I look over at the houses to the left of the sled. They're barely visible in the shadows and if I didn't know they should be there, I probably wouldn't believe that they really are. "We need to keep moving in the direction we're heading. Hopefully, we aren't too far from the golf course."

"What's at the golf course?"

"Shelter."

"But what about one of these houses? Why can't we stay in one of these?" she asks frantically while looking from one side of the street to the other.

I gently wrap my arm around her and walk her closer to the houses on the left that I had been looking at. As we come closer, the shapes of the houses become clearer and clearer until everything is visible. What I imagine was once a very beautiful one story, is now something that's seen in a war-torn city. Only instead of grey ash everywhere, everything is white. The roof is completely caved in and the windows are broken. Debris is everywhere, falling out the windows and even the front door. Emily doesn't move or say anything.

"Hey?" I say as I step in front of her. Her eyes break free from the bleak view in front of her and focus on me. "The clubhouse at the golf course is newer than all of these houses and has cement and steel for its structure. It's our best chance, okay?"

Emily nods her head in agreement, but shows no emotion. She's starting to lose it again.

"You can do this, Emily. I know you've been through a lot, but I know you can do this. All you need to do right now is walk. If you get tired, I will carry you."

I place both my hands gently onto each side of her face. She has a small strand of hair poking out through her beanie, hanging down over her left eye. I gently tuck the strand back under her beanie and smile at her. Surprisingly, she smiles back.

"Are you ready?"

She nods again, but this time with more emotion. I happily accept the response and begin leading her up the dark, snow packed street in the direction of the golf course. The snow is deep and difficult to travel by foot and I tire quickly. I can only imagine how Emily is feeling up to this point. She isn't used to these types of treks.

After we've been walking for several hours, even though it felt like forever, passing house after house, Emily slows down significantly from exhaustion and I begin to question if we're anywhere close to where I thought we should be. Just when panic is building up inside me like a bad cold, I realize there aren't any more houses to my left or my right, only a small cluster of trees just ahead.

"Emily," I pause gasping for my breath. "I think we made it." Just then, I look over and Emily is down on her side with her eyes closed. "Emily!" I quickly kneel down and slide my arm underneath her to pull her close to me. "C'mon, Emily. I need you to stay with me just a little while longer."

The only response she gives is a slight murmur. I know she's exhausted, but I fear she might be getting hypothermia. The hair that is sticking out from her beanie is frosted over. Her cheeks are red and her lips are already cracking from being so cold. She's not going to be able to go on any further, which means I need to carry her the rest of the way. I desperately look around, hoping to see any sign of the golf course that would tell me we are in fact in the right place. Every direction I look, I can only see shadows and falling snow. I can't see a thing and as long as it keeps snowing, I'm not going to. I should keep walking straight in the direction I have been, but where is that leading? I needed shelter an hour ago and without it, Emily won't make it much longer. I need a miracle.

I give Emily one last, quick glance and then I muster up every last bit of energy I have left and pick her up off of the snow. I cradle her in my arms and begin hiking through the snow for the second time in the year we've known each other. Only this time, due to my already exhausted strength, she seems twice as heavy. I'm going off of no sleep or food in nearly a day. Not to mention the strenuous hike I had already been on, which led to us being here in the first place. I barely have any energy left. We're here because I didn't have the courage to say no to all the leaders in the compound. The thought of those men throwing around orders angers me and I clench my teeth. I'm done letting them determine the survival of everyone in the compound.

Suddenly, while I stumble aimlessly through the snow with Emily in my arms, everything stops. I freeze in my tracks and a tingling sensation creeps up my spine as I watch the snow stop falling, like someone turned off a faucet above us. The wind completely ceases at the same moment and I still can't move as I witness the strangest thing I've ever seen or heard of in my entire life.

The visibility around me becomes clearer and clearer in only a few seconds and I quickly find myself standing only a football field's length away from the clubhouse. A dim glow is illuminating the area and I can see the sky for the first time in a year. It's like standing inside a massive pipe that opens up towards the sky. Only the walls aren't cement. I'm surrounded by a thick wall of snow and darkness, swirling around us like a shark waiting to close in and consume us. I look up to the sky and a glowing full moon and many stars are visible. The feeling of hope along with a nervous sensation takes over my body. I now know where I am and can get Emily to safety, but something incredible and frightening is also happening. How can a storm behave this way, and why is it doing so now? I look up to the sky in wonder and Emily shivers from the cold, making me snap out of my trance.

"Emily, wake up," I say to her in excitement. "It's amazing. I can see the sky. I can see the stars."

"Hmm…"

Emily is missing something beautiful inside this awful nightmare we've been stuck in. I had taken her outside the other day to give her something different than the inside of the compound and now I have the chance to show her something bright and amazing even while surrounded by all this darkness, but she's simply too tired and cold to even comprehend I'm actually speaking to her. I reluctantly take my gaze off of the sky, fearing it might disappear when I do and look over to the clubhouse. The building appears to be still standing and completely intact as I hoped it would be.

"I can see the clubhouse, Emily. We'll be there in a couple minutes."

As I come up on the west side of the clubhouse, I can tell that part of the roof has collapsed in the southwest corner. Fortunately, the clubhouse is two levels so the lower level should be completely free of snow. The west side of the clubhouse is built mostly of steel frames for pillars with cement around them and then some heavy wood mixed throughout the building, all the way up into the trusses for the roof. The building is completely covered in white and there are no signs that it was ever made of anything except for ice. I gently set Emily down in the snow, up against a garage door on the lower level. I expect that behind the rollup doors will be equipment and probably even some golf carts. I also know that it will be the driest place in the entire building, because the doors are underneath an upper deck. It's also heavy enough to hold back the weight of the snow that had drifted up against them.

For now, the storm is still clear as I try to lift up one of the doors. The steel is cold and hard to get a grip on. I have to start digging out some snow at the base to even try and get my hands underneath. Nothing. The door still won't budge at all. It, along with the other doors, must have large padlocks keeping each of them secure. I'm going to need another way in. Down on the south side of the building is a normal exterior door that I should at least be able to kick in if I need to. I walk down to the door and try peeking in through the small window in the top. I see a narrow hallway on the other side, but it's too dark to see anything else. I try the handle and I'm not surprised when it won't open. I take a step back and then one step forward and kick the door as hard as I can with my right foot. Nothing happens. I kick the door again, this time using every bit of strength I can find. Again, nothing happens. I then take the stock of my gun and slam it into the heavy glass window. Only a small crack appears on the first whack. I hit the glass several more times, and each time another crack appears while the current ones split and grow throughout the window. Finally, after about twenty hits or so, the glass crashes out of the space it occupied. I reach my hand in through the opening and unlock the door from the inside.

I step into the building, immediately looking for access into the garage area. Inside the door is a little room with stairs leading upstairs and another door to the left. I try the door on the left, but it's locked. I quickly become irritated with all of the locked doors in my way and raise my rifle to teach the door a lesson.

"Don't Alec. They'll hear you," whispers Emily.

I jump from the initial sound of her voice, not expecting her to be there. I turn around to apologize for my carelessness, but she isn't there. It's just an empty doorway.

"Emily?"

I step up to the door to look outside and there she is. Still lying up against the rollup door where I left her, asleep. I bite down on the inside of my lip as I stand there confused. It was her voice I heard, right?

"Apparently, I need to get some rest."

I turn to walk back into the building, but just before I step inside, I spot a light emerge from the trees, a few hundred yards away.

"Shit!"

Almost as if it was working in sync with me, or as if I were in control, the storm collapses around the clubhouse, shielding us from their view. The strange behavior of the weather continues to make the hair on my neck stand up.

I quickly run over to Emily and pick her up, then turn and carry her to the open door. No more time to find a way into the garage. Once inside, I open the second door that leads up into the retail area of the clubhouse to find a place where we can hide and if need be, make a final stance. Inside the retail area it's very difficult to see. I bump into several things as my eyes try adjusting to the darkness. Finally, after I've bumped into probably everything in the store, my eyes adjust and I can make out the layout of the room, enough to get around without bumping into everything else. The store looks as if nobody's been here since the storm began. Everything seems to be that way in the world now. The merchandise is in its rightful place so that the store looks as though it could still be in business. A bit dusty, but not ransacked or a mess. I set Emily down behind the register so I can go and look for a blanket, or anything to try and warm her up. Most of the stuff is golf equipment and completely useless. I find myself walking out of what seemed to be the golf shop and into a hallway and find another store across the hall. From the outside, this one looks like it has more clothes, so I walk in hoping to find something useful.

Trying to focus on the different items on shelves with so little light, strains my eyes. I check shelf after shelf and find nothing but clothes. Mostly clothes people would wear golfing and nothing heavy enough to do any good. Once I feel I've searched the whole store, I head back to where I left Emily. She's still asleep. I sit down on the floor and pull her up so I can wrap my arms around her and keep her as warm as possible. I sit there holding her for thirty minutes or even an hour, I'm not really sure, listening for more soldiers to show up. Nobody comes and it feels like maybe we might have gotten lucky and they can't find the clubhouse in the storm.

"Alec?" Emily says without me realizing she's awake. She'd finally stopped shivering a while ago.

"Yeah?"

"Where's Mya?"

Emily knows me well enough to know that I would take Mya anywhere with me. How can I tell her that I just left her in a hole? Emily loves her as much as I do so I know telling her will upset her.

"Alec, where is she?"

Emily adjusts herself so she can look up at me. I keep my eyes forward and she waits patiently for me to respond.

"She fell into another sink hole. I didn't have time to harness her before we ran after you. I never even had the chance to decide if I was going to climb down and get her or continue after you before I was knocked out."

I feel a tear slide down my cheek as I think about Mya for the first time since I last saw her. I shake my head back and forth and just as I begin to speak again, Emily puts her hand on my cheek.

"I'm sure she's fine. She survived one hole, I'm sure she can again."

"Maybe."

"It's all my fault. If I hadn't let Jake take me, this nev..."

"It isn't your fault, Emily. Jake betrayed us all and he paid for what he did. I'm just glad I got to you before he did anything."

It's hard to make out all the features of her face, but I can just barely see her eyes staring back up at me. I lean down and kiss her. She lifts herself towards me as if she thought the exact same thing and we kiss passionately for the first time since she was taken. The feeling of Emily's soft lips touching mine still makes my skin tingle as if it's the first time. We kiss for a couple minutes until I pull away so I can stay alert. If she's blushing, I can't tell. I am.

"You need to try and get some sleep. I don't know how long we can hide here."

"Do you think they'll find us?"

"Eventually they will. I sa…" I'm about to tell her I'd seen them just before the strange thing with the weather ended, but decide to leave it alone. Telling her the men were that close might scare her beyond being able to sleep and I really don't know how to tell her what I saw anyway. It was too strange. "We just need to rest. We'll need as much strength as possible to make it back to the compound."

She doesn't seem to notice my sudden change of thought and snuggles herself up against me until she's comfortable. "I'll try," is all she says before slowly drifting off to sleep. I follow her, not too long after.

I'm suddenly woken out of a deep sleep by the sound of engines rumbling just outside the clubhouse. We're lucky I heard them at all, exhausted as I am. If I hadn't woken from the noise, they would've cut our throats while we slept. Emily stirs almost at the same moment. She manages to ask "what was that noise?" before I cover her mouth.

"They're here. We need to go now," I whisper in her ear. I help her climb to her feet and grab my rifle. "Stay low and directly behind me. Keep one hand on my jacket so I know you're there."

"Okay," she says softly and I start leading the way.

I walk to the edge of the store and look down the hallway in the direction we had come in. The hallway is dark and I can't see anything. There's no way of telling which side of the clubhouse they're on, but I don't want to go out the way we came. That would just require us to walk all the way around the building. The front of the clubhouse faces the mountain and that's the direction we want to go. The direction we need to go. I look down both ends of the hallway and once I decide there's nothing there, I go left and make my way down the shadowy corridor towards the entrance. I lead us quickly to the end of the hall and stop to peer around the next corner. I can't see anything moving so I start walking again, just as quickly. I can still feel Emily holding on behind me. We're approaching the clubhouse restaurant on our left when suddenly I hear Emily say "into the restaurant, now."

Without questioning her, I turn into the open doorway just as I hear voices coming from down the hall where we were headed. I lead us behind a tall countertop with a cash register, just inside the doorway on the right.

At first the voices are muffled and I can't make out what they're saying. They're talking quietly, but even a soft voice would carry in a place as quiet as this one. A few seconds later I can make out the two male voices.

"Ya need to keep it down."

"I don't see what the big deal is. They're probably long gone by now."

"Shut yer mouth already. How we suppose to sneak up on them with you blabberin' loud enough for them to hear us?"

They stop just outside the door and shine a light into the restaurant. The room lights up well enough for me to see several tables and chairs heavily covered in dust. They're only visible for a second or two before the light moves away to search other areas. A couple seconds later the light comes back and rests on the front counter where we're hiding. It holds there for only a moment before disappearing again.

"See, there's nothing here. This is a waste of time."

"Just shut it and keep lookin!"

I hear them continue back down the hallway.

"That was close," I say softly.

"How did you know they were coming? I couldn't hear anything."

"I thought yo… never mind." I must be going crazy.

I lead Emily back out of the restaurant and continue the way we were going. Hopefully not right into more men. We turn down one more hall and I feel a cold breeze coming towards us. We're getting close to the door the two men used to enter. We approach the glass double doors and I peak outside. Luckily, the blinds are drawn so we're concealed from anyone that might be waiting for us. Directly in front of the doors are two snowmobiles. The weather is still calm, except for a light breeze. Only the snowmobiles are there and I can't see any more men. Just as I go to step outside, a light shines on my back followed by a shout.

"I got em!"

Without hesitation I turn and fire straight into the light and don't stop until it falls away. I grab Emily and lead her out of the clubhouse. We move as fast as we can through the deep snow and climb onto one of the snowmobiles. I quickly fire it up and speed off towards the mountain as fast as the sled will go. We're moving for only a few seconds before more gunfire starts. I turn the sled to the right, towards a cluster of trees I know are there, only from memory. Sure enough, the trees appear almost out of nowhere and I have to jerk the sled to the left to avoid hitting one. I don't react quickly enough though. The right side of the sled clips the trunk of the tree and the impact sends us flying through the air. We land on soft powder, but I land face first and have to fight through the deep snow to get my footing before I wipe some of the snow off my face. I ignore the bitter cold on my face and turn to see what is behind us as Emily struggles to her feet. I raise my rifle and wait for the battle to start. What I wouldn't give to have Brian here with me.

The light from the sled is still on and gives our enemies a beacon for where to go. I motion with my left hand for Emily to take cover behind a pine tree just as multiple lights appear in front of me and I open fire. My gun cracks loudly as each round leaves the barrel. The bright lights from their sleds prevent me from seeing my target so I just aim directly above the light, praying I hit true. Just as quickly as I open fire, bullets crash into the snow in front and to the side of me. I have-to dive behind the tree Emily is also behind for cover.

Gunfire seems to erupt from everywhere. The blinding light from their sleds makes it impossible to see. I keep crouching behind the tree, leaning out every couple of seconds to fire in the direction of a light. After several shots, I strike one and the light around us fades slightly. I see several men to our right approaching. I figure I'm up against ten soldiers at least, and under these circumstances I have no chance. I look down into Emily's eyes just as a bullet strikes me in the side of my left leg, just above the knee. Emily screams as she sees me fall to my knees.

I quickly stand back up, fighting through the pain and fire at a soldier that is only about thirty feet away. The bullet hits him in the arm in the same split second he fires another round. The second bullet hits me in the chest, below my right shoulder and I fall onto my back. Emily quickly moves over to shield me from any more gun fire. I look up as I see the soldier who just shot me moving towards us with his gun aimed directly at Emily. She leans in towards me as she prepares for the shot. Just when I think it's about to end, I hear a loud growl followed by the soldier screaming out in pain. I look up to see a blur of white tearing through the soldier's arm with sharp teeth.

Mya.

The soldier raises his weapon with his unharmed hand to shoot her, but a bullet strikes him in the head and he falls dead onto the snow. Suddenly, gunfire ripples through the trees from behind us and I can only assume Brian came to our rescue. All I can do is lay there in the snow with Emily wrapped tightly around me while I listen to the small war rage on. Everything around me seems to slow down. At this point I can barely hear the gunfire and shouting. It's like listening to something from under water. Out of the distance, I hear a voice that sounds like Brian.

"Cover Alec and Emily. Draw all the fire away from them. Let's show these bastards what we're made of."

Brian had brought help with him.

Finally, after several more minutes of gunfire, I hear one of the soldiers yell "Retreat". I then hear several other soldiers repeat the command. "Fall back you idiots! There's too many of them!"

"We got them on their heels boys, they're falling back," shouts Brian. "Someone needs to check on Alec. It looked like he took a couple hits."

"I got him," replies my father. All the voices are muffled as I fight to stay awake. An instant later my father is at my side. "Damn you, Alec," he says with panic in his eyes.

"Damn me? You… only have your… self to blame."

My father ignores my response and he looks at the wound on my chest methodically, placing his hand on it to try and stop some of the bleeding. "Brian, get over here now!"

"Where's... where's Mya?" I ask as I look up into the dark sky to see snow falling down.

Mya is suddenly at the side of my head, licking my face almost at the same moment I say her name. She lays down onto the snow next to me with her head up against mine and I massage her fur gently with my left hand. She lets out a couple unsatisfied sounds at my condition. My chest feels like it's on fire, along with the rest of my body and I'm having a difficult time breathing. The chill from the snow on my back and the feeling of cold flakes landing on my face is the closest thing I have to comfort. That and the relief that Mya is snuggled up against Emily and me. They're both alright.

"Hang in there, Al," says Brian as he kneels down next to my father. Strangely, the underwater muffled sound disappears and everything sounds clear.

"He's losing a lot of blood. We need to get him back to the compound now," my father says with a shaky voice.

"We can take him back on a sled. I'll take him back on one with me," Brian replies without hesitation. "I can get him there fast."

"Emily, you can ride back with Rider. I'll..." Emily interrupts my father at the same time I shake my head.

"No! I'll ride with you or on the same sled as Alec,"

"The sled can carry all three of us. Besides she can help hold him up," responds Brian. "You should probably bring Mya with you, Paul."

"Alright. Let's get moving," shouts my father like he was a commander giving orders.

Within moments, I'm sitting back on a sled behind Brian, with Emily sitting behind me with one arm wrapped tightly around me and the other hand on top of mine keeping pressure on my chest.

I'd nearly forgotten about the hole in my leg until they pulled me onto my feet. A jolt of pain shoots through my body and I groan from the pain. After a few minutes on the sled the pain fades, along with my thoughts as I slowly slip away.

I awake to a bright light above me. At first, the light is blinding, but within a few seconds my eyes adjust and I can see where I am. I've never been in this room before, but it appears to be some kind of lab with lots of expensive looking equipment. The equipment that I see, I'm not familiar with. I've been inside hospitals and seen just about everything there is out there in the medical field while serving in the military and also growing up with my father as a doctor. Is he a doctor?

My body aches all over and I have sharp pains in my chest and my leg. I can't move enough to look down at my wounds so I just lay there. I'm not alone in the room. My mother is standing next to the bed. She has a look in her eyes that I've seen before. She had the same look when I told her I wouldn't be able to bring Ashlee back. Before, I thought it was disappointment she felt. Now I know that it's sadness. Brian is next to her, but unlike my mother he's keeping his concern hidden behind a mask of calm and focus. He has his hand under his chin like I've always done when I'm nervous about something. Emily is sitting in a chair to my right and when she sees I'm awake, she almost gasps with a look of relief. Her face is red and her cheeks swollen. She's been crying.

"Why does everyone have a look on their face like I died or something?"

"Because you did. Your heart stopped beating for nearly a minute when we first got you down here," my father says in a steady voice. He walks over to the table. "I gave you a shot of adrenaline and an electric shock and neither of those things brought you back."

"Come again?" I say surprised.

I glance at everyone in the room. None of their looks change. Mya hears my voice and I hear her paws on the tile floor move towards me, before feeling her nudge my hand. I struggle to lift my hand up to scratch her head, but Emily notices my struggle and helps my hand the rest of the way.

"Son, there are a lot of things that I need to tell you, but I don't have time for that right now. I gave you an experimental serum that is designed to accelerate the healing process in your body. Fortunately, it jumpstarted your heart, but it isn't enough to heal your wounds or even keep you alive. Your injuries are too progressed for that."

"Well—it worked didn't it? Clearly my heart is beating again." Tears begin to fall down my mother's cheeks almost simultaneously as they do on Emily's.

"That was just the first stage of what I need to do to you. Without the other two phases, your body will pump too much blood into your heart and eventually that, along with every other organ in your body, will basically explode from too much pressure."

"Okay, so start these other two phases already. I don't really wanna burst open like a piñata."

"Alec—the next two phases are extremely painful and could very well kill you," my father says grimly.

"Well, if what you say is true about the first phase, I'll die anyway."

"Alec, there's a second possibility as well," interrupts Brian.

I almost jump at his sudden interjection. I look over at him and wait for him to tell me what the third possibility is, but he hesitates to answer.

"Well, what is it?" I look at each person in the room. Finally, Brian continues.

"You could turn into one of those things that attacked Rider."

"I don't understand," I say softly without looking at my father.

Only I do understand. I hadn't listened to my father when he tried to tell me before because I was so angry. Maybe because I didn't want to believe that everything I thought I knew about him, was a lie. I look up at my father with a cold look in my eyes.

"You didn't?"

"I'm afraid so, Alec. Now we don't have time..."

"You mean to tell me that you created those monsters out there that could have killed Brian and me. They tore a man to shreds."

My voice is now raised as I try and sit up. A burst of pain erupts from my leg and my chest. My heart feels like it's beating faster than it should be. It feels like it wants to burst out of me and jump onto my lap.

"You can yell at me later son," he says calmly as he looks over at the monitor next to Emily. "Your heart rate is already rising. We're out of time."

My father disappears from my view as I suddenly struggle to breathe. Emily is out of her seat with a look of panic knowing there's nothing she can do. She grabs my right hand gently and leans in close to me.

"You're gonna be fine. I know you are. Just try and stay calm," she says shakily. I can hear the doubt in her voice and her eyes confirm it. Bless her heart for trying to be strong for me.

My father returns with two black cylinder containers that look metallic. One is about the size of a Gatorade cooler and the other the size of a two-liter pitcher. He hands the larger one to Brian and moves over to my side.

"What are those?" I ask with strain in my voice.

"Nan-ites. First, I'm going to give you the small container. This cylinder is going to bond with your nervous system, including your brain, muscles and pretty much everything underneath the skin. This is where you will feel pain unlike anything you have before. It will only last for a few seconds before you pass out. The second

144

cylinder will make it so that your body can adapt to any climate and serve as an armor. They will also imitate your skin. Your skin will look and feel normal, but once the Nan-ites detect you're in trouble, they will activate." I nod my head and my father pauses for a moment to look at me with examining eyes. I simply stare back while I try to control my breathing. "We need to start."

"So what happens when I turn into some monster and try to kill everyone in here?"

"This isn't the same serum that was given to the others. I removed those problems and I believe it will do what it's supposed to."

I look over at my mom to try and get a feel for what she's thinking. She still looks worried but nods her head in approval with a weak smile. I look at Brian and all he does is nod his head twice. Finally, I look back at Emily and she's in tears. She forces a smile then leans down and gently kisses my lips. The tingly sensation isn't as strong, but I still feel it. Even while I'm dying, my connection with her is there.

As she starts to pull away from me, she stops and leans in close to my ear. She speaks softly so that nobody can hear but me, and says "I love you."

Hearing those words from her gives me butterflies and fills me with pure joy, helping me almost forget the pain. I've been wanting to say those words to her for some time, but I've been weary of how she might respond. Now that I know, I'm not about to wait to say it back. As I begin to repeat the words, I feel like all the air has been sucked out of me. I try to say it again, but suddenly I can't breathe.

I start gasping for breath and I hear my father shout something, but I'm too focused on trying to breathe to make out the words. The monitor is beeping rapidly and everything sounds like it did when I was on my back in the snow. I glance down at my father just as he presses a button on the canister that I couldn't tell was there and then sets in on my bare chest. As I struggle for breath, I watch the canister dissolve into liquid, but as my eyes focus on the black substance, I see that it's tiny little specks and not actually a liquid. The tiny specks work their way towards my face in a flowing motion as if they're working as one object. I strain my neck, trying to prevent them from getting to my face, but they consume me too fast. There are so many of them that I can no longer see any part of my body, only a sea of flowing blackness. I can feel the blackness crawling down my throat like an ant colony looking to make a home inside my body. If I hadn't already been struggling for breath, I would've gagged from the pressure. Aside from the bizarre feeling in my throat, however, the feeling is bearable. It's not pain I'm feeling, just… discomfort.

Then they start crawling in through my eyes and every other opening they can find in my body. My body convulses from the sudden shock of pain. I lift up off the bed so that the only parts of me still touching are my ankles and back of my head. I'm not sure if I'm screaming because I can't hear anything at all. It's as if all my senses, except for pain, ceased to exist. No sight, no sound or smell. Just pain. It's as if every cell in my body is on the verge of exploding. Suddenly, after suffering a lifetime of hell in complete darkness, the pain stops. It's as if the pain hears my pleading thoughts and I feel my back rest back down on the bed. I still can't see anything because now my vision is filled with a blinding light. Although the light is uncomfortable, I welcome it. The blinding light is better than the darkness. Then I hear that soft, comforting, familiar voice–almost like a whisper.

"It's almost over, Alec."

Not even a second later, I hear the same voice scream. At least I think it's seconds later. I've lost all perception of time.

"You said he would pass out quickly!" another voice shouts.

"He's stronger than I thought. He won't last much longer though. They still haven't entered his brain yet."

They haven't done what?

The pain returns like an explosion of fire through my entire body. Sharp stabbing pains seem to be cutting into me everywhere. My head feels like someone is poking my brain with a knife over and over again and my veins feel like molten lava is flowing through them. I can feel sweat building up on my body and dripping down my face. Then suddenly, the heat is gone and I'm freezing cold. I feel as though I've been tossed out into the snow naked and I've been laying there for hours. All my senses seem to be going haywire and all I want is for the agony to stop. My reality begins to turn upside down as an image flashes of some room. I can see people in the room with me for only a split second and then they disappear.

I start imagining some place beautiful. A place to escape the agony I'm feeling. A place with lots of trees and a waterfall with a pool at the bottom. A place where I can find peace. I imagine myself standing at the top of the falls looking down at the scenery below. Then the pain stops and I am barefoot on some kind of stone with maybe an eighth of an inch of water running over it. To my left, there is a calm river slowly flowing past me until eventually the water falls off the edge only a few steps from where I'm standing. I can feel the warmth of the sun beating down on my face as I look out into a forest that seems to go as far as I can see. I step up to the edge of the falls to see a large pool of water at the bottom, with boulders along the sides and another river disappearing into the dense trees.

Where am I? How did I get here?

Like a sudden shock of electricity, I feel an agonizing pain in my right hand and lift it up to see. There's a gaping hole all the way through as if a blade was stabbed through it. Blood is pouring down my arm and my legs give out on me almost the instant I see the crimson. All my energy is sapped and I feel as though a poison is flowing through my veins. I fall hard onto the wet stone and the area around me quickly turns red. I continue looking over the edge of the waterfall, with my face resting on the cool, wet stone.

I notice something moving down below near the edge of the trees. It looks like a person. The figure steps out into the open and walks over to the pool of water. It's a woman. She doesn't look up right away, instead she just walks up to the edge of the pool and sits down next to it and runs her hand through the water. Images of people appear in the water but I can't make them out. Maybe I'm imagining them. Something in the back of my mind tells me I know her, but I can't remember how. Her hair is long, brown and wavy, hanging down just past her shoulders.

Who is she? What happened to me? How did I get here?

I ignore the pain and try moving my arms so I can lift myself up to get a better look at the woman, but I'm too weak to move.

As I lay there, soaking wet in a pool of water mixed with my own blood, I try focusing on moving my left arm only. I wince from the pain as I try to move again and don't realize I've made a sound, but the woman hears me. She jumps up from where she's sitting by the water and takes a couple steps back, looking up at me. She looks frightened.

Help! I try yelling, but nothing comes out.

The woman's expression changes and she no longer appears frightened. Now she looks as though she's surprised to see me. Her head tilts slightly to the side and she says something softly so I can't hear.

How do I know you?

"Alec?" the woman suddenly yells in a familiar voice.

Is that my name? How does she know me? And why can't I remember anything?

The woman's look of surprise quickly changes to panic as she starts looking for a way to climb up to me.

"Alec!" she yells over and over again like she's worried she might not get to me. "Hold on, Alec! I'm coming."

"Who… are you?" I finally manage to get out, unsure if she even hears me.

The frantic yells from the woman continue and I curl up into a ball, clenching my side as the pain becomes unbearable. I manage to roll over so that I'm looking upstream. Suddenly, the woman is at my side with her arms around me, just in time to see a giant wall of water crashing towards us. I only have a second or two, maybe less, before the wave hits us and suddenly everything stops.

CHAPTER 8

I open my eyes and find myself in a familiar dark room. I turn onto my side and instantly spot a picture of three people with their arms around each other. There's two men and a woman in the middle. My attention goes to the woman. She's blonde with blue eyes and suddenly I'm hit with a wave of images. Memories. The woman is my sister, with Brian and me. I'm back in my room. I remember who I am.

The clock reads 11:23 pm. I slowly sit up, putting my feet down on the ground and scan the room.

Where is everybody? Where's Mya?

"Mya, come here girl!" She doesn't come.

Huh. Where is she? I stand up and walk into the bathroom with a sudden urge to urinate as if I hadn't in days. I wonder how long I've been out. Hours? Days? Maybe even weeks? If only there was someone here who could tell me. When I finish urinating, I stand at the sink gazing into the mirror. My hair is getting long. I know it's been a while since I last cut it, but I hadn't realized it grew out so much. My hair is hanging down over my ears and even my eyes. I also have a pretty good amount of hair growing on my face. A couple more days and I'll have a full beard. Judging by its length, it has only been a couple days. I turn on the water and quickly wet down my hair so I can slick it back out of my eyes.

After I finish in the bathroom, I put on a pair of shoes so I can go find Mya. I gasp from surprise when I walk into the living room. The room looks as though a stampede had run through it. The couch is thrown up against the wall, upside down, and pictures, chairs and the table are scattered around.

"What the hell happened?"

I quickly check my parents' room to make sure they're okay. The room is empty, but also has the same look of destruction. The front door is wide open so I walk over and peak outside. The hallway outside our apartment is empty. I step out into the hall and begin making my way towards the cafeteria, unsure of what I'm going to find. The door to the apartment next to ours is open. Inside is the same chaos as in my own apartment. I continue walking and find apartment after apartment all the same and nobody in sight. I walk towards the main hall with more urgency.

As I near the main hall, I catch the smell of something delicious. Fresh baked bread and mashed potatoes. We don't have mashed potatoes. Or bread.

Do we?

I feel a rumble in my stomach. Whatever it is, I'm hungry. I continue walking again at a quick pace towards the cafeteria, excited to eat something other than soup and rice. Just before I reach the end of the hallway, I stop abruptly in my tracks as I smell something different. Something I haven't smelled in a very long time. Something awful. The smell rotting flesh. The smell of death.

When I turn the corner, my stomach clenches at the same moment I freeze. Bodies are everywhere in the main hall. I instantly have to cover my face with my arm in an attempt to block the smell as I begin to choke. It looks as if an animal had torn everyone to pieces and their corpses have been here for days. There's so much blood that I can hardly see the ground. I begin stepping carefully around the bodies. I peer down at several faces and see people I've

151

known for years. People I used to see every day before the storm hit. My fifth-grade teacher, Mr. Jeppsen, has his throat torn out and multiple incisions all over his body. A woman that worked at the bank—I think her name is Wanita—has similar wounds—but her left arm is missing. I quickly spot Alisha's father, Michael, up against a wall with his throat torn out. Next to him, face down in a pool of blood is Alisha. Her long blonde hair is dark red and her clothes are torn, revealing most of her body.

What the hell did this?

I frantically begin looking around the room for Emily, Brian, Mya and my parents. None of them are here. I turn my gaze to the south hall, leading to the cafeteria and decide that's where they must be. I continue stepping around the mangled bodies until I'm finally free of them in the hallway. I start to feel a knot form in my gut as I fear for the lives of my family and friends. The idea of my mom, dad and Brian lying there torn to pieces makes my heart ache for them. The thought of seeing Emily lying there with her throat ripped open makes the knot in my stomach even tighter and I have to stop. I gather myself quickly and force myself to move on. When I reach the cafeteria doors, I stop again.

There's a dark streak of blood on both of the windows. It looks as if someone slid their hands down them. Afraid to enter and see my family butchered, I take one deep breath before pushing the doors open. I collapse instantly from the sight of Emily sprawled out on the counter top. There's a huge slash down her chest, similar to the one Rider received from the creature in the tree. Her wavy, long brown hair is covering her face, preventing me a full view.

"NO!"

The feelings of confusion, anger and sorrow begin to quickly build inside me. I continue to scream, hunched over, as the sight of Emily quickly overwhelms me to the point of streaming tears. I look down and gaze into the shiny floor of the cafeteria. Only unlike my reflection I saw in the bathroom, the reflection of a monster is now glaring back at me. My hair hasn't changed, other than it looks like it hasn't been washed in months. There are blood stains on both of my cheeks and around my mouth. I look like I've just feasted on a zebra with a pack of lions. But what makes me truly look like a monster, are my eyes.

While I gaze into the bright, yellow, demon like eyes, I hardly even notice that I've started screaming again. Shock is taking over. Now I'm screaming out of anger towards myself and what I've become. *What did I become?* More mixed feelings and confusion flood my thoughts. *Did I really do this? Am I really a monster?* I certainly don't feel like one.

A sharp stabbing pain in my head interrupts my thoughts and makes me double over. Memories flash through my mind of me chasing after Emily, getting captured and leading up to me lying on an operating table. Suddenly, I remember what Brian said. He said I might turn into one of the monsters that attacked Rider. My heart sinks deep within my chest as I realize that Brian's words have come true. My father's serum turned me into a monster and I've killed everyone in the compound, just as I feared would happen. As I continue to look into my reflection, afraid to look back up at Emily, a strange sound catches my attention. To my left, I can hear the sound of flesh being ripped from bone. I slowly look over, and on the far end of the counter, something is eating a person. I can see the legs of a man sticking out from behind the counter.

I gather the strength to stand up and stumble over to see. As I near the end of the counter, more of the man becomes recognizable. The man is wearing a white lab coat over top of a blue polo shirt. Instantly, I'm filled with even more dread as I realize who he is. I take one last step and peer around the corner. Like a man witnessing his worst possible fear, I begin choking on my own vomit as I witness Mya devouring the flesh from my father's face.

I'm frozen. Not this.

Mya looks up at me and starts to growl. Her eyes are the same bright yellow as mine and she's staring at me as if she's never seen me before in her life. She looks hungry. Behind her are two more bodies. One is my mother. She's face down and it looks as though she was trying to protect her face. Hair and flesh are missing from the back of her head and neck. Next to her is Brian. He looks like he has been through the meat grinder. His clothes are torn from head to toe and most of the skin is missing on his face. The only thing that makes it possible to tell who he is, are his dog tags dangling down in a pool of blood. I stare in shock, not able to blink. Not wanting to believe what my eyes are seeing as I force myself to step back towards the door.

No. This can't be happening. This isn't real.

I look back over at Emily and jump from surprise. She's now sitting upright looking at me. Her eyes are also bright yellow and she has an animalistic grin on her face. I try to move further away, but my body is frozen. I'm in shock. Since I can't seem to move, I try to talk to her.

"Em-Emily?" I struggle to get out.

She doesn't respond. Instead, she slowly slides off the counter and steps towards me.

"Emily, what are you doing? It's me… Alec."

She continues to move closer with a monstrous look, so I retreat towards the door slowly, with my eyes fixed on her. Blood is dripping off her lower lip. Her hair is still in her face and some is even caught in her mouth as she stumbles forward.

"Emily?" I continue to plead with her as I raise my hands towards her calmly.

Just before she reaches me, I see my father's legs begin to move out of the corner of my eye. I lose eye contact with Emily for only a split second to see what is going on. Just as I witness my father climb to his feet, with my mom and Brian rising from the dead behind him, Emily lunges forward, biting down on my right shoulder.

"Agh!" I cry out in pain.

I instinctively place my forearm underneath Emily's chin and throw her off as hard as I can. Not knowing my own strength, I send Emily flying across the room, over the countertop and she crashes into the shelf holding all of the dishes. A loud clanging echoes through the room as pots and pans fall to the floor. A chunk of flesh is missing from my shoulder as blood begins to gush out quickly, staining my shirt and my left hand as I press it firmly to try and stop the bleeding. My parents and Brian are already making their way towards me. The flesh on my father's face is practically all gone and the shiny white bone of his skull underneath is visible. I back my way through the double doors and start towards the main hall with my eyes on my family. Emily is already back on her feet and right behind them with the same look of hunger.

Once I'm back in the main hall, I have to take my eyes off my family in order to avoid tripping over the bodies. I quickly, but carefully, step backwards over body after body. As I'm nearing Alicia and her father's body, my father speaks.

"You're gonna pay for what you did to us, Alec," he groans.

"What *I* did?" I shout back. "You made me like this!"

I continue retreating and just as I step next to Alisha, she turns over and bites down on my leg so hard that I feel a bone crack.

"AGH! D-dammit," I choke as I punch down onto Alicia's head. Her head instantly caves in from the blow and she falls to the ground limp just as her father lunges toward my other leg. I dodge his attack by diving out of the way, landing on someone's mutilated body. I'm quickly drenched in blood and guts as I stumble over more bodies trying to break free of the piles of bloody corpses. My pursuer's still right on my tail.

"Come on, Alec," shouts Brian. "Can't we just have a bite?" he asks with a growl.

"Yeah, honey. We're just hungry," my mom snarls.

Finally–after a gruesome minute of crawling through hell–I reach the mouth of the north hall. I climb to my feet, using the wall as support and start limping as fast as I can towards my apartment. I wince from the pain after each step while I drag my right leg along, hurrying as quickly as I can, without looking back. When I reach my door, I look back to see my family and Mr. Wilkinson half way down the hall stumbling towards me. I limp into my apartment, closing the door. I quickly grab the couch and push it against the door along with the chairs and the table to make a barricade. As I set the last chair in its place against the door, my blood thirsty family starts pounding on the door and yelling to let them in.

"Alec! Open the door, Alec," yells my father.

As I stand in the middle of the living room, listening to my family desperately trying to get in, I think of my options. I can either fight my way out, or wait for them to break in. While wrestling with the decisions back and forth in my mind, I limp into my room to grab my gun. I reach under my bed and pull out my 45 caliber pistol and insert a magazine. *I can do this,* I think to myself while tapping the barrel of the gun on the floor. There's a sound of snapping wood in the other room. They're almost through the door. I crawl my way back into the living room to make my stand. I lean up against the back of the kitchen counter, where I can see the front door.

"We're almost in, Alec," my mother says, like she's trying to be sweet. It sounds more like a growl.

Bang! Bang! Bang!

As they continue pounding, I hear more cracking as they break through the wooden door. Only a few more moments now. I sit motionless–with my eyes closed–waiting for the noise to stop and for my family to finally break in. Then–I finally hear her. I open my eyes to see Mya standing in front of me–with her yellow eyes glowing–her sharp white teeth showing–and growling with her eyes fixed on me. She must have slid through a small opening that the others had made.

"Easy, Mya."

I raise my hand. She lets out a loud growl in disagreement as saliva, mixed with some flesh, drips from her mouth.

"Mya, it's me," I continue softly, but she lets out another growl.

I realize this nightmare is about to get worse. I clench my pistol tightly, ready to raise and fire. In one last attempt to calm her, I lean forward.

"It's me, girl."

The next second happens fast. A loud pop from my gun and Mya is draped across my feet. Motionless. I shot and killed my best friend. Tears and snot are streaming down my face as I look up at the ceiling in agony unable to look down at her lifeless body.

"Come and get me!" I yell.

In a flash there is a loud bang as the furniture comes crashing down in front of me. Alicia's father is the first to enter and I shoot him in the head before he makes it a couple feet. Next is Brian and I miss on the first shot because my eyes are too blurry from the tears in my eyes. I fire a couple more rounds and he drops to the ground. My mom and dad come in almost simultaneously. I look my own mother in the eyes as I pull the trigger and do the same with my dad. I roll over as the pain in my stomach becomes so overwhelming that I think something might be clawing its way out of me. While on my side, with my face pressed against the carpet, I see Emily walk in slowly. She isn't alone.

Ashlee is by her side.

My sister is wearing a pair of light green scrubs. Her body isn't torn to pieces like Emily's and everyone else. There isn't a mark on her. She looks like she's been preserved in a freezer. Her skin is snowy white and every inch of her is covered in frost. She froze to death because I failed to keep my promise.

"You said you were coming, Al," Ashlee says in a soft, sad voice. "Why didn't you come for me?"

"You said you would always protect me, Alec," Emily snarls. "Now look at me."

"I'm sorry," I say, unable to control my emotions any longer as tears continue to run down my face. "The storm was too bad. I tried, but I couldn't get to you. I broke my promise and I'm sorry."

Just as the last syllable comes off my tongue, they both leap forward without a sound. Once I start pulling the trigger, I can't stop. I fire several rounds into both of them. Neither falls instantly, but sways back and forth slowly for a second as to torture me a little longer, until Ashlee falls onto her left side, with her pleading eyes looking straight at me. Emily drops to her knees first and then falls over onto her left side, with her body draped over Ashlee's.

"NO!"

I sob uncontrollably. I've just killed my entire family. I lay there on the floor feeling anger towards my father, and especially myself. Yes–my father was the one responsible for me turning into this monster, but I had promised to keep everyone here safe. I failed to protect my sister, and I failed everyone in this facility. They're all dead because of me. It's my fault Emily was taken and my fault I was shot. With the last bit of strength I have left, realizing I have nothing left to live for, I raise my gun and place it against my temple. As I'm about to pull the trigger, I hear a voice echo softly in my mind. A familiar voice.

Alec, wake up.

"Huh?"

Wake up, Alec.

My vision becomes blurred again as the voice continues.

"Emily?"

Wake up, she says in a fainter, softer tone. My reality is really turning upside down and my head starts to spin. How can Emily be talking to me when I just shot her? How can her voice be coming from somewhere else?

"What's… going… on?"

Alec. Please wake up, Alec.

My vision starts to fade until all I see is darkness. I hear Emily's voice in the distance calling for me.

"I don't know how?"

Come back to me, Alec. Now her voice is sad. I hear her crying just as I drift off into nothingness and I can no longer hear her voice anymore.

CHAPTER 9

I'm not sure if I'm back in reality or just another nightmare. I'm on my back and all I can see is a blinding light. I need to squint my eyes from the brightness, so I raise my hand to shield my eyes, but strangely they adjust to the brightness rather quickly. I'm surprised to see that I'm in a dimly lit room and there are no lights directly above me. In fact, the nearest light is several feet to my right on a stand. After I glance around the room, I rest my gaze on someone in a chair next to my bed, leaning over with her head on my chest. The person has long, wavy, brown hair. She must have felt me stir because her head jolts up rapidly but keeps her arms resting on my chest. Looking back at me are Emily's beautiful green eyes. She's been crying. She also looks deprived of sleep and food. Her face is pale, her hair is greasy and matted together like she hasn't taken care of it for days.

"Hi," I say trying to crack a smile.

"Hi," she responds with a smile hidden behind a few more tears that slowly slide down her cheeks.

"I just had the most terrifying nightmare of my life."

"I know. You were screaming out in pain and saying terrible things," she says as she sniffles her nose. "I was trying to wake you, but it wasn't working."

"I heard you," I respond softly as I wrap my arms around her and pull her close. "I heard you."

"Your dad didn't think you were gonna make it the first couple days. *I* didn't think you were gonna make it."

"The first couple days? How long has it been?"

"Six days. Your vitals finally started to level out on the third." Emily starts crying again with her face pressed up against mine. "I thought I lost you."

"You'll never lose me."

I gently pull Emily up so I can see into her eyes. I wipe away a few more of her tears with my left thumb and Emily turns her head into my palm to kiss my hand. The feeling of her skin touching mine feels strange. It's still smooth and wonderful, but I notice a tingling sensation and it's almost as though I can *feel* her reaction. Like my skin is reading the sensations she's feeling on her own skin and sending the responses to my brain. I feel her emotions. I pull away from her quickly at the surprise, like my hand just touched fire. The feeling didn't hurt. It was just bizarre.

"What's the matter?" Emily asks with a hurt look on her face.

"Sorry, it's not you it just... I... I feel different," I reply, trying to put her at ease. "It's like my skin is feeling the same sensations as yours."

"It must be the Nan-ites," she suggests. "Do you not... like it?" she asks again without her expression changing.

"No. I mean I do, I..." Emily pulls away as she cuts me off.

"Maybe we should give you time to adjust," she says as she tries to move away from me.

I quickly grab her hand and pull her back. I sit up in the same motion and pull her in for a kiss. The first moment of the kiss is the same as it has been before. Butterflies quickly fill my stomach and make my skin shiver. Then like a burst of lighting, I can suddenly feel Emily's reaction as well. I can feel the electric impulses her lips send to her brain and back again. At least I think that's what I'm feeling. It's almost as if Emily's sensations and emotions are being conveyed through the touch of our skin. At first the feeling was shocking, but now it feels amazing. I can feel exactly what she's feeling and how much she likes it. And oh how she likes it. Suddenly I can feel her body temperature rising and I hear her heart begin to beat faster. The sudden sound of her heart is like a loud speaker turned on blast, but the sound quickly lowers to a comfortable level. Hearing the quick rhythm of her heart is almost soothing. Suddenly her body begins to give off this aroma that is like a sweet perfume and makes me crave even more of her. I'm so distracted by the new sensations and the passion I can feel from her that I didn't notice Emily had climbed up so she's on top of the bed, straddling me. Just as my hands start to slide under her shirt, the sound of Brian's voice pulls them back.

"Oh boy. Parents coming around the corner in 3, 2…"

Emily slides off my lap and back into the chair just before my parents walk through the door. Mya is right behind them and doesn't hesitate to run and jump into my arms the moment she sees me. She immediately starts to lick my face and whine from excitement. I wrap my arms around her tightly while rubbing her head and patting her on the side all at the same time.

"I was worried about you, big girl," I say to her just as she licks me in the face. "I was worried you wouldn't find her," I say to Brian without looking up at him.

"Find her?" Brian shakes his head. "She found me. I knew the moment I saw her running towards me that something was wrong. I came straight back for help." Brian sits on a table with his legs hanging down.

"But she couldn't…"

"She couldn't what?" Brian interrupts confused.

"Never mind." I quickly try to change the subject. "What matters is she's fine. All of you are."

I glance at everyone in the room. My mom had stopped just beside Emily and placed her hand on my leg. She isn't crying, but she clearly has the look of relief in her eyes. My father had stopped on the opposite side of the bed holding a stethoscope. Everyone is here with me. Well...everyone but Ashlee.

Brian gives me a nod of approval and acts like he doesn't notice my confusion. My father, on the other hand, gives me a curious look.

"How do you feel, son?" he says while using the stethoscope to listen to my heart.

"Great, actually. Now that I'm not dreaming anymore," I say with a sigh of relief.

"Sorry about that," he says with an apologetic look. "I didn't really have time to warn you that could happen. Besides, not all the previous subjects experienced them." He puts his hand on my forehead.

"A heads-up still would've been nice."

"What good would it have done? You still wouldn't have known you were in a dream. How can you even be sure you're not in one now?"

"The nightmare might have felt real, but this feels right. Plus, now that I think back, I can see the parts that gave it away as a nightmare."

I really hadn't thought about that until now. The dream was too systematic and random at the same time. The most random thing of all was my sister showing up like a corpse. As horrible as it was to see, or even remember, it wasn't real. It wasn't possible.

"You don't feel warm," my father says.

"I don't buy that," Brian interjects.

Everyone but Emily looks over at him. He's looking down at Mya before he realizes everyone is wondering why he made the comment. He mouths *sorry*. I crack a smile.

"Now I know I asked you how you feel already, but how do you really?" my father continues.

"At first, I didn't feel anything out of the ordinary. I felt stronger and rested of course, but that was it."

"Go on," he says impatiently. I need to force myself not to roll my eyes at him.

"Then my skin came in contact with Emily's and..." Brian interrupts me with a snort and everyone looks over at him. My father gives him the most irritated look of all because all he cares about is his science project. "When my skin touched hers...it was like her skin was also mine. I could feel what she was feeling." My father doesn't respond. Instead, he just looks at me with a concentrated stare for several seconds until I continue. "I know my explanation sucks, but I really don't know how to say it any better."

"I understand," he replies. "What else? You said you feel stronger, but how? Can you hear better, see better? That can't be the only thing you've experienced so far."

"Paul?" my mom interjects. "Slow down. He's been through a lot."

"It's alright, mom," I say, giving her an approving nod. "Dad, so far what I've told you is all I've noticed. I'll let you know the moment I feel anything else."

"Sorry, Alec. I don't mean to seem as though I don't care. The fact that I do care is why I'm being a little impatient." My father places his hand on my shoulder and looks at me with caring eyes. It's the first time he's looked at me this way in some time. "I can't tell you how relieved I am to see you awake. I was worried that the procedure might not work, like before."

"I know. *That* we can talk more about some other time. Right now, all I want to do is get out of this lab and maybe grab something to eat." *Am I hungry?* I certainly should be.

"Yeah, you and Emily both need some food and probably some more rest," says my mom as she leans down and hugs me. "You, especially." She looks at Emily. Emily smiles back as my mom pats her on the leg and smiles in return.

I look down at Mya, who's made herself comfortable by laying her head on my lap and I start to message the fur on her neck. *How did you get out of that hole, big girl? You couldn't have done it alone.* Emily nudges me in the arm with her elbow and I snap out of my train of thought. I look over at her and she smiles.

"Are we going with them?" she asks.

I look up to an empty room. I didn't realize they walked out.

"Yeah, let's go," I reply as I stand up. Mya jumps down onto the floor and gives herself a shake.

The first thing I notice when I get off the bed is how easy it is. After nearly dying, going through the procedure and then spending a week in bed, I should feel weak in some way. Stiff. I don't at all. In fact, I can breathe better than ever and nothing aches or hurts. I feel amazing.

My parents and Brian are holding open the elevator door, waiting for us as we make our way over to it. Just before the doors close, I look back the way we came, at the doorway leading into the lab we came out of. I was in the Nano-Gen-Research Lab I had seen before. The room next to it, Prototype Weapons, is the one I certainly wouldn't mind going in. What kind of weapons could possibly be in there? A week ago, I didn't know what was really on this floor. I still don't. I still don't know who my father is.

"Dad, at some point, you need to tell us just what the hell was actually going on in this place." I look over at him and all he does is nod.

I have so many questions for him. Questions that I'm probably not going to get answers to right away. Sooner or later though, I will. He's done lying to me. That's just the first of the many changes that will start to happen around here. My view of the small main hall on level two slowly closes with the door to the elevator.

The moment we step out of the elevator, I can smell food coming from the cafeteria. The smell is strong. So strong, it's almost as if I have a plate of food sitting right in front of me. I can smell a hint of chicken broth and salt. The only thing in the compound that would have that is chicken noodle soup. The smell of chicken noodle soup makes my mouth water.

The main hall is buzzing with probably at least thirty people or so taking up most of the places to sit. Just as the thought of how many people might be sitting in the room enters my mind, each person that I can see erupts with a glow around them and a red number 33 appears directly in the center of my vision. I quickly swing my hand in front of me at the giant green numbers and take a startled step backwards. As I swing my hand back and forth, I realize that the numbers and glow aren't in front of me. My hand should have blocked my view of the glow around each person as well as the numbers, but my hand seemed to go through them.

"What is it, Alec?" my father asks excitedly. I try to ignore his annoying giddy attitude about the situation.

When I look over at everyone, they're all staring at me as if I'm a crazy person. All, except for my father who has a grin on his face. I hesitate to answer as I glance back at the crowd. The individual glows and numbers are still showing.

"It's strange. It's almost like I'm looking through some sort of Heads Up Display that's putting information up on a screen for me."

"Good. That means the Nan-ites are operating correctly," my father says without questioning what it is that I'm actually seeing. Brian, on the other hand, has to know.

"What kind of information, bro?" Brian asks.

"Just the exact number of people. Plus, a glow around each person. Only the number is so big that it's blocking most of my vision."

"Badass!"

"Yeah, but I just wish the number wasn't right in the center of my vision like an ugly statue." As I complete the thought, the number quickly disappears. I think of the number again and it comes back just the same. *Gone!* Again, it leaves. Once I realize that I have control of whether or not the number is there, I decide to think of a better place for it. Right bottom corner and much smaller. The number appears down in the right corner, but it's too small to see clearly. A little bigger. Perfect. Now the number looks as if it is only a couple inches tall and just barely visible in the bottom right corner of my vision. I don't like the red and think of a florescent green. The color changes and I decide I'm satisfied with it. Everyone started walking again towards the cafeteria so Emily grabs my hand and pulls me along. I look down at the touch of her skin, which still feels strange and wonderful.

"You alright?" she asks.

"Yeah."

I look back one more time, thinking of the numbers and glows no longer there. They blink out almost simultaneously as if they were anticipating the thought all together. Great. I'm already referring to the Nan-ites as "they".

Mya, Emily and me continue down the hall only a few paces behind Brian and my parents. As we near the double doors to the cafeteria, images of my nightmare flash before my eyes, making me feel like I'm back in the nightmare all over again. I'm suddenly the only one in the hallway, staring down at a bloody door. My stomach begins to churn from the memory of seeing everyone dead. The images of them all torn to pieces. I tell myself it isn't real and everything shimmers back into place. Emily is by my side, holding my hand and Mya at my right, occasionally nipping up at my hand. The others walk through the door and we follow before the doors can swing shut.

The cafeteria is almost as busy as the main hall. I must have woken up during a meal time because otherwise this place wouldn't be so busy. I try to ignore the people in the room and quickly take a seat where Brian and my parents had. They chose a table in the far-left corner of the room and left Emily and I the seats against the wall. So much for trying not to pay attention to everyone in the room. People start coming up and asking me how I'm feeling within seconds of me sitting down. The first is Mr. Wilkinson.

"Glad to see you pulled through, Alec. You had us all worried," he says as he reaches out to shake my hand.

I'm not sure why, but I reluctantly take his hand. I've never really had any issues with him. Only his daughter. Maybe it's because he had been one of those so insistent on us going with Rider to recover nothing. *Rider. Where is he?* The moment the thought of him enters my mind, a series of memories play back through my head on rewind. Images flash back fast, all the way to the moment I first met him. While the images play before me, the room in front of me changes. Everything in the room shifts into new positions, including the people, as if the world is going in rewind. Some new people reappear and others disappear. Everything starts to slow down and when the changes finally stop, the room is exactly as it was when I walked into the cafeteria the night Rider showed up. I can see from where I'm sitting, Rider and Jake both standing only a few feet away from me. Only the images are a week old. I blink, thinking that the room will change back to normal when I reopen my eyes, but it doesn't. I'm experiencing several sensations and feelings all at once. Shock, because of my new abilities, anger at the site of Jake standing steps away from me. Even if he's already dead. My feelings for Rider had been suspicious before. I knew the circumstances of him showing up like he did were strange, but now I know the truth. He was the one in charge the entire time.

The scene around me starts playing at a normal speed just by me thinking it, and I watch the way Rider and Jake both interact with each other. I know why I didn't see it before, but it's clear as day now. Before, with my normal eyes, all I saw was a calm, concentrated face as he pretended to be listening to Jake's story for the first time. Now, I can see Riders vital signs as if they're projected on a screen for me. His heart rate is elevated and he's sweating. He had been trained to control his breathing and look like a statue, but he can't change his vital signs. Nobody can. I watched the week-old interaction play out as I sit in my seat, in deep thought. Rider's been injured, maybe more severely than I was and yet he looked perfectly fine the last time I saw him.

"Alec?"

"Hmm?" I say without realizing it.

"Alec?"

I feel someone touch my arm and everything shifts back to normal. Emily is holding my hand and everyone is staring at me.

"Sorry," I say as I realize I've been ignoring everyone at the table. Mr. Wilkinson is gone.

"What are you looking at?" Emily asks as she and everyone else, except for my father, glances over to where I had been staring. My father keeps his eyes glued to me. "You looked like you wanted to hurt someone."

I shake my head.

"Just thinking." I receive more strange looks from my mom and Brian. My father' expression doesn't change and Emily just looks at me.

"What are you see…" I don't give my father time to probe me as I talk over him.

"Dad, it's important that we find Rider."

"He's not important right now. You are."

"Stop it!" I shout as I hit the table with my fist and ignore the startled looks. "You damn well know it is," I say more gently.

"What's going on, Al?" Brian asks without giving my father time to respond.

"Rider didn't just make some miraculous recovery that night. Did he, dad?" Everyone's startled looks shift to my father, who's sitting there, eyes still glued to me and only a hint of being shaken. Rider could take lessons from him. "Explain to everyone how Rider could have his chest torn open and somehow make a speedy recovery and rush out into a battle as if nothing had ever happened. And after you're finished, I'll tell you how much danger everyone in the compound is really in."

I have to keep my eyes focused on him. I know that if I look at Emily, my wall will come down. I can already feel and see the changes in everyone as they watch me talk down at my father, as if I were the father and he the son. It pains me to speak to him this way, even though I'm angry with him, but it's time for him to give answers.

"After we eat," he says calmly, taking his eyes off me to look at today's options for food, which is the chicken noodle soup. "This isn't the place to discuss that."

My father doesn't look at me again throughout the entire meal. Conversation altogether is even at a minimum. For dinner we have the chicken noodle soup that I had smelled in the main hall. It's as delicious as I remembered it, but for some strange reason I'm not hungry. You'd think after all these days, I would be begging for more food. I really only eat what is in my bowl to avoid questions from everyone at the table. Questions about me can wait. After we're finished eating, my father tells us all to wait for him down in the lab. Emily, Brian, my mom, Mya and me are all down there for only a few minutes before he walks in. Mr. Wilkinson walks in right behind him.

"Are you keeping secrets too Michael, or did you just come to listen?" I ask bitterly.

"Alec, you said you wanted answers, so that's what you're gonna get," my father responds. "Just try to refrain from anymore condescending remarks until we're done."

"As long as we get answers," I reply.

"You all might want to sit down," says Mr. Wilkinson.

Everyone grabs a chair and we sit in a semicircle around my father and Mr. Wilkinson. Mya is on the floor at mine and Emily's feet. Brian sits to Emily's left and my mom is to my right. The four of us sit there staring at the two men in front of us, anxiously waiting for them to begin. My father is the first to speak.

"It all started back when we..." he says motioning towards Mr. Wilkinson, "...were in college. We both were in our second year of medical school at Stanford. I hadn't even met your mom yet. That came a couple years later." My father pauses as he gives my mom a smile. "Michael and I had an idea then that would eventually become a possibility, and eventually change the world. We believed that technology was the key to curing the human body of any ailment that someone might suffer from. Cancer, muscular diseases, mental deterioration, you name it. We imagined being able to implant machines inside the body that would repair the damaged, broken or underdeveloped part of the body. If it went as planned, they would even attack a virus and destroy it without harming the body. At the time, technology wasn't advanced enough to do it. So

Michael and I put that dream on hold and finished school and continued on with our lives."

"Shortly after you and your sister were born, I met Kevin and Michelle Williams. Brian, your dad was speaking at a World Technology Convention in New York. The main focus of his talk was on nanotechnology."

I glance over at Brian the moment my father mentions his dad and nanotechnology in the same sentence. Saying Brian looks like he had been slapped in the face would be an understatement. He looks devastated.

"Please tell me my dad didn't have anything to do with what's happened."

"Of course not, Brian. None of us did." I hear a loud exhale come from Brian at the news. "Your dad died long before any of this happened. Besides, your dad would never have taken part in it. Your dad wanted to better the world, not destroy it." Says my father.

"Brian, your dad was the one who made mine and Paul's dreams possible," interjects Mr. Wilkinson. "It turned out it was every bit as much his dream to change the world as it was ours. The only thing we regret is that he wasn't able to live long enough to see his work finished."

"Seriously. That's all you guys ever do care about, isn't it?" I ask coldly. "How about your greatest regret is that your friend never got to see his son grow up. Instead, it's all about your work. Not people. Your work."

"Alec!" my mom says while giving me a disgusted look.

"It's alright, Susan," my father says calmly. "He has a right to be mad. They both do."

"I'm not mad," responds Brian. "Just confused."

The look on Brian's face says exactly that. I feel bad for him. All his life he's grown up never really knowing much about his parents, other than they were friends with mine. Now he's hearing about them for the first time in a very long while, and he's learning his dad was living a secretive life as well.

"Why are you confused, son?" my father asks him.

"You guys told me that my mom and dad were Professors at the University of Utah."

"They were. Your parents did exactly what I said they did. I never lied to either of you ever. We were working on our research during spare time. It wasn't until the last decade that I was able to be here more than I was at the hospital."

"Now that we know what is more important than your children, we have mo…"

"Dammit, Alec! My research is what saved your life. I deserve a little more gratitude."

"Thank you, *Dad*! Thank you for saving me! Thank you for sending me and Brian on a dangerous mission that nearly got us killed! Thank you for sending us with two psychopaths that were waiting for the chance to slit our throats the moment we walked out that door! Thank you for being the reason Emily was captured! Do you wanna know what Jake was planning on doing with her, dad? Do you even care? If I hadn't broken free, that animal would've had his way with her, and then probably killed her when he finished!" I'm on my feet and I can feel my anger beginning to take control. The room is silent. You could hear a pin drop. Even Mya is looking up at me with concern and I realize that I need to calm down.

"What do you mean, *two* psychopaths? Rider was fighting to help you out there," replies Michael.

"I can't explain why he was out there fighting against his own men, but they were *his* men."

"How can you be so sure?" my father asks unbelieving.

"Because I was there in the mall. Someone there told me so. Jake was second in command and was excited to know that he had been promoted with Rider's death."

My father and Michael both shake their heads at the same time. "I don't believe it," says Michael.

"Neither do..."

"It's true," Emily interrupts my father. "I heard some of his men say the same things."

Emily gives me a supportive nod as we make eye contact and she reaches over and grabs my hand. I nod back grateful for her support.

"And now, since Rider can't leave without one of us opening the door for him, he's hiding somewhere in the compound. Also, he probably suspects we know his secret by now." Both my father and Michael give each other despairing looks. They're finally starting to see the error of their ways. "Now do you guys get it? We need to find Rider now, and we need to protect the compound against a possible attack."

"Those men couldn't get inside the compound with a nuclear bomb," says Michael.

"They don't need one with their leader inside," Brian counters in a calm tone.

"Like Alec said before: he can't open the door without one of us," says my father.

"I was around him just as much as Alec. He's clever. After all, he already fooled you once," Brian says coldly.

"Brian's right. Let's just find him," I reply. "We need to start looking for him now."

"What you should do is go take a shower and get some rest," my father says looking at me. "Besides, we haven't seen him for nearly a week. I think you can take some time to at least clean yourself up a bit."

"What your dad is trying to say is, you smell like shit," says Brian with a serious look on his face.

"Thank you for summing that up for me, buddy."

"It's what I'm here for. I like the beard though. You look less like a pretty girl," Brian smirks.

For the first time since waking up, I reach up and feel my face. I do have a thick beard. I glance at Emily as I move my fingers in it. She shakes her head and gives me a dissatisfied look. She doesn't like it. I'll have to shave it off then.

"Alright. I can hold off on the search long enough for a shower." I look over at Brian. "I want you to begin looking right now though. I'll join you the moment I'm done."

"Sounds like a good plan to me," he replies.

"Brian…" I hesitate to answer. "Make sure you're well-armed while you do. And don't go alone."

Brian nods in response.

CHAPTER 10

Mya and Emily come back with me to the apartment to wait while I shower. I told Emily I didn't want her alone until we found Rider, but I don't think she would've left my side anyway. I don't want to leave her side. As we're walking, I notice that there is an awful smell in the hallway. Without thinking about it, I smell my underarms out of curiosity. The sudden, powerful odor hits me in the face like a load of bricks. Emily doesn't seem to take notice of my awful stench, or maybe she just doesn't care, but I seriously doubt that anybody hadn't noticed. I have to deal with the foul smell the entire way back to the apartment.

When we walk in, Emily instantly takes a seat on the couch and I walk into my room and close the door, but not before Mya follows me in. She seems just as intent on not leaving my side now that she has me back too. I'd rather not have to leave anyone behind for a while. While I'm waiting for the water to heat up, I notice that it's taking unusually long. Normally, after only about thirty seconds the water would already feel nice and hot, but it just feels like normal room temperature water even though I can clearly see the steam. It's not warm or cold. In fact, it never felt cold when I turned it on either. That's odd. Another piece to my new abilities. This will come in very handy in a world that's freezing cold. If my body

176

reacts to the outside like the cold water, I'll be able to go out and bring back important supplies. I like the idea of ice-cold water not feeling cold, but not being able to take a warm shower? I doubt anybody ever wished for something like that. I suppose one day it might come in handy.

I waste no time in the shower, since it's not really all that soothing or enjoyable. I simply wash my body and shave my beard. After I'm finished, I step out of the shower and wrap a towel around my waist and peer into the mirror. Images from my nightmare flash across my eyes like actual memories of a horrific past and all I see is the monster with yellow eyes looking back at me. Relief passes through me when the images shimmer back to normal. Instead of the hungry, yellow eyes that had devoured everyone I cared about, blue eyes are staring back at me. Still normal. While standing in front of the mirror, I examine the rest of my body. My shoulder and chest show no signs of ever being shot. I trace my finger along my skin and can't even find the slightest abrasion of any kind. In fact, I can't even find signs of any of my past wounds. No scars, so scrapes, nothing at all. So far, my father's Nan-ites are doing everything he promised.

"Hey you," Emily says with a smile when I walk back into the living room. "Feel good to shower?"

"Uh…no. Not exactly," I reply with a shrug as I plop down on the couch next to her. Mya jumps up onto the couch next to me and puts her head onto my lap.

"Why not?"

"It seems part of my new change is that I can't feel hot or cold water. It feels the same no matter what the temperature is."

"No hot showers? I would hate that."

"Right? Oh well. At least I'm alive. That's all that really matters, I suppose."

"Agreed," she smiles as she snuggles up to me and leans her head onto my shoulder. "I've never seen you in basketball shorts." She tugs at them with her right hand.

The shorts that she's referring to are a simple black with red stripes down the sides. I also have on a gray t-shirt with a skull wearing an eye patch and a hat, in the center. It makes sense that she's never seen me dressed like this before, since I've always dressed to go outside for either a watch or a scouting trip. I've never left the apartment in something this comfortable. I've always had on a pair of pants and boots in case I needed to go outside.

"I've never seen you in sweats and a hoodie before," I reply.

"I wanted to be as comfortable as possible while I was watching over you."

"Were you really with me the entire time I was down there?"

"Every second," she says with a smile.

Emily tilts her head up so she can look at me. She has a sparkle in her eye and this overall glow about her. Not like the one that the Nan-ites put around those other people, but her body is giving off this energy that is radiating towards me. I give her a smile before leaning down and kissing her. Having her sitting with me, knowing she's safe from danger, at least at the moment, brings me comfort. The agony I felt after having to shoot her in my nightmare is still there, in the back of my mind like a virus waiting to devour me from the inside. I don't know if I'll ever be able to purge myself of that awful nightmare. How does somebody simply forget the most painful thing they've ever seen and done? Sure, it was a nightmare, but it was just as real as the girl sitting next to me is now.

"Is everything alright?" she asks me as she places her hand on my cheek. "I can tell something's been bothering you since you woke up."

The touch of her gentle hands on my cheek makes me shiver. I can feel the electric impulses as they travel back and forth through her hand and my cheek and even feel the emotion she's feeling from the touch. I can't read her thoughts, but I'm sure just as much as I love her that if she ever loses me, it will destroy her. I gently pull her hand down and kiss her again. The same blast of ecstasy I felt when I kissed her in the lab returns, and I have to pull away from her before I lose control. She lets out an unsatisfied sound.

"I need to find Rider," I say softly. "And you're coming with me." I know that bringing her with me can be dangerous, but leaving her behind before got her taken. I fear that if I leave her alone, Rider will somehow circle back behind me and hurt her. Since I don't know where he is, she's safest with me.

Emily returns the smile as I pat Mya on the back to get up. She jumps off the couch and Emily and I begin to follow her. Before we take two steps for the door, Mya stops in her tracks and starts to tilt her head back and forth. She begins whining and looks back at me for support.

"What is it girl?" I ask as I kneel down beside her.

I put my arm around her and rub the soft fur at her neck. Just as I'm about to ask her what is bothering her, everything around me goes quiet. I can't hear anything. It's as if my ears are somehow filtering out all sound. I can't even hear my own breathing or the rustling of Mya's feet on the floor. I feel a tingling sensation across the entire surface of my skin. It's like an alarm has been triggered in my body and suddenly I'm aware of something bad happening. I don't know how I know, but something tells me that whatever is happening, it's in the cafeteria. The room is still silent and the three of us aren't moving. Mya has her eyes on the door like she's watching for prey and I mimic her exactly. I feel Emily place her hand on my shoulder and just as she starts to speak, I hear a blood curdling scream. I jump back into a standing position as the loud scream pierces my ears like an explosion from within the room. I quickly turn around to find the source of the scream. Emily is staring at me with a concerned look on her face.

"What is it?"

"You didn't hear that scream?"

"No. What are you talking about? You and Mya are acting weird."

"How did you not hear it? It was so loud," I say as I turn back to the door. Mya's eyes are still locked on the door with her hair standing straight up.

"Alec, I didn't hear anyth…" Emily is interrupted by a loud roar, unlike anything I've ever heard before. The roar is as loud as the scream had been, but yet somehow Emily hears it. "What was that?"

I look over and find her wide eyed and pale. Without thought, I walk past her and back into my room and go straight for my bed. I kneel down and pull out my gun case and quickly remove my pistol. I insert a magazine and step back out into the living room after being gone less than thirty seconds.

"Alec, what is it?" she asks as she grabs my arm when I try to go past her.

"I don't know, but I have to go."

I kiss Emily on the lips and walk over to the door. Mya is now growling and scratching at the door.

"Mya, you're staying here," I say as I pull her away from the door. As I hold her back with one hand, I open the door with the other.

"Be careful," Emily says as she folds her arms and looks at me nervously.

"I'll be back before you know it," I say, just before the door closes. Now that I'm sure of the direction Rider is, I know Emily will be better off in the apartment.

I quickly look down both ends of the hallway to make sure there isn't anything waiting for me. Once I see that it's clear, I start sprinting down the long, cinder block walled corridor towards the main hall. I blur past the apartments so fast that I can feel wind hitting my face as if I were riding a motorcycle on the interstate. Now I'm experiencing the improvements in my physical abilities. My feet barely make a sound as they make contact with the tile floor. I stop instantly when I reach the end of the hall and peak around the corner. At first, I don't see anything, but I can hear someone coming towards me from the direction of the cafeteria. I listen closely until I hear a thumping sound. The thumping has a rhythm to it and sounds familiar. As I listen to the sound, I can suddenly smell something awful and strange. Something I've never smelled before. The footsteps get closer until a frightened woman comes around the corner.

"Alisha," I say softly as I grab her by the arm and stop her. "What is it?"

"He's dead! He's dead!"

"Who's dead?"

"I… dunno him, but he's dead!" Alisha is crying hysterically to the point I think she might pass out from lack of breath. The strange smell is very strong on her. I have to resist the urge to cover my mouth.

"Where is…"

Another big roar floods the main hall. Alisha runs off down the hallway heading for what I assume to be her apartment. I keep still and listen as I press up against the wall. Loud, heavy breathing is now around the corner. Animal like breathing. It sounds as though there is a bull around the corner waiting to gorge me with his horns. I stand quietly and slow my breathing to avoid making any sounds. I hear the creature begin to move towards the wall I'm hiding behind. As I wait anxiously, trying to decide if I should step around the corner and face whatever it is, the breathing stops. What seems like several moments pass by and I can feel my heart beating faster. Whatever is waiting around the corner, knows I'm here.

Suddenly, I can hear another thumping sound. Only this one is different from the other. It's much faster and has a different rhythm. A heartbeat maybe? It must be. The thumping I heard before must have been Alisha's heart, followed by that horrible strange smell. Now I smell something else, along with another beating heart. The smell is nothing like the smell that was coming from Alisha and it's certainly nothing like the sweet smell from Emily. The Nan-ites put danger up in my vision and it's flashing red. I think the Nan-ites are telling me that the smell is another predator. The heartbeat that I hear is powerful. It has a rhythm unlike a human. It beats quickly twice and pauses before giving three equally quick beats. Then the rhythm starts over.

While standing there, I listen to the sounds from around the corner and the same female voice I've heard several times now, tells me to kneel down. I know Emily isn't behind me, but I do what she tells me to without hesitation, only to see a large, clawed looking hand smash into the side of the wall with enough force to damage the cinderblock. I dive to my right, somersaulting to another crouched position and turn to face my attacker with my gun up and ready to fire.

Before me stands a creature unlike anything I've ever seen or imagined before. The creature's back is to me and it appears to be a good seven or even eight feet tall. It has long muscular arms that hang down to its waist with razor sharp claws, two or three inches long. The rest of the body is also muscular, but looks as though it's been stretched out from a smaller frame. There appears to be spikes protruding from its body in an even fashion on its shoulders leading down the back of the arms and stopping at the elbows. More of them are running down the center of its back along the spine. Its skin is a faded red tint, with patches of greyish white, throughout the body. Whatever this thing is, it's very large and looks deadly. The creature spins to face me and the moment its piercing yellow eyes lock onto me, I freeze.

Staring back at me are the same yellow eyes that I had seen in the trees the night Rider was attacked. The same yellow eyes had glared back at me in my nightmare. Neither one of us move or make a sound. We just stand there studying one another for an eternity. Then it speaks.

"What's the matter, Alec?" says a deep rumbling voice. "Don't you recognize me?"

It speaks with a fearsome smirk. The light glistens off shiny, white, razor-sharp teeth. I lower my gun to my side, but keep my defensive stance.

"How could I forget that bogus smile of yours, Rider? Were you waiting for me to cut your throat like I did to that spineless coward Jake?" I say through clenched teeth.

Rider chuckles and the sound echoes off the walls. You can no longer see who this once was, behind the square, muscular chin and heavy eyebrows. His hair is long and thin, falling down to his shoulders in a big mess like a dirty, black, mop. His eyes give off a glow, even in the bright light.

"He was spineless. I'll give you that," he says as he straightens himself so that his head nearly touches the ten-foot ceiling. "If he really is dead, like you say, then you did me a favor. The fool always was too quick to make poor decisions. One of which, was taking your girl."

"Don't pretend like you had nothing to do with that," I say through clenched teeth.

"I didn't. That was never part of my plan." The creature begins walking to his left, towards the center of the main hall, but never moving closer to me. Then he stops and looks at me with a devilish grin. "Taking this facility will be easy. Even you can't stop me now."

183

"I guess there isn't anything left to talk about then, is there?"

I'm much smaller than Rider is now. Before, I had no doubts in my abilities to beat him in a fight. Now, even with my new strengths, which I know very little about so far, I don't know if I'll be a match for him. I have no idea what I'm really up against. The two of us stand there like a pair of statues, waiting for the other to make his move. No matter what Riders current abilities may be, I have one thing in my favor. I'm holding a gun in my hand. Rider eyes the weapon for a split second and grins one last time. He moves fast. Too fast for a body that size. I react just as quickly and begin firing straight into his chest. Rider stops in his tracks as soon as the first round strikes flesh, followed by several more. Each round strikes his center mass and blood begins to ooze down, dripping onto the floor. His painful screams echo through the main hall. He drops to all fours and starts spitting blood out onto the white tile. I don't stop firing until I empty all fifteen rounds into him.

Rider looks up at me in pain, attempting to shroud it with anger. The fact that he isn't dead already, is frightening. A single round would have stopped a normal man. I just put fifteen into him and he still has fight in him. I only grabbed one magazine of ammo, so I toss the gun to the floor on my right. He's still on all fours, breathing heavily and continuing to spit blood onto the floor. Maybe thirty seconds had gone by since he first dropped, then he looks up at me again. The pain in his eyes is gone. Only the look of murder remains. Rider climbs to his feet and wipes some of the blood from his chest. Where there should be gaping wounds and shredded flesh, his skin is smooth and unharmed. He healed.

"Well, well," he says, followed by a chuckle. "This makes things interesting." I can feel my heart rate quicken at the sudden realization that my opponent is even more dangerous than I thought.

184

The next few seconds happens quickly. He lunges towards me, quick as lightning, as if he were shot out of a gun. I narrowly avoid a blow to the head from the spikes on his arm. I dodge the attack by stepping to the side, only to be struck on the right cheek by a follow through punch with a closed fist. I can feel the bones shatter in my face as I'm sent sailing through the air, then slamming into the wall near the large, steel door. The wind is knocked out of me and I groan from the pain in my face, but no sound comes out as I struggle to breathe at the same time. The creature is laughing loudly while looking over his body, admiring his new strength.

"The power," his voice booms. "It's incredible."

I reach a hand up to my face and pull it away quickly when I feel it's disfigured shape. I can't see myself, but I know my face looks mangled and smashed in. Now it's time to see what my body can do. Almost the instant I finish the thought, the bones in my face begin to reset and mold back together. The sensation is equally painful as the initial punch from Rider and a groan slips out as I regain my breath. Rider stops boasting as soon as he sees my face reshaping into what it's supposed to look like.

"It seems you're more than you appear as well, Captain Winter."

I climb to my feet and realize I'm next to the control panel for the door. This could be my best and only chance to get him outside. Rider grins as I turn and enter the code on the panel to open the door. I pull the door open just before I'm struck from behind and sent flying through the air, landing hard in the snow with Rider on top of me. Rider hit me so hard I imagine being hit by a truck would've felt similar. I feel something isn't right and I look down at my left arm. It's broken and just dangling there. Just as quickly as my face had healed, I feel my arm being put back together. Knowing I need to act fast, I kick my legs at Rider as hard as I can and send him tumbling and then slamming hard into the jagged rock wall near the opening of the cave. He staggers to his feet quickly and charges for me. He stops in his tracks instantly with shock in his eyes.

A shotgun blast erupts from behind me and puts him down on his back.

"Alec, move!"

I pivot in the snow and turn back to the door. Brian is standing in the doorway holding a shotgun and fires again. Everything slows down to the point that I can make out every individual pellet from the shell. As they pass by me, each one lights up with a glow in a rapid fashion, just as the number 410 appears, indicating the total amount of pellets. Brian is using a 12 gauge shotgun. Before the second shot has time to reach Rider, I scramble quickly and dash towards the door. Brian fires off one more shot just as I make it inside. Rider is roaring behind me, clearly more angry than damaged by the shotgun. Brian enters the code and shuts the door just as I step in, locking Rider outside. The pounding and screaming is loud, but the door was designed to stop a nuclear blast. Rider will never break through and everyone is safe. For now.

"What the hell was that?" Brian asks in a shocked, and concerned voice.

"That... was Rider," I reply as I run my hand along my face. It feels normal, as if nothing ever happened.

"Dude, you had me worried for a second there, bro," he says patting me on the shoulder. "Are you hurt?"

"No. Not anymore," I reply. Brian gives me a confused look. "Let's just say I heal quickly. Just like our large friend out there. I'm just glad you showed up when you did." I return the pat on the shoulder and we begin making our way towards the cafeteria. The same, awful smell that was on Alisha is coming from down there. "Have you been down here yet?"

"No. I came from my room when I heard the roaring."

"I think he killed someone," I respond as the double swinging doors come into view. One of them is barely hanging from its hinges.

"Aside from the fact that he looks like something from a horror movie, what makes you think that?"

"When Alisha ran past me she said "he's dead" more than once and that she didn't know who the person was."

"Oh," is all Brian replies with.

Walking into the cafeteria feels like walking into a giant wall of rotten sewage. All the people that are inside the cafeteria reek of the foul smell that had been on Alisha. Some of them still have terrified looks on their faces. After seeing a monster kill a man, I can hardly blame them.

That's it. The smell is fear.

I'm smelling fear on everyone because of what happened. In fact, now that I know what it is, I had smelled it on Brian too, even if it was only for an instant. Back in the cave, just before Rider was shot the first time, I caught a hint of that smell for only a split second. Had Rider really frightened him that much?

I look over at him and he appears calm as ever, but focused on the room, watching to make sure there aren't anymore surprises waiting to attack us. Brian did say I had him worried. Maybe he was more afraid for my safety than he was of Rider. I look away from Brian without giving it another thought.

Several people are crowded around a table in the center of the room. My parents, Emily's mom, and Alisha's dad are among them. As I approach the table, I'm able to make out the shape of a man on his back, with his arms falling over the sides of the table. I don't know him and I can't hear his heartbeat. His head looks as though someone tried to twist it off like a bottle cap. My father looks up when he notices us standing there and doesn't say a word. My mom also looks up, wondering what my father is looking at.

187

"Alec. Brian," she says moving towards us. "You're both alright." She puts one arm around us both.

"Where's Emily?" Emma practically blurts out.

"She's fine," I assure her as I place my hand softly on her shoulder when she runs up to me. "She's back in my apartment. Safe."

"Alec?" says Mr. Wilkinson, "Did you see Alisha?"

I nod in response.

"She's fine too."

"Is he still in the compound son?" My father asks with worry in his voice.

"No. Brian and I were able to lock him outside."

"Good."

"Dad, where did Rider come from?"

My father points towards the kitchen.

"From somewhere back there. The freezer, maybe?"

"Who is this man?" asks Brian, pointing to the dead man slumped over the table.

"His name is Alex," replies Emma. "I don't really know much more about him. Emily might be able to tell you more. She's the one who always made sure she got to know everyone."

"Do you know if he had any family," I ask.

"I think a wife and son," Emma replies.

I nod my head. Someone is going to have to tell his family the bad news. The kind of news nobody should ever have to hear. Especially a child. My father starts to walk towards the kitchen and I move to follow him. I give Brian a glance and motion for him to follow with a tilt of my head.

"Where are you going?" I ask as I catch up to him in the back by the ovens. Brian stops next to me when my father turns around.

"I need to see where he's been hiding all this time. I might learn something from it" He turns back around and goes down the short, narrow hallway towards the freezer door. It's open.

Brian and I follow close behind him as he steps inside. Brian quickly makes a comment about it being cold and wishing he had on a jacket. My father says nothing. I don't feel any different than before we stepped into the ice-cold box. Before we go more than a few paces into the large freezer, I catch the awful sent of fear and quickly start listening for any sounds. I hear something faint coming from towards the back, behind a large pallet of food about twenty feet away. I grab my father's shoulder with one hand and put my other in front of Brian.

"What's the matter," my father asks.

"There's someone in here," I reply softly. I listen carefully for the sound I heard. As if my ears are listening to my thoughts, the sound grows louder and louder until I can make out what it is.

A heartbeat.

The thump, thump sound isn't as loud or strange as Riders had been. It sounds completely normal and similar to the others that are here with me. Only maybe a little smaller. Or just not as strong as if belonging to a smaller person. Without hesitation, Brian pulls out a pistol from his waistband and hands it to me. He's still holding the shotgun.

"Dad, get behind us."

"Rider's gone now. You said so yourself," he argues. "It's probably just someone that was scared and ran in here to hide."

"You're probably right," I respond in a softer tone than he. "Get behind us anyway," I say while pulling him back so I can move past him.

He is right. I know it probably is just someone that is scared, but considering everything that just happened, being safe is the only option. Brian and I move slowly as one, further into the freezer.

189

Once we reach the spot I can hear the heartbeat coming from, I point towards it, indicating to Brian we're there. He nods his head and moves quickly. He steps behind the pallet of food, with his gun ready to fire at anything, but quickly lowers it. His look is of concern, but calm and he motions for me to step up and see. I'm expecting to see a frightened woman or even a man, but instead, it's a child. A little boy. A boy I've seen plenty of times before, playing with his friends in the main hall. The name Jesse pops into my head. He has a frightened look on his face, and he reeks of fear.

"Hey buddy? What are you doing in here?" I ask with a soft voice.

"I ran in here when the monster came out," he replies with a squeaky voice.

"You're Jesse, right?" He nods his head. "Well, I'm Alec. This is Brian and Paul. You'll be safe with us okay. The monster is gone now." Jesse nods again and I reach out my hand to help him up. He reluctantly reaches towards it, still unsure if he is going to be safe. "You can trust me, Jesse. We'll take you back to your parents."

Once I mention parents, Jesse grabs hold of my hand and I pull him up. I notice he's shivering, so I decide to pick him up and hold him. I hand the gun back to Brian with a free hand. I hold Jesse tightly as I try to warm his body. At the thought of wanting to warm him up, the words 'Radiant Heat' pop up in my vision. I quickly think about hiding the words and they disappear. I let out a smile at this new discovery. My father gives me what looks like an approving smile and I can't help but think he's smiling because he misunderstands the reason for my smile.

"Alright, let's keep going." I say to Brian. "Dad, you can lead the way." I motion with my eyes up ahead to the right and Brian moves ahead in front of me and Jesse, with my father in the lead.

The four of us keep moving quietly as we make our way towards the back right corner of the freezer. The freezer is very large like everything else here. This facility had been built to keep people alive for a very long time so it had a large storage. Unfortunately, food is the only thing the facility doesn't produce. So even with as much food that was and is still here, eventually it will run out. Someone will need to calculate how long that will take in order to prepare.

"Man, it's *really* cold in here," complains Brian.

"I'm fine," I reply. "What about you, Jesse?"

"I'm okay now," he chirps with more calmness in his voice. The nasty stench isn't as strong on him anymore, but still there.

"Well… not all of us are *super*," Brian says.

"Super?" asks Jesse. "Like a superhero?"

"Alright you guys. Keep it down," my father cut us off. "*This* is what we came in here for."

We're at the end of the freezer now. The lighting is dim, and probably difficult for everyone else to see. Amazingly, I can see just fine, as if the room is well lit. Covering the entire wall, which is fifteen feet wide and ten feet tall, is some kind of red gooey looking thing. It has some sort of slimy substance dripping down from the inside onto the floor. Almost looks like jello.

"What the hell is that?" asks Brian.

"That my boy is a cocoon," my father says with a grin on his face. His grin bothers me.

"A cocoon?" Brian asks. "Like the kind a caterpillar goes into?"

"Yes. Exactly."

"Are you sure? I thought a butterfly was supposed to come out. I don't know if you saw that thing, but he wasn't very pretty. He was kind of an asshole too."

My father gives Brian an agitated look. He isn't always so patient with Brian's humor at times.

"It seems the wound he suffered mutated his body. He went through a similar metamorphosis as Alec," says my father.

"You can't get any uglier, Alec. That's why you didn't change," Brian says with a wink.

I stare at Brian with a blank face, holding back a smile. *Someone* needs to find a way to laugh about all this. Brian is the perfect person for it.

"Rider was infected by a different form of the serum that had already taken hold in someone else. Alec has a better version inside of him, plus the Nan-ites. The original serum mutated its subjects as well. I never imagined that the same serum would evolve even further if transmitted to another." My father's excitement is gone. Now, he sounds serious and concerned. A dead man wasn't enough, but somehow this is.

"Dad, if Rider was mutated from the original serum into what he is now, what would happen if he infected someone in the state he's in now?"

"I'm not sure." My father shrugs his shoulders. Having Rider running around like some creature from somebody's nightmare is bad enough. Now there's the possibility that he can make others like him.

"I'm leaving. It's too cold in here," Brian says as he turns to leave. He's obviously had enough.

"Yeah, I need to get Jesse back to his parents."

"Hey, did you guys see my dad? He was in the cafeteria." Jesse's light brown eyes are probably barely visible in the low light to others. His dark black hair is long and wavy. It's grown out, covering his ears and he's starting to look like he has a mullet. Brian and I give each other worried looks at the mention of his dad in the cafeteria. Even my father stops looking at the cocoon and glances over at us. The fact that nobody asked about their missing child before, explains everything.

Jesse's dad is the dead guy on the table.

His mom was probably in their apartment or somewhere else when it happened.

"Uh... no, Jesse. I didn't see him," I reply, trying to hide any emotion.

As we approach the entrance to the freezer, I hear what sounds like a crowd of people talking, coming from the cafeteria. There's a lot of people in there now. We walk through the kitchen and back into the eating area to find it full of people. There's barely enough room for anyone to walk.

Thankfully, you can't see Jesse's dad either.

My mother comes up to us when we walk in.

"Is this Jesse?" she asks, pointing to the boy in my arms. I nod and lower him down onto his feet.

"Where's my dad?" Jesse asks, scanning the room.

My mom looks like she's on the verge of tears.

"I-I'll get his mother," she says as she moves away quickly.

A few seconds later a woman shouts.

"Jesse!"

A distraught woman, in her late twenties or early thirties, comes running up to us. She has short, black hair that doesn't quite reach her shoulders, and the same light brown eyes as Jesse. She isn't a large women, but she's a little plump. She's wearing a pair of jeans that don't look flattering on her, and a long sleeve green shirt. It's obvious she's been crying. She comes up and practically rips Jesse out of my arms. She hugs him tightly and falls to her knees. Jesse can tell something is wrong and starts crying himself.

"Mom, what's the matter? W-where's dad?"

I walk away, not wanting to witness a young boy mourn the loss of his dad. Just as I make it to the doorway, I hear the painful screams of a little boy and they echo through the cafeteria and out into the hallway. I walk through the doorway with a now missing door, and try to shut out the noise. The last thing I hear is Jesse

193

crying out for his daddy, before I'm able to turn off all noise completely. I can't wait to go in my apartment and lock myself away from this day.

CHAPTER 11

Emily and Mya are both waiting for me on the couch when I walk into the apartment. Emily jumps up and throws her arms around me at the same moment Mya puts her front paws on my side.

"What happened? Is everyone alright?"

I hesitate briefly before I answer.

"One man was killed in the cafeteria. Nobody else was hurt."

"Oh no," she says covering her mouth. "Who was it?"

"I'm not sure. I didn't know him. Brian and I found his little boy hiding in the freezer though. I didn't really get a chance to meet his mom once she found out her husband was dead."

"What made that sound?" Emily asks. "I heard gunshots too." I assume she's referring to the roaring noise Rider made before I left.

"Rider. Apparently, he had some sort of reaction to the serum that was in the other creatures system…" I hesitate again as the image of Rider flashes in my mind. "And it wasn't a good reaction."

"What do you mean?"

"He changed into something big and very dangerous." I decide not to describe Rider's appearance to avoid making her any more frightened than she already is. She's starting to smell like everyone else. Scared.

"Where is he?"

"He left the compound. With a little… motivation from me and Brian," I say as I scratch the back of my head.

"Did he hurt you?"

The feeling of having my face caved in is still fresh in my memory. That hurt a lot. Not as much as having millions of tiny robots enter my body, but a lot.

"No, he didn't. I'm fine," I smile. It isn't entirely false. Yeah, he hurt me, but I healed from it. So technically it's like he didn't. "I need to get back down there. There were a lot of people in the cafeteria when I left, and everyone will be in a panic."

"I'll come with you."

"Are you sure? Remember there is a dead body and it isn't pretty."

"I'm sure, Alec," she says without hesitation. "Won't be the first one I've seen."

"Alright, then let's go."

The three of us start to make our way to the cafeteria. As we're walking down the hallway, I begin to feel warm. Feeling my body temperature rise certainly isn't a new sensation to me, but I haven't felt warm or cold since my change. Besides, most of the warmth is in my face and my eyes. That part is odd.

"You feel really warm all of a sudden, Alec," Emily says as if she's reading my mind.

"Yeah, I know. I was just noticing that myself."

"Are you feeling okay?"

"Yeah, I feel fine. It just suddenly feels like it's really hot in here. That's all."

"The temperature feels fine to me. Do you think it has something to do with the Nan-ites?"

"I don't know. Let's just keep going."

As we continue walking, I hear a commotion coming from the main hall. People are voicing their concerns about the evening events and they have good reason to. I continue listening as we get closer and realize that probably every person in the compound is in the main hall. Just before we reach the end of the hall, James comes running around the corner.

"Alec? Emily?"

"What's going on?" I ask as he comes to a stop, panting.

"They're... all... freaking out about what happened. Everyone's here. I was coming to get you guys."

"Well, we're here now."

We walk around the corner to see about a hundred people in the main hall, shouting and pointing their finger at anyone they can put the blame on. Most of the people are only voicing their concerns about the incident with Rider tonight, but others are even talking about the night Emily was taken and the night I was brought back to the compound nearly dead. Anyone who saw me would know that I shouldn't be alive right now.

In the center of all the frantic people, I see my father and other council members are trying to calm them down. I spot Brian standing behind my father with a concerned look on his face. Emily and I begin making our way through the crowd so we can talk to him. Mya, as always, is right by my side. While making our way through the crowded space, I receive several looks as we walk through. Some of the looks are frightened, others are angry. Even one of the council members is giving me a disgusted look as we approach.

"You and your stupid dog are the reason this has happened!" He takes a step forward and kicks Mya hard in the side.

Mya lets out a loud yelp as she tucks her tail between her legs and moves behind me. She's whimpering. I immediately bend down to comfort her and make sure he hasn't broken any ribs. I'm rubbing her side softly when I feel my face getting even hotter. Hot as if I were standing too close to a fire. My anger is starting to boil

197

up inside me and my breathing quickens. After all that I've done for these people, and this man claims I'm the one to blame for all of this, and then to kick Mya? I stand up to confront the man and Emily quickly steps in front of me.

"No, Alec. He isn't worth it."

I can't see my own face, but I know it's red. It has to be. My face literally feels like it's on fire.

Emily hurries and places her hands on my chest before I lunge at him. I burn a death stare into the man's eyes for several seconds.

This is the same man who has been one of the biggest motivators for me and Brian to go on all the searches.

The main hall is quiet. You could hear a pin drop. I hadn't noticed their focus change to me when Mya was kicked. As I continue to look into this man's eyes, the room quickly erupts with a thump, thump as I become aware of all the heartbeats in the room. I close my eyes to concentrate on silencing out the sounds and also because my face feels like it's going to melt off my skull. Once I've calmed myself down, I force myself to turn and continue walking towards Brian and my father.

"That's what I thought. You and that *whore* just keep walking."

The heat in my eyes erupts like an explosion as I go from standing next to Emily, to grabbing him by the throat in a flash. A look of horror flashes across his face as soon as he realizes what's happening. I let out what sounds like a growl as I throw him as hard as I can. The man goes sliding along the tiled floor and doesn't stop until he slides almost thirty feet. He stops just before his head smashes into the wall. I go to run over to him, but before I take a step, I'm punched in the face by a rush of foul stench and I realize that I've frightened the entire room.

"Look at him," shouts a man just to my right. "Look at his eyes," shouts another. They're talking about me, as if I'm some animal.

I glance over at the person closest to me. The man's eyes say he's terrified every bit as much as the odor coming from him. My vision zooms in on his dilated pupils just by thinking about it and I see my reflection looking back at me. I see what has him so frightened.

I turn away from him and look over to my family. Everyone else in the room gasps as my eyes sweep past them. Brian's look is just a blank stare, like nothing is wrong at all. My father has a perplexed look, like he's looking at a project gone wrong. My mother covers her mouth, and I smell a hint of fear coming from her. Once my eyes rest on Emily, I'm surprised. She isn't frightened at all. I would smell it, if she was. Instead, she looks sad.

I start backing away from everyone.

"Alec, wait," Emily cries out to me.

My stomach feels sick. Not just from the looks everyone's giving me, but from what I saw in that man's eyes. My nightmare came true. I turn and run towards my apartment, not knowing what to think. I have to get away from everyone. Away from the frightened stares and the awful smell.

I reach the door in only a couple seconds and step in as quickly as possible. I walk straight into the bathroom so I can look into the mirror. I flip on the light switch as I enter and freeze in my tracks as I look into the eyes staring back at me. I slowly inch my way closer as I focus on the alien eyes.

When I had seen the reflection in the frightened man's eyes, all I could see was a bright blue. Now that I can see my reflection clearly, I see that they are a bright, fluorescent, blue color. And they are glowing. At least they appear to be. Even my pupils no longer look human anymore. Now they're elongated and look like they belong to an animal.

Or a monster.

While looking at my alien-like features in the mirror, I begin to see images of the people in the main hall. The looks of fear on their faces makes my stomach churn.

Have I really become the monster of my nightmare?

My eyes may be a different color than the Lurks or Riders, but they still have the same characteristics. I didn't kill anyone, but I did lose control. I can't lose control like that. I can't let the Nan-ites turn me into a monster.

I continue gazing into my reflection when I hear the front door open and close. I step out of the bathroom just as Emily comes walking into my room, breathing heavily. She doesn't say anything. She simply walks up and wraps her arms around me. After we embrace for about fifteen seconds and her breathing goes back to normal, she places her right hand on my cheek and looks into my eyes.

"You're not afraid?" I ask with curiosity, even though I can tell by her smell.

The expression on Emily's face changes to a puzzled and yet almost offended look.

"Why would I be afraid? Just because you look a little different now, doesn't mean you *are* different."

"I look like a monster," I say as I look away.

"But you're not one. I think your eyes are beautiful. Intimidating—but beautiful. Besides, you're a *good* person. You would never hurt someone. Especially me." I look away from her, but she gently turns my head back and smiles before giving me a kiss.

"Thank you," I say as I pull away. She smiles. "Where's Mya?"

"She's with Brian."

Emily continues looking into my eyes with the same expression she always has. She really isn't scared and she really doesn't seem to mind them. If she does, she's good at hiding it. People ignore things about the ones they love all the time.

"What's everyone saying down there?"

"I don't know. I ran after you the moment you left," she replies. "You're fast. You practically disappeared, you were so fast."

"I didn't notice." I hear voices out in the hallway.

Emily and I walk out into the living room just as my parents, Brian and Mya come walking through the door.

"Mya, come here girl," I say like I always do when I see her.

I ignore everyone else, not wanting to see their expressions.

"Come here, baby."

Rather than coming to me like usual, she backs away and lets out a low howling sound that she makes when she's unsure about something. She's hearing my voice, but seeing a different set of eyes, and it's confusing her. I continue talking to her, trying to comfort her, as I slowly move closer. She backs herself into a corner and realizes she has nowhere to go.

"Come on girl," I say again as I reach for her.

She tilts her head as she smells my hand. I place my hand on her head and start to scratch behind her ears. After a couple of seconds, I pull her towards me with my other hand and give her a hug.

"It's okay big girl. It's still me." She gives me a kiss by licking my cheek and I know we're going to be alright. I then stand up and acknowledge the rest of my family.

"Does your vision look any different son?" asks my father.

"No. Not so far."

"Bad ass man," Brian says. "Now you can win a staring contest with a lion."

"Funny," I reply, dryly.

"Oh, it doesn't look bad," says my mom in a soothing tone. "Now you just look different that's all."

"Maybe, but everyone in this compound is going to be afraid of me now. Especially after that man was killed tonight."

"You could've hurt that man," my mom says.

"After what he did and said he got off easy," I reply.

"What did he do?" She asks.

"First, he kicked Mya for no reason. Then he called Emily a whore," I reply as I feel myself getting angry again.

"It's okay, Alec," Emily says as she grabs my arm gently.

Instantly I start to relax.

Everyone in the room appears to be completely at ease around me. I might be the only one in the room that's tense. I now realize that while my immediate reaction to everything may have been understandable, now I need to focus on being calm.

"Alec, are you feeling any more symptoms of possible changes right now?" asks my father.

"No, I feel fine. Earlier though, right before this happened, my eyes and face felt really hot."

My father has a confused yet focused look as if he's trying to understand everything. Clearly—I'm going through changes or experiencing things that he didn't expect.

"Is that all?" asks my father.

I shrug my shoulders.

"Just before Emily and I started to walk down to the main hall, my body started to feel really warm. Emily even noticed and commented on it." I glance over at her and she smiles. "I didn't really notice my body was warm because I was too focused on my eyes. They felt like they were on fire. Especially in the moments before they changed. I didn't *feel* the change though. Just relief as the heat started to go away."

My father looks at me for several seconds as he searches for an answer. I know when he thinks of a response, it will sound like something that makes sense, but how can he really know why this happened? He says the serum is supposed to create the perfect soldier, but I doubt my eyes changing like this is supposed to be part of it.

"I have to be honest son," my father says with a brief pause, "there aren't supposed to be any visual changes like this. The Nanite's purpose is to regulate what the serum cannot. They are what keep you human."

"I was afraid of that."

"Don't the Hulk's eyes turn green?" asks Brian with a grin on his face.

I look over at him with a glare. I don't usually mind his jokes, but right now I don't feel like being funny.

"Yeah... I'm just gonna go. Let you guys... finish your conversation without me," Brian says as he pats me on the shoulder and walks out.

Once the door closes, my father continues interrogating me more about the changes my body's gone through. I tell him about all the differences in my vision, smell, hearing, and even how I no longer feel varying degrees of temperature anymore. He nods in satisfaction at all of it. He says all of these side effects are expected to happen with the serum, except the visual changes.

"Son, make sure you tell me if you experience any more changes. I need to know about everything."

"I'll keep you updated," I reply solemnly.

"Paul, I think we should go to bed. It's been a long day," my mom says to my father as she puts her hand gingerly on his shoulder.

"Sounds good to me. You two don't stay up too late. Your body could use more rest too, son," he says with a nod. I nod in return.

"Good night, Emily," says my mom.

"Good night, Susan," Emily responds while giving her a hug.

"Good night, Alec." My mom smiles and then hugs me before heading to her room. My father follows close behind her.

Once they close their door, Emily and I both take a seat on the couch. Emily leans into me so I can put my arm around her. I hold onto her tightly. Mya climbs up on the other side of me and rests her head on my lap as usual. We both sit there for quite a while without saying anything. I think we both keep silent because we're just enjoying our time alone together. I certainly am.

Emily and I still haven't been able to spend any real time alone since the mall and we were a little too busy trying not to die then. Sitting here with her is relaxing and comforting. It seems like we sit for hours, looking at the blank cinderblock wall. Eventually, I lose myself in the rhythm of her heartbeat and fall asleep.

A couple hours later I wake and Emily and Mya are still in the same positions. I look over at the clock on the wall. It's two in the morning. I slowly slide out from under Emily and get off the couch. Mya opens her bright blue eyes and looks up at me.

"Go back to sleep, big girl," I whisper.

I reach down and gently lift Emily off the couch, cradling her in my arms, and carry her into my room. Emily was always a slim girl, but particularly tonight, she feels as light as a feather. I set her down in my bed and pull the covers over her after I remove her shoes. Once she looks comfortable, I kiss her on the forehead, then grab an extra pillow and close the door behind me. I shut the light off in the living room and lay back down on the couch. This is the first time I've been in total darkness since I awoke from my coma and what I see is amazing. The room appears to have a light blue, glow to it. It's as if someone turned on a blue halogen light, and the light is filling up all the darkness.

"Well, my new eyes might not be so bad after all," I say to myself. Mya looks up at me again. I rub her head with affection before resting my head on my pillow.

I stay awake for probably another twenty minutes or so, enjoying my ability to see in the dark. My head is full of memories of everything that's happened recently. The past couple weeks have been the most intense and unbelievable weeks of my life. That's saying something, considering my time in the military. I've seen and learned a lot since the night the grizzly attacked. Two strangers have shown up. One was a psychopath, and the other is the leader of the psychopath and a small army of men. My father and his friends created new soldiers that mutated into something they weren't supposed to, and *they* turned a man into something even worse. And then there's me. I'm not the same anymore. I'm no longer just a soldier with all my training and skills that I've learned over the years. I've been changed into something. My eyes are proof that I'm no longer just a man anymore. What am I? Am I as dangerous as the creatures that are outside? Those creatures are probably trying to find a way inside the compound at this very moment. I need to find a way to keep everyone safe. I need to keep Emily safe. The only question is, what do I need to protect her from? The creatures outside? Or the darkness inside of me?

CHAPTER 12

The next morning I wake to Emily snuggled up against me on the couch. I slept so well, I didn't even hear or feel her climbing back onto the couch with me. Mya is still asleep at our feet. I slowly sit up and try not to wake Emily, but this time she does.

"Hey..." she says quietly while sitting up. She has lines on her face that match the pattern in the couch. "Where you going?"

"Just to the bathroom," I reply as I lean in and give her a quick kiss on the forehead.

I have to climb over her since she's on the outside of the couch. I hurry into the bathroom so I can take care of my business. As I stand there, I look over into the mirror so I can see my reflection. My eyes still have the same animal-like look to them and bright glow. I'm not sure how long it's going to take to get used to my new look. I just hope it doesn't take everyone in the compound forever.

After I finish up in the bathroom, I walk back out to sit with Emily on the couch. When I discover she's passed out again, I decide to let her sleep and go take a shower. I don't take my time enjoying the shower like I used to, but rather make it a quick one. Not being able to enjoy a hot shower is another thing I'm going to have to adjust to. Once I have on a clean t-shirt and a pair of basketball shorts, I go back to the living room where Emily is still out cold. I sit down and lightly shake her with my hand to try and wake her. She doesn't budge so I try whispering in her ear.

"Emily, wake up."

"Oh, why? What time is it?" she groans.

I look over at the clock and I'm surprised to see how early it actually is. 6:00 AM. Even that's early for me, especially since I didn't fully go to sleep until almost three in the morning. I feel as if I slept for ten hours though, not three. "Uh… I guess it's earlier than I thought. Go back to sleep."

"Aren't you tired?" she asks with her sleepy voice.

"No. I'm just gonna go to the council meeting. I might as well since I'm up. I'll come back when it's over."

"Alright, don't be long."

I kiss her tenderly on the forehead again and slide on a pair of flip flops I have sitting by the door. I step outside of the apartment quietly and start walking to the main hall where the council members usually hold their meetings. I never really understood the importance of the council meetings, or even the council for that matter, but I guess if it satisfies the needs of the older men in the compound, it really doesn't matter.

The compound is very quiet at 6:00 in the morning. A lot different than later in the afternoon when people are moving back and forth between the cafeteria and their apartments. Even the few kids that live here are usually running around acting crazy, trying to have fun. At this early in the morning, you'll only find a group of men who have nothing better to do than argue with one another. While walking down the long hallway, I can already hear the council members arguing loudly about last night. Nothing new. I'm not surprised to hear them arguing, especially after everything, but as I draw closer to hear their actual conversation, I am shocked to hear my name.

"My son is welcome here every bit as much as anyone else! How can you of all people be so willing to kick him out?!" my father shouts.

"Your son *isn't* normal. You saw what he did last night. What if he kills someone like that monster Rider did? What then?" I recognize Mr. Wilkinson's voice.

I turn the corner just as Mr. Wilkinson finishes talking. All the council members turn and look at me as I walk into the large room. None of them have the same expression of fear upon seeing me like last night, but most of them have a look of anger or concern on their faces.

"Oh look, the man of the hour. If he even *is* a man anymore."

I'm not surprised to see the man who I confronted last night, sitting with the council members. I hadn't really taken the time to notice his features before, but now that I'm not being caught off guard by either my body changing, or him kicking my dog, I can actually look at him.

He's bigger than most of the men in the compound. If it weren't for my martial arts training and the fact that I have super strength now, I might actually be concerned about his aggressive attitude towards me. I ignore his comments and walk over to my father's side.

"What's going on, dad?"

"We voted and decided it's in the best interests of the people that you should leave," the man replies.

"Other than being the asshole who kicked my dog last night, who are you again?" I sneer in response, taking a step closer to him.

"I'm the one who's having you kicked out," he smirks.

Who does this guy think he is? Just because he's a council member doesn't give him the right to decide my fate. In fact, why do any of the council members think they have that right? I have just as much right to live here as anyone. I actually have more, if we want to get technical. Afterall, I'm an Army Captain. None of these men are even employed by the government in any official capacity. Last I checked, this was a government facility.

"What is your name?" I ask.

"Joe Anderson," he replies. "And you *are* leaving. It's already been decided."

"Do you think you can make me, Joe?" I say coldly while staring at him with my new eyes. I see them reflecting in his own.

Joe frowns at my response and takes a step back. Rather than argue with him any longer, I simply smile and turn away from him. I look around at all the different council members and each one of them keeps their eyes down at the table. Neither one of them has the courage to look me in the eye as Joe gives me their verdict.

"You agreed to this too, Michael?" I ask confused as I step away from Joe.

He hesitates to respond when he looks up. I can tell as he looks at me with a blank face that he's really just looking at my new appearance. I'm having a hard time with my new eyes. I'm sure I look alien to everyone now.

"The people are afraid, Alec. They fear you're going to end up like Rider and kill more people. I'm sorry, but..."

I cut him off.

"That's not what I meant. You *want* me to go?"

He nods his head. I can see in his eyes that he is struggling with his decision. He really is just a coward. I look over at my father, hoping that he will stand up for me. He sits there calmly like a statue as if he's incapable of speaking.

"Dad!" I exclaim in exasperation, loud enough to make sure I get a startled reaction from him.

"I'm sorry, Alec," he says as he gets up from his chair. He looks me in the eyes as he speaks his next words. "You know I would never agree to this, but the council voted on it. There's nothing I can do," he says softly.

"Not the first time," I scoff.

My father looks down ashamed and I don't look at him again. Since the first few days we arrived here, everyone has agreed to have a council for decisions. They all believed it would be beneficial for everyone living here to have a group vote on actions that would have an impact on quality of life rather than one person in charge. I can certainly refuse to go. Nobody can stop me, but that would do no good.

"We expect you gone within the hour," Joe says with satisfaction after a long moment of silence. No one else has the audacity to speak up and go against the council's decision.

I glower at him as I feel my blood begin to boil. I want so badly to choke the life out of him. That would only give them another reason to see me as a monster.

But I'm not.

"I just need to change and pack some supplies. I'll be gone before that," I say softly and begin to walk out. I stop just before exiting the room and look at everyone one last time. The only one willing to make eye contact is Joe and he has a smirk on his face. Everyone else has their eyes down. I give my father one last glance hoping for some change, only to be disappointed. I shake my head and walk out.

As I make my way solemnly back to my apartment, I try thinking of how I'm going to tell Emily that I've just been exiled from the compound. She'll most likely be angrier than me, and want to leave with me. There would be an uproar among the community if that happened; I would be painted as the manipulator. Emily's parents would be devastated.

The walk back seems as though it's in slow motion. Time doesn't really matter to me anymore as I think of what to say to her. When

I reach the door to the apartment, I place my hand onto the brass handle. The handle which once felt cold to the touch every time I grabbed it, now doesn't even feel like it has a temperature.

I enter the apartment quietly, hoping that Emily is still sleeping. As I close the door, the room goes dark and my vision instantly turns into blue, night vision mode. I walk over to the couch and find Emily still asleep, so I go straight into my room to change into something more appropriate for the harsh outdoors, even though it probably doesn't matter. I don't expect the cold to be a problem now, with the inability to not feel temperatures, but I'd rather be prepared. I decide to go with my white camo. Blending in with the environment is going to be important. In the event that I run into Rider or other creatures. When I'm fully dressed, I pack my backpack with extra clothes to sleep in, and the typical toiletries for keeping clean. I don't have everything I'll need to hunt and cook food, so I'll stop by the armory to gear up. The only weapon I have in my room is my knife and my pistol, and those aren't going to be enough to face Rider again.

When I have everything I need in my room, I walk back out to the living room. Mya pops up the moment she sees the pack in my hand, knowing I'm leaving. Only this isn't a trip that she can come on either.

"Hey big girl," I say as I kneel down to say goodbye. "You're gonna have to sit this one out."

I give her a hug and rub her under belly. I let her lick my face as I say goodbye to her and then I give my attention to Emily. I sit down on the end of the couch and whisper to her.

"Emily?" She opens her eyes and smiles up at me. Her eyes immediately dart to my backpack and become alert.

"Where are you going?" she asks as she bolts into a sitting position.

"Outside for a bit. I'll be back in a little while."

Lying to her tears me apart inside, but I don't have the heart to tell her that I'm not going to be back any time soon. She would make me let her come along, and I just can't put her in that kind of danger again. I smile and give her a kiss on the lips.

"I love you." My heart aches as I say the words. I let my lips linger on hers for a second longer.

"Love you too," she replies, with eyes open and burning into mine the entire time. She knows something is wrong. I can feel her eyes watching me as I avoid eye contact.

I stand up and walk over to the door and open it. Mya follows me, thinking she's coming. I kneel down and hug her before I gently push her back inside and just before I close the door, I see Emily jump up from the couch. I close my eyes with my hand on the handle. I'm leaving my whole world inside this room and it feels like a huge chunk of my heart is being left behind too. I have to will myself to let go of the handle before turning and walking away. I feel one tear slide down my cheek as I get further away from the apartment.

I make my way down to the armory so I can grab the last of the supplies I'll need on the outside. Once I'm in the armory, I grab a tent, some basic cooking supplies (a small pot and metal silverware and a cup), a flashlight (even though I probably won't need it), a few small explosives, my M4 and another .40 caliber pistol and plenty of ammo. I'm in and out in five minutes.

I chuckle as I enter the main hall and see the audience waiting for me. All the council members, excluding my father, are there—arms folded and solemn as if it were execution day.

"Here to kiss me goodbye?" I smirk as I walk up to Joe.

"Good. You're going to need a sense of humor while you're all alone out there," he grins.

Not even a second later, Joe's mouth meets my fist and he hits the ground hard. I had to concentrate on making my jab to his mouth soft enough that it wouldn't do permanent damage. Blood splatters to the ground as he lets out a weasel like laugh and stumbles, trying to climb back to his feet. I keep walking past him as he tries to gather himself.

Just as I reach for the door, I hear the sound of steel rubbing against fabric. I hadn't been focusing my hearing, so I really don't know why I even heard it. Time slows to almost a stop as my body switches into defense mode. I quickly turn around and see everything like time is frozen. Several of the council members have expressions of utter shock beginning to form across their faces. I rest my eyes on Joe and his expression is one of anger. Like a rattlesnake lunging to bite someone, I snatch the knife from Joe's hand before it's completely free of the sheath. I then thrust the knife into the back of his hand and he lets out a loud scream.

Joe continues screaming as he runs in the direction of the cafeteria. All the other council members just stand by with terrified looks on their faces. None of them even move to offer Joe help. The room smells terrible. Fortunately, my parents and Emily weren't here to witness what just happened.

"You're all making a huge mistake," I say through clenched teeth as I enter the code on the panel. The moment the door is open, a gust of wind rushes past me. The ice-cold wind doesn't affect me at all, but quickly startles the remaining council members. "Make sure this door stays closed no matter what! Do you understand me!?" I shout at them.

A couple of them nod their heads, but most of them are still frozen in place after what they just saw. One member that I don't know the name of, steps forward to close the door behind me, nervously watching my movements. I turn to face the dark, frozen landscape. I step outside and hear Emily's voice calling out my name, just as the door slams behind me. I hear it lock in place and

I'm suddenly trapped outside with Mother Nature and whatever lurks in the shadows.

Only now, nothing can hide in the shadows from me.

CHAPTER 13

The weather today is mild in comparison to the normal blizzard like conditions. The snow is lightly falling, and the wind isn't blowing. Of course, the weather *would* be calm, now that I don't care. My night vision kicks in instantly when I step into the cave. I hadn't turned the light on before I came outside, but it no longer matters. It seems that darkness will no longer be an issue for me. The bitter, cold air doesn't have any effect on me, but I am still curious about the temperature. I walk over to where the thermometer is, but it's destroyed. It must have happened last night when Rider was out here. As I almost feel disappointed at not knowing the temperature, a white number pops up in front of me. 17 degrees Fahrenheit.

"What can't these Nan-ites do?" I say out loud.

I walk over to the mouth of the cave so I can look out over the valley. Judging by the amount of light, I would wager that the sun isn't up very high in the sky. It is only a little after 6:00 in the morning, after all. The compound is on the east side of the valley, between the cities of Farmington and Layton. It's on the east bench, above Highway 89. Nobody knew that it existed before the storm. I've driven by the road that leads up to it thousands of times over the years and never had any idea. The road that leads to the compound is right off the Highway with a fence and gate stopping regular traffic from driving on it. A sign is posted that reads *City and Management*. The perfect cover that nobody would ever question.

My vision has the same blue glow as before in my apartment and I can see all the way down to where Highway 89 would be. Before I would have been lucky to see thirty feet in most conditions with the storm. Now, I can see as far as the fog will allow. It has to be a good 300 yards from where I'm standing to the highway. Another white number pops up as I think of it. The highway is actually 360 yards away and the number is taking up almost all my vision. I imagine the numbers in a different location and smaller like when I was in the cafeteria. I look out across the valley below and spot where the sinkholes are. The number 151 in yards appears in the upper right corner in green. It works. I think of other measurements to make sure it isn't a fluke and the total circumference of the hole appears, in the same color and in the same spot. The hole is 15.6 feet by almost an equal 15.1 feet wide.

My abilities are incredible.

While standing there, gazing around the valley and marveling at my new honed ability, I spot a small group of five deer, north of the compound, heading in that direction. One of them is very young. I can tell which deer is the mother by the way she is still very protective of the young one. She keeps close and looks around in all directions for danger. Food is scarce, so any predator would likely be starving and searching for an easy kill.

Before the storm, all a deer would need to worry about this time of year would be poachers or a large mountain cat, like a cougar or bobcat and a car of course. Now there are a lot more things to be afraid of.

I continue watching the family of deer make their way north and I start walking in the same direction. I don't know why I start following them, I just do. We're heading in the direction of my house in Layton so I start jogging. Traveling by foot in the snow is easy for me now. Prior to the Nan-ites, it would become more and more difficult with each step, making my legs ache from the strain of sinking into the snow, but it's actually getting easier as I go. I quickly learn that with my new sense of control, strength, and balance, I can move through the snow without falling in too deep, where I might get stuck. I feel as if I'm gliding along the top because I'm able to take the next step before my foot sinks to the bottom. I imagine I'm like Jesus on water.

After jogging for ten minutes, I catch up to the family of deer. At first, they don't notice me because I'm still too far back for them to see, but once I'm within about 50 yards, they don't hesitate to dart off in a different direction and disappear after a couple minutes.

The compound is about five miles from my house. (4.8, according to the Nan-ite's.) What usually would've taken me at least half a day or more will now be under an hour at the casual jogging pace I'm going.

It seems like it was only yesterday that we left the house and came to the compound. My father had just returned from the hospital, or at least that's where he said he was. He said he was told of a place we could hide from the storm. Now it's pretty apparent that when he said he was at the hospital, he was actually at the compound doing his experiments. It's no surprise we, and many others that lived near us, were able to find shelter in a Top Secret government facility. At first, the only people that were there, were the people from our neighborhood and families and friends of other workers. Brian and I found Emily and her parents the day we came. Others started showing up weeks and even months later. Some of them had heard of the compound and came searching for it. Most of them Brian and I had found lost in the snow and rescued. How anyone found out about the place is a mystery to me.

It's amazing what people will fight through, when they are fighting to survive.

I start running along the highway at a much faster pace. I pass by trees that are frozen solid, their branches struggling with the weight of the snow piling onto them. Houses are in even worse shape. I pass house after house that have either a caved in roof, or the house is collapsed all together. The world that we once lived in is a frozen ruin. If the storm ever stops, there won't be anything to come back to. After only fifteen more minutes of gliding through the snow, I'm able to see the exit I used to take for my house. It's barely recognizable. I can barely distinguish between one place from the next anymore. Everything is dark. Granted the dark is no longer dark like it used to be, but there isn't any color anymore. Just, black, grey, and white.

Our street has twenty houses on it. Most are ruined now. So many homes with families that are probably still inside because not all of them made it to the compound. I knew most of these people. Sure, some of the families had changed over the years, but most have lived here since I was a child. They were just left to die cold and scared, not knowing what to do or what was going on. I feel a sudden sadness for all of them. Being trapped in the facility made it easier not to think about the people that didn't have somewhere to ride out the storm. If only they were still inside having dinner with each other, or watching a favorite movie. The thing is, they're no longer homes anymore. They're frozen tombs.

I continue walking down the street looking for signs of life. My heart begins to beat faster as I feel for those who didn't make it. The chances of anyone surviving in this weather with no electricity, is bad enough, but now there are creatures beyond imagination waiting in the darkness. I stop in the street, about halfway from my house when I smell something burning. It smells like a fire.

Odd.

I love the smell of campfires. I have so many good memories of camping up in the mountains. A good fire to sit around, or roast some marshmallows was my favorite part. We used to go on family camping trips all the time growing up. We would always go to Spirit Lake, high up in the Uinta Mountains. It was an easy place to get to. The only downside was it took about four hours to get there from home. The drive was worth it though. A nice quiet campground sitting right next to a lake. There were only about 10-15 sites so it was never very busy. A small lodge sat next to it where you could go inside and get simple fishing supplies, like bait and hooks. If you got bored of fishing in Spirit Lake, it was just a 2 mile hike to two more lakes that sat just below the timberline. It was rare that you didn't see a moose on a trip up there. Sometimes you might even see a bear.

I focus my sight, looking around for any sign of where the fire is coming from. My vision instantly alerts me to the location of the burning, by highlighting the smoke in red. It isn't a campfire at all. It's a chimney fire and it's coming from *my* house. Someone is there.

I pull my rifle off my back and approach the house slowly. As I get closer, I can hear chatter from inside. Two people are having a conversation. I stop 30 feet from my house and listen to them talk. They're arguing about who should go hunting today. I listen to them go back and forth for a few minutes until I'm sure they aren't Rider's men. I continue moving towards the front of the house again and realize that the moment they see me, they'll be frightened. Seeing a man pop up out of nowhere would be more than enough, but my eyes are sure to send them into a frenzy. If they have guns, they'll most likely shoot at me, and I want to avoid that at all costs. I need to figure out a way to conceal my identity. Or at least my eyes.

Our house isn't like the others in the neighborhood. All the houses on our street are one story homes, but they all have plenty of space for a nice patio, maybe a pool for those that can afford it, and a good sized grass area for kids or a dog to play on. Our home is a two-story home. Not originally, but my father always wanted a two-story home, and loved the neighborhood too much to move anywhere else. So, he added a floor, but in the process, he also had the framing changed. Most houses are built with the standard pine wood, but ours is built with a special kind of steel and fiberglass. The steel was designed to make a home more structurally stable in the event of an earthquake. Living in Utah along one of the worst fault lines in the world made my father paranoid. As a result, our home is the only one in the neighborhood still standing. Turns out his paranoia had a benefit.

I make my way to the back of the house through the side gate. The gate is already open so I don't need to worry about climbing over it and making noise. I never would have got it open with how deep the snow is anyway.

Once I'm in the backyard, I go straight for the stairs to the second floor deck. It was one more thing my father had to have. It was a walkout balcony from his room, with stairs leading down to his pool. I really can't blame the guy for wanting his house a certain way. He had worked really hard his entire life for it. Even if it wasn't the work we all thought he was doing.

I step lightly as I move up the spiral staircase, pausing on each step to make sure I don't make any sound before moving on to the next one. The snow is six feet deep, and that doesn't include the areas with high drifts. I fall down to waist deep snow with each step until I make it to the top. I walk up to the French doors, where the snow only reaches to about my knees and try the handle. Locked. I stand there for a moment thinking of what to do. French doors are easy to force open, but it might make too much noise. This is the only way inside, short of knocking on the front door. I focus my hearing on the two men talking again, and wait for a moment in their conversation to get loud. They're still arguing. While waiting, I see two red silhouettes of the two men appear in my vision on the first floor in the living room. It's as if I'm seeing them through some sort of heat vision through the floor and walls of the home.

"You know what Bobby, I'm sick of your whining. If you're that damn hungry, you can go hunt yourself."

"I always do the hunting around here. All you do is sit on your fat ass and eat when I bring back food."

I push on the door the moment the second voice shouts. Luckily, the locks hadn't been secured in the frame. The doors move inward, and the bolt pops free. The sound isn't very loud, but in a world where there isn't any noise, except for the wind, anyone could hear it if they are listening, so I stop to see if they heard me. The house is quiet. I focus my hearing so I can hear their heartbeats. Their heart rates are normal. The silence is finally broken only a couple seconds later.

"I'm going back to sleep. Wake me when you have food," mutters the first guy, who apparently is fat and lazy.

Once I'm sure they aren't coming, I slowly push the doors inward. They might feel the cold air coming in so I have no choice but to shut them. I turn the lock so I can close them with no interference, then relock it. My parents' room is a mess. All of their stuff is scattered everywhere, thrown onto their bed and dresser. Even the different pictures of the family that had been on the walls are torn down. The bedroom door is open, so I step lightly out into the hallway. My parents loved the idea of an open concept house, so from the upstairs, you can look down into the main living room where the fireplace is. I peer over the railing and see a dim glow coming from the fire, barely bright enough to light up the room. Both men are already back to sleep on the couches.

The man that is on the love seat is tall and skinny. His legs are dangling over the side of the couch and he looks extremely uncomfortable. The second man, the "fat ass" I presume, is on the larger couch. Judging by the lump under the blanket, the other guy was right. He is fat.

I move slowly down the hallway to my right, towards my room and find the door to it open as well. My room is a disaster just like my parents. Clothes are hanging out of the drawers in my dresser and in piles everywhere all over the floor. I step over to a chest where I keep all my military and old Martial Arts equipment. The chest is mostly empty except for a couple of awards I won when I was younger in Taekwondo. One of the awards is a first place trophy in the USA Martial Arts Youth Championships for hand to hand combat. Another is second place in the weapons using two Katanas. Katanas weren't a big part of Taekwondo, but I always wanted to learn how to use one. I found a man in town that taught me how to fight with any type of sword, so I would go to his class right after Taekwondo. The two Katana's I used at the Championships are no longer hanging on the wall. They don't appear to be anywhere in the room either.

I search my room for anything else I might be able to use. I find my old snowboarding goggles in the closet. Surprised that they're still there, I put them on and look into the mirror above my dresser. I can see my eyes as if the goggles aren't there. I try relaxing my vision so I don't have my enhanced vision. I need to know what it will look like if someone without my abilities looks at me. Once I'm able to stop my vision from having any enhancements, I can't tell my eyes are different through the lenses. Hopefully this will be the case with anyone I come across. It will come in handy when I encounter anyone that I might frighten, or if I want to conceal them so as to not give away my advantage with an enemy.

Once I finish searching my room, I step out into the hallway and look at the door across the hall.

Ashlee's room.

I reach for the door handle to go inside, but stop just before my hand touches it. I feel a knot in my throat and my stomach tighten at the thought of seeing her on the bed reading a book like back when we were kids. I suddenly have a realization that there's nothing in here other than memories that will bring me more sorrow—so I turn away.

I begin making my way back down the hall to my parent's room. As I'm walking by, I glance back down into the living room, where the two men are sleeping. I spot one of my katana's leaning up against the fireplace. I pause for a moment, unsure of what to do. The sword could come in handy the next time I face Rider. I could also wake up these two men and cause them to panic. After thinking about it for a good minute, I start descending the stairs quietly. I slowly move to each step hoping that none of them will creak. None of the steps made any noise before, so I continue down the staircase. I place my left foot onto the last step and I know I'm clear. All I need to do now is navigate through the mess in the living room over to the fireplace. I take my last step onto the surface of the main floor and the hardwood lets out a loud creaking sound that would have woke a hibernating bear. Both men jump to their feet in an instant, panicked looks on their faces and guns ready.

I don't move. Both men stare at me, with one gun pointed toward my chest.

"And who the hell are you?" shouts the taller man. His cheekbones stand out and he has a pointed nose. His hair is a long, shaggy blonde and his eyes are blue. He has a full beard that looks like he hadn't brushed in days.

"Looks like we have ourselves an intruder Kyle," responds Bobby. Bobby is quite the overweight man, as if he hasn't seen a shortage of meals in the last year. Calling him fat as Kyle had, really didn't do him justice. The man looks like he had spent his life in a donut shop. His cheeks are puffy and he's trying to grow a full beard like his friend, but he has a bunch of patchy looking scruff. Someone might as well have stuck random pieces of wax paper on his neck and pulled some hair free. His hair is brown, along with his eyes, and even though he's glaring at me, he looks frightened. He smells frightened.

"I just came to get some of my things. That's all," I reply calmly.

"Your things?" Kyle laughs. "You're packing some pretty serious hardware there." He motions towards my M4.

"This is our house now," shouts Bobby.

"I don't want any trouble. I'll just take my stuff and go."

"We searched a long time for this place, mister. It's no longer yours anymore," mutters Kyle.

"No offense pal, but you really can't stop me," I say calmly.

Bobby is the only one of the two holding a gun. He snatched it up in the same moment he jumped off the couch. Kyle had his leaning up against the fireplace—next to my sword. Both their heart rates are elevated.

"You forget that I'm pointing a gun at you." He lowers his voice aggressively.

Just as Bobby utters the last syllable, I move like lightning. I'm getting used to my ability to move fast, and I cover the fifteen feet between the two of us in the blink of an eye. I snatch the hunting rifle out of Bobby's hand and grab a handful of his shirt with the other.

"H-how did you d-do that?" Bobby stutters as he starts to shake while trying to move his face as far away from me as possible.

"We want no trouble sir," says Kyle in a shaky voice. "Take whatever you want. H-hell, you can have your house back." I look over at him and he's raising his hand in a calming gesture.

Both men are scared out of their minds now. The foul aroma from their fear is filling the room quickly, making me want to plug my nose. It's like a gas line had burst open. I release Bobby and step back from him.

"That won't be necessary." I look over at Kyle. "I don't want any trouble either. As I said *before*, I just came to get a couple things that belong to me, that's all." I lean the rifle against the couch.

"Really mister. We'll just go, if that's okay?" says a still frightened Bobby. He's still frozen in place. His eyes keep darting back and forth from the door, Kyle and me.

I stand there in silence for a moment and consider their offer. This *is* my house and I really don't have anywhere else to go. I'm also sick of people trying to push others around and not help them.

"No. Judging by the looks of you two, neither one of you would last a day out there."

Both men give each other confused glances as I walk past them and pick up my sword. The smell in the room isn't as strong as both their heart rates begin to slow down. I look at my reflection in the sword blade with my back to them both. The fireplace is giving off low light, but that doesn't matter. I can see myself clearly in the steel and my goggles are still concealing my eyes.

"You look like a soldier," Kyle says in a much calmer voice.

I turn around and face them. They both eye the sword with caution.

"I was. Before the storm anyway." I glance around the room, examining the mess.

"We're sorry mister, but the house was already a mess like this when we got here," responds Kyle.

"No matter. Now I'm just like you. Trying to survive in this world." Both men are still unsure of me. They keep eyeing the sword in my hand as if they expect me to use it on them. "You guys have no reason to be afraid of me."

Kyle appears to relax his body, but he still looks tense. I hear him let out a loud exhale as he straightens his posture and lowers his hand. After a few seconds he starts breathing normally and the smell of fear stops coming from him. Bobby is still frozen, but glaring at me. He's also still leaning backwards in an awkward position as if he's still trying to separate himself from me. I decide to ignore his distaste for me for at least a while, considering he really can't hurt me anyway. A thought comes to my mind as a way to win his trust.

"You guys look hungry. When was the last time you ate something?"

"Couple days," replies Kyle. "Hunting has been a little scarce lately."

"Well, I'm pretty hungry myself. Keep the fire going until I bring back some fresh food." I slowly walk past them to the front door. I pull my rifle off of my back and lean it against the door. I would like to use my rifle to go hunting, but I don't want to alert any danger that might be in the area. Not only could Rider hear the shots and come looking, but I still have the creatures that attacked him to worry about.

"You're not taking a gun?" asks Kyle.

"Don't want to waste the ammo," I lie. "I shouldn't be gone long. Make sure you keep the fire going." I close the door behind me without another word.

The weather is still calm when I step outside. It's also still early morning, so the sun is still behind the mountain. Not that it matters. A light breeze is blowing down from the north as I stand there in silence, trying to pick up the scent of an animal. Maybe those deer I had seen earlier are still nearby. I'm not sure how strong my sense of smell really is, but it's time to find out.

"I don't trust him," I hear Bobby whisper inside the house. My hearing amplifies his voice so that it sounds like he's whispering directly into my ear.

"I don't think we really have a choice, Bobby."

"I don't take orders from no one," Bobby says with disdain.

"Just leave the man be. If he wanted to hurt us, he would have already." Bobby scoffs at Kyle's response. "You saw what the man could do. He probably could have killed us in our sleep."

I start off on a jog and shut them out. Being able to hear as well as I do, has its advantages, but I can see disadvantages in it as well. A few minutes later, I find myself on the edge of my neighborhood. A strange smell forces me to stop. I think it's human, but it's musty at the same time. A sweet, salty smell with something else. It's coming from the south, towards the compound, but I don't think it's very far away. I continue jogging in that direction to see if I can find it. I focus my hearing as I run, to see if I can hear anything. After a few seconds, I hear a faint heartbeat in the distance. It can't be more than a couple hundred yards away. With my ability to see great distances, I should have no issues seeing what it is, but trees and houses are blocking the way. A couple seconds later, I pick up the sound of another heartbeat, and then another and another. They're coming towards me, and fast.

Nearly a dozen deer come galloping around a corner like a stampede. The smell of fear slams into my face as I jump out of their way. Something frightened them, and whatever it is, it's close behind. I suddenly hear the sound of another heartbeat as the deer blow past me, but whatever it belongs to, it stops as if it knows I'm there as well. I'm frozen in my stance like a snowman as I listen to this other beating heart of... *something* just around the corner of a house. I'm caught in a waiting game with some unseen stranger that could be anything.

NEGATIVE in bold letters appears in my vision as I imagine the possibility of it being Rider. The Nan-ites are right. This heartbeat is different. The smell is even different. Whatever, or whoever it is that is waiting for me to make a move–it's making it so that the food is getting away from both of us. I am hungry, but

I can last longer. Kyle and Bobby are starving. Well–Kyle is starving. Bobby could probably miss a few more meals, but I still need to take care of them both. If I can't help the people in the facility then I need to help the people that are still left out here. There's no telling how many people are left.

I slowly start backing away, listening closely to see what the unseen stranger might do. It doesn't move at first, but then slowly begins to back away as well. Once I know it isn't going to follow, I turn and start to sprint towards the herd of deer. The stranger runs in the opposite direction as well until it's out of my reach of hearing and smell.

I'm stronger and way faster than the deer now. I catch up in only twenty seconds as I blast through the snow with my powerful legs. I quickly imagine myself as a lion hunting a gazelle. I've seen plenty of documentaries that show lions hunting the elusive beasts before, but I've always used a rifle to hunt. Now, I truly am the lion and I'm only steps behind a large buck. My heart is racing from the excitement and pure exhilaration of the moment. The stench of fear coming off the animals is strong. The buck is terrified as it tries to run for its life. I raise my sword up with my right hand, with the hilt facing up. The buck lets out a strangled, horrific sound as the blade strikes home, directly behind the head. The smell of fear doesn't vanish until the heart stops beating. It was scared until the very last moment. This is my first experience of the negative side of having heightened senses. I've really never thought of how terrifying it could be for an animal to be hunted in this manner. Being able to know how afraid it was makes me feel sick. I'm grateful for the sacrifice it made, since the food is needed, but I don't like what I just experienced. Being able to feel how another animal feels when you're about to kill it, shouldn't be possible. I'm never going to hunt like this again. Since I won't want to use my rifle, I'll need to get a bow.

Dragging the lifeless animal back to the house is much easier than it had been when Brian and I have gone hunting in the past. Even after breaking the animal down for meat, the weight of it, carrying it back to the car would sometimes be a lot of work. Since then, we both have hated bringing a kill back to the facility. Now, I barely notice I'm dragging anything at all. This will make hunting way easier. Providing food for the compound will be possible now. I don't take my time going back to the house. I move as quickly as possible and the deer leaves a crimson path behind me. Luckily, nothing follows.

When I make it back, I walk right in without giving them any warning. They're both on the couch waiting for me and Bobby is holding my M4 and points it directly at me when I walk in.

"Bobby, don't!" shouts Kyle, running toward Bobby to get him to lower the gun.

I ignore them both and walk past them to the back door leading into the garage. The garage is the perfect place to store the meat. It's cold enough to keep it fresh, but it will also protect it from other animals. I release the lock so I can manually lift up the garage door and then drag the body inside.

"What are you?" asks Bobby. Both men scurry behind me to observe from a safe distance. "A normal man couldn't get close enough to kill a buck with just a sword in the summer on a sunny day. You did it in the dark, in the middle of a blizzard. I think it's time you explain yourself."

Both men are standing in the doorway as if trying to prevent me from coming back inside. Bobby still has the rifle, but he isn't pointing it at me. Without responding, I turn and pull the garage door down to stop cold air from blowing into the house. When the door is closed, I turn back around and walk straight towards both men. Bobby raises the rifle–my rifle–as I walk towards them.

"I'm not gonna let you hurt us," he says. I hear Bobby start to pull the trigger, so I dash forward and snatch the gun out of his hands. Fear quickly spills out of him.

"What were you thinking, Bobby?" says Kyle.

"You have a terrible attitude. And since you do, you can prepare the food," I say calmly as I pat him on the back. His body tenses at my touch and his face has a combined look of scared and irritated. "Kyle and I will be waiting by the fire." Kyle smiles. He's probably relieved to not be taking orders from the fat guy anymore.

We both head back into the living room and sit down. I take a seat on the long couch and Kyle sits on the smaller one. Even though he's completely relaxed and doesn't smell afraid, it's clear that he's still a little weary of me. He'll warm up to me eventually. As I'm sitting down, my hand brushes up against my pant leg and I notice how wet I am. My boots and pants are soaking wet along with my jacket. I hate wearing wet clothing almost more than anything. Too many bad memories of missions where I was wet for days. My clothes are also caked in ice and would most likely make someone else cold. With my body now able to regulate my temperature, I could probably swim in the arctic without getting cold. I unlace my boots and set them next to the fire so they can dry off.

"I'll be right back," I say to Kyle as I get up and walk upstairs. I feel Kyle's eyes on my back the entire time as I ascend the stairs.

I walk into my room to look for a pair of shorts or sweatpants to wear, so my wet pants can dry. I hadn't packed all my clothes when we were all rushing to get to the compound, so there should be something. I dig through the pile of clothes that are tossed on the floor in my closet. Even my nice business suit was thrown on the floor. I would probably never wear it again, but seeing it on the floor like it is junk feels strange, so I pick up the dark grey suit and hang it back up. It's the only thing hanging from the rod when I step out of the closet. I continue sifting through the scattered clothes on my floor and find an old pair of black jogger pants that I would sometimes wear to do my martial arts training. I pull my wet pants off and put on the joggers and head back downstairs.

Bobby is still in the garage, hacking away at the deer, and Kyle is still on the loveseat. I take off my coat and set it and my pants down on the floor in front of the fire so that they can dry. I sit back down in the same spot as before. Kyle continues looking at me like a child staring at a strange new animal in a zoo. He even starts to tap his fingers on the couch in anticipation for food, and maybe even for Bobby to come back inside and start his grumpy ramblings. He would probably take anything to avoid the awkwardness he's most likely feeling. We both just sit quietly, avoiding conversation for about fifteen minutes when Bobby finally emerges from the garage, with three good sized steaks for us to eat. He's carrying them on a plate, one he likely grabbed from the kitchen, and tosses them onto the cooker that was already set up in the fireplace. He also has a nasty look on his face.

"Make sure you flip those, every couple minutes. I don't like mine black," I tell Bobby. "Also, there should be some good spices in the kitchen to add some flavor."

The plate makes a crashing sound as Bobby slams it down onto the ground with anger. Pieces of broken glass go everywhere.

"Dammit, I'm not someone to be ordered around like a child!" he shouts. "Cook your own damn food!"

"This is my home," I reply calmly. "You may have found it while I was gone, but it's still my home. Now I got you enough food to last you a couple weeks, so you will do exactly as you are told until you stop acting like a child and learn some manners and respect. I could throw you out into the snow and let you fend for yourself. Seeing how you were doing such a great job of it already. And don't make me point out the fact that you were ordering Kyle around like a child."

Bobby lowers his head and looks down at the ground. He isn't huffing and puffing with his chest out for the first time since I arrived.

"You know our names. At least tell us yours," he replies softly with his eyes still on the floor.

"My name is Alec Winter."

"Why are you wearing those goggles?" asks Kyle. Bobby looks at him, surprised he has the courage to say something.

I look at both of them as I consider what to say. What explanation can I possibly give that will make sense? Showing them my eyes might only make matters worse with Bobby. He already doesn't trust me. They both watch me, waiting for my answer. I slowly reach up and grab my goggles with both hands. I close my eyes before I remove them and set them down next to me. A loud gasp fills the room when my eyes open, revealing my bright fluorescent blue animal like eyes. Neither Bobby or Kyle say anything at first. They just stare at me wide eyed as if they're seeing me for the first time. Oddly though, I don't smell fear coming from either of them. They're just looking at me, trying to puzzle out why someone would look the way I do.

"What are you?" Bobby asks again, as he glances over at Kyle as if to see his reaction.

"I'm a man, just like you." I don't move at all so I don't frighten them.

"I've never seen a man with eyes like that before," Kyle says as he tilts his head with wide eyes.

"You sir are the strangest man I've ever met," adds Bobby. "Why are you... how can you do the things you can?"

"How about we talk after we eat?" My stomach growls.

232

Bobby looks as though he's about to argue, but then nods his head slowly and goes back to preparing the food. Over the next ten minutes I watch him prepare our food with a particular attention to detail. He checks on the food precisely every three minutes to the second. Flipping each steak over every time until they are cooked to perfection. He even took the time to grab some spices from the kitchen like I suggested. Bobby isn't so bad after all. He just needs to relax a little.

We eat in silence. The meat is oddly delicious. I haven't eaten a full deer steak like this very often because we always sold the meat or dried it out for jerky. The spices Bobby chose are perfect. I can taste some garlic, onion and a hint of pepper. I finish eating before the other two and take my plate into the kitchen and set it on the counter. The kitchen is a disaster. It's clear that people have been ransacking the place in search of food. All the cabinet doors and drawers are open. There's trash everywhere and the shelves are mostly picked clean. More so than the rest of the house. I decide not to linger in the kitchen any longer than I have to, and walk back into the living room. Both Bobby and Kyle are on the loveseat.

For the first time since I came back home, I step up close to the fire and look up at the few pictures that are still hanging on the wall. None of them have been touched. I'm grateful for that. I grab a small family picture that has all of us in it. Brian, my parents, me...and Ashlee. Even Mya is in this family photo.

"Who are you really, Mr. Winter?" Bobby asks politely from where he's seated.

I take my seat back on the couch, still holding the picture. I haven't taken my eyes off of Ashlee since pulling the picture from the wall. The pain mixed with regret and anger is still festering like an old wound. I miss her terribly and wish there had been more I could have done to help her. She could still be alive now, even after all this time, yet it's impossible for me to reach her. At least it *was*

233

impossible. Until now. I can't help but smile as I realize for the first time since going through my change, that I can finally reach Salt Lake City without endangering myself or anyone else. And I can get there quickly.

"Mr. Winter?" says Kyle.

I forgot I was being watched and my mind quickly reminds me of Bobby's question a moment ago. Apparently, I really did lose my focus while looking at the picture. I might not have really heard him at all, but the Nan-ites might have.

"Sorry," I apologize as I set the picture down next to me. "I didn't mean to ignore you. Old memories came flooding back. What I'm about to tell you will be hard to believe."

I go on for nearly an hour telling them my story and about everyone in the compound. I even tell them of Rider and the other creatures. They deserve to know of the dangers that are potentially lurking in the shadows, just waiting for the right opportunity to strike. When I'm done explaining the dangers, I tell them that I have to go and that I don't know exactly when I'll be back. I tell them that I *will* come back for them and take them to the compound, where they can have better shelter. More secure shelter. They both nodded their heads during my story, accepting everything I had to tell them, like it was perfectly normal. Their trust for me seemed to grow during the last hour. Seeing me for what I am and what I'm capable of doing, must have helped convince them. During that time, I learned a bit about both of them as well.

Bobby and Kyle are both hunters and friends. They have been for years. Kyle had grown up in Utah and Bobby moved here when he was a teenager. When the storm hit, they both decided that they would ride it out in their trailer that they lived in, near the interstate. Eventually the snow was too much for the trailer and they realized that they would need a better place to ride out the storm. They just started searching homes that looked stable and that also had a fireplace. Eventually they settled on mine.

As I'm getting ready for my trip, I grab my pack from upstairs and put the picture from the wall in it. My parents hadn't taken the time to bring any photos with them, and I know they would want at least one of the family. If I'm able to get back inside, I want to have it with me. I also grab both of my swords and decide to leave the M4 with them. All they have are hunting rifles, so I figure they could use something extra in case they have any unwanted visitors after I'm gone. Not that it would matter, but anything could be the difference in their survival. I tell them to stay in the house and not to go outside for any reason whatsoever. They ask if I'll be gone more than a week. My response is simple.

"If I'm not back within a week, I won't be back." They don't ask for an explanation and I exit the house without another word.

CHAPTER 14

I'm leaving the house before mid-day and don't conserve any energy while I sprint towards Salt Lake, as fast as my legs and the terrain will allow. The distance from Layton to Salt Lake City is 24.2 miles. I basically have to run a marathon distance in knee deep snow, and that's just to downtown Salt Lake. I'll still need to run the extra couple miles up the East bench where Primary Children's hospital is located. Also, since it is on the East bench, it sits near the base of the mountain. The snow will most likely be deeper up there than in the city. It always was back during a normal winter. I want to get to the hospital as quickly as possible. I still have Rider and his men to worry about, so I need to go there and be back by the end of the day. I'm not really sure if I can manage that, but based on how fast I made it to my house from the compound, it shouldn't be a problem. The Nan-ites quickly calculate an ETA to the hospital. It's based on a route going along the 89 highway, pretty much the whole way there. It will take me almost two hours to get there. I wonder if the ETA the Nan-ites came up with is based on my casual jog from the compound to here. If it is, then I can shave that time down significantly by going full speed. The question is, can I maintain a full sprint? I'm going to find out.

Running at such a fast speed through the snow is indescribable. The Nan-ites put up a miles per hour when I think of speed. 53 mph. I can nearly run at freeway speeds through knee deep snow. I never would've imagined being able to do something like this. The Nan-ites also re-calculate my ETA. 32.5 minutes. Much better than the original estimation. I'll be there in no time.

After only two minutes, I come up on the compound. I start to feel a strong sense of longing as I pass by. I'm missing Emily more and more as the hours go by. Mya too. The only thing that's helping me get through it is the thought of finding Ashlee. I go by the compound without even glancing up in its direction. I have to go to Salt Lake. Even if I don't find anything, I need closure. I need the peace of mind, so I can move on.

As I run towards Salt Lake City, with the small hope tucked in the back of my mind, I pass house after house, and building after building, that are completely engulfed in snow and ice.

Everything is dead.

No life of any kind appears to exist, aside from the group of deer I saw earlier. The fact that there are any deer is a miracle. Even the deer need food to eat, but the plants are dead and underneath the snow. The lifeless cities of Farmington and Bountiful, places that were part of my childhood up to adulthood, are no longer cities at all anymore. It's overwhelming to see. All they are now, are just permanent monuments of ice spread out over a frozen landscape. Seeing these cities in such ruin makes it hard to focus on what my task is.

Get to the hospital and find Ashlee. Or a body to bury.

Finally, I start to make my way around the point of the mountain, along the old gravel pits and gas refineries, as I approach the Salt Lake valley. What I find when I come into the valley, is exactly what I expected and feared.

Downtown Salt Lake appears even more lifeless. It looks like a scene from an old science fiction movie. Only this is reality. All of the buildings appear to be intact. The tall business buildings and even the massive Mormon temple are still standing. The oldest and largest structure in the city. The temple is also the only thing about the city that could be considered beautiful. The stone building was always beautiful before, but now the temple looks like a giant ice castle out of a fairy tale. The entire city has an eerie feeling to it. I quickly make my way down to the corner of State Street and 400 south. Both courthouses are still standing. The newer one that had been built within the last thirty years, and the older one that looked more like a massive church or cathedral. The streets are packed with frozen cars. People were probably trying to use them to get out of the city once the panic began. The snow is covering them all. Now they just look like oddly shaped bumps in the snow.

I stop to listen for any signs of life. I feel like I can hear something, but I'm not sure. There's something about it that just doesn't feel right. I feel like someone is watching me. I mentally ask the Nan-ites if there are any people within eyesight. NEGATIVE. I trust the scan to be correct, but it still doesn't put me at ease. Could be my own fears playing with me. Or maybe I want there to be people so badly that I'm imagining they're all still up there looking down. I decide to ignore it and start running again as fast as I can. I want to get to the hospital and be done with why I came here.

I run up the main intersection at a fast pace as I blow past the Salt Lake City library. The giant glass structure, intended to be a place for children and adults to read and learn, or just find a place to ponder about life, is no more than a frozen, empty glass box now. My run continues to take me up the long road leading to Medical Hill, taking me past abandoned restaurants, grocery stores and even homes. The middle of 4th south continues to be a frozen junkyard for cars. Some of them, the ones that aren't completely covered in snow, have lifeless, frozen corpses inside them. People who froze to death with nowhere to go, waiting for help to come. I clear snow off of one vehicle to look inside and regret it instantly. Inside the vehicle is a mother on the back seat holding her two small children. I can't see the children's faces, but I can see their small bodies from under the blanket. Seeing people in their frozen tombs, churns my stomach as I fear for the worst.

Blocking out the images of Ashlee frozen to death inside a hospital room like I saw in my nightmare is challenging.

After I make my way up the steep, winding road, a road that used to have many accidents during the winter, I begin passing the University of Utah and a cemetery. The cemetery might still be a good place to hunt for food. Deer used to always hang around in there. I pass the University where Ashlee went for medical school, and continue the last half mile up to the hospital. The storm had started picking up as I ascended the hill. Now, the wind speed is up to 27 miles per hour, and starting to make a thin layer of frost build up on top of my clothes. Surprisingly, it isn't sticking to my skin or hair at all. Must be the Nan-ites superhuman abilities assisting me again.

The wind doesn't bother me at all, as far as temperature is concerned, but it is affecting my hearing and smelling. Two of my biggest new strengths at detecting nearby life. Visibility is becoming more difficult as well. A fog starts to roll in and appears to get thicker and thicker the closer I get to the hospital.

The weather isn't making any sense. It's like the golf course all over again. When I was at the golf course, there was an opening in the storm that allowed me to see my destination as well as the stars. Only instead of helping me now, it's like some unseen force is trying to stop me from reaching the hospital. The closer I get, the worse the storm gets. I'm less than a quarter mile away when the wind starts blowing harder than anything I've ever experienced. It's almost like I'm witnessing the first hurricane in Utah. The wind speed quickly picks up and increases to 65 mph and continues rising at a rapid pace. Even with my new strength, I begin to experience difficulty moving forward. I can feel my muscles tightening as I strain to continue on. As I fight with everything I have to go on, I think back to the strange phenomenon at the golf course with Emily. I remember the wall of storm, in a giant circle around me, like someone had been watching me then.

Can someone really be watching me? How else can that occurrence be explained, or the unnatural winds now? Why would the storm help me before when I needed shelter, and now it's trying to stop me? It doesn't make sense. Or maybe what is happening now, is just bad weather picking up at a bad time. Either way, my muscles are getting tired for the first time since going through my change.

I feel tired.

I continue battling the strong winds for nearly an hour, as they reach top speeds of over 100 mph. I need to make it to the hospital. I need to find Ashlee. It doesn't matter if she's alive anymore. I just have to find her so I can finally put it to rest and so my family can also move on. I continue fighting the wind for another hour. My love for my sister and the hope of finding her helps to keep me going. Eventually the wind hits 210 mph and I feel something tear in my left leg. I wince from the pain as I feel the Nan-ites start to mend it back together. Just as it heals, I feel a burst of pain in my right. This tear is much worse and I fall onto my chest with my face buried in the snow. I try to climb to my feet as every muscle in my body begins to ache. I think of the family photo I looked at earlier. I'm letting my family down. I'm letting Ashlee down all over again. After shedding a few tears and apologizing to my sister out loud, I drop into the snow from sheer exhaustion and black out.

I wake to the winds beating down on my back. The wind speed hasn't dropped. I'm covered in a thin layer of snow that's frozen to my clothes. My hair and skin are still dry.

I sit up and wonder how long I've been out. 17.3 minutes appears up in front of me. I'll never get used to that.

I climb to my feet and discover that my muscles no longer ache. They've already recovered from the tears that happened only 17 minutes ago. With the winds not slowing down, I look up towards the hospital. I can just barely see the large, glass building that's been a place for children across the world to go to for healing for years. It had been one of the leading children's hospitals in research and healing. That's what inspired Ashlee to go there in the first place. She volunteered her junior year in high school there one summer and she made up her mind on the first day. For now, I'll need to come up with a different plan for visiting the hospital later. I'm clearly not meant to go now. I turn around and never look back as I descend the steep and cold landscape back down into the city. Heartache and failure are the only things I'm feeling now.

Once I'm back downhill toward the city center, I continue through the snow packed street towards the highway. I'm about to pass the library when suddenly all my senses start sounding like fire alarms in my head. I hear a whisper in the wind, telling me to *stop*. It's that same familiar voice I've heard many times, instructing me to do something that's always in my favor. I do exactly what the voice says.

Instantly, I smell fear floating across the snow like rotting food, making the street smell rancid. I focus my senses to find the source, when screams suddenly echo loudly in my head. Screams from multiple people, all crying for help. The Nan-ites direct me towards the Salt Lake City Police station, next to the library. The Nan-ites illuminate the building in a white glow.

I waste no time in running to the station. The voice in my head, or wherever it is coming from, always seems to have a knack for spotting danger and now isn't a time to ignore it. The Nan-ites are clearly picking up the danger in the station as well. Someone needs help, and people are going to be hard to come by in this world now. I have an obligation to protect people even more so than ever before. It's my duty.

The Salt Lake City Police station is a beautiful, state of the art building. I remember back when it was first built and had tours for the open house. The building has its own back-up power supply, powered by generators and even solar panels and a wind turbine. The solar panels will be useless with the black sky, but the turbine, with the nonstop wind, could provide enough electricity for a small group. I approach the building from the front, where it has a modern walkway with pillars leading you up to the front door. The pillars are supporting awnings that are slanted downward for a unique look to match the building and also for rain water to run off. The entire front of the building is nothing but glass. I can see into the front lobby and even up to other floors. I can see into the gym, the locker room area and some offices that are along the outside in the front and on the side. Nobody is visible in any of the rooms and all the lights are off. I walk up to the front doors and pull on them. Locked. This particular building only has a few points of entry. I remember from my tour of the building when it first opened, that there is a loading dock in the back and also two ramps that lead down into a two-level parking structure beneath the building. One garage entrance is on the north end of the property, just off of the road that leads to the hospital and the other is on the southeast corner, right next to the loading dock.

I'm closer to the garage entrance on the north so I head there first. The heavy doors are down in the locked position. Realistically, I might be able to break in with my new strength, but the doors look like they were designed to prevent unwanted guests. They look more like vault doors than ones for a garage.

As I stand there and think of a possibility to get through, the Nan-ites put the question to rest. NO POSSIBLE ENTRY. That answers that question. I begin making my way towards the loading dock and the other garage entrance. The loading dock is where the generators and turbine are located. The generators aren't running at the moment, but the turbine appears to be working properly. As I approach a manned access door in the loading dock, I hear the screaming again. It's clearly a woman's voice.

"Pl… ease.. stooop!"

"Shut your mouth," shouts a man's voice, followed by the sound of a hard slap. "The longer you fight, the longer it takes to be over." The man chuckles.

I try the door and it's locked. I make my way out of the loading dock and try the south ramp entrance. Also secured. All the entrances are locked. I stand there in the snow, pondering how I'm going to get inside without them hearing me. I can easily break in through the front, or even the loading dock door, but they will likely hear me. Whoever is inside, will likely have an arsenal of weapons. It is the police station, after all. I'm fast and strong, but surprise will be my best friend today. I need to navigate the building quickly to find where the woman crying for help is, and if there are any other hostages. It's been a long time since I went on the tour, and I barely remember the exact details of the inside.

The Nan-ites quickly jog my memory of the building. Images of the station from when I went on my tour flash before me. I can see myself walking down the ramp, into the first level of the garage to see where they keep all their department vehicles, even motorcycles. I'm then on the second level, viewing where they keep their K-9 units in their kennels and a service area for vehicles. I can now remember each and every room like I just walked through the building. What I'm seeing is incredible. If the Nan-ites can search my memories and help me recall any moment from my life, there's no limit to what I can do with it. If only I had actual schematics of the whole building. That would be more ideal. Especially since I didn't see every inch of the place on the tour. Instantly, blueprints of the building flash in front of me. The schematics are burned into my mind as if they were just downloaded into a file. Now it feels like the Nan-ites are just showing off and they don't stop there either. The sounds of every beating heart in the building sound off in my head as the Nan-ites map out the location of each one, and place markers in my field of vision to let me know where they are. The Nan-ites even mark the location of the woman that's crying out for help. It's almost like a holographic map that's only visible to me.

Brian would love this.

I walk around to the back of the building. According to the schematics of the station, I can get inside through the ventilation system on the roof. There's an access point directly up the wall in the loading dock area. The generator is fifteen feet high, but not a problem for me to reach with my new abilities. I jump as high as I can and end up jumping too high by four feet. I come down onto the generator with a loud clang that echoes pretty loudly. I hope nobody heard that. I look up at the ledge, just above the door. It's more like a small lip that sticks out by only a couple inches from the wall. If I miss, I'll fall over thirty feet onto the snow packed ground. The Nan-ites might be able to heal me, but I still very much feel pain.

My heart starts pounding as I prepare for the jump.

I push off the generator, using the same amount of effort as I did to get where I already am and blast off the generator. I hit the wall hard, but manage to grab onto the tiny ridge with my fingertips. Now, I have to launch myself another twelve feet onto the lower part of the roof, using only arm strength. I dangle against the cement wall of the loading dock area and look up to the edge of the roof. How I'm going to make that distance with just arm strength? I do not know.

I hear the familiar voice trying to give me confidence. I shake my head as the voice speaks over the wind like a watchful guardian. I lower myself so that my arms are extended all the way and heave myself up with every ounce of strength I can muster. I launch into the air like a rocket. I end up launching myself higher than the roof and I come down hard onto the snow packed ledge and I quickly start to slip. I try to grab onto the icy snow. As I'm sliding off the roof, I pull one of my katanas out from behind my back where I stored it between my pack and stab hard into the snow, like it's an ice pick. The blade cuts through the snow like butter and I continue sliding. I then pull out my other katana from the same place and thrust it into the snow, but this time turning the blade so that both sides of the blade are facing up and down. The blade anchors into the snow and I'm able to start pulling myself up. I pull the first katana out and repeat what I'd done with the second, and alternate the same thing over and over again as I work my way onto the roof.

Wasting no time, I move over to the ventilation system and gently pop off the outer panel. It makes a clanging noise, but hopefully, not loud enough to reach the lower levels of the station. I then start working my way down the shaft using my arm strength, by pressing my hands up against each side and lowering myself down by crawling downward with only my hands. Once the shaft levels out, I continue my way to the nearest vent and come out inside the gym on the third floor. The room is empty.

I exit out the gym door quietly, and end up in the outer hallway that only has a wall on the left side. To my right is the grand hall and front door, which will be three floors to ground level. The only thing separating me from the three story drop is a glass wall that's only a few feet high with a railing attached. I walk over to the stairs at the end of the walkway and begin to make my way down. My holographic map shows that there's only one person on the main level and the rest of the people are down on one of the sub-levels.

The staircase is one of those "floating staircases" where you can see through each step to the other side. It's lined by a glass railing. I take each step softly to make as little noise as possible as I descend the stairs. I notice that the air is musty, but it's being overpowered by the rotten smell of all the terrified people inside. I try to block out the awful smell as my boots lightly make contact with the floor, barely making any noise as I come down onto the second level.

Suddenly, all the screaming downstairs stops.

The woman that was screaming is no longer making any noise. As I descend down to the first level, I stop just before the bottom. A door opens and closes. A man in a police officer's uniform comes walking into view, but doesn't see me. The lighting is low, due to the lack of light coming from outside and there being no inside lights on. The officer is using a flashlight to help him see. The fact that this man is wearing a police officer uniform means nothing to me. He has to be part of whatever is going on below.

He's kind of a heavy-set man, with a shaggy head of black hair. He isn't wearing all the normal duty gear that an officer would normally carry, but he does have a gun holstered. I can't smell fear on him. At least not yet.

"What are you doing to those people downstairs?" I asked softly from the shadows. He still hasn't seen me.

The officer whirls around and flashes the light in my direction. I move before the light is on me, by jumping down over behind a motorcycle that's used as a display item like a museum piece.

"Who's there? How'd you get out of your cell?"

Cells? So, they are keeping people locked up. I'm not sure if this guy is a real police officer, but he definitely isn't a good person. A woman screaming for someone to stop doing something and here he is on what appears to be a patrol. With my enhanced vision I can see him clearly as if I was up close to him. He has the look of murder in his eyes.

"I asked you a question," I growl at him.

The stalky man flashes the light over to my direction, but again I'm too fast. This time, I silently dash over to the windows and creep up behind him.

"Come out, you coward! You'll be punished for this."

I move up so that I'm directly behind him. The man is only 5'7 so with my 6'4 frame, I tower over him. I remove my goggles so the man will be able to see me for what I really am.

"Do I look like one of your prisoners?" I say softly.

The man spins around and simultaneously starts reaching for his gun. Only he's too slow. I pull his gun from the holster before his hand is even close and grab him by the throat. He tries to scream, but I'm cutting off his air flow. The horrified look is all I need to know he's terrified. The nasty odor that comes from him is just an unwanted confirmation.

"If you try to warn the others, I'll snap your neck. Do you understand?" The man nods as much as he can with how I'm holding him. "Now, tell me who you are and what is going on here."

The man doesn't take his eyes off of mine. He's beyond frightened and I can hear his heartbeat pounding loudly.

As I lower him down and release my grip around his throat, images start appearing in my head. Images of people flashing rapidly from one person to the next. CRIMINAL DATABASE appears in my vision. They're images of people with criminal history. Some people have violent pasts, others just petty crimes.

Is there a limit to what the Nan-ites can do?

Finally, the images stop on a picture that matches this man's face perfectly. I look down at a name tag on his shirt. It says J. Olsen, but that isn't his name at all. Nicholas Sandoval is a common criminal with a pretty long list of crimes he's committed since he was eighteen. Assault, burglary and drug possession.

"Actually, Nicholas… I think I've figured it out."

"H-how do you kn-know my name?" he chokes. "And what are you?" Nicholas is shaking as he steps backward trying to separate himself from me. He's beginning to breathe rapidly.

I close the distance between us and grab him by the shirt, just below his chin. I lift him up so he's eye to eye with me. His heart is pounding harder than a drummer in a band.

"Are there others like you, pretending to be something they're not? Or is it a real officer hurting that woman downstairs?" I say through clenched teeth.

"Th-they're all l-like me sir?" Nicholas tries to wiggle free without success.

"Are any of the real ones still alive?"

"Barely s-sir. We beat em all pretty good when we got free."

"Last question. Do you take part in what is happening to that woman as well?"

Nicholas's heart starts to beat even faster. I didn't think that was possible. I was already sure he was participating in what's going on downstairs without him answering, but he seals his fate by talking.

"No sir. Of course not," he says, putting emphasis on each word as his eyes flicker away for a split second. A normal person wouldn't have seen it, but I'm not a normal person.

"Thanks pal. You've been a big help."

"S-so will you put me down then?" he asks with doubt in his voice.

"Of course," I grin.

I grab Nicholas with my other hand after I tuck the pistol into my pants and throw him across the room. He slams into the thick bulletproof glass window at the registration counter. A loud crash echoes through the large open room. His mangled body is dangling there, suspended in the air as he hangs from the glass with his body partially through. Blood is spilling onto the floor from the shards of glass penetrating his skin as his body spasms.

The noise is sure to alert the others, so I sneak my way into the hallway to wait for them to come up the stairs.

Two men come running up only a few seconds later. They're also wearing police uniforms. I don't get a good view of their faces as they come through the door. I replace my goggles so I can hide in the shadows as they begin shining their flashlights around the main hall. One of the men walks over and picks up Nicholas's flashlight that's still by the front door. The second points his light right at Nicholas's body when he enters the room and I get a view of his face.

Pictures of more criminals start flashing in my head as the Nanites search for him. Only a fraction a second passes before the pictures stop on a Jose Ramirez. He's a 5'11 Hispanic man, with a teardrop tattoo and several other tattoos to signify the gang he's a part of. Jose had multiple run-ins with the law for burglary and gang affiliations. He has even faced charges for murder at one point, but they couldn't prove he did it so he was let go. My brain is operating like a computer.

I don't give Jose a chance to alert his companion. I move quickly, like a ghost in the darkness, as I slit Jose's throat with one of my katanas. His body collapses to the tile floor and the other man spins around at the noise.

The Nan-ites find the second file instantly. Another gang member with known ties to white supremacists. He has tattoos on his neck and all over his hands and arms. His name is Byron Freeze. His head isn't bald now, but I'm sure it was before the storm hit. Now his fading blonde hair is hanging down over his eyes and ears. It's filthy. Freeze's light shines on Jose's already lifeless body and he freezes. His name suits him. The smell of fear fills up the room instantly as I move closer to him. His pistol is drawn.

"Drop your weapon and I'll consider letting you live."

Freeze flashes his light towards me, but I don't move. He shines the light right into my eyes.

"You made a big mistake in coming here," he says as he raises the pistol.

"You're the one who made the mistake."

Freeze's arm drops to the ground with the pistol still grasped in his hand. I moved so quickly he didn't see the sword as it sliced his arm off clean. He looks down in shock as blood starts squirting onto the floor. He falls to his knees and I kneel down and place the tip of my blade against his throat.

"Now, how many more of the people downstairs are garbage like you?"

Freeze's face is turning white as the blood drains from his body. He's bleeding out quickly.

"Answer me!" I grab a fistful of his hair and pull him closer, carefully avoiding the large amounts of blood. I pull my goggles off, so he can look me in the eyes. Shock had already taken over before fear could come out of him. One look at my eyes though and the shock disappears. Freeze tries to push away as he looks away from me. The smell continues to spew from him, rapidly.

"Answer me, and I'll kill you quickly."

He never looks at me again. He keeps his eyes focused on something to his left, or maybe it's nothing at all. A muffled "four" comes out just before I ease the blade into his chest. I wipe the blade on his pants before walking over to the door leading downstairs.

The Nan-ites are picking up nineteen heartbeats downstairs and four of them are criminals, according to Freeze. I go down a flight of stairs and come out into a hallway. I've been in this part of the building before. Aside from the parking garage, there really isn't much to the lower levels, except for some small rooms. Some were probably used as briefing rooms and others for meetings. There's even a room for the building's computer servers.

The last room on the right houses the kennels. I'm not hearing any heartbeats from anything but people. I try to avoid any thoughts as to what might have happened to the K-9's.

The hallway has a plain tile floor and white walls. There isn't any need to make the lower levels look ornate like the upper ones. Down here, only officers and city employees would come. The last room on the left is where I originally heard the woman. I can see her attacker is still in the room with her.

I move down the hall silently, but quickly. Once I reach the door, I enter without waiting.

I turn the handle and the door squeaks as it opens. Inside, is a scrawny, white male. He doesn't have his shirt on. The Nan-ites pull up his file and I have all his information instantly. Dirk Kondri is by far the worst one in comparison to the other three I encountered tonight. He's known for assaulting over a dozen girls and even children over the course of twenty years. I have images and files of every known crime he's committed. He's a 36 year old immigrant from Romania. The file says that he was getting ready for a sentencing hearing, where he was finally going to be put away for life. He deserves worse, but since he never took a life, or at least hadn't been caught, he never received the death penalty. Crimes against women such as the one he just committed, are unforgivable, but the same crimes against children should be an automatic death sentence.

A death sentence that I'm about to give him.

Kondri freezes like a statue when I enter. His hair is long and shaggy and he has a full beard. I'm still holding my katana as I approach the female. The only thing she's wearing is a dirty blue sun dress, and she's face down on a table. She has small cuts all over her body. She isn't moving and her eyes are closed. Fortunately, I can still hear her breathing.

I only glance at her before returning my fiery gaze back to him. Kondri is still holding a knife and he's eyeing my katana like he's staring down a poisonous snake. He probably expects me to kill him quickly and be done with it. He's dead wrong. I slide the katana back into my bag on my back and pull out my knife. When I killed Jake, I thought I had enjoyed it. Only I killed him quickly. This will truly be the first time I take pleasure in killing a man. I want him to suffer and cry out for help like all his victims.

The first thing I do is casually walk up to him. He tries to slash the knife at me, but I knock it from his hand with a quick flick of my hand. I grab him by the hair and slowly slide my knife into his gut. Kondri cries out in pain as I twist the knife around as it's inside him. After I turn the blade once, I slowly put an upward pressure as I cut toward his rib cage. Kondri's screams are ear piercing. At first my ears hurt from the high-pitched shrieking. The Nan-ites recognize my pain and seem to lower the volume, but completely mute all sound.

"NO. I want to hear him suffer," I say aloud to them.

"Alec, stop," I hear the familiar female voice whisper.

I ignore her

The Nan-ites restore my hearing, but keep it low enough so that it doesn't hurt. Kondri starts to slump over, but I hold him up as I pull my knife out and then stick it into his leg, over and over again. I keep at it for a while. Eventually I lose track of how long. All I know is that Emily's voice retreats into a deep spot in my mind. I take my time in making this monster suffer, even long after he died. Now I know what kind of darkness is inside of me.

There isn't anything in the room for me to cover the woman up with. She's unconscious, but breathing. Once I finish with Kondri, I pull out a light wool blanket that I always pack with me, and place it over her body. Before I'm able to walk out of the room, the remaining three guys come in.

I was so busy with Kondri, I forgot about them.

I don't look up at them at first. Instead, I roll the woman over onto her side so that she's in a more comfortable position. I tuck her black hair that had fallen over her face, back behind her ears. She's pretty. Even underneath all the old and fresh bruises and cuts, I can tell. I gently move her hair to the side and reveal her oval shaped face and slightly elongated ears. Like most people nowadays, her skin has a fair tone to it from the lack of sunlight.

I glance up at the three men to see only one of them holding a gun. They all have shock and confusion on their faces as they look back and forth from me, to the crimson, butchered mess on the floor. All three of their files come up at the same time.

Hector Sanchez, Bud-Ryan Reschke, and Jeff Kleven. All three of them have non-violent pasts. In fact, the only reason any of them have criminal history is because all three of them had theft problems. Hector had just been booked on his third and final strike for retail theft. His most recent activity was at a Walmart. Bud-Ryan had a couple breaking and entering's in the Salt Lake area. He never had weapons on him when he broke into homes. He would just wait around for people to leave during the day and then he'd strike. He had only been caught so far on two occasions, but he was a suspect in a few dozen other cases. Jeff is the car thief. He had just been booked on his first joy ride in a stolen car. Neither one of these guys deserves to be butchered like the others. Unless they *had* taken part in violence like what was done to this woman here. By the looks in their eyes, I suspect they hadn't. They don't just seem frightened at the sight of me, but somehow relieved at the same time.

"This woman here," I say softly. "Do you guys join in on the party or just stay back and let it happen?"

Neither one of them speak up. They glance at each other as if they're waiting for the other to speak. My eyes are clearly visible in theirs, as they let off a light glow.

"Answer me!" I yell.

"Uh, no sir. We never did," answers Bud-Ryan. "I might have been a thief before, but I would never do this."

"But you'll stand by and watch!"

"They would've killed us if we tried to stop them," says Jeff.

"So you were half assed criminals, but even bigger cowards."

Bud-Ryan and Jeff lower their heads. Hector is still looking at me, as if he's offended by my comments and still has his gun pointed at me.

"Lower. Your. Weapon. Hector Sanchez," I snarl.

Hector's eyes widen when I call him by name. The other two give me quick, surprised looks as well, but return their attention to Hector.

"Dude, you saw what he did to those guys upstairs," says Jeff. "Put it down."

"Yeah man. Put it down," Bud-Ryan pleads.

Hector reluctantly lowers his weapon at Bud-Ryan's pleading. He tucks his pistol into the back of his pants and starts to relax. Bud-Ryan and Jeff relax as well and take deep breaths of relief.

"Is there somewhere more comfortable we can put her?" I say, looking down at the woman.

"Yeah," answers Bud-Ryan. "Down the hall, there's a couple cots."

"Show me."

I gently pick the woman up. I follow the three of them out as they lead me down the opposite end of the hall to the last room on the right. The woman is very light in my arms. If it weren't for the feeling of touching her, I wouldn't know I was carrying anything at all. My strength has increased that much even just in the past few hours. I seem to be getting stronger in every way by the minute. Too bad I didn't have this strength when I carried Emily several miles in the snow, or even when Brian and I carried Rider. It certainly would've come in handy then. We continue down the narrow straight hallway that's littered with all sorts of trash. There are office supplies, leftover wrappers from food and even ammo casings. I look up at the walls and see bullet holes. There was a shootout here. Once we reach the room, the three of them stop outside to let me go in first.

"After you," I say, looking at Hector.

He nods and goes in. Once inside the room, I quickly notice that the room has been modified from a meeting room, to a sleeping room. There are five cots set up, lined around the room in a circle. Five cots mean that two of these guys have to sleep on the floor or on something else. Or at least they did. I suspect that Bud-Ryan and Jeff are the ones that had to deal. I place the woman down on the first cot in the room. As I lay her gently onto the cot, her eyes jolt open and she flings her arm out at me as if to strike me. I don't try to stop her. I simply take a step back to see frightened, brown eyes looking up at me.

"It's alright, ma'am. You're safe now," I say as softly as possible.

Her discomfort seems to grow as she glances over at the three other men.

"Out. Now." I order them.

All three of them leave without saying a word. They even close the door behind them. The woman relaxes a little once they're gone, but she's still eyeing me with caution. She also still smells frightened.

"I'm not going to hurt you," I say as I slowly take my backpack off. "My name is Captain Alec Winter, of the United States Army. I'm sorry I didn't get here sooner, but nobody is going to hurt you again."

I pull out a bottle of water and offer it to her. She eyes the bottle nervously, then slowly reaches out her hand and takes it. She drinks the water quickly as if she hasn't had a drink in a while. I imagine their only way of getting fresh water is to grab snow. That isn't exactly a bad idea, but the water in my bag is filtered and likely tastes much better than melted snow.

"What's your name?"

"Shirley," she says with a raspy voice. "Did... you kill him?"

I nod my head. She doesn't need any more of an explanation. Besides, what am I going to say? I gut the man like a fish for what he did. The fact that he's dead is all that matters.

"I've killed four of the men here. Including those three out there in the hallway, that's seven. Are there any more of them?"

Shirley shakes her head. I can only imagine the suffering she's been going through over the past year and I don't want to.

"Anyone else still alive here are the officers or other city employees that worked in the building." Shirley is looking at the floor and she has my water bottle clenched between her hands. I gently place my right hand over hers and she flinches, but doesn't pull her hand away.

"Do you feel up to taking me downstairs to the other survivors?" I ask even though I don't need her to show me. The seven remaining people are each locked up in the holding cells. Probably starving and in terrible condition with how everyone here looks. Shirley certainly isn't in good shape. I wonder how long it's been since any of them had a decent meal around here. "It might help if they see a familiar face that they trust. I might frighten them."

"You don't frighten me," she replies. She's telling the truth. The smell of fear from her is gone. "What are you going to do with those other guys?"

"Were they involved in hurting you or anyone else here?" I ask.

Shirley looks away.

"No. I guess not."

"I can't justify hurting someone just because they were let out of their cells."

Shirley looks up at me.

"I agree. I'll show you where the others are."

I help Shirley off the cot before walking over to the door. When I open it, Bud-Ryan jumps to his feet, startled, and the other two jump from being startled as well. Hector isn't holding his gun. Shirley quickly grabs hold of my jacket, pulling herself in tight at the sight of them.

"Shirley, are you sure none of these men ever hurt you?"

She keeps her eyes on Hector for several seconds without answering. Fear quickly fills the hallway and Hector starts to sweat. His right hand is twitching and slowly moving towards the back of his pants.

"I can remove your hand, before you have time to blink, Hector. Don't be stupid."

257

"He's the one that broke free. He let that monster Dirk out, along with the others," she trembles.

"Really?" I say, as I place my hand on my knife. "Did he hurt you, or anyone else?"

I don't take my eyes from him. The light in the hallway is dim, but I have no trouble seeing the frightened look on his face, or the terror in his eyes. He knows that his life depends on Shirley's response and is likely waiting to find out if he will have to fight for his life.

"I told you none of..."

"Shut your mouth!" I interrupt Bud-Ryan. "I didn't ask you."

Hector's eyes go from me to Bud-Ryan for only an instant, before returning back to my gaze. He's right to be afraid of me. All Shirley has to do is say "yes" and I will kill him. I will do it in front of all of them too. That way Bud-Ryan and Jeff will know how serious I am.

Jake, as much as I hated him, was right about one thing. The world *is* different now. Different, because I will punish those who commit crimes that are done to Shirley, and crimes that were nearly committed against Emily. Finally, after everyone in the hallway waited to hear their fate, Shirley finally answers.

"No," she says, finally taking her eyes off him. "None of them did."

All three of the men instantly relax. Hector the most. He lets his hand fall to his side and the smell of fear in the room starts to dissipate.

"Alright then. Take me to the others," I say as I relax my hand as well. "You three can lead the way."

With that, Bud-Ryan, Jeff and Hector lead me and Shirley down the hall, where we start to make our way down to the bottom level. Shirley is still holding on to my jacket as if she'll never let go. Once we're on the bottom level, they walk me over to a door in the middle of the hallway that leads into a room with some holding cells. These holding cells were never meant to be for long term. Only for short periods of time, while prisoners waited for initial booking, or waiting for transport to more permanent homes.

"Hector, you first," I order him. He steps up to the door without hesitation and before he grabs the handle, I remove the gun he had tucked in his pants. He glances back at me, probably wondering if I intend to use it on him. "I think you've lost your firearm privileges for a while."

He glances at the 40-caliber pistol only once, before returning his attention to the door. He opens it and we all follow him in. Shirley shows no patience as she releases her death grip on my arm and quickly runs over to the first cell in the room. Each cell is a private individual room and has a heavy steel door with a small window. Shirley looks frightened as she tries to look inside, while smacking the glass on the small window to get the person's attention.

"Where is the key to open them?" I ask without directing the question at one particular person.

Bud-Ryan quickly moves over to the wall, next to the door and grabs a set of keys that are hanging up on a hook. He doesn't wait for me to tell him what to do next. He walks straight for the cell Shirley is at and unlocks the door. Shirley can barely wait to get inside and disappears in the cell.

"Unlock the rest of them, and then wait outside," I say to Bud-Ryan. He nods and quickly moves on to the next cell.

"Shirley?" cries out a man's voice. "Are you alright?"

"Jay," responds Shirley. "We're saved," she says as she starts to cry.

"What do you mean, we're saved?"

"Come."

A few seconds later, Shirley leads out a man that looks like he's been beaten for a very long time with the mix of old and new bruises. His brown hair is filthy, matted together and grown out, falling into his bruised face. All he's wearing is a white t-shirt and underwear and appears to be starving. His skin is pale and his cheek bones are visible. The t-shirt looks like it's a couple sizes too big for him. One glance at Bud-Ryan and rage quickly comes across the beaten man's face.

"No," I say to Jay calmly, as I step up and gently place my hand on his shoulder.

"Who are you to stop me?" he says trying to swat my hand away and looking at me with sharp eyes.

"The same man who just rescued you from this hell," I say just as calmly.

"This is my station. Nobody gives me orders here, Stranger."

"It belonged to Dirk Kondri less than thirty minutes ago, Sgt. Olsen."

"Do we know each other, Stranger?"

"No, we don't. Now why don't you lower your voice?"

Sgt. Olsen takes a step towards me and gives me a shove. Or at least, he tries.

He's a decently sized guy. Six feet tall, but only weighs approximately 150 pounds. His shove would've moved most men, even in his condition. Not me. Sgt. Olsen is shocked and looks ready to fight.

"Who are you, Stranger?" he says angrily as he steps back and takes a defensive stance.

"My name is Captain Alec Winter and I'm starting to think you belong in that cell," I say coldly.

Bud-Ryan finishes unlocking all the cells and nods to me as he walks out of the room. Sgt. Olsen gives him a vengeful stare as he walks by. The other six people start coming out of their cells at the same moment Bud-Ryan leaves the room. None of them are in any better shape than Sgt. Olsen.

"You're all free now. Those men won't be hurting any of you again," I say loudly for all of them to hear.

Most of them have confused looks on their faces. A few of them look frightened when they see my eyes. I don't blame them. Everybody has that look on their face when seeing me for the first time.

"Olsen, this man freed us. We owe him our thanks," says a much shorter man than Olsen. His hair is also dark brown, but with patches of grey. He looks like he's in his late forties or even fifties.

"Look at him, Captain. Look at his eyes."

"I can see them fine, Olsen," says the Captain as he walks up to me. He still has on decent clothes. A pair of raggedy, grey, dress pants and a dirty, white polo shirt. He also has bruises and cuts on his face and long hair hanging down over his almost black eyes. Everyone else has similar wounds on their faces.

"Thank you, Captain," he says as he reaches out his hand and I take it. "My name is Brandon Silber. We are in your debt. All of us," he says while looking over at Olsen.

"None of you owe me anything."

"Yes we do, I'm afraid. Kondri and those other three have been... well I suspect you already know what they were up to." He gives Shirley a painful glance. "We all owe you our lives."

"I'm grateful for your appreciation, but I don't require anything of you. I was only passing by when I hear...when I decided to check in here for any survivors."

Captain Silber gives me a sideways look when I change what I was going to say. He doesn't think about it long though, and just continues on.

"Where are you coming from, Captain?"

"Layton, Sir. I just came up here hoping to find my… hoping to find my sister." Images of her lying dead in the snow come into my mind and I try to force them away.

"It seems we all lost someone in this storm," Silber says as he gives me a pat on the arm. "I suspect you will be moving on, then?"

"I'm afraid so. I have some things in Layton that I need to tend to. The rest of my family is still there," I say while looking over at Shirley. She's helping one of the other women in the group. The woman is likely in her late 50 or 60's and has grey raggedy hair that's down to her shoulders.

"Really? Are you guys holding up in a station as well?"

I look back at Captain Silber.

"No, actually. There's a Top Secret government building up on the east bench. It's a large facility, and self-sustaining. We have running water—hot running water, food, and good medical facilities."

Captain Silber raises an eyebrow and before he's able to respond Olsen does.

"Layton? Do you really expect us to believe you came all the way here from Layton?" questions Olsen accusingly. "And this facility you speak of, I've never heard of it."

"You've never heard about it because it's *Top Secret*. Plus, I don't really expect you to believe anything, Sargent. Just know that it's true."

"I believe you," says the Captain. "I don't think a man with eyes like yours would have any reason to lie."

Captain Silber looks around at the others. There are seven of them in total. Three women, counting Shirley, and two other men. I suspect they were all officers or at least employees of the station. Maybe some are spouses. All of them look like they're on the brink of starving to death and I can't just leave them here to die. I can bring them back some food to last them at least a week. Long enough for me to handle the situation back home. At least I hope it will be handled by then.

"You all look very hungry. Before I go, I'll hunt and bring back enough food to last you until I can come back. Do you have somewhere that you can prepare it?" I say addressing Captain Silber.

"We do. Surprisingly, the gas is still on, and that turbine out back generates enough electricity for us to have some power," replies Captain Silber. "Why? What do you have in mind?"

"Any of you opposed to deer?" I ask. This time I look at all of them.

I don't get any opposition on the food choice, except for a few snide remarks from Olsen. I do my best to ignore him and ask Captain Silber if he has any rifles in the building for me to use. I don't want to experience a hunt like the one earlier. He says they do have some and takes me to their armory. Bud-Ryan and the other two aren't in the hall when we come out.

"Did you kill Kondri?" the Captain asks as we walk.

"Yes."

"What about the others?"

"Freeze, Ramirez, and Sandoval are dead too. I kinda made a bit of a mess near your main entrance, as well as a meeting room on the floor above us."

"I see," he replies as he furrows his brow. I can sense a displeasure in his voice and his posture now looks tense. "I guess things are different now, aren't they?"

"There are good people and then there are people like Kondri. It's hard enough for people to survive in this world now. Would you rather be always looking behind you, wondering if the monsters like him are going to attack? Feed them, trust them, and then one day end up in a cell? Or worse, not wake up at all?" I don't wait for an answer.

"I don't think you and the rest of your people want to go through that again. Killing Kondri might be a question mark for you, but for me it was an easy choice. I walked in on him after he had just finished doing monstrous things to Shirley. I could hear her screams… hear her *pleading* for him to stop and he only enjoyed it the more she fought him. If I had let him live, you would have been stuck with the hard choices of locking him up, and giving him food you all would have needed to survive, or letting him starve or simply executing him altogether. Now all you need to worry about is keeping everyone in here who deserves saving–alive." After saying all that to him, I begin to think about everyone back at the facility, the mall and Bobby and Kyle. There are likely more out there that are struggling to survive and I need to find them.

We're at the armory door now. Captain Silber puts his hand up to stop me from walking in.

"I'm grateful for you freeing us from the atrocities they were committing… and I'm not even judging you for killing them. But when I look at you, I don't see an executioner. I see a man who always looks to do the right thing. No matter what the situation might ask for. I don't think you joined the military so that you could kill people. I think you joined so you could make a difference in this world. So that you could help people that are in need. I think you've seen some awful things happen since the storm began and maybe even lost people you care about. Like your sister. Just because the world is changing, doesn't mean you have to change who you are along with it."

He lowers his arm and lets me pass without saying another word.

I walk into the armory and go straight for the rifles that are locked behind a fence with a gate. The fencing goes from the floor to the ceiling. The rest of the room has some standard looking lockers on one wall and an armorer's table on another. I look at the Captain and all he does is shrug his shoulders.

"The lock doesn't work," he says. "Something to do with losing the main power in here. I'm afra…"

I step up and rip the fencing off the door like it's nothing. I don't see the look on Captain Silber's face, but I'm assuming it's astonishment at the sheer ease at which I removed the fence. I set the fencing down against the wall and walk back over and grab an AR15 with a holographic sight. After I have the rifle, I grab a box of ammo from the cabinet next to all the weapons and load only a few rounds. When I turn around, Olsen and Shirley are in the room. They're both looking at the chain link fencing to their right. Captain Silber has a satisfied look on his face.

"Can we open up one of the garage doors?" I ask.

"Sure. Right this way," responds the Captain. "Olsen, go find some clothes. You look ridiculous," he finishes as we leave him and Shirley standing there looking confused.

I think about what the Captain said to me as we make our way into the parking garage. I know my actions may seem harsh, but it's not like I'm going around looking to find people to kill. The men at the mall were trying to kill me and hurt Emily and the men here were basically doing the same. I put his words to the back of my mind and try not to think about them again. The station's garage is very large and open. In the center of the garage you have the different office spaces and rooms like the armory and kennels. Otherwise, you can see from one end of the garage to the other with only a few concrete beams in between. They designed it this way, so that the department could set up different types of vehicle courses for training purposes. The Captain is leading me to the southeast exit. We have to walk up a slight incline to get to the large, steel garage doors, intended to prevent anyone from getting in from the outside.

"Do you have enough power to open them automatically?" I ask as we approach the exit.

"Maybe, but it will take a lot of power to get them open. These doors are extremely heavy."

"It won't be a problem. I can lift it myself," I say with a nod. Captain Silber shrugs his shoulders.

I walk up and examine the mechanism that operates the heavy door. Releasing a garage door so that you can open it manually is simple. All you have to do is pull on the cord that is attached to the main unit. These types of doors are a different matter. I can easily force it open, but I don't want to damage it in any way. This door is not only keeping the cold out, but also making the building more secure from unwanted guests. The door is fixed to a chain, similar to the one on a house garage, only much bigger and stronger. The concept appears to be the same, however. There are two motors, one on each side of the door, with a lever that releases the tension on the door. I pull both of them, and then have to also pull the heavy pins that are locking the doors in place.

"You don't honestly think you can lift that do you?" the Captain asks as I bend down to grab the door.

There isn't any space for my fingers to fit, so I have to wedge my knife into the bottom in order to create enough space for them. Once the door is up enough, I slide my left hand under the door and lift. There's a little resistance at first, but with a little force, the door lifts up to let the ice-cold air blow in. I turn and look at the Captain and find him looking back at me, wide eyed with his mouth hanging open for the first time since he was free from his cell. I turn back to look at the doorway and there is a perfect wall of snow, three quarters of the way up the door. The snow isn't really that deep, but the door is the perfect place for the snow to drift into as the storm rages on. I turn around one more time and face the Captain.

"Wait here for me. I won't be gone for more than fifteen minutes."

"Whatever you say, Captain," he says with a nod.

I turn back around, grab the rifle that I leaned against the wall and launch myself off into the shadows, landing in fresh powder just outside the door. I don't move right away, but focus on listening to my surroundings. I don't want to waste time running around the city, or outside the city for that matter, trying to find them food. I need to get home fast. I concentrate on focusing my sense of smell and my hearing and try to reach them out, like extended hands, feeling around for food. Nothing. This could take longer than I thought.

I run north to the edge of the city, up on the bench where the Capitol is located. I stop on what would be the front lawn of the Capitol and look up at the 100 hundred plus year old marble structure. It's breathtaking to see such a pivotal part of Utah's history, so still and so empty. The capitol building was built between 1912 and 1916. It was completed twenty years after Utah earned its statehood.

I focus my senses again, hoping to catch the smallest hint of animal life, only to be disappointed. The wind is too strong and blowing back and forth in all directions, so it's next to impossible. I'm becoming agitated as I stand there like a corpse in the snow. If the Nan-ites my father put inside me can't do something as simple as find some deer for me with all their so-called capabilities, then how can they do everything else so far?

Suddenly, something happens and throws me off guard. As if the Nan-ites are listening to me yet again, red indicators begin popping up in my field of vision as if I was seeing enemies in a video game. The blue indicators tell me there are deer directly east of where I'm standing, up wind. They're down in Memory Grove Park. I start to make my way down there, when a feeling makes me look north, towards Layton. There are more blue indicators, between me and Layton, scattered in groups along the way. There are two green indicators right where the compound is located. There's also a red indicator just a little northwest, beyond the facility. Something about the red makes me feel uneasy, and alarms suddenly go off in my head. Even though the alarms are in my head, I try covering my ears anyway. They're loud and sound like a fire alarm. I ask for them to stop and they do instantly.

Quickly, I run down the hill into Memory Grove Park where the deer are. They're bundled up near an old stable where horses were kept, laying in the snow. They can't see or hear me, so this is going to be an unfair hunt. I begin feeling sick, as I had before when I used my sword on that last buck, since this kill will be equally unfair. They're just sitting there, most likely starving and not expecting anything to be out hunting them. I point my rifle at the largest one and fire. The buck goes limp instantly from my kill shot, the rest panic and start to scatter. I have another one in my sights though, before any of them are on their feet I take that one down as well. I waste no time and sprint over to where both my kills rest on powdery, soft snow. I strap the rifle to my chest and grab each deer with one hand. The entire time I'm dragging them back to the station, I'm constantly aware of the red indicator, still moving, slowly towards the facility. The two green indicators are still outside the compound. I know who they both are.

I drag both deer up to the garage and slide down the wall of snow. The Captain is still waiting for me, along with a few others. Olsen, who is now wearing better clothes, and Shirley are among them. They all have looks of surprise and excitement on their faces. Olsen is glaring at me.

"You really are something special, Captain Winter," speaks Captain Silber.

"And a hero," adds Shirley smiling.

I nod my head to them all. I wish there was more I could do for them, but I don't know what else I can do, even if I had more time.

They all look so tired and worn. Unlike everyone at the facility, these people truly have had to fight to stay alive. Me and everyone else at the compound have been blessed to have such a place to call home during this nightmare. Now though, these people are the ones that are fortunate. They're at least miles away from another storm that is coming. A storm that's on its way to my family.

"I'm sorry. This is all I can do for you right now. I have to go," I say anxiously as I give each of them a nod.

"You've done more than enough, Captain. Just remember what I told you," he says, returning the nod.

"Lock this door," I say, avoiding his comment. "There are things out here that you don't want coming inside."

"Thank you," says the Captain.

CHAPTER 15

I'm almost two blocks down the snow covered street before I hear them pull the door closed. I need to get back to the compound as fast as possible. I run hard and push myself beyond what I think I'm capable of. Back in Salt Lake, when I was trying to reach the hospital, I pushed myself to the point that my muscles ached and felt like they were even tearing. Now, I'm running like I'm fighting the storm, only my legs feel like they can go farther and harder than before. And the storm is fighting back making it harder.

I wonder if somehow the Nan-ites are learning from everything that I experience and feel. It's as if they're adapting to my weaknesses and correcting them. It took me just over a half hour to reach Salt Lake. I'll be back to the compound in twenty minutes. The red indicator is still moving towards the compound, getting closer every minute, but taking its time. The Nan-ites calculate that the red indicator will arrive only seconds after me. The two green indicators are still there as well. After only 22 minutes of charging through the snow since leaving the station, I start coming up on the facility. I'm already on the east side of highway 89 and about to pass the sink hole. I can also just barely make out the two shapes moving near the opening of the cave, leading to the entrance to the facility. One of the shapes is much smaller than the other.

It's Brian and Mya.

"I told you to stay inside, Brian," I mutter to myself, as I sprint towards them.

The valley in front of the compound is quiet. There isn't a single animal in sight and the family of deer I had seen earlier in the day are long gone by now. Just as I approach the ledge next to the cave, I see a dark, bulky figure coming out of the clearing of trees on the north end, about 200 yards away. The figure is walking at a casual pace. I shout before Mya has time to even growl or bark at me.

"Brian, get back inside now!"

Brian turns towards me, with an alarmed look on his face. I move past him, getting in between him and the danger. The Nan-ites are still sounding the alarm, but I've been able to keep the alert confined to the top right corner of my vision and only a small red flashing dot. Mya quickly becomes overly excited as she realizes I've just arrived. She quickly runs to me and starts jumping on me, oblivious to what is coming. I kneel down and pull her close, so that Brian can get a hold of her to take her inside. I never take my eyes off of the figure moving towards us and I put my goggles on to conceal my true self.

"Let's go, Mya," says Brian, now aware of the danger, even if he can't see it.

He grabs Mya's collar and begins to pull her towards the door. She wines and fights back, confused why she can't stay with me. I stare into the distance while the figure I thought was Rider begins to move towards us. As he comes closer, I realize it isn't Rider at all.

It's someone else. Or something else.

This creature is much smaller than Rider and has a much darker shade of red to its skin. The closer it gets, I can see that it has a scar on its left cheek. I find this unusual because the Lurks as well as myself aren't supposed to have scars of any kind. It only makes

271

sense that Rider and whoever else is mutated by the serum wouldn't be any different. Now that the creature is closer to the compound, Mya notices that something is coming towards her and starts to growl. Brian gave up on fighting her and is now pounding on the door, trying to get someone's attention.

"Nobody's coming, Brian. Get ready to fight," I say anxiously.

"Shit!" Brian curses as he comes out of the cave with his M4 ready.

Mya is by my side as Brian walks up and joins us, and we all wait for our enemy to arrive. The creature is now coming over the snowbank, only thirty feet away from where we are standing. Mya starts barking ferociously.

"Isn't Rider like eight feet tall? He's shorter than me," mutters Brian.

"He is. This isn't Rider," I respond. "That's far enough!"

The short version of Rider stops fifteen feet away. He has a devilish grin on his face as he stands there in the shadows staring back. His bright yellow eyes glow in the darkness and remind me of the first time I saw similar yellow eyes, looking up at me from the sink hole. The creature's appearance is eerily similar to Riders in many ways. Aside from its height and color, this creature is structurally identical. His arms are long with sharp jagged claws on his hands that look as though they could tear through a car door. His legs are big and muscular like a world class bodybuilder. Or maybe a powerful animal. The mutation turned this person, or soldier, into the perfect killing machine. Brian and I both look at our enemy, marveling its physique, when suddenly it speaks.

"Are you Alec?" he asks in a deep, growling voice. He's standing in an aggressive stance and seems as though he's deliberately trying to show off his claws.

"What do you want?"

"I came to see who was responsible for killing my friends," he says sharply, with his eyes focused on me.

"Were you at the mall?" I ask.

"I was," he says through clenched teeth.

"Well, now you've seen him, so I suggest you leave," I say as I nod my head in the direction he came.

"You're not in a position to be shouting orders, Alec."

I watch as the soldier stands there, poised with arrogance. The stout, ugly creature is wearing what is left of his military pants and jacket. The pants appear to be stretched to their maximum, like a pair of spandex. The jacket is unbuttoned with the sleeves torn off. It's clear that his service in the military is important to him or else he wouldn't have gone through the trouble to keep it on when it no longer fits. His rank is still visible.

"You Army, Private?"

"Yeah. Why does that matter?"

"I'm Army… We both are," I respond while glancing at Brian. "Have you forgotten what the Army stands for? We're supposed to serve and protect this nation. Not make it worse."

My last statement seems to light a fire inside the soldier. He starts breathing heavily and paces back and forth, while keeping his eyes on me.

"This is a new world. The United States of America doesn't exist anymore. The strong survive and the weak do what the strong want." The soldier stops pacing and looks down at Mya.

"Things didn't go so well for the last person that said that to me," I say calmly.

"You better shut her up," he says, ignoring me as he takes a step forward. His eyes are still on Mya.

"Easy man," I say while putting one hand up for the soldier and lowering another for Mya. Mya stops barking after I put my hand out, but continues after only a few seconds. "Look... we don't want any trouble. Tell us Rider's business and be on your way."

The soldier smirks and takes a step back, relaxing his posture.

"Rider didn't send me here," he chuckles.

"Then why the hell are you here?" shouts Brian.

Mya's bark becomes more intense and she starts to move towards the soldier.

"Mya, no!"

I step in front of her at the exact moment the soldier lunges forward. The impact from the soldier crashing into me, sends me tumbling through the snow past Brian. I hear a loud yelp and time slows almost to a stop. I roll to my feet to see Mya flying through the air and slamming into the wall with incredible force almost immediately going limp.

"NO!"

Brian pulls his trigger and a flash erupts from the barrel of his gun as the soldier charges him. I watch as the bullet barely misses the soldiers face and he knocks the rifle out of Brian's hands. The soldier grabs him by the throat and lifts him off the ground. I dash to Brian's aid with a sword already drawn. I'm so fast that the soldier doesn't see me move or the flick of my wrist. The soldier laughs as Brian dangles from the air, but Brian quickly drops to the ground with the hand still grasping his throat.

"Aghh!" the soldier yells, as his blood stains the white snow. "How... that's impossible!" he shrieks in confusion as blood continues spraying from his bloody stump.

It seems Rider didn't have time to tell his men that I've changed too. I remove my goggles and reveal my eyes to the defeated soldier. My glowing blue eyes reflect off of the snow and encompasses the bright yellow in his eyes. The soldier looks at me in horror, as he collapses to his knees, when he realizes he underestimated his opponent.

"What are you?" he chokes.

I raise my katana as I step closer to him.

"Your executioner," I say through clenched teeth. I bring my sword down with lightning quick speed, severing the soldier's head from his body. I move to Mya's side before the head hits the ground.

She isn't moving, except for a slight up and down motion of the chest as she struggles for breath.

"Easy girl." A quiet whimper barely escapes.

Brian struggles to his feet and moves to my right side.

"She looks pretty bad man. We need to get her inside quickly."

Brian notices the trickle of blood that is starting to form underneath her. The same trickle of blood that I'm trying to ignore. He runs back into the cave and starts banging on the door. The sound of his fist hitting steel almost seems like a whisper to me as I watch Mya suffer. The faint sound of her beating heart begins to drown out everything around me as it echoes through my head. I know I need to get her inside quickly, or she'll bleed out. All I can do is try and soothe her by massaging the fur around her neck and ears. Suddenly, the sound of a familiar, soft, worried voice pulls me out of my trance.

"Oh no, Mya," Emily says when she sees the blood-soaked snow.

I give her a worried glance, as I reach down and gently place my arms underneath Mya. I slowly lift her off the ground, trying to avoid causing her too much pain as she whimpers from discomfort. I carry her into the compound with Emily at my side.

"Brian, get dad," I say loudly as I cross the main hall towards the stairwell. Brian starts to run toward my parents apartment. Emily pushes the door open and I gently, but quickly descend the dark staircase. Once at the bottom, Emily opens the door to the lower level. We move into the open room and continue our way to the

Nano-Gen Research lab. Emily opens the last door and I walk over and gently lay her down onto a table. Blood is all over my clothes, as well as on my arms and hands.

"Emily, grab me some towels." I point to a cabinet behind her.

She runs over to the cabinet and returns with a handful of towels in only a few seconds. I grab one and press it onto the gash in Mya's side that she received from the soldier's long claw. Emily sets the rest of the towels down on the edge of the table and moves over to comfort Mya. She places her hand on Mya's head and gently rubs her fur while talking to her by calmly saying her name and trying to tell her everything is okay. Finally, after only a couple dreadful minutes, my father comes in with my mom and Brian. I turn my head the moment the doors open. I can tell by the looks in their eyes how bad the situation appears. My mom puts a hand to her mouth the moment she sees Mya.

"Dad, she's dying. What do I do?" I say in a pleading voice trying not to break down.

My father places his hand on Mya's stomach to check her breathing.

"Brian, grab me the stethoscope over on that table," he orders, while pointing to a table next to the cabinet with the towels.

Brian moves over to the table quickly and rummages through a couple drawers before returning with the stethoscope. My father takes it from him and quickly starts checking Mya's breathing. He moves it around in a couple different places until he finds a spot he's satisfied with and holds it there for about ten seconds. I also listen to the *thump, thump* Mya's heart is struggling to make.

"Alec, I'm afraid there's nothing I can do," he says in a sorrowful tone. "She's lost too much blood, and the impact of hitting the wall caused a lot of internal damage," he says regretfully with a slight shake of his head. "Her heart is already too weak."

"Can't you stitch her up, or something, to at least stop the bleeding?"

My mother starts to cry and even Brian has tears begin to slide down his cheek.

"She's already lost too much, son."

The knot in my stomach tightens as I look around the room desperately as if I'll see something that might help. "Wh-what about the serum? The serum can save her right?"

My father shakes his head.

"We don't have anymore. I only had enough for you."

"But if we had some. Would it work?" I say more seriously.

"The serum was never tested for dogs, Alec."

"Would. It. Work?"

"I don't know," he says, folding his arms in defeat. "We don't have anymore, so it doesn't matter."

I pull my nine inch knife from its sheath.

"Alec, what are you doing?" Emily asks with concern in her voice.

"Giving Mya some serum."

"Alec, do…" My mother starts to say.

I slice open my hand, allowing my blood, which is flowing with the serum and the Nan-ites, to pour freely. I can see Brian begin to pace back and forth and his breathing, along with everyone else accelerates. I know I have to be quick, because my accelerated healing will close the wound fast. I remove the towel and hold my hand over Mya's wound, so my blood can mix into hers. I use my other hand to squeeze it, to try and help the blood flow out faster, but the cut on my hand starts healing after only a few seconds and the blood flow stops. I make several more deep cuts into my hand all the way up my arm to create as much blood flow as possible. I grimace from the pain while biting down hard, as each slice sends a shock through my entire body making me tremble. I try to fight back any signs that I'm in pain.

"Al…" Emily starts to say as she reaches her hand up to stop me.

"It's going to work. It has to!" I say to her with pleading eyes.

She pulls her hand back.

Blood continues to gush from my body as I continue cutting deep slices into my arm for several minutes, each time having to cut different spots because the spots that had already been cut heal quicker than spots that hadn't. I keep this up until I no longer even notice the pain. Everyone watches in horror as I butcher my own arm, over and over again, like a psychopath in a mental hospital.

"Alec, that's enough son!" shouts my mom.

I ignore her and keep cutting to ensure the blood continues to flow. I start to get dizzy from the loss of blood and stagger. Emily quickly places her hands on my side and stabilizes me.

"Stop, Alec!" my mom yells again.

I glance over at her and tears are streaming down her face. I look over at Brian and see the pain in his eyes as he shakes his head. Finally, after ten agonizing minutes of watching, Emily places her hand on mine to stop me.

"You need to stop, baby," she says softly. Her eyes are swollen with tears sliding down her cheeks.

I reluctantly allow her to take the knife from me and she sets it on the table. I then place my hand on Mya's neck, just below her jaw, where her fur is the softest and begin to massage her gently. The memory of when I held her for the first time as a puppy flashes into my mind and I'm no longer in the room.

I'm sitting at my computer in my bedroom in my house. I just found a post online about a litter of husky puppies for sale. I'd been looking for months trying to find the one I wanted to take home.

With a quick flash I'm in a small house in Cache Valley, where I held her for the first time when she was only three weeks old. I decide she's the one I want to take home the moment I cradle her in my arms.

A flicker and now I'm home again—here in Layton—and she's a few weeks older and so on as every memory I have with her plays back like a blur, reminding me of every wonderful moment I shared with her.

I continue massaging her neck, like I always have and she opens her bright, blue eyes to look at me. I lean in close to her and she licks me across the face.

"Good girl," I say softly, as I press my forehead against hers.

Emily rests her hand on my shoulder as she begins to cry. All I can do is listen as the beat of Mya's heart becomes fainter, and fainter, as her life slowly ebbs away and she closes her eyes for the last time. When I no longer hear her heart anymore, I, who has been so strong and poised during my entire adult life and never shown any sign of emotional weakness ever, begin to cry uncontrollably as I let out not only tears for Mya, but also for Ashlee. Ashlee had been there with me when I got Mya and Mya was my only real connection left to her. Now, I've lost them both and the shock of it all is too much for me to bear.

CHAPTER 16

I sit on a chair, motionless, with my head resting in my hands for quite a while. My father, my mom, Brian and Emily aren't moving or saying anything. They sit there silent with me, also feeling the loss of someone close to them. Mya had been a part of our family for seven years. Even my father, who almost never showed emotions towards anyone was attached to her. When I first brought her home, he was kind of put out by it, but after my first tour away from her, he grew attached to her and he would sometimes even take her with him to work. Everyone loved her.

"This is all my fault," I finally say aloud.

"Alec..." Emily starts to say.

"If I hadn't been so concerned about my own selfish needs, the false hope of finding Ashlee, I never would've gone to Salt Lake. I never would've wasted time helping others when my family needed protecting too. I let someone like Joe force me out. I was weak. And Mya paid for my weakness."

"You go too far, Son," my father replies, with a disappointed look on his face. "This is *my* fault, I'm afraid."

I look over at him without responding. Hearing him admit his mistakes catches me off guard. After holding his gaze for a few seconds, I get out of my chair and somberly walk over to the cabinet, where Emily had grabbed the towels. I return holding a sheet and drape it over Mya's lifeless body and then place my left hand on her one last time. Finally, the tears that had poured down my face had stopped. I pull my hand off of her and walk over to my chair. I lean down and put my weight on the chair and close my eyes for a moment as I try to regain my composure. I stay like this, breathing in and out for a couple minutes before I can't take it anymore. I open my eyes and take hold of the chair and heave it into the wall with enough force that the chair explodes with metal and plastic ricocheting in every direction.

"Nobody is to touch her," I say with a mixture of anger and heartache.

I start walking towards the door and Emily reaches out and gently grabs my hand. I stop long enough to pull her from her seat and we walk out of the lab together. The others follow behind us. When we walk through the door into the main hall, there's a loud commotion coming from a very large gathering of people. Everyone in the compound seems to be here, due to the lack of space between bodies. Joe is in the middle of it all, shouting out his hate towards me as usual.

"Alec and that stupid dog of his, have brought nothing but trouble to this compound since they brought back those two men! If it weren't for them, no one would be dead and there wouldn't be any freaks running around," he says with hatred in his voice. "Speak of the devil. Here he comes now!"

The four of us walk right into the middle of the room, but I keep walking past Joe, straight to the exit. Apparently in the chaos, nobody had decided to lock the front door to the compound. It's cracked open. I open the door, letting all the cold air into the main hall and everyone cowers from the freezing temperatures. I hear several gasps as I disappear into the dark, cold outdoors for only a few seconds, before returning, dragging the soldiers' body in one hand and holding the severed bloody head in the other. I kick the heavy door closed, as if it were lighter than paper and a loud bang echoes in the room. I toss the corpse and head onto the floor in front of Joe. He jumps back as if avoiding a striking rattlesnake. More gasps come quickly, along with a few shrieks and screams.

"I'm not the one you need to be afraid of! I know I look different now, but I'm still the same person that went looking for your family and spent every second of every day in the freezing cold, either searching or waiting for more people!"

The room falls silent at my shouting. Even Joe stays silent as he gazes down at the mutated, dead body.

"This was not the only one out there! There could be a small army of these coming this way at any time! If one came here to attack us, then the rest will be coming as well. They are coming here to take our home away from us, and they will kill anyone who gets in their way!"

"How can you know this for sure," says Joe.

I start to answer, but Brian does first.

"It's basic military strategy. Rider and Jake came here alone with a bogus story to gather intel. They learned about our schedule and how the facility operates and tried to gain our trust. And then when we were distracted, they snuck in and grabbed Emily."

I give Brian an approving nod and he returns the gesture just as the room explodes into a panic. The commotion becomes so loud that even I have a hard time telling who is saying what. I look over and see my father speaking with other members of the council and focus my hearing to figure out what they're saying. I try to concentrate and block out all of the noise, but can't pick up more than a few words from each of them. After they speak for about a minute, they nod to each other and then Mr. Wilkinson shouts for everyone to calm down.

"Everyone, calm down! Please, everyone calm down!" Mr. Wilkinson uses his hands to gesture for them to quiet down.

The crowd noise begins to dissipate as they all realize he's yelling. The room once again falls to a silence. The room is so quiet that I can hear the heartbeat of every individual in the room. I listen to the sound of the beating hearts, as each one makes its own rhythm, for only a couple seconds before Mr. Wilkinson interrupts the silence.

"Now—I know with everything that has happened today, and in the days prior, that you all have questions, but unfortunately I cannot answer them for you," he says, slightly shaking his head as he glances at my father.

"Well, who can!?" shouts someone from the crowd as the commotion starts up again. "Yeah, we want to know what's going on, and why Alec's eyes look like a tiger's and glow like a damn neon light!" The bickering and complaining go back and forth as they wait for Mr. Wilkinson's response.

"I'll handle it from here, Michael," says my father as he steps forward. He turns to everyone and addresses the crowd. "There are some things that have been kept from you, because some things are better left unsaid. However, due to the recent events, I feel that you deserve to know the truth." He pauses for a moment as he searches for the right way to tell everyone he's to blame for their situation. "Michael and I are research scientists for the United States government and I've been coming to this compound for over a decade now, helping to develop a means of making soldiers better. Our employment here is the only reason we were all able to use this place as a shelter from the storm."

"Tell them why I look different and why *this* body looks the way it does," I interject.

"I...figured out a way, using genetics research and Nanotechnology, to make the human body faster, stronger, invulnerable to temperature, and many other unknown possibilities.

Unfortunately, my first test subjects didn't react to the serum the way I had hoped."

"Did they die?" asks another random person in the back of the room, near the south hall.

"No," my father says, shaking his head. "The serum was actually a success, as far as making all of those things I mentioned happen." Now his expression turns to disappointment and I can see sorrow behind his eyes. "But their physical appearance changed. Now their skin has a black, silky, polished shine to it, and scales like a snake or even a lizard. Their skin acts like an armor and protects them from anything, like the weather or even a physical attack. Now they no longer look human, so they stay away from the compound in order to avoid causing alarm or panic."

"Then what is that? It doesn't look anything like what you described. It's not even black. And you still haven't explained why your son looks like a freak," shouts Joe.

"To start with the freak," I snap as I jump in, no longer able to tolerate Joe's hatred. "I was going to die from gunshot wounds I suffered while rescuing Emily from Jake and the rest of the psychos at the mall. My father injected me with the serum because he knew it was my only chance of survival. The fact that I'm standing here is proof that it worked. My body didn't react to the serum like the others did. My eyes are the only visible difference. As for this guy here," I point to the decapitated body, "I'm pretty sure Rider went back to the mall and turned all his men."

"And how would he be able to do that?" replies Joe with a cold expression.

"That giant red creature that killed the man in the cafeteria was Rider. He's the way he is now because one of my father's *experiment's* tried to kill him. As a result, he was infected with the serum and it mutated his body. Now all of his men will look like this, and they will be coming here," I finish as Joe stares at me with a perplexed expression on his face.

During the explanation of events, Emily had made her way through the crowd to stand at my side. She cringes at the site of the mutilated body in front of her and uses my body to shield herself from having to continue looking at it. I notice her discomfort and put my arm around her. We stand there together, listening to my father and Joe go back and forth with their own opinions on the situation. The two men begin arguing after only a couple of minutes and then eventually, they're just full-blown yelling at each other. Joe takes shots at me, essentially blaming me for everything, but even stoops as low as bringing Emily into the discussion as well. My father shouts back, accusing Joe of being a coward for even mentioning Emily.

"Alec is none of those things, mister!" shouts the little boy Jesse, the one I had found in the freezer. "You don't know what you're talking about!"

Jesse is standing opposite of Emily and me on the other side of my father and Joe. I hadn't even noticed him squeeze his way past everyone to see what was going on. The room is quiet, including my father and Joe, as they all stare at the small boy. Jesse's mother runs up to him, in shock at what her son had just said.

"Jesse, that's enough! He didn't mean that," she says, apologizing to Joe.

"Yeah, I did! He's a stupid jerk!"

"Jesse!" snaps his mother while pulling on his arm. "I'm sorry, sir," she apologizes again as she pulls him away. Jesse yanks his arm free of his mom's grip and runs over to me. I bend down to greet my five-foot-tall hero, as he gives me a hug.

"Thanks buddy, but you need to listen to your mom," I say in a soft voice.

"But… that man is saying bad things about you."

"I know, but what he says doesn't bother me and you can't let it bother you either, okay?" I ruffle his hair.

"If you say so," he responds after hesitating briefly. "Is your dog alright?"

"No Jesse, I'm afraid she's not. That bad guy right there killed her."

"Is that why you killed him?"

"No. I killed him because he was going to hurt everyone else if he had the chance. Killing is never a good thing Jesse, but sometimes you have to do a bad thing for a good purpose. You do it in order to protect yourself and the people you care about. Understand?"

"I think so."

"Good. Go back over to your mom."

I pat him on the back before he runs back over to her and I can hear him tell her sorry as he gives her a hug. She gives him a kiss, saying she loves him and he says the same thing back. As I watch the young boy and his mom, I'm interrupted by more shouting from Joe.

"Enough!" My voice reverberates through the room startling everyone. The Nan-ites must have magnified the volume of my voice. Everyone falls silent again.

"How dare you speak to me that way, boy?" snaps Joe.

"*Boy*?! I am Captain Winter of the United States Army. I am the highest-ranking member of the United States military in this facility and since none of you are employed by the government, that makes me the only one who is authorized to shout orders around here! I have listened to your *shit* for far too long out of respect for my father, but now I am done! I did not bring Rider and Jake back here. They came here on their own." I glare at Joe as my blood begins to boil from the pain of losing Mya and my ever-growing hatred for him. At least now we have our hatred for one another in common.

286

Joe starts to speak, but I cut him off.

"And let's not forget that all of you so-called council members making decisions for us, are the ones who wanted Brian and I to go with them. You've all been blinded by your ignorant ideals to see the big picture. The safety of this place is no longer a discussion. You no longer speak for anyone in this compound, and from this moment forward you will do as Brian or I say, or you can take your chances out there." I point to the door.

"What do you want us to do, Alec?!" yells someone in the back.

"Yeah!" shouts several others.

Joe looks as though he might explode, now that he realizes he no longer has the support from anyone in the compound.

"Tell us your plan, son," my father says.

"For now, I need all of you to stay here and keep the door locked," I reply. "I'm gonna go ask your nine test subjects for help." My father looks surprised at me mentioning them. Everyone in the room begins to talk loudly again as I finish my statement.

"But, what if they kill you?!" shouts one of them.

"They already tried to kill that other guy!" shouts another.

"Everyone quiet down!" my father shouts. "Quiet!" The commotion slowly dies down until it's quiet enough for him to speak. "They won't hurt him."

"How can you be sure?" asks Emily.

"Yeah, dad. How *can* you be sure?" I ask sarcastically. He looks over at me, realizing that I've figured out the truth. I don't know why I didn't sooner, but for some reason, now everything makes sense. "Come on, dad. It's time we all know the truth about the Lurks and everything else that is going on."

I've been trying to piece it together for some time now. Why would these creatures only attack Rider? And then when Mya and I ran after them, they didn't try to hurt her or me. All the things they were saying to me. They knew me. Mya knew them, because she stopped barking once she got close enough to see them. Then she fell back down into the hole. The only way for her to get out of there was for one of them to let her out. Then the Nan-ites pinged their heartbeats down underground near the sinkholes as I was killing this soldier in front of me. The thing that made it the most obvious to me though was my father when I brought up their appearance. He really was in pain for what happened to them.

"They won't hurt him, because they know him," my father says. A few people begin to whisper, but for the most part, everyone keeps quiet. My father and I continue to stare at each other. He looks ashamed. "The first nine subjects… are… your men," he struggles to say.

I nod my head. Finally. He actually told the truth.

Brian looks over to me to respond and I nod my head.

All this time, I've wondered why they made no attempt to harm me in the forest when they had been given several opportunities to do so, even before the night they attacked Rider. If they were as ruthless as they seemed, they would have killed me the first time Mya fell into the sinkhole. That also explains the grizzly attack and it having a broken neck.

"I know why you didn't pick me and Brian to be part of your experiment, but how did you keep it from us?"

"I didn't pick anyone. They were given orders. I got word of which unit we were getting and I told them I wouldn't proceed if they didn't exclude my sons from it." He's looking at the ground.

"I was their commanding officer. I should have been there with them," I say bitterly. "They trusted me."

"I was only trying to protect y…"

"It doesn't matter now," I say and start to walk away. "I'll be back within a few hours. Everyone stay inside and keep the door locked." I give my father one last glare before turning to the door. He's looking at me with a sort of sadness mixed with regret.

Emily walks with me holding my hand as we walk over to the door. I can sense the stress in her breathing and by the rate of her heartbeat. Her hand is sweating more than normal and the impulses I'm getting from her skin confirm it. Oddly, there isn't a foul smell.

"I just got you back and you're already leaving me?"

"I won't be gone long. I'm not even going that far," I say in a soothing voice. I look into her eyes as we stop at the opening of the cave. "I have to go. I can't stop Rider and his men alone."

"I know. It's just that every time you go out there, something bad always happens," she says with a slight roll of her eyes as she looks away.

I pull her close and put my arms around her.

"This will be the last time... I promise." I whisper into her ear that I love her. I then give her a kiss on the lips and turn to face Brian as he walks up, holding an M4 rifle.

"I thought you might want this." He holds out the rifle.

"No. I won't be needing that," I say as I put my right hand onto his shoulder. Brian returns the gesture.

"If you say so. Don't be long."

Don't be long is our way of saying good luck to each other. We don't like to bring luck into anything. We have our training, and training alone is what will bring us back. So, we say "don't be long," as a way of saying it without saying it. I let go of Emily's hand and open the door. I only open it wide enough for me to fit through, to prevent too much cold air from filling the room full of people. I step through the narrow gap and turn one last time to face Brian and Emily.

"Remember... only open this door for me." With that, I turn away and start walking into the darkness without looking back.

I hear the door close behind me and once again I'm locked outside in the frozen world. I hear the locking mechanism activate the moment the door is closed all the way. I walk out of the cave and over to pick up my katana and goggles that I had left lying in the snow after I killed the soldier. They're right outside the mouth of the cave where I left them. The snow-covered ground is drenched in the soldier's blood, causing the snow to melt. I put on my goggles, covering my eyes and tuck the sword back into my pack, which I had never taken off while I was in the compound. I'd been so distracted with... I simply forgot I was wearing it. The second sword is also still there so I return it to its place on my back with its twin. I begin my descent down the side of the mountain, towards the sink hole. The Nan-ites are still pinging all nine of them down there.

Suddenly, after I take only a few steps, images burst into my mind like an explosion. It happens so abruptly that I have to stop and take a knee because images are flashing through my mind so fast, it makes me dizzy. The images are strange.

I see a mixture of images that appear to be memories of my own, mixed in with someone else's. It isn't until about fifteen seconds into the experience that the images start to slow down and I can make out what I'm seeing. I see images of myself, running through the snow the night Rider was attacked. Only, I'm oddly too low to the ground for it to be me. I see our tents set up in the cluster of trees, and our fire burning. Everyone is there. Jake, the dead coward, Rider, the clever mastermind behind it all, Brian and... *me*?

I'm seeing myself from a different point of view. It's like looking into a mirror, only something else comes along with the images. Feelings. Emotions. I can feel what the person that is looking at me is feeling. When the images stop on Rider and Jake, I get this feeling of anger and distrust. Not really a surprise because I've felt that way about them both from the beginning. Then it stops on Brian and I feel a sense of happiness. I feel a love for him which also isn't a surprise. Brian is my friend. My brother. The feelings become even stronger when the images stop on me. I feel a powerful love for myself. A strong feeling of longing and wanting to protect me.

"What the hell is this?"

What is happening? I have an idea but… can it really be possible?

More memories of recent events pop into my head, including tonight when I had to kill the soldier. Again, everyone is present, like in the camp. The soldier is there. Brian is there. I'm there. Then the memories flash to what I thought about just before Mya died. My first memories of her in my life. It's like my love for her is being combined with her love. Now I'm looking at myself again, only from someone else's point of view. I feel a love so powerful that I'm the only thing in this world that matters. I'm the center of the universe and everything else is just there. Impossible.

Could I be seeing Mya's memories? Feeling her emotions?

I'm not sure, but it's the only thing that makes sense. Besides, I'm seeing everyone from down low. I'm seeing as Mya sees things. Always having to look up at the people around her.

The memories continue and I watch myself from seemingly Mya's eyes, carrying her through the compound and setting her on the table. I even feel the anger towards the soldier. How she wanted to attack him, but was unsure of herself. Her feelings are like mine, when I feel unsure of myself, or angry towards someone. Then the feelings quickly change to fear and pain. She's in so much pain, and yet all she is thinking about is me the entire time. She's so terrified of the unknown and the possibility of losing me is going through her head. I can feel her body trembling and her heart failing like it's my own. All those feelings seem to lessen a little as I carry her. Then I see the several, agonizing minutes of myself cutting my arm, over and over again, attempting to heal her with my blood. Her emotions don't change during those minutes, but finally do once I finish and move close to her head. I see what it was like for her to lick me in the face and express her love for me one last time, before slowly fading away.

Then the images of all her memories suddenly stop, but for only a split second. Now I'm back in the medical lab on the table. My confusion grows even more because I'm seeing what I think to be Mya, getting up from the table and jumping down onto the ground. I feel excited and a longing to go find myself like I'm the one in the lab. To see what I am doing. I feel a curiosity to try and get out of the lab. It feels as though it's really me, jumping off of the table and frantically looking back and forth as if I'm lost or confused. She's walking around the room, trying to get out. Mya is trying to get out. After a couple seconds of looking around and even trying to push open the door, Mya jumps up, resting her paws onto the handle and looks through the window into the small hall. I can see her paws and I get the first real confirmation that it's really her point of view. She looks out the window for only a few seconds before giving up, realizing nobody is coming for her. I can feel her disappointment as she walks over and curls up in a corner. The images and feelings stop a few seconds later.

"What was that?" I gasp, almost as if I need to catch my breath.

How can I see Mya's memories and feel what she's feeling? More importantly, why did it feel like those last images were new and happening right now? It must be the Nan-ites. Somehow, they tapped into her mind and allowed me to see and feel through her. Just another curse for me to live through, I guess. It's already hard losing her. Now I must relive moments in her life. Only I don't know what that moment was. It felt new.

I look around the valley for a moment, trying to gather myself, since the images are still fresh. Once I'm composed, I continue walking towards the very first sinkhole that Mya had fallen into. The walk to the sink hole only takes me a few seconds and when I reach the edge of the hole, I look down to the bottom to find nothing below. No yellow eyes looking up at me. Just the darkness that I can now see through. I glance one last time at the compound. It's shrouded in darkness and swirling snow from the wind. I haven't actually stopped to look at it like this, now that I can. I get an eerie feeling from the grim circumstances that even we live in. I have to pry my eyes away from the scene and I step over the edge. I land on the bottom with enough force that the ground crumbles beneath me, leaving a small indent. The force at which I land would have easily broken both my legs before, but now I feel as though I had simply jumped off the third step of a staircase.

I peer down the long tunnel that I had once looked down before, when I could only see darkness. Now I can see everything and there is nothing looking back at me. The tunnel appears to open up into a cavern at the other end. Although I can see with no issues, I turn the light on that is attached to my gear just below my left shoulder. I want to keep the Lurks, my men, in the dark as much as possible about my new strengths. Just in case I need to use them. I might not get a welcoming reunion from them. Hopefully, they will still be my men and see me as their Captain and friend.

I begin walking down the tunnel, prepared for anything to jump out. They may have been my friends once, but I can't be sure as to how much the serum could have affected their minds. So I'm going to expect anything. The tunnel is lined with really thick, black rock that I'm not sure of the name of. It's smooth, almost with a polished look. The word OBSIDIAN pops up in front of me. I've never heard of such a large amount ever being found before. Then again, I really don't know much about rocks at all. I wouldn't have heard anyway. Normally though, I would still be excited to find something like this, but right now I have more important things to worry about than a bunch of rock. As I approach the end of the tunnel, only about fifteen feet from the cave, I hear the same hissing sound that I heard that night in the trees. And then someone calls out to me.

"Alec..." the voice echoes.

I stop walking to try and focus my hearing. While standing in the tunnel, I begin to hear the faint thump of a heartbeat. I listen to the faint beating until it gets louder and louder and eventually, I can hear another heartbeat. And then another. And another, until I can hear nine distinct heartbeats, all thumping with one another as if they're beating to a similar rhythm. I continue listening to the sound of each heartbeat in order to try and gauge where each of them is standing.

The Nan-ites quickly map each of them out for me. They're spread out in a circle. Not just a random circle, but a tactical one. Apparently, they're expecting anything as well. Or they simply just want to kill me. One of them even appears to be hiding just above the entrance from the tunnel. Whoever it is that's waiting, thinks they will have the element of surprise. I think for one more brief moment about all the people relying on me, expecting me to bring an end to the violence and keep them safe. They all need me to succeed. We also need the help of these men. Without another thought, I step into the cavern.

"You've got a lot of nerve coming down here, Winter," says one of them with a deep voice, similar to the soldier I killed outside the compound.

"Calm down, Frank. Alec is the first guest we've ever had. Besides, he's our *friend*," another says sarcastically.

I quickly recognize both voices the moment each of them speak. The first is clearly Frank Walker. Frank is a First Lt. in our unit and is known as the big, buff guy from Alabama that nobody wants to mess with. He stands about 6'5" and could throw almost anyone around like a rag doll when he was human. He's also the unit's weapons expert and has a slight obsession with big guns. Now, you can't even tell what he looked like when he was human. His skin now has a jet black and leathery appearance like a snake.

The second voice is Taylor Wilcox and he's much smaller than Frank. Taylor is only 5'11" and is your typical redneck farmer from Tennessee. He used to always wear his cowboy hat everywhere he went. Now he isn't wearing much of anything, except for a pair of military grade boots and pants. His skin has the exact same color and texture to it as Frank and the rest of them.

In fact, every single one of them is dressed almost the same except for a few who either still have on a shirt or a jacket. They're spread out evenly in the cavern and have me surrounded. Even with my abilities, I doubt I could take all of them.

"Well, are you just gonna stand there or are you gonna say something?!" says Frank. I glance over to my right where he's standing.

"I came here because whichever one of you tried to kill Rider, didn't succeed," I say in a calm voice as I take my eyes off Frank.

"What do you mean, I didn't succeed?!" hisses a voice from behind and above me. The same voice that said my name when I was still in the tunnel.

I turn around to see who was sitting on a ledge above the opening. He's crouched down like a gargoyle statue on the roof of a building, ready to strike at any moment.

"I mean he's still alive. The serum in your blood infected him and turned him into a monster."

"That's impossible! No human could've survived the wound I gave him!" he says with a chuckle, only his menacing yellow eyes take any humor out of his voice.

"I guess you're still just as bad a killer as you were when you were human," Frank says with a grin.

The Lurk on the ledge doesn't make a sound after Frank's comments. Frank always talked to his younger brother Jermaine that way. Jermaine is smaller than his older and much bigger brother. He's only six feet tall, but very muscular himself, although he looks puny next to Frank. Everyone does.

A few of the others let out a chuckle at Frank's poke to his little brother and I watch each of them closely through my goggles. I wonder if any of them has any clue that I'm different too.

I'm able to examine the cavern for a moment while everyone laughs. The cavern is about three times the size as the main hall in the compound. The ceiling is twenty feet high in most areas, but one section looks much higher. *32 feet high.* There's more obsidian like in the tunnel, scattered throughout the cavern. Finally, everyone stops laughing.

"Listen. The situation is much worse than you think," I say taking a moment to look at each one of them individually. "After Rider mutated into whatever he is, he went back and infected all of his men. Now there's an army of soldiers with your speed and strength coming to take over the compound. And judging by the fact that you attacked Rider, I'm guessing you already know what this guy is about."

"Why should we help you? Your father turned us into monsters!" shouts Taylor as he stands there with his arms folded.

Some of them look away when I try to make eye contact with them. Others keep their eyes on me, but don't say a word.

"You're right. My father turned you into what you are, not me. And you should help me because it's the right thing to do."

"You're just as guilty since you chose not to be a part of it," Taylor continues.

"The first I heard of my father's crazy experiment was barely over a week ago. I didn't choose not to join you. I had no choice or knowledge of what was going on at all," I say in a pleading voice.

"Well, none of us will help you regardless. You're on your own," responds Taylor, but in a calmer voice.

"Is that an order? Because the last time I checked, I was the commanding officer in this unit," I snap back.

"You were, but now I am. I was second in command to you and always the better fighter when we were human. Now, nobody can challenge me," Taylor says with pride in his voice.

Now I know that none of them can see my eyes enough to question if I'm normal or not. If they could see my eyes even just a little, I doubt Taylor would be so confident.

"Since when did fighting ability and strength determine if you were a leader?" I ask.

"Since you abandoned us, and we became stronger than anyone that ever lived," he says with piercing eyes. Until this moment I had tried to ignore the bright, yellow predator eyes. Now, with Taylor looking at me as if he wants to kill me, I have no choice but to acknowledge them. After all, there are nine sets of those eyes looking at me.

"Well—since I'm here, that still leaves me in command. You wanna command this unit, you have to take it from me," I challenge him.

All of the Lurks, my friends and soldiers of war, stand there in silence. Some of them look at each other with confused looks on their faces. None of them have any idea that I still have the advantage over all of them in the skill of fighting, so it's natural that they all think I'm crazy. No ordinary human would stand a chance against Taylor, but I'm no ordinary human and I'm about to teach him a lesson.

"Alec, he'll kill you," says one of them.

"We'll see."

"I hope you enjoy the taste of your own blood, because you're about to have a mouthful," Taylor says with a grin on his face.

I reach my left hand over my shoulder and pull one of my swords from its sheath and hold it behind my back with the blade pointing upwards. I look Taylor straight in the eyes and smile. Taylor's grin quickly disappears and he lets out a loud shriek just like the one I had heard in the distance the night of the bear attack. He crouches down into an attacking position, similar to that of a predator on a hunt, and lunges towards me. In the split second it takes Taylor to travel fifteen feet to where I stand, he would have appeared like a glimmer to any normal person watching, but to me he appears slow. It seems like I have all the time in the world to plan my counterattack. The Nan-ites are adapting like I thought. Nobody can lunge at me from straight on again. I'm sure of it. Just before Taylor reaches me, I step to the right and put the palm of my hand into Taylor's face with as much force as I can. As my right hand connects, blood splatters onto his face and on my jacket, just before he is sent flying into the rocky wall.

Everyone in the cavern lets out a gasp of surprise.

"How?! That's... impossible!" mumbles Taylor as he staggers to his feet.

"You're not the first person to say that."

"How can you move like that!?" he demands.

I reach up and pull the goggles off and toss them onto the ground. I watch the reaction on Taylor's face go from surprised to furious, as my bright blue eyes glow in the darkness.

"How do you like the taste of your own blood, Taylor?" I sneer, crouching down slightly in preparation for another attack.

He lets out another loud shriek and charges. This time I step to my left and bring the sword down, slicing at Taylor's right arm enough to cause him pain, but not enough to seriously hurt him. Just a small cut.

"Keep this up and you're gonna lose a lot of blood." The slice in Taylor's black reptilian arm heals as I speak.

"Give it up Taylor. I think your challenge is over," orders Frank. Taylor shoots Frank a nasty look.

"That's Captain to you," he says while spitting blood onto the ground.

"Enough, Taylor! If you don't stop, I'll kill you myself!" Frank continues.

"Yeah, I think you proved your point," adds Jermaine.

"I don't know why you're so mad at me, but I swear to you, I had no idea you were all ordered to be a part of my father's experiments. Hell, I didn't even know he worked for the military until recently." I try to defend myself, showing my hands outward at my sides as a sort of white flag.

"Then explain why you're faster and stronger than me! Not to mention those bright, blue bulbs you have for eyes!" yells Taylor. Everyone else in the cavern seems to agree with Taylor's question because all nine sets of eyes are fixed on me.

"I was dying and my father had no choice but to inject me with the serum. He included the Nan-ites that were supposed to go into you guys, but the government wouldn't allow him to." I pause for a moment then continue in a softer tone. "Luckily for me, the serum, when combined with the Nan-ites, worked and my eyes were the only thing that changed. I'm sorry, Taylor. I'm sorry to all of you." I put my sword away and stand there as I wait for someone to respond. Several of them are looking down at the ground. Even with their new eyes and appearance, I can see the shame on their faces. Only, they have no reason to be ashamed.

"Alec would never abandon us guys. You all know that," says the same voice that pleaded with me not to fight Taylor. I turn and look up at another ledge to my left. He's sitting about ten feet above me. It's Justin Price. Justin was blonde haired and blue eyed before his change. He's just under 6'4" and a very honorable person. Justin never talked badly about anyone behind their back and always looks for the good in people. He's also loyal to a fault. He was only eighteen years old when I met him, but instantly became one of my friends due to the fact that he loves basketball just as much as I do and he grew up in Springville, Utah. We would always run the court on base and were known as the unstoppable duo. He's always had my back, no matter the circumstances and I always know I can count on him for anything. After Ashlee, Brian and of course Mya, I would say Justin is my closest friend. He and Ashlee always had a thing for each other, but for some reason nothing ever happened. Justin would always ask about her and then when he'd see her, he wouldn't do anything. I don't know if it was out of respect for me or not, but I wish he would have.

The other five members of the unit who hadn't spoken yet are Derrick Martinez, Jason Adams, Cole Spencer, Seth Richards and John Vincent. They've all now moved into a semicircle around me. Derrick is 6'1" and from L.A. He's also one of the craziest bastards I've ever known. He was once arrested for getting into a brawl in a bar because a guy looked at him wrong. After a few broken ribs, several broken noses and about a thousand dollars in damage later, I had to bail him out of jail. He's lucky he wasn't discharged from the military. The only thing that probably kept him in was his unmatched skill with a sniper rifle. He's just too valuable to the United States to let go.

Next to Derrick is Seth Richards. Seth is 5'11" and a big dude. Not big like Frank, but a big heavy guy. Seth is a solid 260 lbs. and has a really short crew cut. He's also a real asshole. Seth is new to the unit and nobody in the unit really likes him at all because of his mouth. He never knows when to shut up and always talks trash about other guys in the unit behind their back. In a way, he's the complete opposite of Justin. The only reason he's in our unit is because he was reassigned from his former one, where he kept fighting with the men. He was basically on a final strike with the military. One more incident and he would be out. I approved his transfer, only because I hated to see a valuable soldier get wasted for his attitude. I hoped I could change that. Plus, although none of us like him, anyone of us would want him going into battle because he's simply one hell of a soldier. I knew that I just needed to find a way to harness his skills and give him a leader he could believe in.

The last three standing next to Seth are Jason, Cole and John. Jason is the shortest in the group at 5'6" and has curly red hair. Jason grew up in a small town in Colorado called Granby and originally only joined the military to help pay for his medical school. He already had a love for shooting guns and dreamed of going to different places, so the military was a perfect fit for him. Not only did he still get to be a trained medic, but he also got to carry a gun at the same time.

Cole is also from Colorado, but from Boulder City. He's 6'0" tall and average in build. He was always in excellent shape, but only waying around 170 lbs meant he wouldn't be able to throw his weight around. Cole has light blonde hair and is definitely the nerd in the group. He's very good with anything electronic. That's why he's the unit's communications expert and a decent shot with any kind of gun. Seems those Colorado boys spend too much time in the mountains, having a little too much fun.

John is from San Diego and is your typical surfer type, golden blonde hair and a total lady's man. Being 6'5" and a sound athlete also give him the advantage in most hand-to-hand combat situations. He's the only one who could give me a real fight, even though Taylor always says otherwise. John is a warrior in every sense of the word. There's no quit in him. I never had any doubt that he could survive a storm like this. If I were to pick which member of the team would outlive the rest, it would be him.

"You know I'm always up for a fight," says Justin. "And it sure is good to see you," he says as he walks up and gives me a hug.

"You can count me and Jermaine in as well," adds Frank.

I nod my head to each of them in approval as the rest of them also agree to help. All except for Taylor. I look at him patiently and wait for his response. I'm really not sure what he will say, but I need his help. After a long wait and utter silence with everyone watching him, he slowly turns his back to everyone and walks off into a corner of the cavern and disappears behind a wall of rock. I shake my head in disbelief at my friend's cowardly act. I can accept Taylor's anger towards me, but not being willing to help save innocent lives? That is not what we stand for. I decide I won't let Taylor say no and start after him.

"Let him go," Justin says as he puts up a hand to stop me. "He'll come around. He just needs some time."

CHAPTER 17

I reluctantly allow Taylor to deal with his issues alone and take in the view of all my men. I'm looking forward to having them all back. This is the first time we've all been together since the storm hit. We were all on a six month leave, having a nice long vacation from war. At least Brian and I were. It was during this time that me, Brian and Ashlee went on our trip together. Since our trip was to California, John met up with us. The only reason he isn't in the picture by my bed is because there wasn't anyone else around to take it.

The thought of my father being responsible for all of this, still makes me angry. He can put blame on someone else all he wants. He was a puppet and therefore a coward. The only thing that makes it easier to think about is the fact that I would be dead if it weren't for him. Then again, had none of this ever happened, I wouldn't have been shot saving Emily. Mya would still be alive.

I spend the next couple hours talking with them. They all tell me about the day they received word of my father's experiment. All of them tell me how they figured I had turned it down and was allowed to because of my rank and that I had used that rank to get Brian out as well. I feel bad that they thought I abandoned them. Additionally, the fact that I'm now changed makes me feel even worse. I have all the added strengths that they do and more because of the Na-nites, with none of the negatives.

I go on to tell them everything that has taken place for me since it all started. Everything from gathering all the people that we could from town and bringing them to the compound, to what brings me to them. I fill them in on Emily and they all quickly begin making obscene comments and jokes. They can't wait to meet her. The last thing I tell them is how Rider went through his change and likely turned all of his men as well. I'm just about to tell them about the soldier and Mya, when Justin beats me to it.

"Where's Mya at bro?" he asks. "Haven't seen her since I pulled her out of that other hole."

That's how she got out of there.

Having him bring up her being down in the hole takes me back to when she fell in. I was sure she wouldn't make it out of there or something would kill her. The relief I felt to get her back only to then lose her all over again has really taken its toll. I remember about the ache in my stomach as I start thinking about her again. I hesitate to answer. I'm not sure if I'm ready to talk about her yet. It did happen only a couple hours ago. I guess now I don't really have a choice. Justin doesn't mean anything by it. He knew her before the storm, which explains why she wasn't afraid that night Rider was attacked.

"She's dead," I finally say. "One of Rider's men killed her, not even an hour before I came down here."

"Oh shit," Justin says as he puts his hands on his hips and lets out a sigh. "Sorry, Alec. I know how much she meant to you." Justin whispers quietly.

"It's fine. We have more important things to worry about right now," I say as I place my hand on Justin's shoulder. I really don't have time to think about her. Or the images that I saw. I can't think about anyone in particular. Only the task at hand. Suddenly, an idea pops into my head. "How about we introduce you guys to everyone upstairs? They're expecting me to be back by now, anyway."

"Lead the way," shouts Frank as he jumps up from where he's been sitting. "I could use some food. I'm starving."

"Yeah, let's go scare the hell out of that prick Joe," adds Jermaine.

"Forget Joe, I wanna meet Emily," smiles John as he gives me a wink.

"In your dreams, John," I say as I take off on a dead sprint.

I'm faster in the tunnel than I am out in the snow, since I have firm ground to plant my feet on. I speed through the tunnel like a blur, making it to the sinkhole in less than two seconds. Once in the hole, without slowing down, I jump at an angle as hard as I can, landing on a small stone nearly half way up. I then plant my feet against the jagged rock and launch myself the rest of the way up, soaring into the air. I land ten feet from the hole, with my legs digging deep into the snow, up to the middle of my thighs. The others land next to me, one by one, each sinking deep into the snow as I did. Once we're all on the surface, we make our way to the compound as a unit.

"Imagine if we had this strength back when we were deployed," says Frank with excitement.

I can't help but feel the same. We really would have been deadly like this. We would've finished skirmishes before they ever began.

"Just so you guys know, not everyone is going to give you a very big welcome," I say as we enter the small cave that leads to the front door of the compound—the home I've grown to appreciate over the last year.

"Let us worry about that," chuckles Frank. "We'll just tell them we thought we were coming to a costume party."

I can't help but crack a slight smile at Frank's humor. It sure is good to have them all back again. I begin pounding on the door for someone to let us in as we wait in the cave. I can't hear any commotion coming from inside. Everyone most likely got tired of waiting and left. At least I hope they did.

The light isn't on, so we all wait there in the dark cave. I walk over and look at where I killed the soldier. The blood stained, icy ground is now covered with a fresh layer of snow. There's no longer any signs that anything happened here—that I'm thankful for. I quickly return my gaze to the door and walk back over to wait, as an image of Mya, laying up against the wall bleeding, flashes into my mind. I try to shake it out of my head. My heart is heavy.

After only a few seconds of standing there, the images are interrupted as I hear the light footsteps of someone walking up to the door from inside.

"Alec, is that you?" asks Emily in a soft voice, knowing that my enhanced hearing will allow me to hear her.

"Yes Em. It's me!" I shout.

The locking mechanism instantly releases and I help push the heavy door open. Emily throws her arms around me tightly the moment it opens. She lets out a sigh of relief and I can hear her heart rate begin to slow. She really was anxious the entire time I was gone.

"Are you okay?" she asks as she looks up at me, the concern quickly fading away.

"I'm fine. How's everything in here?"

"Fine for now. I was worried about you. You were gone longer than you said you'd be. Did you fi…" Emily jumps back a step as she realizes I'm not alone. The dark skin of my men makes them blend in with the shadows.

"It's ok, Emily," I say as I grab her hand. "They're my friends. They won't hurt you."

"How you doin, ma'am? Justin Price," Justin says without hesitation and extends his dark reptilian hand.

"Em… ily," she replies, cautiously accepting the gesture. Her eyes are still slightly suspicious.

"Alec told us a lot about you. You're a lucky girl," Justin adds. "Or at least he's lucky," he smiles.

"Alec told me a lot about you as well. He's told me about all of you guys."

"I hope it was all good stuff," blurts out Seth.

"Are we kidding, Seth? There's nothing good to say about you," laughs Frank in his deep, booming voice. Everyone joins in on the laughter just as Seth pushes Frank in the chest.

"I thought there were nine of you," Emily says. The laughter stops and Emily looks around at everyone's reaction. I can see that she's wondering if she shouldn't have said that. "Did I say something wrong?"

"No, Emily," I reassure her. "Taylor decided, for his own reasons, to stay behind."

"Oh. Sorry you guys," she apologizes.

"No worries, ma'am. Name's Frank Walker. And this is my younger brother Jermaine," Frank says casually as he elbows Jermaine in the shoulder.

"Nice to meet you guys. All of you," she says, glancing at each one of them. "But call me Emily. Please."

The rest of them finish introducing themselves to Emily and talk with her for a few minutes. While we're all chatting, someone comes walking by from the cafeteria and notices us all standing there. It's an older woman, whom I've seen before. The Nan-ites quickly play back images of her heckling me from the background, always nearby Joe during the group altercations. I hadn't noticed her because I was always focused on Joe and the other council members. Seeing her now makes a thought pop into my mind as to who she is and the Nan-ites quickly play back all the sequences where she was in the background fanning Joe's flames. She's one of the biggest haters after Joe that wants me gone. One glance at all of us standing there, black creatures with yellow eyes, she quickly runs back towards the cafeteria screaming.

"Monsters," she shouts over and over again as she runs away from us. "He brought back monsters!"

"Stupid old woman," mutters Emily. "I hate her."

"Well, that went exactly the way I expected it to go," I say. "Come inside so we can close the door."

One by one, each of them walk into the main hall, probably for the first time since their change. They've all been out in the snow for the past year surviving on their own. I only have a small taste of that for a few days here and there. As they enter the facility, the lights shine off each and every one of their shiny bald heads. Being bald is another reaction to the serum I'm thankful I didn't get. All of them have been through far more than I have. I should be grateful for my condition and I have an even greater respect for them than aver.

"Emily, stay here with them. I'm gonna go put out that fire before the compound burns down."

"Go on. I'll just hang here with the guys," she says as she gives me a slight squeeze of my hand.

Frank gives me a childish grin.

"Behave yourselves boys. I'll be right back," I say and walk away.

I quickly run down the hallway and slow just outside the cafeteria doors. Inside, I can hear the woman yelling frantically that "Alec has brought more monsters and we're all in trouble." I listen for a moment as her and (none other than) Joe try to rile up everyone inside. Emma tries to calm everyone down, but to no avail. Once I decide I've heard enough, I push open the doors. All the eyes in the room switch to me as I walk in and the room falls silent. Even the woman and Joe don't move or speak and I walk right up to them both.

"Emily is in the main hall with my friends, Emma," I say without looking at her. Emma quickly puts the dishes she's holding on the counter and starts for the door. "Emma?" This time I look over to her. "Don't be frightened. They look different, but they won't hurt you."

Emma smiles like Emily, and for that moment she looks just like her. "I trust you Alec," and she turns and walks out.

I return my attention to the old woman and Joe, the one man I hate more than anyone, including Rider. Joe has been nothing but hateful towards me from the beginning. Plus, he said hurtful things about Emily and kicked Mya. I would love nothing more than to throw Joe and the old woman out in the snow to fend for themselves, but I know that isn't the right thing to do.

"I told you I was going to get someone who could help us," I say in a soft, but angry tone. "Not only that, but you also knew who I was bringing back, so why this continued spewing of hate?"

"You're an abomination!" responds the old woman without hesitation.

An abomination? That hurts. Why do they hate me so much? I can understand the fear they have, but not the hatred. I haven't done anything to them. It doesn't make sense.

"Well, I guess the only chance any of you have at survival is me and the other eight abominations in the other room. They are my friends and they will stay. Anyone that has a problem with that, can take it up with me." Without another word, I turn and walk out of the cafeteria. I casually walk back to the main hall at a normal speed and ponder about everything that's taken place in the past week.

Everything was completely normal before Jake and Rider showed up. Sure, some people were hearing strange noises outside, but that was just my men the entire time. Nothing to be concerned about. Now, I feel as though I'm living in a nightmare and all I want is for it to end. I want to wake up in my bed at home and for Mya to be there. I want Ashlee to walk in the front door and ask me to go do something. I want life to be normal again.

While I approach the end of the hall, I can hear Brian and the other's laughing. I'm glad that they are welcoming Brian back into the group like nothing happened. The men mean just as much to him as me. When I walk around the corner, I discover that Brian isn't the only one in the main hall having a good time with the guys. There are over a dozen other people in the main hall, including most of the members of the council and my father. Surprisingly, none of my men seem confrontational towards my father, despite even being forced to be part of his experiment. The fact that they aren't being volatile towards him shows their own level of character.

I lean against the corner and watch as people from the compound interact with the strange and frightening looking people. Emily's parents, Jesse and his mom and a few others are present. To my surprise, most of the people in the room aren't even afraid. They actually seem comfortable with them. Even little Jesse is chatting up a storm with Jermaine. I listen as Jesse tells Jermaine about the night he was hiding in the freezer and how Brian and I found him. He sure does like us. Jermaine even goes as far as letting Jesse feel the texture of his skin. Jesse looks as though he's at an amusement park or a toy store for the first time. Here's this new thing in front of him that he's eager to enjoy. No fear whatsoever. I guess being around me must have rubbed off on all of them. Emily turns around and sees me standing by the hallway watching. She quickly cuts her conversation short with John and hurries over to me. She reaches out and grabs my hand and I pull her in for a kiss. After, she looks up and smiles.

"I have something to show you," she says with wide eyes.

"What?"

"Follow me." She begins leading me over to the door to the stairs.

"No, Emily." I take a step back. "Please. I don't wanna go back down there right now." I'm not ready to see Mya's lifeless body again. Not yet. I'd rather wait until this conflict with Rider is resolved so I can take the proper time to cope with it.

"Trust me. You *want* to see this." She grabs my hand and I reluctantly nod in agreement and she leads me into the stairwell.

I hesitantly walk with Emily through the door and down the wide staircase, unsure of what she could possibly want to show me down here. There's *nothing* good down here. Heartache is all I'm going to find. When we reach the bottom of the stairs, she leads me over to the door for the Nano-Gen Research. She stops just outside the door and looks up at me.

"Not too long after you left, I couldn't stop thinking about the look in your eyes when Mya died, so I came down here hoping that…" Emily pauses for a moment searching for the right words to say. "Well… I guess I just came down to check on her. This is what I found."

Emily turns and pushes the double doors open, leading me into the room. The images from earlier come back. Mya getting up from the table and walking over to the door, then going into the corner. Before I can ask myself if the images can possibly be real, I look at the table that I left Mya on. It's clear. Nothing, except for the sheet that I covered her with is there. A knot quickly forms in my gut as the emotions of losing her overcomes me and the feelings of hope and anxiety flood through me. I turn to my left and I almost stop breathing, but my heart is pounding.

"It… was real," I finally say as I step up to a large cocoon, similar to the one Rider came out of. Only this one is the same bright blue color as my eyes.

"What was?" Emily asks, curiously.

311

I look over at Emily and smile wider than I ever have in my life. Tears of joy start to form in my eyes as I place my hand on the large, bright blue cocoon. Instantly, I'm hit with sensations I haven't felt since going through my change and I laugh.

"It feels... warm," I say surprised.

I keep my hand on the large, blue cocoon for several minutes without saying a word as I listen to Mya's powerful, living, beating heart. The cocoon is much larger than the one that Rider came out of. This one is just over twelve feet high and eight feet wide. Whatever she's changing into, she's going to be big. I lean into the cocoon and place the side of my face up against it and enjoy the wonderful sound and the warmth. I feel like I could fall asleep as I stand there listening to the wonderful rhythm of her heart. Emily patiently watches me as I take in the sensational moment of relief that my friend is still alive. She lets out a cheerful laugh and smiles just as big as me all while fighting back tears of her own.

"What did you mean before?" she asks me again.

"When I left the compound earlier, images of things she had seen and experienced in her life started flashing through my mind at a very rapid pace. I had a hard time following it, they were coming so fast. At first, I thought they were my own memories, then I realized they were all from a different point of view. Then it started getting weird. I was no longer seeing just a memory, but I was watching her movements through her own eyes. I saw her get up from the table and walk over to the door," I say as I point over to it. "She jumped up and looked out the window and then came over here and curled up on the floor. After that, the images stopped."

Emily is wide eyed as she listens to my story. Even I know how crazy it sounds, but how can anyone deny what I saw? Especially if they see what we're looking at.

"Do you think that your blood being inside her has something to do with you being able to see what she does?"

"There's no other explanation," I reply. "It has to be the Nanites that gives us the link. I also think that she cocooned because she was also infected by that soldier. The combination must also be what's making her change so fast. Rider and I both took a week to go through our changes. The combination of my blood and the soldier's DNA must be accelerating everything." I can barely conceal my excitement. "It's amazing."

"Yeah, and it looks as though she's going to be huge too."

"Yeah, she is. As big as Rider. No. Bigger," I reply. "Now we just have to hope she's still *her* when she comes out."

"Alec, you know Mya would never hurt anyone."

"I know that Mya would never hurt anyone, but what if she isn't Mya anymore when she comes out?"

"You're the same after your change and as far as we know, so is Rider," responds Emily in Mya's defense. "Your friends upstairs are the same as well."

"Yeah, I guess you're right. Emily, I don't want you to tell anyone about this." I look at her for the first time since walking into the room.

"Why?"

"We need to keep as much as we can secret. We don't know who we can trust in the compound right now and everyone who lives here is already on edge. This will just make it even worse. Besides… I don't want Joe or that nasty woman finding out about her either. At least not until she comes out. I can't risk losing her again." I look back at the cocoon.

"You don't even want to tell Brian?"

"No. He'll wanna come down here. So will my father and my mom. Then everyone will start to wonder why we're all coming down here again. Someone might follow."

"I see your point. I don't want the wrong people down here either," she replies.

I reluctantly remove my hands from the cocoon and put my arm around Emily. We watch the cocoon together for a few more minutes until I decide we need to head back upstairs to avoid any suspicion. Before walking out of the laboratory doors, I place my hand on the cocoon one last time and smile from the warmth I continue to feel from it. Finally, I lead Emily by the hand and we exit the lab. We walk back up to the main hall quietly, both of us unsure of what to say, and join everyone in the main hall. We find even more people there waiting. Now it seems as though everyone in the compound is there again, including Joe, who is now doing the talking. Again. The scene looks like a political rally with Joe campaigning for the biggest douchebag of the century.

"How can any of you trust these abominations? Look at them!" Joe points his finger at my men angrily. "They're no longer even human!"

I look over to where my men are all standing, only a few feet away from Joe, and I'm surprised to see them all keeping their cool. Frank is laughing and pointing at Joe.

"Who does this fool think he is?" Frank asks as we walk up next to him. Being this close to Joe makes me anxious and I have to focus on not taking a few steps and killing him.

"How dare you insult me?" Joe shouts in anger. "We were all here long before any of you. You want your stupid war? That's fine, but we're all staying in here where we're all safe."

"Technically, they were here first since this is where they were kinda made. No offense guys," Brian says, glancing at them. "So doesn't that make this their place?"

"And you, you stupid little smartass!" Joe snaps, pointing his bandaged hand at Brian. "I've had about enough of your childish comments."

The look on Brian's face changes to a confused one, as if someone just said a joke to him that he doesn't understand. I heard him ask Frank if he thinks he's "little". Frank says "yes" without hesitation.

"Hmm," is the only response Brian gives.

Frank gives him a playful elbow jab to the ribs.

Everyone in the room quickly starts arguing with each other. Some are in favor of us and others in favor of Joe. The room isn't completely divided, but enough to cause problems. I already showed them who the enemy is. They've never been given a reason to fear me, or any of the men. The fact that they look scary has nothing to do with it. Joe and the woman are the ones acting like monsters.

"Let me see if I can explain this to you better this time!" I shout with a different mindset than I had earlier. The emotion from losing Mya is gone and I'll soon have her back, so now I can think clearly again. "We are not going anywhere!" The room quiets down. All except for Joe and the woman. "You're all trying to call them monsters because they look different? All of you that think that way should all be ashamed of yourselves. You might have been able to get away with that kind of behavior back when the world still had order, but you will not get away with it here. You're all fortunate to even call this place a home. You're also only here because of my father. So, either you welcome all who come here peacefully, or get out!"

"That's up to the council and the people to decide! Not you!" shouts Joe.

"You think because you're a member of some silly little council, that you can give orders? Your council doesn't mean *shit*. You're a group of people that all want to be in control. You order people around, talk to them however you like, treat us like we're expendable." I calmly step up to them both. "You both have forked tongues and I've let you guys act like this place belongs to you, long enough."

"No one here will follow you," growls the woman.

"Is that so? And before we get carried away, does anybody here even know what your name is?" I ask.

"My name is Michelle Weaver, but you can call me Ms. Weaver," she says with a hateful tone.

"Consider yourself lucky if I don't refer to you as a walking pile of garbage," I reply. Michelle's face turns red and before she explodes, I continue. "These men behind me have followed me into many battles. They're going to follow me into another one, probably tomorrow and one that some of us might not live through."

"None of *these* people will follow you," she growls again indicating with her eyes towards the crowd.

"Let's find out. Shall we?" I turn my attention towards all the people. "Everyone listen up! Joe here thinks he can do a better job keeping you safe! He thinks he can do a better job keeping you alive! Well, since our country was all about voting in a leader and since Joe here wants to be a leader so bad, we're going to vote for who's going to lead us. All of you will decide!"

"This is absurd," Joe mumbles so the crowd can't hear him.

"It's what you wanted," I say back to him.

"Who's in favor of Alec?" shouts Emily.

I look over at her and she grins as she looks back. I can't help but smile in return. The room erupts as people cheer in support for me. Joe's demeanor, along with the hag woman, become aggravated and nervous. Joe and the woman are already unhappy, but I'm now monitoring Joe's vital signs. His heart rate is highly elevated and he's breathing heavily. The woman is too. The small number of people that cheer in favor of him isn't enough to satisfy his pride.

Eventually, I have to shut out the noise. Between Joe, Michelle and the rest of the room, the thumping sound of nearly a hundred heartbeats and screams becomes too much. Learning to control what I want to hear or see is challenging, but I'm learning. All I have to do is think "silence" and I get it. I concentrate on blocking out all noise except for voices. Being able to do something like this is strange and incredible. It's like putting yourself into a zone. What a professional ballplayer might do in order to focus on the game and not the noisy crowd. All I have to do is think of the people I want to hear or not hear and the Nan-ites will mute or even raise or lower the volume of the voices as I wish. This is the first time since going through my change that I'm getting a grasp on this particular skill.

"Let's ask Alec what to do!" yells someone from the crowd. "Yeah!" yells another. "What do you want us to do?!"

"I need anyone who knows how to use a gun to hold here in the main hall," I responded. "My men and I are trained for battle. We're even more deadly than we were before, but we are greatly outnumbered by Rider and his men."

I glance over at Brian and I can see the look in his eyes. The one we usually give to each other when we know we might not survive the battle we're going into. All of us have managed to survive this long and we've never lost someone before now. Sure, some of us have suffered serious injuries, but we've always come back.

"We will do our best to stop them and keep them from getting inside, but if they make it past us, or if they get inside the compound, they will either kill you, or infect you." Most of them look frightened. I can't hardly blame them. Some of the women begin sobbing uncontrollably the moment they grasp how serious our situation is. "I'm sorry to frighten all of you. That's not my intention. You all are choosing to trust me, and with that trust I won't start by lying to you. I will die before I let anything happen to any of you. All of us are prepared to do that for you."

"If they get inside, how will we stop them?" asks an older man in the front. His hair is dark with patches of white and he has the appearance of a very wise man. I've never spoken to him before.

"You won't." I have no other way to put it. They really won't be able to stop them if they get inside. "But as long as none of you open that door, they can't get in here. That door was designed to withstand a nuclear blast. Your responsibility as members of this compound will be making sure nobody in here lets them in."

"Who would do something like that?" asks someone in the back.

"People do crazy things when they are scared," replies Brian. "Some of the best people will betray others when they are faced with no other option."

The room falls quiet again. Nobody seems to know what to say in response to Brian's words. Who would? Several people look at the person standing next to them as if they don't know who they're looking at. They're wondering who could possibly be a coward and a traitor. This is a good thing, as sad as it might be.

"Those of you that are going to stand by and protect the door, follow us to the armory. We'll get you a weapon. The rest of you, go back to your apartments or the cafeteria, or wherever you want to. If I see anyone try to open this door, I'll consider you the enemy and you will be locked up until this is over." I pause and look at all of them. "When it's over, you'll be put out in the snow."

I look over at Joe and Michelle and keep my eyes focused on them as they glare at me. They both hold their gaze for several seconds before walking away, likely thinking of some way to get revenge.

I motion for Brian and the rest of the men to follow me to the armory. Emily takes hold of my hand and walks with us.

"Thank you," I whisper in her ear.

She responds by kissing me on the cheek.

"We need to make some preparations. I'll come find you as soon as we're done," I say softly to her.

"How long will you be?" she asks.

"Couple hours at most," I say as I rub my eyes.

"You need some sleep," she says with a motherly tone.

"I'll sleep when this is over."

"If you don't rest, how can you expect to be useful?"

"I've gone longer without rest before."

"If you say so," she says, wrinkling her nose at me. "I'll wait for you in your apartment."

"K. I'll try to hurry."

I kiss her and watch her continue down the hallway as I stand at the entrance to the armory. I wait outside the door and allow all the men to go inside. Only five people followed us. My mom and dad, along with three other men. Mr. Wilkinson, the old man with black and white hair that introduces himself as Peter, and James.

We spend the next several hours planning and prepping those who will stay inside for the upcoming battle. I'm outside with Frank and Justin setting traps in the snow for Rider and his soldiers. The armory doesn't have a large supply of explosives, but it does have about a dozen grenades and a couple of C4 explosives. We set up a perimeter with a trip wire directly in the line of path the first soldier had taken to get here. We separate the two explosives by about fifteen feet so that when the timer is triggered, there will only be five seconds for several of Riders men to walk in and get sandwiched by the explosion. The five seconds, however, means that they have to be taking their time. If they're running, the explosives will go to waste. Hopefully, Rider will be arrogant and they'll stroll on up here with no worries and in no hurry.

Inside, Brian and the rest of the men are getting my parents and the other three as ready as possible. First, they find each of them a weapon that they can handle. James keeps his AR15 that he always carries with him during his watch and the others are given semi-automatic hunting rifles. We don't have enough assault rifles to spare, so they will have to make due. Luckily, all of them already know how to use a weapon. Even my mom knows how to handle one and actually looks more comfortable with hers than my father does. She always wanted to come shooting with me when I had gone to the range or just up in the mountains in a remote place. She's pretty good with a rifle and loves shooting an AR15. I wish I hadn't left my M4 with Kyle and Bobbie, but they needed a better weapon as well. Now I'm thinking that we probably need it more. I would go get it, but I don't want to risk leading Rider to them, or worse, be gone when he attacks.

After several hours of preparing, I send the five volunteers to get as much sleep as possible. I spend a little more time with my men, reminiscing about old times. I also need to find a way to protect Brian. He's going to be very vulnerable to direct attacks, since he's still human. After several ideas from everyone, we decide to place him up on top of the compound with a sniper rifle. Luckily, we happen to have a thermal scope in the armory. We attach it to a Barrett 50 caliber rifle.

Rider and his men still aren't completely aware of my men. Rider will no doubt have them on alert for something, since he was attacked by one of them, but he won't fully grasp the levity of the situation. There are eight of them and he won't see them coming. All of them, except for Taylor and Derrick, are going to stay down in their cavern until the last second to surprise Rider as much as possible. As soon as the explosives detonate, they will attack. Derrick volunteered to be the one to stay with Brian and watch his six. Plus, having the extra sniper will come in handy. I pray that Taylor will come to his senses and join the fight. We need him.

"They won't even know what hit 'em," laughs Frank.

"Yeah, you guys just need to make sure you wait until the explosives go. Any sooner and it won't work," I reply.

"When should I take a shot at Rider?" asks Brian.

"The moment you see them cross the trip wire," I reply. "Try and shoot him at the same time as the explosion and that will cause even more confusion for him. He won't have time to see where the shot came from."

"How 'bout I just shoot him in the head and end it right then?" he asks.

"Make that shot," I nod, "and you might just end the battle right then."

"If it doesn't kill him, he might go after the shooter in anger. He'll be a sitting duck up there," says Derrick.

"That's why you'll be up there with him," I reply. "That way you can keep him safe and also be his way of communicating with us."

"Will do. Now we can see who the better shooter is," he smiles with sharp, pointy teeth. His yellow eyes beam with arrogance. That smile would scare most men. Brian simply grins back.

"While you guys are playing a game, let's just hope everything goes as planned. Remember, kill anything that comes close to the door. Our number one priority is the compound. Nothing gets inside. Understood?"

"Yes sir!" they all say together.

"Brian, it's time you go and get some rest. You can't stay awake like we can," I say as I rub my own eyes. "I need you as rested as possible."

"Are you sure you don't need rest too?" he responds. "I've never seen you look so exhausted before."

"He's right Alec," adds Justin. "You've been through a lot today. Losing Mya, and God knows what else you did before that."

"Go spend some time with that girl of yours, Alec," says Frank. "Maybe… sleep a little too," he smiles. The last remark sends everyone into a frenzy as they all laugh and crack jokes.

"Alright, alright. As long as you guys stop with the perverted comments about her."

"Uh oh," says Justin. "I think somebody's in love. You've never been so defensive of a girl before."

I wink at him with a grin and start to walk out.

"Make sure you guys come get me if something happens."

"We got this. Get some rest, Captain," Frank says with a salute and putting emphasis on the title. The rest of them join in on the salute, including Brian. I salute back with a feeling of gratitude. I'm lucky to have men like this to follow me into battle. Men that will lay down their lives for me. I turn and walk out and Brian follows.

All of the men have strict orders to be out of the compound by midnight. All of them except for Derrick. If Rider and his men decide to show up in the middle of the night, the whole plan would be a bust if they're still inside. I told Derrick to make himself at home and that if he wants, he can crash on my couch for the night. He was grateful for the offer, but said he was going to head down to the cafeteria to find something to eat and that he'd hang with Brian so he won't bother me. Once we make it to my apartment, I'm surprised to see who's waiting outside.

"What the hell does she want? When will she get the hint?" I mutter softly.

"Actually, she's not here for you," Brian adds.

I look over at him, unsure of how to respond. Brian and Alisha? I never even thought of the combination. Ever. Brian doesn't look back at me, not even when he says she isn't here for me. I stare at him for a good thirty paces as we approach the door. When he finally notices, his expression looks more like a puppy looking for approval. I finally grin and he relaxes, also with a grin. I pat him on the back and just laugh. He joins me and we're both laughing even as we approach her.

"Alisha," I say with a nod and a smile.

"Alec," she says back with a less friendly expression.

"Good night, bro," Brian says as I turn the nob.

"Night, bro." I pause and watch them as they walk away. My biggest concern, going into the battle tomorrow, is Brian. Brian isn't like the rest of us and can easily be killed if one of Rider's men gets a hold of him. He was only a split second away from being choked out by the soldier that killed Mya. Even at that moment, I thought I had been too late. His only chance in the upcoming battle is to keep as much distance from them as possible. When the battle does come, I will have a difficult time not worrying about him. I close the door behind me without looking back at them. I do, however, concentrate my hearing and I hear them kissing and giggling. That happened quickly. Typical Brian. Whatever makes him happy.

The light is off in the living room, but I have no trouble seeing the room is empty. A feeling of disappointment hits me, but quickly vanishes when I hear the lovely sound of Emily's heartbeat, coming from my room. I can also smell the sweet aroma from her perfume. I quickly walk to my bedroom door and enter. The light is on, but she's sound asleep, comfortably on the bed. I walk over and take a seat on the edge of the bed. The slight movement doesn't wake her.

Seeing her sleeping peacefully gives me comfort to know, at least at the moment, she's safe. Tomorrow, tonight, or whenever we have to fight will be the most important battle of my life. I won't be fighting to help people in other countries or to kill some terrorist. I'll be truly fighting to keep those I care about most, alive. I lean down and kiss her on the cheek. She opens her eyes slowly and once she realizes it's me she's staring at, she bounces up into a sitting position like she shot out of a cannon… and in a mock attack, smothers me with kisses.

"The d-door." I barely get the words out.

She pulls away from me, clearly perturbed with the fact that I interrupted her. "Well, you better hurry and close it then," she says while waiting impatiently. I jump off the bed and cover the distance to the door in one step.

"Turn off the light too."

The last thing a normal person would have seen before the light turned off, would have been Emily pulling her shirt over her head. Only I'm not normal, so the lights might as well have been on. Fortunately, she can't see me blushing as we start kissing again.

CHAPTER 18

"How come you left without telling me?" Emily whispers. She's lying beside me, with her hand on my bare chest.

"You would've wanted to come with me," I reply somberly. Those feelings of leaving without her come flooding back.

"Would that have been so bad?"

"It was too dangerous out there when it was just the storm we had to worry about. Now, inside the compound is the only place that will be safe until Rider and his men are killed," I continue softly. "Even after he's gone, I'm not so sure the world will be a safe place for anyone. I could never forgive myself if something were to happen to you."

"I know you won't let anything happen to me." She smiles and kisses me on the cheek. "Where did you go while you were gone?"

"I went home. There were two men living in my house. They were scared at first, but it didn't take long to gain their trust. After spending a couple hours there, I went to Salt Lake."

"You ran all the way to Salt Lake?" she asks as she sits up.

"It took me less than an hour to get there too." Her eyes widen in surprise.

"Why did you go there?"

"I was going to the hospital," I continue without looking at her, but instead I stare into the ceiling.

"Oh." She says quietly.

I notice her sudden change in mood, so I go on to give her some peace of mind.

"I wasn't able to go there though. The… the weather was really bad. The wind was really strong and… I couldn't go to her even when I could see it," I say as I start to fight back tears. Emily quickly throws her arm around me.

"You need to stop blaming yourself for that."

"How can I? I told her I was coming and I didn't. She's dead because I failed."

Emily pulls away from me with a disgusted look on her face.

"Because I got in your way?" she asks as she sits up, holding the blanket to cover herself.

"What? No. That's not what I'm sayi…"

"You're right. That wasn't fair. But you need to stop moping around feeling sorry for yourself, or blaming yourself or anyone else for Ashlee's death. She made her own decisions and that's nobody else's fault." She glares at me with her arms folded.

I slowly climb from the bed without looking at her.

How can she snap at me like that? And to talk about Ashlee that way? I put pants and a t-shirt on and walk out of the room. Hearing Emily say that to me, hurts. But why does it hurt so much?

I leave the apartment and walk towards the main hall. All the lights are off, but I can see the glow from the lights in the main hall as I approach. When I reach it, I'm relieved to find it empty. I walk down to the cafeteria to see if maybe Derrick is there. The lights in the south hall are off as well, so I'm not surprised to find the cafeteria black and also empty. I stand there in the darkness wondering what to do or where to go. I don't move for several minutes when suddenly images flash before me. I know the images are in my head, but I can see them clear as day like the world in front of me is changing.

Images of me and Mya. The images stop on one memory—a specific time when Mya could see that I was in a bad mood and she had jumped up onto my lap and showed me affection. The image replays itself and I can feel a sense of comfort coming from it. The feeling is strange like when I touched her cocoon. I can feel her trying to comfort me right now. Being able to feel what she's feeling is bizarre, but it also feels natural at the same time. The feelings aren't like when I touch Emily's skin. When that happens, I'm simply sensing her emotions. Mya and I are actually sharing our emotions and thoughts. We are almost one in the same now. Without thought, I find myself walking in that direction, going down to where she slumbers.

I don't turn on the lights in the stairwell and take each flight of stairs in one easy leap. Once I'm in the main hall of the second level, I cross the corridor and walk into the lab. Mya's cocoon is letting off a glow similar to my eyes, but illuminating the entire room. Her cocoon looks undisturbed, but I don't need to see it to know she's alright. I can simply feel it. I walk over and place my hand onto the smooth, blue surface of whatever the cocoon is made of, before sitting down and positioning myself so that I can lean my head against it, with my skin making contact with the smooth surface . I close my eyes while enjoying the warmth and the comfort from her thoughts and hypnotic sound of her heartbeat until I fall asleep.

I quickly start dreaming about my upcoming battle with Rider. The dream feels real, just like it had when I went through my change, but I have no trouble in recognizing it isn't real this time. Mya is in the dream with me and we're both feeding off each other's emotions towards Rider. We dream several different scenarios where I dominate Rider without any problem and then others where I lose. Where *we* lose. The sensations of battle feel so real that each time I suffer a wound, I scream out in pain like it's really happening.

It isn't until the last scenario of the battle when I actually feel afraid for the very first time in my adult life. We're right outside the compound. Rider and I are going back and forth, over and over again, landing significant blows to one another. Both of us are worn down and just waiting for the other to slip so one of us can end it.

Mya isn't present during this particular dream, but at one point I cut off Rider's arm and I think it's over. I'm dead wrong. Rider picks his arm up off the ground and puts it up to its rightful place. I watch as the bone mends itself back together, followed by the muscles, arteries, veins and other tissue. Rider continues his attack as if nothing happened and comes at me with more anger and ferocity. I struggle to match his strength, but not his speed. He's fast, but I'm faster. All I need to do is avoid his long arms and sharp claws and I can defeat him. I'm about to charge Rider when I hear a scream. I look to my left and see Emily being dragged in the snow by one of Rider's goons. Rider's expression instantly goes from fierce to pleased. I quickly toss my swords in front of me and drop to my knees. Emily already has tears streaming down her cheeks.

"Rider, please let her go," I beg. All he does is grin back.

I watch in horror as Rider, without hesitation, drags his claws down Emily's face, leaving deep incisions in her flesh. The screams from Emily frighten me beyond anything that I've ever imagined possible. This is worse than my nightmare during my change, simply because I am witnessing Emily's suffering. Rider continues his horrific attack on her, all the way down her body and she continues screaming in agony, begging for him to stop. All I can do is watch because two of his men are now holding my arms. Rider grins at me one last time, after torturing Emily for several minutes, then reaches his hand up and grips her neck.

"Alec…" a voice whispers and I open my eyes, startled from the dream. When I realize I'm back in reality I grab her and pull her close and hold her tightly.

After a moment I reluctantly pull away and look into Emily's eyes. She's kneeling down beside me, holding onto my hand. She looks concerned. I'm surprised to see her.

"What are you doing down here?"

"I was worried when you didn't come back," she says looking down at her hand and my hand, clasped together. "I went to Brian and he said he hadn't seen you."

I place my other hand on top of the one she's using to hold mine, while looking down at them.

"If I can't be with you, this is the next place I'd rather be."

"Can't be with me? When did I ever say you couldn't be with me?"

"You didn't, but you seemed pretty upset before, like you didn't want me there."

"Look at me," she says softly. I look up at her and she gives me a smile. "I never want you to leave my side, Al. I love you." A tear slides down her cheek. "And I'm sorry for what I said about Ashlee. I didn't mean to…"

"I know what you meant." I gently place my fingers on her lips. "You're right." I look down again. "I shouldn't be blaming myself or even… my father. I am mad at him, but it isn't his fault. I'm so *angry* with her… and no matter what, I'll never be able to reconcile it. I'm angry with her and I can't even talk it out with her. I'll never get to."

"I never had the blessing of getting to meet her, but based on what I've heard you say about her, I know she wouldn't want you to go on punishing yourself like this." Emily sits down on the floor and leans into me, resting her head on my shoulder. "I know how much you love and miss her, but it's time for you to move on."

Emily and I sit together as we lean up against the cocoon for a while. All I'm able to do is ponder about the things I need to do as Emily suggested. The relationship with my father will take some time to fix, but Emily put the big picture in focus for me. Ashlee chose her profession because she wanted to take care of children. I guess she did that until her last moments. She wouldn't abandon them even to save herself. Her reasons for staying at the hospital are honorable and she deserves credit for sacrificing her life for the people she cared about. That's how I should remember her. It's how I *will* remember her.

"I love you too, by the way," I suddenly say.

"I know," she replies and sits up to look at me. She has the same bright smile as always. "Let's go get some sleep."

"Alright."

We climb to our feet and Emily walks over to the door. I place my hand on Mya's cocoon as she waits for me.

"Make sure you take care of her for me, big girl," I say softly so Emily can't hear me. "I might not make it tomorrow and you'll be the only one that can do that."

An image of Mya licking me across the face touches my mind and I know she hears me. Whether she hears my voice out loud, or simply hears me in her thoughts, I know she at least understands what I'm feeling. I reluctantly remove my hand from her cocoon and walk over to Emily and we leave the lab together.

Once we're back in my apartment, she climbs into bed with me. Neither one of us bothers to change into something more comfortable. I just hold her in my arms, and we sleep soundly for the last few hours of the night.

CHAPTER 19

"Alec..." whispers Derrick. I wake to see him staring down at me. At first his bright yellow eyes startle me, but I quickly recover. If he noticed my surprise, he shows no sign. I glance over at the clock and see it's a quarter after five. I look back up at Derrick and he looks concerned. "It's time," he whispers and glances at Emily's still body and walks out.

I sit up and place my feet on the floor. I hate waking her when she sleeps so peacefully, but I promised her I wouldn't leave again like I did last time. I shake her gently and say her name. She wakes with a startled look on her face, like she's expecting to have to fight. Maybe she wasn't sleeping peacefully after all.

"You have to go, already?"

"I'm afraid so."

She sits up into a sitting position and hugs me tighter than ever before. I hug her back, just not quite as hard, to avoid hurting her. After a short embrace, I have to gently pry her arms loose.

"I love you, beautiful."

"I love you too." She forces a smile.

I kiss her for possibly the last time and put on the pants and jacket I set aside in the night and then my boots. I look back at Emily and smile one last time and then walk out of the room and out of my apartment without looking back.

"Get some sleep?" asks Derrick when I step into the hallway and close the door.

"Yeah. Where's Brian?"

"By the main entrance. Your mom and dad and the others are there too."

"Good."

Derrick and I walk down to the main hall quickly. Brian and the others are there as Derrick said they would be. When we walk into the room, all of them are waiting by the door, holding their guns and prepared for battle. Brian is dressed in his white camouflaged gear like me, to make himself as invisible as possible. He has an M4 slung over his shoulder so that it's hanging down in front of him. He's also holding the 50 caliber Barrett sniper rifle. The perfect weapon for killing someone as large and powerful as Rider and his mutated army. The other volunteers are wearing the same exact thing they were during the hours that they were being prepped for the battle. Each of them appears tired, frightened and unprepared to try and defend the compound. But they'll have to. At least until my secret is ready. Hopefully she's ready in time.

"Alright," I say nodding to each of the men. "Remember, your job is simple. Keep that door closed at all costs. It doesn't open unless one of us opens it. Understood?"

"Got it," says James. The rest of them simply nod their heads.

"Then it's time."

I left all my gear by the front door to be ready for me this morning. I grab my two swords and tuck one of them into a small loop on the back of my jacket, intended for something else. The second one I will have to carry. I used my backpack to hold them previously, but I don't want any restrictions. Brian hands me a couple grenades and the AR15 I also set aside. I don't know if Rider's men will come armed, since the soldier I killed wasn't, but I'm not taking any chances. If I have to kill all of them with a gun,

I have no problem with that. Once I'm all geared up, I look over at my father. My first initial thought when I look at him is anger, but I quickly remember my conversation with Emily and I force the thought out. I walk over to my mom first and give her a hug.

"I love you, mom."

"I love you, son," she says as she wipes away some tears.

I turn and step over to my father.

"I love you too, dad." Saying it is hard, but at least I did. He responds the same way as my mom and I turn and walk away without saying another word. I hear Brian repeat the same exact process with them while I wait at the door next to Derrick. Once he joins us, I enter the code to open the door. Ice cold air fills the room instantly, making everyone behind us, including Brian, cover their faces. I don't know if Brian is going to wear a mask, but he isn't wearing one now. Derrick and Brian step out into the cold, dark cave first and then I follow. I pull the door closed and lock it behind me.

The wind is blowing extremely hard this morning. Brian has to pivot on his back foot in order to keep himself from being knocked over. Luckily, he's dressed warm enough to shield him from the cold. Derrick isn't wearing much. Not that he needs to. He has on his black military jacket and matching pair of pants, but he isn't wearing any shoes.

"Alright fellas. Stay focused and alert," I say as we approach the mouth of the cave.

I step up to the opening slowly and peak out into the dark valley. The darkness isn't an issue for me, but unfortunately, it's snowing just enough to obscure my vision. I can't see anything nearby, so I step out into the open. I motion for Brian and Derrick to stay back for a moment while I double check to make sure it is in fact clear. I stand on the edge of the snowbank, just outside the entrance of the cave and focus my hearing and my sense of smell. I reach it out as far as I can, trying to pick up any signs of life. Even though the Nan-ites have been detecting life from great distances, I need to be sure. After extending my senses as far as I possibly can, I hear the sound of a heartbeat a mile out. A red indicator pops up in my field of vision. Then I hear another heartbeat and another indicator pops up. And another and another until there are twenty-two indicators approaching the compound and getting closer.

"There's twenty-two of them and they're getting close," I say as I look back at them. Brian and Derrick give me confused looks.

"How do you know that?" asks Derrick. "I can't smell or hear them."

"The Nan-ites. Let's get you guys up on the ledge. They're only a couple minutes out."

They both nod and step out of the cave. All three of us look up at the same time, towards the ledge. I can see it easily, even in the storm. The Nan-ites measure it to be 24 feet above the mouth of the cave.

"Can you make that jump?"

"I don't know. I haven't tried to jump that high before," Derrick responds without looking at me. He's still looking up at the ledge.

"I can't see the ledge and I definitely can't jump that high," says Brian.

"I'm gonna throw you. Derrick will catch you."

"I'm sorry. Can you repeat that?" Brian says alarmed.

"It'll be fun," I smile at him. All he does is shake his head. He's going to be mad about this for a long time.

Derrick crouches down as low as he can in order to jump higher than any man that ever lived has done before. His eyes are focused on the ledge above as he blasts off into the air like a rocket. The Nan-ites had been monitoring his chances of making it because they alert me when he's coming up short, about halfway through the jump. WARNING flashes above him as he stops in mid-air, a couple feet shy of the ledge. Just when I think he's going to come falling back down, he lashes out at the rock with his razor-sharp claws. He looks down at us with satisfaction on his face.

"For a moment there, I thought you were gonna wimp out on me," I say to him.

"Brian's the one that should be worried about wimping out. That's a pretty long fall."

"What's he saying about me?" Brian asks.

"Nice knowing you, Brian!" Derrick shouts.

I laugh as I step over to Brian and wrap an arm around him.

"Seriously though, what's he saying?"

"He said it was nice knowing you." Brian squints his eyes at me. "Hold still. This is gonna be quite a ride."

Brian pins the rifle to his chest and stiffens up. I put my hands on his hips and make sure I have a secure hold. I launch off the ground, harder than any previous time I have before. Harder than when I jumped onto the roof of the police station. Brian and I clear fifteen feet almost instantly, but lose momentum fast and come to a stop a few feet shy of where Derrick is standing. I throw Brian the last couple feet and Derrick snatches him out of the air. I fall to the snow covered, stone ground, using the strength in my legs to absorb the impact. It feels as if I simply jumped off of the first couple steps of some stairs. I can hear Brian laughing about how much fun it was. Only my guys can joke and act like nothing is happening when we're about to go to battle. Hopefully, we'll be joking when it's all over.

"Watch him, Derrick. He won't last two seconds if one of them gets their hands on him."

"They'll have to come through me first."

"Hey, you just worry about yourself," shouts Brian.

While I'm making my descent down the slope, to the place where I'll wait for Rider's arrival, images pop into my head. I can feel Mya is getting anxious. She's picking up on my emotions and the fact that I'm worried about Brian more than I ever have been before. I sense a similar worry from her. I have to keep Rider's men away from him. He's my priority during this battle, but I can't be up there with him. I need to face Rider myself. Not because I have hard feelings towards him for what happened, but because I'm the only one that has a chance against him. He's just way too big for any of the other men to fight. He's too big for me. I'll need to outsmart him in order to have a chance.

The red indicators indicate that he and his men are about to emerge from the trees on the other side of the clearing. The air is still too thick with fog and snow for me to see anything beyond the sink hole. I walk up and take my spot, 50 yards away from the explosives. The soldier that came the night before is on display, waiting to greet the rest of his friends. His head is resting on a hanger rod from one of the apartment closets. Now it's being used as a pike. One of the explosives is underneath the body so that it can't be seen. With some luck, the explosion will take out nearly half of Rider's men. If it only takes out Rider, I'll be satisfied.

I continue waiting in the dark, snowy clearing—out in the open for anyone to see. Waiting for an army of mutated, trained killers that had once been a beacon of hope to this country, men who once served to protect people in need and stood for honor. Now, they're no longer men and have no honor. Not because they look different. Not because they've changed on the outside. They're no longer men because they've abandoned humanity. They chose to be animals, to inflict suffering on people that are weaker than them. To take life when they can help protect it better than they ever could have dreamed before. Now it's time to put them down like the animals that they are. It's time for us to show them what a soldier is supposed to stand for. Our special forces unit is called the

Reaper's. We call ourselves that because we are the bringers of death.

The indicators stop moving just beyond where I can see. They're in the clearing now, only about 50 yards from their greeter on a stick. None of them have the Nan-ites, so they have no idea if I'm really here or not. The only way they can possibly know that someone is waiting for them is if they can smell me. No doubt they probably do, but why stop? If their sense of smell is as strong as my men, then they know that I'm the only one here. Unless they can smell Derrick and Brian, which I doubt. They should be just out of range.

The indicators begin moving again after a short pause, but they split off into three groups. A small group of four goes to my left, another group of four to the right. The remaining fourteen continue on the same path they were already going. Right where I want them to. Within a few seconds I can see who is coming towards me. The soldiers that appear, mostly look just like the one I already killed. Average height, thick legs and arms like a roided out bodybuilder that turned into something really ugly. Some with grey skin, others light red. They have long hair all over their bodies, with some spikes of different shapes and sizes protruding from their arms. A few of the soldiers are tall. Long, lanky and awkward looking. Rider is long and lanky, but still well built. These guys look like they would snap in half at the slightest impact. They're the most unnatural looking ones out of them all. Standing right in the middle of them, with his red skin, long hair and jagged spikes, is Rider. He grins at the first sight of me and holds the grin until they come to a stop, only a few feet from their decapitated friend. Rider takes one glance at the head on the pole, then returns his now emotionless gaze back to me.

"I was wondering why he didn't return last night," Rider says calmly with his deep voice. "Looks like I underestimated what you're capable of."

"You underestimated me the moment you showed up with your puppet, Jake," I say coldly. "You two and your phony act."

Rider chuckles and his voice echoes through the air.

"Looks like you've been through a change yourself, Captain. I could see those eyes from a mile away."

"I can see the eight men you sent around to flank me."

"No matter. Knowing where they are won't help you. You don't really think you can stop all of us alone, do you?"

I bring my sword into view and take a defensive stance. "There's only one way to find out."

"Make him squeal like a pig."

All thirteen men that stayed with Rider break off into a dead run before he finishes his command. The first couple manage to avoid setting off the explosives, but the third soldier, one of the tall ones, steps right on the wire. The explosion is loud and deafening. At first, the noise hurts my ears, but the Nan-ites quickly adjust the volume so that I don't have to plug them. When the smoke from the explosion dissipates enough for me to see, all fourteen of them are on the ground, including Rider.

At first, none of them move. I quickly check my flank and the remaining eight soldiers are still holding their positions. I can hear them discussing their options. They're worried about triggering another explosion, so they remain still.

After a moment, Rider begins to move and a knot forms in my stomach. Rider's men would be weak without him, but I'll just have to accept whatever loss they had. The Nan-ites start scanning the bodies that lay before me in the snow. Five out of the fourteen are dead. Their hearts have stopped completely, without even the slightest pulse. Others have severe injuries, including missing hands, legs or severe burns. The other eight soldiers are still holding their positions as Rider climbs to his feet. A deep gash is across his bare chest, right where he had suffered his life changing wound. The one that would go on to change him into what stands so close to me now. I hear a shot come from the ledge behind me. Just before it strikes true, Rider moves his head to the right. He missed? Brian missed with the 50. Cal.

Rider grins at me just as another shot rings out. Rider turns his body just in time. Another miss. Rider glares at me with his bright yellow, predator like gaze. He no longer has a grin on his face. Instead, a snarl replaces it and he starts to charge and I open fire. I empty my entire clip into him and he doesn't even slow down.

"Reapers, now!"

More shots ring out instantly as a swarm of black, serpent-like creatures erupt from the sink hole. I look over to the first four soldiers that split off to my left. Two of them are down, but the other two are heading straight for the main swarm in front of me to join their comrades. I look to my right to see the other four, already closing in on me, a few steps ahead of Rider. The soldiers that are with him, the ones that survived, are up and fighting with my men. I see Frank and another large soldier going toe to toe. The tall, lanky, yet muscular soldier slices at Frank's chest with his sharp claws, spraying blood onto the white snow. Frank roars in anger and tackles the tall soldier to the ground. The two of them roll around as they toss each other back and forth.

I return my gaze over to where I last saw Rider and he isn't there. I scan the area trying to find him, when suddenly I'm struck in the back by a hard kick that sends me flying face first into the snow. I quickly climb back to my feet, only to be surprised by Rider again, who grips one of his large hands around my throat. He lifts me off the ground so that I'm eye level with him and he pulls me close so that our faces are only a couple inches apart.

"I underestimate no one." He spits in my face.

Rider starts squeezing my throat even tighter, completely cutting off my air flow. Just as I can feel the bones in my neck are about to give, I draw my knife with lightning speed and slice Rider's hand, making him release his grip. I quickly jump away from him, giving me a moment to catch my breath and allow my neck to heal back to its normal structure. Feeling it expand is strange and extremely uncomfortable. More so than the squeezing had been. The deep cut on Rider's hand already healed without a mark to show for it. I retake a defensive position as Rider paces back and forth, like an animal waiting to pounce on its prey.

"You're not going to imprison these people like the ones in the mall," I growl.

"Who's going to stop me?!" he yells back. "You and your pathetic Reapers? Oh yes, Captain. I knew about you and your *legendary* men from the beginning." Rider smiles at my surprise. "How do you think I knew about this place to start with? I doubt even you knew of its existence before the storm. There are many things you don't know. We're taking this facility even if we have to kill all of you."

"Not if I stop you."

"Your men couldn't kill me when I was human. Do you really think they can stop me now?!" Rider roars as he puffs up his chest. I put my knife back into its sheath and draw the one sword I still have with me. The other one is in the snow only a few feet from Rider. His laugh is so loud and deep that I'm sure even Brian probably hears it. "That's not going to help you."

"What are you waiting for then?" I grin.

I charge Rider at full speed. He quickly swipes down at me with his sharp claws, but I sidestep the blow like I did in the cavern with Taylor. I slash the sword down onto Rider's back, leaving a large incision. Rider screams in pain as I slash at his left arm not even a second later. The blade cuts through Rider's arm like butter and the bloody limb falls to the ground. I step around him to see the look on his face. He's shocked and in pain, but recovers quickly and surprises me. He picks his arm up off the ground and holds it in place just as the healing starts. It only takes a few seconds for the bone to rejoin and the tissue to heal so that there isn't any sign of damage. Rider grins at me as he clenches his fist to make sure he still has full use of his hand.

"See? I'm Invincible!"

He charges me again. I quickly step to my left this time, trying to avoid the heavy blow, but I'm not fast enough. Rider's sharp claws come down on my right shoulder, ripping through my jacket and exposing muscle tissue. I grimace from the pain and swipe at Rider with my other hand, barely grazing his chest with my sword. The wound on my shoulder takes a little longer to heal than his did, leaving me vulnerable for several seconds. I have to dodge several more attacks as I wait for tissue and muscle to mend back together. Rider is faster than I anticipated and requires me to be quick and precise with every decision I make. As the wound on my shoulder finally heals, allowing me to continue full attacks, I suddenly can't see what is taking place on the battlefield.

Mya's looking through the hard-shelled cocoon she's in. She's growling ferociously as she watches and feels me battling Rider. I'm instantly vulnerable and incapable of fending off any attacks as Mya wiggles around inside the cocoon, trying to find a way out. I feel a blow to the side of my head as I try to gain control of my vision. Then I feel an agonizing pain as something sharp digs into my chest, making blood spatter onto my face. Either through the sudden burst of pain or by simply taking control of my vision, I can suddenly see from my own eyes again, but only in time to see Rider grab me again by the throat. I quickly slash down at Rider's arm, but he knocks my hand away and then pulls the sword out of my hand and tosses it to the ground. I try to do the same with my other sword, but Rider beats me to it and grabs my arm. He squeezes tightly and makes me let go as I feel the bones in my hand and wrist break.

Just as I'm blacking out from the pain and lack of oxygen, something crashes into Rider's side, knocking him to the ground and I drop to my knees. I struggle to look up and see one of my men, tangled with Rider on the ground, clawing at Rider's chest. As my vision clears and I look over at the two tangled bodies, I see Taylor is the one wrestling for his life with Rider.

Taylor roars loudly. The same shrieking noise that I heard in previous nights, echoing through the dark sky. Now he's wrestling with someone twice his size, thrashing his arms around wildly trying to inflict as much damage as possible. He takes chunks out of Rider's chest and all I see is a flurry of red spraying everywhere. Rider roars back as Taylor continues his assault until Rider suddenly grabs hold of both Taylor's arms and snaps them in half like twigs. Taylor screams out it pain as his arms dangle to his side, swaying back and forth. Rider grabs Taylor's throat and squeezes with enough force to bend steel, until a loud popping sound echoes across the battlefield. Taylor's entire body falls limp as Rider throws him to the ground next to me. I don't need the Nan-ites to put deceased in bright red letters to know Taylor is gone.

"No!"

"Look around Alec," Rider shouts as he walks over to me. "I told you. Your men are too weak for my army!"

The wounds in his chest are already healing. In a moment there won't be anything left to show what Taylor had done. I take a moment and look around for the first time since the fighting started, to see three more of my men, lifeless in the snow. I can't tell which ones they are. Four of my men are dead. I look in the other direction to see the five Reapers that are still alive, including

Brian. Each of them has one of Rider's men holding them submissive. Two more soldiers are holding guns, making sure none of my men try to fight.

"You lost this battle before it even began!" he continues to boast.

The bones in my hand reset themselves and the rest of my wounds start to heal as I kneel down in the snow, unsure of how to continue the fight. Half my men are dead, the rest are captured. I don't have any weapons. I could beat Rider to one of my swords, but what then? He might just order his men to execute mine.

The battle is over. We lost.

At least they still don't have access to the facility.

"No! Let go of me!" a female voice suddenly cries.

The sound of the familiar voice makes my heart stop at the realization of how wrong I am. I look up and I'm forced to witness Joe dragging Emily through the snow by her hair, with several followers behind him, all carrying guns. The guns my parents and the other three were using to secure the inside.

"Well, well. What have we here?" Rider smiles as he looks over at them.

Joe pushes Emily down into the snow in front of Rider. She looks over at me with tears streaming down her already bruised face.

"We've come to offer the surrender of the compound in return for our freedom!" Joe says.

Rider laughs.

"Finally. Someone with some sense." He looks down at Emily as she's trying to crawl over to me. "And what's this?" He reaches down and snatches her up off the ground.

"We knew Alec wouldn't continue if you had her," Joe replies with a shaky voice.

"I see. Come here," he orders Joe as he pushes Emily over to one of his soldiers. Joe's stance quickly becomes weak as Rider studies him. "Don't be afraid."

I can see right through Rider's lie as Joe cowers in his presence.

"You're a fool Joe! You should've stayed inside!"

"I'm trying to keep everyone alive," he shouts back. "Unlike you."

"You just gave them access to the compound! All you had to do was stay inside!"

Everything is compromised. All our planning and preparations for this battle and we're defeated from the inside. Joe, a man who's been nothing but heartache for me since first meeting him and now he's betrayed everyone in the compound. There has to be a way I can remedy this. A way to prevent Rider from seizing control of the compound. I need to get Brian and Emily free somehow and back inside. I'm faster than anyone out here, but Rider is between them and me.

Mya, I need you.

"Enough jabbering, you two. Come here… Joe? Is that your name?" Rider has a devilish grin on his face. This is about to get bad for Joe. He's only a couple steps from him, so Rider reaches out and grabs Joe by his shoulder. He instantly starts pleading for his life.

"W-we ha-have a d-deal, right?"

"No deals were ever made," Rider responds. "But I'm not gonna kill you." He's still holding his grin. Rider raises his left hand to Joe's face and puts one of his sharp claws up to Joe's cheek.

"No! No!" pleads Joe. He screams in horror as Rider leaves a deep gash in his cheek and then another in his other cheek so that he has two identical markings on his face. I know Rider isn't marking him like this for no reason. He only gave each of his own men one cut. He clearly has something sinister in mind for the coward. Once he's finished scarring Joe's face and infecting him, he releases him. Joe collapses to the ground crying like a child as he looks in horror at the blood on his hands.

"Now you'll get to see what it's like to be an abomination." I chuckle, just as Mya's sight takes over again.

Now she's moving her powerful paws while trying to swipe at the cocoon containing her. She's almost free.

Rider returns his concentration to me as Joe scurries off with his followers. Emily is squirming, trying to free herself from the soldiers' grip, but to no avail.

"It's too bad, Alec." I hear him moving closer to me. "All that trouble you went through to save her." I can hear the pleasure in his voice. "I'm gonna enjoy killing her in front of you. Or even better… maybe I'll turn her into something a little more pleasing," he says with the same laugh as the one before.

Mya must have sensed my feeling towards Rider's words because I can feel her growling and slashing around violently. She's ramming her head into the wall of the cocoon with a lot of force. She rams it again and again until a crack appears and eventually the whole cocoon looks like it's going to shatter. My sight returns as Rider is taking a step towards Emily. "This is your last chance to surrender, Rider," I laugh.

"Surrender? Do you have some master plan you're waiting to unleash or something?"

"Actually… yeah I do." I chuckle again with my head down as I feel Mya finally break through the cocoon wall. "She's coming for you."

"Who's coming for me?"

"Mya."

"What? Your stupid dog? Too bad I didn't bring her a treat," he laughs loudly. Some of his men laugh with him. "Well, prepare to watch me turn your pretty girlfriend into a monster." He takes one last step towards her.

A low howl echoes over our heads. Everyone on the battlefield stops and looks towards the compound. Not a single soldier on either side is moving except for myself and Emily. She looks over at me with concerned eyes, hoping to read my expression. I simply nod my head as I slowly stand up.

I continue watching through Mya's eyes again, as she slams her way through the double doors, knocking them off their hinges and breaking the glass windows. She runs fast, ramming her head into the stairwell door, also knocking it off its hinges, sending it crashing into the wall. Mya leaps each flight of stairs in one effortless bound and pounds through the door at the top and sends the door flying into the main hall with more glass and metal going everywhere. Several people are there in the hall as Mya enters the great room.

Every single one of them has the look of horror on their faces as they gaze up at her. She looks around, only stopping to look at each person for a fraction of a second. They begin to flee in every direction to escape her. I catch a glimpse of my parents, James, Mr. Wilkinson and Peter are still alive. My parents look more surprised than scared to see Mya, but the other three take cautious steps backwards. Fortunately, all of them appear to be alright. Then Mya looks straight at the wide-open steel door and charges towards it like a speeding freight train.

I regain control of my vision so that I'm no longer seeing through Mya's eyes. I look over to the entrance. I can tell she's huge from the moment I see her because she's standing higher than the top of the opening of the cave. The flame from the explosion is reflecting off of her bright, glowing, blue eyes. She looks like a giant white werewolf from a horror story, while she lurks in the shadows like a predator on the hunt. I marvel at the sight of my loyal canine friend as she slowly moves forward with her tail sticking straight

346

up. Her long, razor sharp, white teeth glistening in the light. Her body structure still looks for the most part like before, except now her legs are much more massive and muscular. Instead of a typical scrawny leg like a normal dog, her front and rear legs look like they belong on a giant tiger. Her fur also still appears to be normal, except for the dark stripe on her back. The stripe is sticking straight up in the air like it always used to when she's ready to attack, but now it has sharp spikes that could cut flesh, blended in with the fur. Mya stops just as she emerges from the cave and lets out a loud, ear piercing howl that makes everyone cover their ears. I felt from our connection the howl was coming and lessened the volume so that the sound wouldn't hurt my ears. Since doing it at the beginning of the battle, it happens naturally now.

"Impossible!" Rider yells. He's trying to act angry, but I can smell the fear on him.

Rider crouches down into an attack position as Mya bolts towards him like lighting. Mya runs with grace as she kicks up snow after each powerful step, blasting through the snow, growling as she approaches her prey. Rider tries to brace himself, but she slams into him like a train hitting a small car. The impact sends Rider flying through the air in the direction of the sinkhole.

Mya quickly turns towards the soldier who is nearest to Emily. She quickly knocks the soldier down with her powerful paws before sinking her teeth into him, tearing at his grey flesh. The soldier desperately tries to fend her off with his hands, but she grabs one of them and tears it off. She then picks him up and starts shaking him back and forth like he's one of her toys. She opens her jaws and the soldier falls to the ground dead, with blood splattered everywhere. There are two soldiers holding guns and they fire at her, but only succeed in making her mad. The rounds bounce off the side of her like she's wearing armor and she leaps towards one of them, grabbing him by the head and removing it instantly. She kills the second soldier the same way. He continues firing until even a few seconds after his head is gone.

I look over to see Frank, Jermaine, John and Justin fighting with the soldiers that had been holding them. Brian is still being held by one, but Mya is moving slowly towards them. One soldier looks frightened and appears to be weighing his options. He's one of the short, stocky ones—just like the one that had nearly killed Mya. He makes his decision and throws Brian at her like a ball. Mya catches him out of the air with her mouth and gently sets him down before bolting after the soldier, who is now on a sprint for his life.

I stop watching Mya as Emily runs over and jumps into my arms. I hold her tightly, relieved she wasn't harmed. I notice she's only wearing a t-shirt and somehow not shivering from the cold. I take off my blood-stained jacket and put it around her.

"I need you to stay here," I say as I kiss her on the forehead and start to walk away. She grabs my arm to stop me.

"No, don't go!"

"I have too," I reply softly as I wrap my arms around her tightly one more time. "I have to find Rider and end this. I'll be fine. This time I have her." I point over to Mya who is now walking towards us. I walk over and pick up a rifle and the one sword I can find and start for the sinkhole.

"Let's go, big girl." *Big Girl* now has a whole new meaning.

Mya doesn't hesitate and leaps over to my side in one bound and walks next to me towards the hole. She's several feet taller than me now, so when I look directly at her, I'm looking at her shoulder. We stop 20 feet from the hole to try and pick up Rider's tracks or scent. Mya crouches down low, like she used to when she would stalk something hiding in the bushes. She moves towards the sink hole, slowly, like a wolf on a hunt for food. I move with her, as we each move closer and closer to the edge of the hole and look down to the bottom.

"Are you sure he's down there, Mya?" I ask quietly.

She starts clawing at the snow with her giant tiger like paws, just as the Nan-ites place a red indicator in my field of vision. He's definitely down there. Mya's looking straight at me, awaiting my approval to go inside. She's still Mya after all. I smile.

"Go."

Mya leaps into the hole the moment she hears the command. She lands on a stone about halfway down and then jumps a second time, landing at the bottom. I land on the ground beside her almost at the same time, since I didn't use the extra step. Mya most likely could have done it in one step as well, but probably chose to do it the way she did because it's something she isn't comfortable doing yet. She did only come out of the cocoon a few minutes ago, as opposed to me who had had days to get used to my strength.

We wait at the bottom of the hole for a few seconds until Mya suddenly catches Rider's scent and she lets out a loud growl that shakes the tunnel. Pieces of obsidian, along with other rock and dirt, fall to the ground as her growl echoes into the cavern and back.

"Mya, wait!" I call after her. She doesn't listen and bolts down the tunnel, like she did the first night she chased after what ended up being a Reaper.

I follow behind her as closely as I can, but she's too fast. Incredibly fast. In just the short 40 feet of the tunnel the Nan-ites measure her speed at 62 miles an hour. I can only imagine what she would get up to with more space to run. Just as she reaches the end of the tunnel, Rider steps out from the right side of the cavern where he was hiding, hitting her in the head with a giant slab of rock. Mya doesn't make a sound as she slams into the wall and falls to the ground motionless. A split second later, I leap into the air and force my knee into Rider's face. His head snaps sideways in a way that would have killed a normal man, but he recovers quickly and I land at the opposite side of the cavern. I quickly begin firing my rifle at him and the bullets shred through his body like a paper target. He collapses to the ground as I empty an entire magazine into him. He lays motionless on the ground when I run out of ammo.

"Get up, Rider! GET UP! Your great army is dead, Rider! I guess we weren't as weak as you thought." I draw my sword as his wounds began to heal rapidly. Rider moves slowly, waiting for them to be done.

"You haven't beaten me yet!"

He tries lunging at me, but I easily step around his blow this time and slice him deep down his back. The wound starts healing so I go to thrust my sword through his back, straight into his heart. Somehow Rider sidesteps my attack. It's as if his body is learning to adapt like mine is. He deflects my blow before grabbing me by the throat. I punch him hard in the face and all he does is laugh at me while prying the sword out of my hand.

"It seems you have a habit of underestimating me. Game over, Winter," Rider grins.

Rider slashes the sword downward towards my head. I watch the glistening steel move towards me in slow motion. Time is now moving so slowly, I'm able to examine the perfection of the Japanese-made steel that is about to split me in two. I have all the time in the world to think of another way out.

Or await my death.

How can I stop Rider from killing me? I can put my hand up to try and catch it, but it will slice right through my hand and continue to my head anyway.

He's too strong for me to break free. There's nothing I can do to stop what's coming.

Suddenly, something strange starts happening. My skin, all over my body, trembles for barely a fraction of a second and I look into Rider's eyes. My skin is black like the skin on my men, but it doesn't look like the flesh on a reptile with scales. Instead, it's smooth and polished like a carbon fiber or other metal. Like the obsidian in the tunnel. It looks like armor. Rider doesn't have time to react to my sudden change. Without the Nan-ites, his mind can't process as quickly as mine. He doesn't even see the change until it's too late. The blade makes contact with the crown of my head and shatters into pieces, sending shards of steel in all directions. While Rider is caught off guard, I pull out my knife and slash at Rider's throat. He lets go of me just as blood splatters on us both. I follow up with a spinning back kick, making contact with the side of his face and he slams into the rocky wall.

Mya's regained consciousness and waiting patiently as Rider starts to climb to his feet. His back is to her and he's clearly forgotten about her. She's creeping up behind him, slowly. I keep my eyes on Rider, trying to hold his attention, but I'm no longer seeing through my own eyes. I'm seeing through the eyes of my dog as she stalks her prey like a hunting predator. Her emotions are all over the place, but I can feel the anger and revenge boiling through her as she waits to sink her teeth into him.

"How could you turn against humanity the way you have? How could you violate your oath as a soldier?" I say calmly, but seething with anger.

"Who are you to judge me?" Rider spits blood at my feet, still trying to gather himself.

"I'm not the one judging you, but you have a meeting with Him in a few minutes."

"You may have beaten me, but at least I managed to kill some of your men," Rider chokes as his throat is healing. "You think that your troubles are over? You don't know half of what's coming. None of you do." He spits more blood onto the stone ground.

Rider's laugh sounds like pure evil as he relishes in his accomplishment, even though he knows he's about to die. A man that can find joy in taking lives needs to be put down. Mya is still waiting on my command. I feel pity for Rider and the kind of person he is and will be remembered as. His lack of respect for life reminds me of Joe, as he continues his unforgettable laugh. They're the same people. Just from different worlds.

"You outnumbered us more than two to one. You're the one who was weak." Rider looks as though he's about to make one last ditch effort at attacking and lunges at me, but I step back too quickly. "Go ahead, Mya."

Rider stops his attack at my mention of my furry friend and I turn to walk away. I release my connection through Mya and concentrate on my own thoughts to shield myself from seeing her rip him apart. The last thing I see is Rider's frightened look when he turns around to face her. Mya snarls ferociously as she tears Rider to pieces and she rips his arms from his body. After removing his arms, she rips out his throat and then throws what's left of his body into the wall.

I remember back to a time she captured a rabbit and shook the little creature around violently and ripped at its flesh until she decided it was no longer any fun.

Rider is the rabbit.

As I reach the beginning of the tunnel, Mya stops her violent attack. She looks over at me as I wait for her. I look back to see a crimson coat instead of her shiny white fur.

"Time to go, big girl."

I pull out the two grenades I've been waiting to use. I pull both the pins and toss them over to where Rider's motionless body is resting. His heart is somehow still beating, but slowly coming to a stop as it fails to win the fight for life. I turn and run as fast as I can to escape the blast.

Mya runs right beside me just as the grenades explode and shake the entire cavern, all the way through the tunnel. A ball of flame rushes after us like a tidal wave of fire, right on our tails. We both jump off the wall into the air, narrowly avoiding the blast, as we launch ourselves off of the side of the rocky hole onto the surface. The flame is minimal by the time it reaches the surface, but tons of dust and smoke explode into the air above us, just as we land on the edge. Smoke is emulating off our bodies.

Everyone who survived the attack is waiting for us when we reach the top. Jermaine, Derrick, Frank, John, Justin, Brian and Emily. All of them, except for Emily, are holding a rifle. Probably just in case it had been Rider that came out of the hole. They're all staring at us, going back and forth between me and then Mya, like they don't know what to think. Like they're looking at two alien creatures. I almost forgot about my transformation and I look down at my hands and then then touch my face. My face feels more like a metallic mask than anything. I can't even feel my lips or my mouth. It's firm and feels impenetrable. How I'm able to breath and talk is beyond my knowledge. The Nan-ites are incredible.

"No one else made it?" I ask in a solemn tone.

"No sir. We lost Jason, Seth, Cole and Taylor," responds Frank. All of the men are fighting back tears as Frank mentions the names of our fallen friends. All I can think about is Taylor and how he chose to join the battle at the moment I needed him the most. He saved my life.

"The men we lost today were our friends," I say. "They were the finest men I've ever known. All of you are." I stand straight and tall and salute my men. Each of them returns the gesture, holding their positions until I relax.

CHAPTER 20

The men and I clear the dead from the battlefield over the course of the next few hours. We remove Rider's dead soldiers by throwing them into the bottom of the sink hole and setting them on fire. As for the four men we lost, we begin preparing a funeral service, which most of the compound will attend. Everyone except for Joe and his followers. Joe ran off somewhere. Not in the compound, but somewhere out in the darkness. The Nan-ites picked him up somewhere west of here, only a couple miles away. I imagine he'll find some place to stay while his body changes into the very thing he hated. The rest of his followers will be allowed to stay, but will also be watched closely. They're not allowed to attend the funeral.

We decide not to burn our friends like the coward trash Rider and his soldiers are, but to bury them the traditional way. We want them to have a hero's funeral. Most of the cleanup time is spent digging the graves for them. Removing the snow and then digging through the frozen solid dirt is a long task, even with our strength. Brian insisted on helping as well, even though we told him he should stay inside where it's warm. We don't argue once he made his choice. When the holes are dug, we wrap Jason, Seth, Cole and Taylor in white sheets and place them in their respective graves.

Later in the evening, we hold the ceremony in silence. Every person is given the opportunity to stop by each grave and throw a handful of dirt onto each soldier. The process takes nearly an hour as each person has their chance to show respect for those who had fallen protecting them. Once everyone is done paying their respects, we fill the holes back up. We then fire off four shots, each one dedicated to one of our friends.

Mya is lying down in the snow just a few feet back from where we stand, attending the entire service. Everyone in the compound gives her nervous looks as they pass by. Even lying down she's intimidating. I suspect it will take a long time for them to grow comfortable around her again. Some probably never will. Emily is by my side during the entire service with her arm around me. I can tell by the way she's holding me that you would need to pry her hands off of me in order to get her to let go. Knowing she'll hold on to me so tightly is the only thing giving me a sense of relief during the funeral. She's making it bearable.

After the funeral is over, everyone heads back inside the compound except Emily, Mya, the rest of the men and me. We stand there for a while longer, spending a little extra time saying goodbye. One by one, each of the men eventually walk away after finishing their goodbyes, until it's only Mya, Emily and me remaining outside in the freezing cold. Luckily, the wind isn't blowing too hard and the snow is lightly falling. We're curled up against Mya's thick, warm fur, overlooking the valley. Emily can only see a short distance, but I describe what I can see as best I can. Now having the ability to see more than what's a short distance away makes the world around me seem a little less bleak. So long as I'm not looking at some abandoned building or collapsed home. Now, all I see is a clearing of snow and some trees not too far to the left.

Even with Mya lying down and me sitting up against her, I can't see over her head. Her size is incredible. The Nan-ites measure her to be eight feet and three inches tall on all fours. She's six feet long and weighs 935 lbs. Her fur is the strangest part of her. It still has that same soft, fluffy feel to it, but somehow managed to deflect bullets from a high-powered rifle. My father said he would have to do some research to learn more about how the changes affected her. I wonder if somehow her fur activates in defense as my skin did when Rider nearly killed me. My skin changed back to normal shortly after the battle once I had relaxed. I could feel the change as it took place and it was sort of uncomfortable. Not painful, but more like an itch. One thing I'm grateful for is the ability to still feel warmth when I make contact with Mya. Feeling warm as I sit up against her and the sensations and feelings I can feel through our mental connection, as well as the sensations from contacting Emily's skin... all of it is hard to cipher through and absorb. So many different things to comprehend at once. Another thing I might not ever get used to either, but I'll certainly enjoy every second of it.

"What's the matter?" Emily asks softly. I didn't realize I was staring at her.

"I just think you're beautiful," I say with a smile.

I raise my hand to touch her cheek, but stop myself. The bruises on her face look extremely uncomfortable and make me grimace in pain for her.

"I'm fine," she says and takes hold of my hand, then presses it up against her cheek. "They will heal," she assures me.

She leans in and kisses me. I can feel a slight discomfort coming from her through the contact, but she's hiding it well. Her face is really bothering her. Mya lets out a loud, echoing howl and we both start laughing, even though the sound probably hurt Emily's ears. Seeing Emily laugh and smile fills me with joy. Being around her and Mya makes me feel whole again. I thought I lost one and almost lost the other. I can spend every second of every day with them for the rest of my life and I'll be perfectly happy. There's nothing I want more.

An idea forms in my mind and I think about it over and over again. I'm certain Emily feels the same way I do, especially now. I can feel it in her just as I can feel and understand Mya's thoughts and emotions. I can't read her thoughts exactly, but the contact of our skin tells me that much about her. I'm a part of her just as much as she's a part of me now. I want to spend the rest of my life with her. Now I just need to plan out how to ask her to be my wife. I'll work that out later.

Rider hinted that something else might be coming. He was only the first of what will likely be more enemies to come and try to take the compound. Losing some of my men is hard. Losing them was a good reminder of who we all are and what we stand for. We are soldiers. Even if our country or even if the world doesn't go back to the way it was before, we all still have a duty—a duty to serve and protect those who might not be able to.

I am a Captain in the United States Army Special Forces.

We call ourselves Reapers. I am a Reaper. If anyone tries to come here and hurt those that I care about, they will find out who I am. They will know me and they will fear me.

I am Alec Winter.

EPILOGUE

"What's happening?" the harsh voice asks.

"I think he's remembering something," responds the female. Hearing the man's voice for the first time since blacking out, makes me uncomfortable. The woman's soft voice somehow provides some feeling of comfort.

"What is it?"

"I don't know."

"What do you mean, you don't know?"

"His mind is... fighting the machine. I'm only getting blurry images. It will ta..."

The woman's soft voice is interrupted by a loud slap.

"This machine allows you to extract info from any other person! What's holding you back with him?"

"He's... n-not a normal person, sir," she says in a shaky voice. "It will take me some time to be able to get around the defenses in his mind and get... clear information from him."

"Well, you better have something for me the next time I come visit you. I won't accept failure again, Doctor. Do you understand me?"

I understand, but she doesn't answer. I can only assume she nods her head, afraid to say anything more. Afraid he might hurt her again. It's clear now that this man is dangerous and won't let anything or anyone get in the way of his goal. He's going to kill this woman if she doesn't give him what he wants. He might kill *me*. If only I could help her by giving her what he needs. Sadly, I don't know how to give it to him, let alone what it is that he wants. We are both doomed unless I can free myself before that happens. I need to get free from this place before it's too late. I need to find Mya. I need to find my sister.

Made in the USA
Las Vegas, NV
18 September 2023

77763717R10207